Alice of Old Vincennes

by
Maurice Thompson

PREFACE

To   M.   PLACIDE   VALCOUR

M. D., Ph D., LL. D.

MY DEAR DR. VALCOUR: You gave me the Inspiration which made this story haunt me until I wrote it. Gaspard Roussillon's letter, a mildewed relic of the year 1788, which you so kindly permitted me to copy, as far as it remained legible, was the point from which my imagination, accompanied by my curiosity, set out upon a long and delightful quest. You laughed at me when I became enthusiastic regarding the possible historical importance at that ancient find, alas! fragmentary epistle; but the old saying about the beatitude of him whose cachinations are latest comes handy to me just now, and I must remind you that "I told you so." True enough, it was history pure and simple that I had in mind while enjoying the large hospitality of your gulf-side home. Gaspard Roussillon's letter then appealed to my greed for materials which would help along the making of my little book "The Story of Louisiana." Later, however, as my frequent calls upon you for both documents and suggestions have informed you, I fell to strumming a different guitar. And now to you I dedicate this historical romance of old Vincennes, as a very appropriate, however slight, recognition of your scholarly attainments, your distinguished career in a noble profession, and your descent from one of the earliest French families (if not the very earliest) long resident at that strange little post on the Wabash, now one of the most beautiful cities between the greet river and the ocean.

Following, with ever tantalized expectancy, the broken and breezy hints in the Roussillon letter, I pursued a will-o'-the-wisp, here, there, yonder, until by slowly arriving increments I gathered up a large amount of valuable facts, which when I came to compare them with the history of Clark's conquest of the Wabash Valley, fitted amazingly well into certain spaces heretofore left open in that important yet sadly imperfect record.

You will find that I was not so wrong in suspecting that Emile Jazon, mentioned in the Roussillon letter, was a brother of Jean Jazon and a famous scout in the time of Boone and Clark. He was, therefore, a kinsman of yours on the maternal side, and I congratulate you. Another thing may please you, the success which attended my long and patient research with a view to clearing up the connection between Alice Roussillon's romantic life, as brokenly sketched in M. Roussillon's letter, and the capture of Vincennes by Colonel George Rogers Clark.

Accept, then, this book, which to those who care only for history will seem but an idle romance, while to the lovers of romance it may look strangely like the mustiest history. In my mind, and in yours I hope, it will always be connected with a breezy summer-house on a headland of the Louisiana gulf coast, the rustling of palmetto leaves, the fine flash of roses, a tumult of mocking-bird voices, the soft lilt of Creole patois, and the endless dash and roar of a fragrant sea over which the gulls and pelicans never ceased their flight, and beside which you smoked while I dreamed.

MAURICE   THOMPSON.

JULY, 1900.

CHAPTER I
UNDER THE CHERRY TREE

Up to the days of Indiana's early statehood, probably as late as 1825, there stood, in what is now the beautiful little city of Vincennes on the Wabash, the decaying remnant of an old and curiously gnarled cherry tree, known as the Roussillon tree, le cerisier de Monsieur Roussillon, as the French inhabitants called it, which as long as it lived bore fruit remarkable for richness of flavor and peculiar dark ruby depth of color. The exact spot where this noble old seedling from la belle France flourished, declined, and died cannot be certainly pointed out; for in the rapid and happy growth of Vincennes many land-marks once notable, among them le cerisier de Monsieur Roussillon, have been destroyed and the spots where they stood, once familiar to every eye in old Vincennes, are now lost in the pleasant confusion of the new town.

The security of certain land titles may have largely depended upon the disappearance of old, fixed objects here and there. Early records were loosely kept, indeed, scarcely kept at all; many were destroyed by designing land speculators, while those most carefully preserved often failed to give even a shadowy trace of the actual boundaries of the estates held thereby; so that the position of a house or tree not infrequently settled an important question of property rights left open by a primitive deed. At all events the Roussillon cherry tree disappeared long ago, nobody living knows how, and with it also vanished, quite as mysteriously, all traces of the once important Roussillon estate. Not a record of the name even can be found, it is said, in church or county books.

The old, twisted, gum-embossed cherry tree survived every other distinguishing feature of what was once the most picturesque and romantic place in Vincennes. Just north of it stood, in the early French days, a low, rambling cabin surrounded by rude verandas overgrown with grapevines. This was the Roussillon place, the most pretentious home in all the Wabash country. Its owner was Gaspard Roussillon, a successful trader with the Indians. He was rich, for the time and the place, influential to a degree, a man of some education, who had brought with him to the wilderness a bundle of books and a taste for reading.

From faded letters and dimly remembered talk of those who once clung fondly to the legends and traditions of old Vincennes, it is drawn that the Roussillon cherry tree stood not very far away from the present site of the Catholic church, on a slight swell of ground overlooking a wide marshy flat and the silver current of the Wabash. If the tree grew there, then there too stood the Roussillon house with its cosy log rooms, its clay-daubed chimneys and its grapevine-mantled verandas, while some distance away and nearer the river the rude fort with its huddled officers' quarters seemed to fling out over the wild landscape, through its squinting and lopsided port-holes, a gaze of stubborn defiance.

Not far off was the little log church, where one good Father Beret, or as named by the Indians, who all loved him, Father Blackrobe, performed the services of his sacred calling; and scattered all around were the cabins of traders, soldiers and woodsmen forming a queer little town, the like of which cannot now be seen anywhere on the earth.

It is not known just when Vincennes was first founded; but most historians make the probable date very early in the eighteenth century, somewhere between 1710 and 1730. In 1810 the Roussillon cherry tree was thought by a distinguished botanical letter-writer to be at least fifty years old, which would make the date of its planting about 1760. Certainly as shown by the time-stained family records upon which this story of ours is based, it was a flourishing and wide-topped tree in early summer of 1778, its branches loaded to drooping with luscious fruit. So low did the dark red clusters hang at one point that a tall young girl standing on the ground easily reached the best ones and made her lips purple with their juice while she ate them.

That was long ago, measured by what has come to pass on the gentle swell of rich country from which Vincennes overlooks the Wabash. The new town flourishes notably and its appearance marks the latest limit of progress. Electric cars in its streets, electric lights in its beautiful homes, the roar of railway trains coming and going in all directions, bicycles whirling hither and thither, the most fashionable styles of equipages, from brougham to pony-phaeton, make the days of flint-lock guns and buckskin trousers seem ages down the past; and yet we are looking back over but a little more than a hundred and twenty years to see Alice Roussillon standing under the cherry tree and holding high a tempting cluster of fruit, while a very short, hump-backed youth looks up with longing eyes and vainly reaches for it. The tableau is not merely rustic, it is primitive. "Jump!" the girl is saying in French, "jump, Jean; jump high!"

Yes, that was very long ago, in the days when women lightly braved what the strongest men would shrink from now.

Alice Roussillon was tall, lithe, strongly knit, with an almost perfect figure, judging by what the master sculptors carved for the form of Venus, and her face was comely and winning, if not absolutely beautiful; but the time and the place were vigorously indicated by her dress, which was of coarse stuff and simply designed. Plainly she was a child of the American wilderness, a daughter of old Vincennes on the Wabash in the time that tried men's souls.

"Jump, Jean!" she cried, her face laughing with a show of cheek-dimples, an arching of finely sketched brows and the twinkling of large blue-gray eyes.

"Jump high and get them!"

While she waved her sun-browned hand holding the cherries aloft, the breeze blowing fresh from the southwest tossed her hair so that some loose strands shone like rimpled flames. The sturdy little hunchback did leap with surprising activity; but the treacherous brown man went higher, so high that the combined altitude of his jump and the reach of his unnaturally long arms was overcome. Again and again he sprang vainly into the air comically, like a long-legged, squat-bodied frog.

"And you brag of your agility and strength, Jean," she laughingly remarked; "but you can't take cherries when they are offered to you. What a clumsy bungler you are."

"I can climb and get some," he said with a hideously happy grin, and immediately embraced the bole of the tree, up which he began scrambling almost as fast as a squirrel.

When he had mounted high enough to be extending a hand for a hold on a crotch, Alice grasped his leg near the foot and pulled him down, despite his clinging and struggling, until his hands clawed in the soft earth at the tree's root, while she held his captive leg almost vertically erect.

It was a show of great strength; but Alice looked quite unconscious of it, laughing merrily, the dimples deepening in her plump cheeks, her forearm, now bared to the elbow, gleaming white and shapely while its muscles rippled on account of the jerking and kicking of Jean.

All the time she was holding the cherries high in her other hand, shaking them by the twig to which their slender stems attached them, and saying in a sweetly tantalizing tone:

"What makes you climb downward after cherries. Jean? What a foolish fellow you are, indeed, trying to grabble cherries out of the ground, as you do potatoes! I'm sure I didn't suppose that you knew so little as that."

Her French was colloquial, but quite good, showing here and there what we often notice in the speech of those who have been educated in isolated places far from that babel of polite energies which we call the world; something that may be described as a bookish cast appearing oddly in the midst of phrasing distinctly rustic and local,—a peculiarity not easy to transfer from one language to another.

Jean the hunchback was a muscular little deformity and a wonder of good nature. His head looked unnaturally large, nestling grotesquely between the points of his lifted and distorted shoulders, like a shaggy black animal in the fork of a broken tree. He was bellicose in his amiable way and never knew just when to acknowledge defeat. How long he might have kept up the hopeless struggle with the girl's invincible grip would be hard to guess. His release was caused by the approach of a third person, who wore the robe of a Catholic priest and the countenance of a man who had lived and suffered a long time without much loss of physical strength and endurance.

This was Pere Beret, grizzly, short, compact, his face deeply lined, his mouth decidedly aslant on account of some lost teeth, and his eyes set deep under gray, shaggy brows. Looking at him when his features were in repose a first impression might not have been favorable; but seeing him smile or hearing him speak changed everything. His voice was sweetness itself and his smile won you on the instant. Something like a pervading sorrow always seemed to be close behind his eyes and under his speech; yet he was a genial, sometimes almost jolly, man, very prone to join in the lighter amusements of his people.

"Children, children, my children," he called out as he approached along a little pathway leading up from the direction of the church, "what are you doing now? Bah there, Alice, will you pull Jean's leg off?"

At first they did not hear him, they were so nearly deafened by their own vocal discords.

"Why are you standing on your head with your feet so high in air, Jean?" he added. "It's not a polite attitude in the presence of a young lady. Are you a pig, that you poke your nose in the dirt?"

Alice now turned her bright head and gave Pere Beret a look of frank welcome, which at the same time shot a beam of willful self-assertion.

"My daughter, are you trying to help Jean up the tree feet foremost?" the priest added, standing where he had halted just outside of the straggling yard fence.

He had his hands on his hips and was quietly chuckling at the scene before him, as one who, although old, sympathized with the natural and harmless sportiveness of young people and would as lief as not join in a prank or two.

"You see what I'm doing, Father Beret," said Alice, "I am preventing a great damage to you. You will maybe lose a good many cherry pies and dumplings if I let Jean go. He was climbing the tree to pilfer the fruit; so I pulled him down, you understand."

"Ta, ta!" exclaimed the good man, shaking his gray head; "we must reason with the child. Let go his leg, daughter, I will vouch for him; eh, Jean?"

Alice released the hunchback, then laughed gayly and tossed the cluster of cherries into his hand, whereupon he began munching them voraciously and talking at the same time.

"I knew I could get them," he boasted; "and see, I have them now." He hopped around, looking like a species of ill-formed monkey.

Pere Beret came and leaned on the low fence close to Alice. She was almost as tall as he.

"The sun scorches to-day," he said, beginning to mop his furrowed face with a red-flowered cotton handkerchief; "and from the look of the sky yonder," pointing southward, "it is going to bring on a storm. How is Madame Roussillon to-day?"

"She is complaining as she usually does when she feels extremely well," said Alice; "that's why I had to take her place at the oven and bake pies. I got hot and came out to catch a bit of this breeze. Oh, but you needn't smile and look greedy, Pere Beret, the pies are not for your teeth!"

"My daughter, I am not a glutton, I hope; I had meat not two hours since—some broiled young squirrels with cress, sent me by Rene de Ronville. He never forgets his old father."

"Oh, I never forget you either, mon pere; I thought of you to-day every time I spread a crust and filled it with cherries; and when I took out a pie all brown and hot, the red juice bubbling out of it so good smelling and tempting, do you know what I said to myself?"

"How could I know, my child?"

"Well, I thought this: 'Not a single bite of that pie does Father Beret get.'"

"Why so, daughter?"

"Because you said it was bad of me to read novels and told Mother Roussillon to hide them from me. I've had any amount of trouble about it."

"Ta, ta! read the good books that I gave you. They will soon kill the taste for these silly romances."

"I tried," said Alice; "I tried very hard, and it's no use; your books are dull and stupidly heavy. What do I care about something that a queer lot of saints did hundreds of years ago in times of plague and famine? Saints must have been poky people, and it is poky people who care to read about them, I think. I like reading about brave, heroic men and beautiful women, and war and love."

Pere Beret looked away with a curious expression in his face, his eyes half closed.

"And I'll tell you now, Father Beret," Alice went on after a pause, "no more claret and pies do you get until I can have my own sort of books back again to read as I please." She stamped her moccasin-shod foot with decided energy.

The good priest broke into a hearty laugh, and taking off his cap of grass-straw mechanically scratched his bald head. He looked at the tall, strong girl before him for a moment or two, and it would have been hard for the best physiognomist to decide just how much of approval and how much of disapproval that look really signified.

Although, as Father Beret had said, the sun's heat was violent, causing that gentle soul to pass his bundled handkerchief with a wiping circular motion over his bald and bedewed pate, the wind was momently freshening, while up from behind the trees on the horizon beyond the river, a cloud was rising blue-black, tumbled, and grim against the sky.

"Well," said the priest, evidently trying hard to exchange his laugh for a look of regretful resignation, "you will have your own way, my child, and—"

"Then you will have pies galore and no end of claret!" she interrupted, at the same time stepping to the withe-tied and peg-latched gate of the yard and opening it. "Come in, you dear, good Father, before the rain shall begin, and sit with me on the gallery" (the creole word for veranda) "till the storm is over."

Father Beret seemed not loath to enter, albeit he offered a weak protest against delaying some task he had in hand. Alice reached forth and pulled him in, then reclosed the queer little gate and pegged it. She caressingly passed her arm through his and looked into his weather-stained old face with childlike affection.

There was not a photographer's camera to be had in those days; but what if a tourist with one in hand could have been there to take a snapshot at the priest and the maiden as they walked arm in arm to that squat little veranda! The picture to-day would be worth its weight in a first-water diamond. It would include the cabin, the cherry-tree, a glimpse of the raw, wild background and a sharp portrait-group of Pere Beret, Alice, and Jean the hunchback. To compare it with a photograph of the same spot now would give a perfect impression of the historic atmosphere, color and conditions which cannot be set in words. But we must not belittle the power of verbal description. What if a thoroughly trained newspaper reporter had been given the freedom of old Vincennes on the Wabash during the first week of June, 1778, and we now had his printed story! What a supplement to the photographer's pictures! Well, we have neither photographs nor graphic report; yet there they are before us, the gowned and straw-capped priest, the fresh-faced, coarsely-clad and vigorous girl, the grotesque little hunchback, all just as real as life itself. Each of us can see them, even with closed eyes. Led by that wonderful guide, Imagination, we step back a century and more to look over a scene at once strangely attractive and unspeakably forlorn.

What was it that drew people away from the old countries, from the cities, the villages and the vineyards of beautiful France, for example, to dwell in the wilderness, amid wild beasts and wilder savage Indians, with a rude cabin for a home and the exposures and hardships of pioneer life for their daily experience?

Men like Gaspard Roussillon are of a distinct stamp. Take him as he was. Born in France, on the banks of the Rhone near Avignon, he came as a youth to Canada, whence he drifted on the tide of adventure this way and that, until at last he found himself, with a wife, at Post Vincennes, that lonely picket of religion and trade, which was to become the center of civilizing energy for the great Northwestern Territory. M. Roussillon had no children of his own; so his kind heart opened freely to two fatherless and motherless waifs. These were Alice, now called Alice Roussillon, and the hunchback, Jean. The former was twelve years old, when he adopted her, a child of Protestant parents, while Jean had been taken, when a mere babe, after his parents had been killed and scalped by Indians. Madame Roussillon, a professed invalid, whose appetite never failed and whose motherly kindness expressed itself most often through strains of monotonous falsetto scolding, was a woman of little education and no refinement; while her husband clung tenaciously to his love of books, especially to the romances most in vogue when he took leave of France.

M. Roussillon had been, in a way, Alice's teacher, though not greatly inclined to abet Father Beret in his kindly efforts to make a Catholic of the girl, and most treacherously disposed toward the good priest in the matter of his well-meant attempts to prevent her from reading and re-reading the aforesaid romances. But for many weeks past Gaspard Roussillon had been absent from home, looking after his trading schemes with the Indians; and Pere Beret acting on the suggestion of the proverb about the absent cat and the playing mouse, had formed an alliance offensive and defensive with Madame Roussillon, in which it was strictly stipulated that all novels and romances were to be forcibly taken and securely hidden away from Mademoiselle Alice; which, to the best of Madame Roussillon's ability, had accordingly been done.

Now, while the wind strengthened and the softly booming summer shower came on apace, the heavy cloud lifting as it advanced and showing under it the dark gray sheet of the rain, Pere Beret and Alice sat under the clapboard roof behind the vines of the veranda and discussed, what was generally uppermost in the priest's mind upon such occasions, the good of Alice's immortal soul,—a subject not absorbingly interesting to her at any time.

It was a standing grief to the good old priest, this strange perversity of the girl in the matter of religious duty, as he saw it. True she had a faithful guardian in Gaspard Roussillon; but, much as he had done to aid the church's work in general, for he was always vigorous and liberal, he could not be looked upon as a very good Catholic; and of course his influence was not effective in the right direction. But then Pere Beret saw no reason why, in due time and with patient work, aided by Madame Roussillon and notwithstanding Gaspard's treachery, he might not safely lead Alice, whom he loved as a dear child, into the arms of the Holy Church, to serve which faithfully, at all hazards and in all places, was his highest aim.

"Ah, my child," he was saying, "you are a sweet, good girl, after all, much better than you make yourself out to be. Your duty will control you; you do it nobly at last, my child."

"True enough, Father Beret, true enough!" she responded, laughing, "your perception is most excellent, which I will prove to you immediately."

She rose while speaking and went into the house.

"I'll return in a minute or two," she called back from a region which Pere Beret well knew was that of the pantry; "don't get impatient and go away!"

Pere Beret laughed softly at the preposterous suggestion that he would even dream of going out in the rain, which was now roaring heavily on the loose board roof, and miss a cut of cherry pie—a cherry pie of Alice's making! And the Roussillon claret, too, was always excellent. "Ah, child," he thought, "your old Father is not going away."

She presently returned, bearing on a wooden tray a ruby-stained pie and a short, stout bottle flanked by two glasses.

"Of course I'm better than I sometimes appear to be," she said, almost humbly, but with mischief still in her voice and eyes, "and I shall get to be very good when I have grown old. The sweetness of my present nature is in this pie."

She set the tray on a three-legged stool which she pushed close to him.

"There now," she said, "let the rain come, you'll be happy, rain or shine, while the pie and wine last, I'll be bound."

Pere Beret fell to eating right heartily, meantime handing Jean a liberal piece of the luscious pie.

"It is good, my daughter, very good, indeed," the priest remarked with his mouth full. "Madame Roussillon has not neglected your culinary education." Alice filled a glass for him. It was Bordeaux and very fragrant. The bouquet reminded him of his sunny boyhood in France, of his journey up to Paris and of his careless, joy-brimmed youth in the gay city. How far away, how misty, yet how thrillingly sweet it all was! He sat with half closed eyes awhile, sipping and dreaming.

The rain lasted nearly two hours; but the sun was out again when Pere Beret took leave of his young friend. They had been having another good-natured quarrel over the novels, and Madame Roussillon had come out on the veranda to join in.

"I've hidden every book of them," said Madame, a stout and swarthy woman whose pearl-white teeth were her only mark of beauty. Her voice indicated great stubbornness.

5

"Good, good, you have done your very duty, Madame," said Pere Beret, with immense approval in his charming voice.

"But, Father, you said awhile ago that I should have my own way about this," Alice spoke up with spirit; "and on the strength of that remark of yours I gave you the pie and wine. You've eaten my pie and swigged the wine, and now—"

Pere Beret put on his straw cap, adjusting it carefully over the shining dome out of which had come so many thoughts of wisdom, kindness and human sympathy. This done, he gently laid a hand on Alice's bright crown of hair and said:

"Bless you, my child. I will pray to the Prince of Peace for you as long as I live, and I will never cease to beg the Holy Virgin to intercede for you and lead you to the Holy Church."

He turned and went away; but when he was no farther than the gate, Alice called out:

"O Father Beret, I forgot to show you something!"

She ran forth to him and added in a low tone:

"You know that Madame Roussillon has hidden all the novels from me."

She was fumbling to get something out of the loose front of her dress.

"Well, just take a glance at this, will you?" and she showed him a little leather bound volume, much cracked along the hinges of the back.

It was Manon Lescaut, that dreadful romance by the famous Abbe Prevost.

Pere Beret frowned and went his way shaking his head; but before he reached his little hut near the church he was laughing in spite of himself.

"She's not so bad, not so bad," he thought aloud, "it's only her young, independent spirit taking the bit for a wild run. In her sweet soul she is as good as she is pure."

CHAPTER II
A LETTER FROM AFAR

Although Father Beret was for many years a missionary on the Wabash, most of the time at Vincennes, the fact that no mention of him can be found in the records is not stranger than many other things connected with the old town's history. He was, like nearly all the men of his calling in that day, a self-effacing and modest hero, apparently quite unaware that he deserved attention. He and Father Gibault, whose name is so beautifully and nobly connected with the stirring achievements of Colonel George Rogers Clark, were close friends and often companions. Probably Father Gibault himself, whose fame will never fade, would have been to-day as obscure as Father Beret, but for the opportunity given him by Clark to fix his name in the list of heroic patriots who assisted in winning the great Northwest from the English.

Vincennes, even in the earliest days of its history, somehow kept up communication and, considering the circumstances, close relations with New Orleans. It was much nearer Detroit; but the Louisiana colony stood next to France in the imagination and longing of priests, voyageurs, coureurs de bois and reckless adventurers who had Latin blood in their veins. Father Beret first came to Vincennes from New Orleans, the voyage up the Mississippi, Ohio, and Wabash, in a pirogue, lasting through a whole summer and far into the autumn. Since his arrival the post had experienced many vicissitudes, and at the time in which our story opens the British government claimed right of dominion over the great territory drained by the Wabash, and, indeed, over a large, indefinitely outlined part of the North American continent lying above Mexico; a claim just then being vigorously questioned, flintlock in hand, by the Anglo-American colonies.

Of course the handful of French people at Vincennes, so far away from every center of information, and wholly occupied with their trading, trapping and missionary work, were late finding out that war existed between England and her colonies. Nor did it really matter much with them, one way or another. They felt secure in their lonely situation, and so went on selling their trinkets, weapons, domestic implements, blankets and intoxicating liquors to the Indians, whom they held bound to them with a power never possessed by any other white dwellers in the wilderness. Father Beret was probably subordinate to Father Gibault. At all events the latter appears to have had nominal charge of Vincennes, and it can scarcely be doubted that he left Father Beret on the Wabash, while he went to live and labor for a time at Kaskaskia beyond the plains of Illinois.

It is a curious fact that religion and the power of rum and brandy worked together successfully for a long time in giving the French posts almost absolute influence over the wild and savage men by whom they were always surrounded. The good priests deprecated the traffic in liquors and tried hard to control it, but soldiers of fortune and reckless traders were in the majority, their interests taking precedence of all spiritual demands and carrying everything along. What could the brave missionaries do but make the very best of a perilous situation?

In those days wine was drunk by almost everybody, its use at table and as an article of incidental refreshment and social pleasure being practically universal; wherefore the steps of reform in the matter of intemperance were but rudimentary and in all places beset by well-nigh insurmountable difficulties. In fact the exigencies of frontier life demanded, perhaps, the very stimulus which, when over indulged in, caused so much evil. Malaria loaded the air, and the most efficacious drugs now at command were then undiscovered or could not be had. Intoxicants were the only popular specific. Men drank to prevent contracting ague, drank again, between rigors, to cure it, and yet again to brace themselves during convalescence.

But if the effect of rum as a beverage had strong allurement for the white man, it made an absolute slave of the Indian, who never hesitated for a moment to undertake any task, no matter how hard, bear any privation, even the most terrible, or brave any danger, although it might demand reckless desperation, if in in the end a well filled bottle or jug appeared as his reward.

Of course the traders did not overlook such a source of power. Alcoholic liquor became their implement of almost magical work in controlling the lives, labors, and resources of the Indians. The priests with their captivating story of the Cross had a large influence in softening savage natures and averting many an awful danger; but when everything else failed, rum always came to the rescue of a threatened French post.

We need not wonder, then, when we are told that Father Beret made no sign of distress or disapproval upon being informed of the arrival of a boat loaded with rum, brandy or gin. It was Rene de Ronville who brought the news, the same Rene already mentioned as having given the priest a plate of squirrels. He was sitting on the doorsill of Father Beret's hut, when the old man reached it after his visit at the Roussillon home, and held in his hand a letter which he appeared proud to deliver.

"A batteau and seven men, with a cargo of liquor, came during the rain," he said, rising and taking off his curious cap, which, made of an animal's skin, had a tail jauntily dangling from its crown-tip; "and here is a letter for you, Father. The batteau is from New Orleans. Eight men started with it; but one went ashore to hunt and was killed by an Indian."

Father Beret took the letter without apparent interest and said:

"Thank you, my son, sit down again; the door-log is not wetter than the stools inside; I will sit by you."

The wind had driven a flood of rain into the cabin through the open door, and water twinkled in puddles here and there on the floor's puncheons. They sat down side by side, Father Beret fingering the letter in an absent-minded way.

"There'll be a jolly time of it to-night," Rene de Ronville remarked, "a roaring time."

"Why do you say that, my son?" the priest demanded.

"The wine and the liquor," was the reply; "much drinking will be done. The men have all been dry here for some time, you know, and are as thirsty as sand. They are making ready to enjoy themselves down at the river house."

"Ah, the poor souls!" sighed Father Beret, speaking as one whose thoughts were wandering far away.

"Why don't you read your letter, Father?" Rene added.

The priest started, turned the soiled square of paper over in his hand, then thrust it inside his robe.

"It can wait," he said. Then, changing his voice; "the squirrels you gave me were excellent, my son. It was good of you to think of me," he added, laying his hand on Rene's arm.

"Oh, I'm glad if I have pleased you, Father Beret, for you are so kind to me always, and to everybody. When I killed the squirrels I said to myself: 'These are young, juicy and tender, Father Beret must have these,' so I brought them along."

The young man rose to go; for he was somehow impressed that Father Beret must wish opportunity to read his letter, and would prefer to be left alone with it. But the priest pulled him down again.

"Stay a while," he said, "I have not had a talk with you for some time."

Rene looked a trifle uneasy.

"You will not drink any to-night, my son," Father Beret added. "You must not; do you hear?"

The young man's eyes and mouth at once began to have a sullen expression; evidently he was not pleased and felt rebellious; but it was hard for him to resist Father Beret, whom he loved, as did every soul in the post. The priest's voice was sweet and gentle, yet positive to a degree. Rene did not say a word.

"Promise me that you will not taste liquor this night," Father Beret went on, grasping the young man's arm more firmly; "promise me, my son, promise me."

Still Rene was silent. The men did not look at each other, but gazed away across the country beyond the Wabash to where a glory from the western sun flamed on the upper rim of a great cloud fragment creeping along the horizon. Warm as the day had been, a delicious coolness now began to temper the air; for the wind had shifted into the northwest. A meadowlark sang dreamingly in the wild grass of the low lands hard by, over which two or three prairie hawks hovered with wings that beat rapidly.

"Eh bien, I must go," said Rene presently, getting to his feet nimbly and evading Father Beret's hand which would have held him.

"Not to the river house, my son?" said the priest appealingly.

"No, not there; I have another letter; one for M'sieu' Roussillon; it came by the boat too. I go to give it to Madame Roussillon."

Rene de Ronville was a dark, weather-stained young fellow, neither tall nor short, wearing buckskin moccasins, trousers and tunic. His eyes were dark brown, keen, quick-moving, set well under heavy brows. A razor had probably never touched his face, and his thin, curly beard crinkled over his strongly turned cheeks and chin, while his moustaches sprang out quite fiercely above his full-lipped, almost sensual mouth. He looked wiry and active, a man not to be lightly reckoned with in a trial of bodily strength and will power.

Father Beret's face and voice changed on the instant. He laughed dryly and said, with a sly gleam in his eyes:

"You could spend the evening pleasantly with Madame Roussillon and Jean. Jean, you know, is a very amusing fellow."

Rene brought forth the letter of which he had spoken and held it up before Father Beret's face.

"Maybe you think I haven't any letter for M'sieu' Roussillon," he blurted; "and maybe you are quite certain that I am not going to the house to take the letter."

"Monsieur Roussillon is absent, you know," Father Beret suggested. "But cherry pies are just as good while he's gone as when he's at home, and I happen to know that there are some particularly delicious ones in the pantry of Madame Roussillon. Mademoiselle Alice gave me a juicy sample; but then I dare say you do not care to have your pie served by her hand. It would interfere with your appetite; eh, my son?"

Rene turned short about wagging his head and laughing, and so with his back to the priest he strode away along the wet path leading to the Roussillon place.

Father Beret gazed after him, his face relaxing to a serious expression in which a trace of sadness and gloom spread like an elusive twilight. He took out his letter, but did not glance at it, simply holding it tightly gripped in his sinewy right hand. Then his old eyes stared vacantly, as eyes do when their sight is cast back many, many years into the past. The missive was from beyond the sea—he knew the handwriting—a waft of the flowers of Avignon seemed to rise out of it, as if by the pressure of his grasp.

A stoop-shouldered, burly man went by, leading a pair of goats, a kid following. He was making haste excitedly, keeping the goats at a lively trot.

"Bon jour, Pere Beret," he flung out breezily, and walked rapidly on.

"Ah, ah; his mind is busy with the newly arrived cargo," thought the old priest, returning the salutation; "his throat aches for the liquor,—the poor man."

Then he read again the letter's superscription and made a faltering move, as if to break the seal. His hands trembled violently, his face looked gray and drawn.

"Come on, you brutes," cried the receding man, jerking the thongs of skin by which he led the goats.

Father Beret rose and turned into his damp little hut, where the light was dim on the crucifix hanging opposite the door against the clay-daubed wall. It was a bare, unsightly, clammy room; a rude bed on one side, a shelf for table and two or three wooden stools constituting the furniture, while the uneven puncheons of the floor wabbled and clattered under the priest's feet.

An unopened letter is always a mysterious thing. We who receive three or four mails every day, scan each little paper square with a speculative eye. Most of us know what sweet uncertainty hangs on the opening of envelopes whose contents may be almost anything except something important, and what a vague yet delicious thrill comes with the snip of the paper knife; but if we be in a foreign land and long years absent from home, then is a letter subtly powerful to move us, even more before it is opened than after it is read.

It had been many years since a letter from home had come to Father Beret. The last, before the one now in his hand, had made him ill of nostalgia, fairly shaking his iron determination never to quit for a moment his life work as a missionary. Ever since that day he had found it harder to meet the many and stern demands of a most difficult and exacting duty. Now the mere touch of the paper in his hand gave him a sense of returning weakness, dissatisfaction, and longing. The home of his boyhood, the rushing of the Rhone, a seat in a shady nook of the garden, Madeline, his sister, prattling beside him, and his mother singing somewhere about the house—it all came back and went over him and through him, making his heart sink strangely, while another voice, the sweetest ever heard—but she was ineffable and her memory a forbidden fragrance.

Father Beret tottered across the forlorn little room and knelt before the crucifix holding his clasped hands high, the letter pressed between them. His lips moved in prayer, but made no sound; his whole frame shook violently.

It would be unpardonable desecration to enter the chamber of Father Beret's soul and look upon his sacred and secret trouble; nor must we even speculate as to its particulars. The good old man writhed and wrestled before the cross for a long time, until at last he seemed to receive the calmness and strength he prayed for so fervently; then he rose, tore the letter into pieces so small that not a word remained whole, and squeezed them so firmly together that they were compressed into a tiny, solid ball, which he let fall through a crack between the floor puncheons. After waiting twenty years for that letter, hungry as his heart was, he did not even open it when at last it arrived. He would never know what message it bore. The link between him and the old sweet days was broken forever. Now with God's help he could do his work to the end.

He went and stood in his doorway, leaning against the side. Was it a mere coincidence that the meadowlark flew up just then from its grass-tuft, and came to the roof's comb overhead, where it lit with a light yet audible stroke of its feet and began fluting its tender, lonesome-sounding strain? If Father Beret heard it he gave no sign of recognition; very likely he was thinking about the cargo of liquor and how he could best counteract its baleful influence. He looked toward the "river house," as the inhabitants had named a large shanty, which stood on a bluff of the Wabash not far from where the road-bridge at present crosses, and saw men gathering there.

Meantime Rene de Ronville had delivered Madame Roussillon's letter with due promptness. Of course such a service demanded pie and claret. What still better pleased him, Alice chose to be more amiable than was usually her custom when he called. They sat together in the main room of the house where M. Roussillon kept his books, his curiosities of Indian manufacture collected here and there, and his surplus firearms, swords, pistols, and knives, ranged not unpleasingly around the walls.

Of course, along with the letter, Rene bore the news, so interesting to himself, of the boat's tempting cargo just discharged at the river house. Alice understood her friend's danger—felt it in the intense enthusiasm of his voice and manner. She had once seen the men carousing on a similar occasion when she was but a child, and the impression then made still remained in her memory. Instinctively she resolved to hold Rene by one means or another away from the river house if possible. So she managed to keep him occupied eating pie, sipping watered claret and chatting until night came on and Madame Roussillon brought in a lamp. Then he hurriedly snatched his cap from the floor beside him and got up to go.

"Come and look at my handiwork," Alice quickly said; "my shelf of pies, I mean." She led him to the pantry, where a dozen or more of the cherry pates were ranged in order. "I made every one of them this morning and baked them; had them all out of the oven before the rain came up. Don't you think me a wonder of cleverness and industry? Father Beret was polite enough to flatter me; but you—you just eat what you want and say nothing! You are not polite, Monsieur Rene de Ronville."

"I've been showing you what I thought of your goodies," said Rene; "eating's better than talking, you know; so I'll just take one more," and he helped himself. "Isn't that compliment enough?"

"A few such would make me another hot day's work," she replied, laughing. "Pretty talk would be cheaper and more satisfactory in the long run. Even the flour in these pates I ground with my own hand in an Indian mortar. That was hard work too."

By this time Rene had forgotten the river house and the liquor. With softening eyes he gazed at Alice's rounded cheeks and sheeny hair over which the light from the curious earthen lamp she bore in her hand flickered most effectively. He loved her madly; but his fear of her was more powerful than his love. She gave him no opportunity to speak what he felt, having ever ready a quick, bright change of mood and manner when she saw him plucking up courage to address her in a sentimental way. Their relations had long been somewhat familiar, which was but natural, considering their youth and the circumstances of their daily life; but Alice somehow had

9

kept a certain distance open between them, so that very warm friendship could not suddenly resolve itself into a troublesome passion on Rene's part.

We need not attempt to analyze a young girl's feeling and motives in such a case; what she does and what she thinks are mysteries even to her own understanding. The influence most potent in shaping the rudimentary character of Alice Tarleton (called Roussillon) had been only such as a lonely frontier post could generate. Her associations with men and women had, with few exceptions, been unprofitable in an educational way, while her reading in M. Roussillon's little library could not have given her any practical knowledge of manners and life.

She was fond of Rene de Ronville, and it would have been quite in accordance with the law of ordinary human forces, indeed almost the inevitable thing, for her to love and marry him in the fullness of time; but her imagination was outgrowing her surroundings. Books had given her a world of romance wherein she moved at will, meeting a class of people far different from those who actually shared her experiences. Her day-dreams and her night-dreams partook much more of what she had read and imagined than of what she had seen and heard in the raw little world around her.

Her affection for Rene was interfered with by her large admiration for the heroic, masterful and magnetic knights who charged through the romances of the Roussillon collection. For although Rene was unquestionably brave and more than passably handsome, he had no armor, no war-horse, no shining lance and embossed shield—the difference, indeed, was great.

Those who love to contend against the fatal drift of our age toward over-education could find in Alice Tarleton, foster daughter of Gaspard Roussillon, a primitive example, an elementary case in point. What could her book education do but set up stumbling blocks in the path of happiness? She was learning to prefer the ideal to the real. Her soul was developing itself as best it could for the enjoyment of conditions and things absolutely foreign to the possibilities of her lot in life.

Perhaps it was the light and heat of imagination, shining out through Alice's face, which gave her beauty such a fascinating power. Rene saw it and felt its electrical stroke send a sweet shiver through his heart, while he stood before her.

"You are very beautiful to-night Alice," he presently said, with a suddenness which took even her alertness by surprise. A flush rose to his dark face and immediately gave way to a grayish pallor. His heart came near stopping on the instant, he was so shocked by his own daring; but he laid a hand on her hair, stroking it softly.

Just a moment she was at a loss, looking a trifle embarrassed, then with a merry laugh she stepped aside and said:

"That sounds better, Monsieur Rene de Ronville much better; you will be as polite as Father Beret after a little more training."

She slipped past him while speaking and made her way back again to the main room, whence she called to him:

"Come here, I've something to show you."

He obeyed, a sheepish trace on his countenance betraying his self-consciousness.

When he came near Alice she was taking from its buckhorn hook on the wall a rapier, one of a beautiful pair hanging side by side.

"Papa Roussillon gave me these," she said with great animation. "He bought them of an Indian who had kept them a long time; where he came across them he would not tell; but look how beautiful! Did you ever see anything so fine?"

Guard and hilt were of silver; the blade, although somewhat corroded, still showed the fine wavy lines of Damascus steel and traces of delicate engraving, while in the end of the hilt was set a large oval turquoise.

"A very queer present to give a girl," said Rene; "what can you do with them?"

A captivating flash of playfulness came into her face and she sprang backward, giving the sword a semicircular turn with her wrist. The blade sent forth a keen hiss as it cut the air close, very close to Rene's nose. He jerked his head and flung up his hand.

She laughed merrily, standing beautifully poised before him, the rapier's point slightly elevated. Her short skirt left her feet and ankles free to show their graceful proportions and the perfect pose in which they held her supple body.

"You see what I can do with the colechemarde, eh, Monsieur Rene de Ronville!" she exclaimed, giving him a smile which fairly blinded him. "Notice how very near to your neck I can thrust it and yet not touch it. Now!"

She darted the keen point under his chin and drew it away so quickly that the stroke was like a glint of sunlight.

"What do you think of that as a nice and accurate piece of skill?"

She again resumed her pose, the right foot advanced, the left arm well back, her lissome, finely developed body leaning slightly forward.

Rene's hands were up before his face in a defensive position, palms outward.

Just then a chorus of men's voices sounded in the distance. The river house was beginning its carousal with a song. Alice let fall her sword's point and listened.

Rene looked about for his cap.

"I must be going," he said.

Another and louder swish of the rapier made him pirouette and dodge again with great energy.

"Don't," he cried, "that's dangerous; you'll put out my eyes; I never saw such a girl!"

She laughed at him and kept on whipping the air dangerously near his eyes, until she had driven him backward as far as he could squeeze himself into a comer of the room.

Madame Roussillon came to the door from the kitchen and stood looking in and laughing, with her hands on her hips. By this time the rapier was making a criss-cross pattern of flashing lines close to the young man's head while Alice, in the enjoyment of her exercise, seemed to concentrate all the glowing rays of her beauty in her face, her eyes dancing merrily.

"Quit, now, Alice," he begged, half in fun and half in abject fear; "please quit—I surrender!"

She thrust to the wall on either side of him, then springing lightly backward a pace, stood at guard. Her thick yellow hair had fallen over her neck and shoulders in a loose wavy mass, out of which her face beamed with a bewitching effect upon her captive.

Rene, glad enough to have a cessation of his peril, stood laughing dryly; but the singing down at the river house was swelling louder and he made another movement to go.

"You surrendered, you remember," cried Alice, renewing the sword-play; "sit down on the chair there and make yourself comfortable. You are not going down yonder to-night; you are going to stay here and talk with me and Mother Roussillon; we are lonesome and you are good company."

A shot rang out keen and clear; there was a sudden tumult that broke up the distant singing; and presently more firing at varying intervals cut the night air from the direction of the river.

Jean, the hunchback, came in to say that there was a row of some sort; he had seen men running across the common as if in pursuit of a fugitive; but the moonlight was so dim that he could not be sure what it all meant.

Rene picked up his cap and bolted out of the house.

CHAPTER III
THE RAPE OF THE DEMIJOHN

The row down at the river house was more noise than fight, so far as results seemed to indicate. It was all about a small dame jeanne of fine brandy, which an Indian by the name of Long-Hair had seized and run off with at the height of the carousal. He must have been soberer than his pursuers, or naturally fleeter; for not one of them could catch him, or even keep long in sight of him. Some pistols were emptied while the race was on, and two or three of the men swore roundly to having seen Long-Hair jump sidewise and stagger, as if one of the shots had taken effect. But, although the moon was shining, he someway disappeared, they could not understand just how, far down beside the river below the fort and the church.

It was not a very uncommon thing for an Indian to steal what he wanted, and in most cases light punishment followed conviction; but it was felt to be a capital offense for an Indian or anybody else to rape a demijohn of fine brandy, especially one sent as a present, by a friend in New Orleans, to Lieutenant Governor Abbott, who had until recently been the commandant of the post. Every man at the river house recognized and resented the enormity of Long-Hair's crime and each was, for the moment, ready to be his judge and his executioner. He had broken at once every rule of frontier etiquette and every bond of sympathy. Nor was Long-Hair ignorant of the danger involved in his daring enterprise. He had beforehand carefully and stolidly weighed all the conditions, and true to his Indian nature, had concluded that a little wicker covered bottle of brandy was well worth the risk of his life. So he had put himself in condition for a great race by slipping out and getting rid of his weapons and all surplus weight of clothes.

This incident brought the drinking bout at the river house to a sudden end; but nothing further came of it that night, and no record of it would be found in these pages, but for the fact that Long-Hair afterwards became an important character in the stirring historical drama which had old Vincennes for its center of energy.

Rene de Ronville probably felt himself in bad luck when he arrived at the river house just too late to share in the liquor or to join in chasing the bold thief. He listened with interest, however, to the story of Long-Hair's capture of the commandant's demijohn and could not refrain from saying that if he had been present there would have been a quite different result.

"I would have shot him before he got to that door," he said, drawing his heavy flint-lock pistol and going through the motions of one aiming quickly and firing. Indeed, so vigorously in earnest was he with the pantomime, that he actually did fire, unintentionally of course,—the ball burying itself in the door-jamb.

He was laughed at by those present for being more excited than they who witnessed the whole thing. One of them, a leathery-faced and grizzled old sinner, leered at him contemptuously and said in queer French, with a curious accent caught from long use of backwoods English:

"Listen how the boy brags! Ye might think, to hear Rene talk, that he actually amounted to a big pile."

This personage was known to every soul in Vincennes as Oncle Jazon, and when Oncle Jazon spoke the whole town felt bound to listen.

"An' how well he shoots, too," he added with an intolerable wink; "aimed at the door and hit the post. Certainly Long-Hair would have been in great danger! O yes, he'd 'ave killed Long-Hair at the first shot, wouldn't he though!"

Oncle Jazon had the air of a large man, but the stature of a small one; in fact he was shriveled bodily to a degree which suggested comparison with a sun-dried wisp of hickory bark; and when he chuckled, as he was now doing, his mouth puckered itself until it looked like a scar on his face. From cap to moccasins he had every mark significant of a desperate character; and yet there was about him something that instantly commanded the confidence of rough men,— the look of self-sufficiency and superior capability always to be found in connection with immense will power. His sixty years of exposure, hardship, and danger seemed to have but toughened his physique and strengthened his vitality. Out of his small hazel eyes gleamed a light as keen as ice.

"All right, Oncle Jazon," said Rene laughing and blowing the smoke out of his pistol; "'twas you all the same who let Long-Hair trot off with the Governor's brandy, not I. If you could have hit even a door-post it might have been better."

Oncle Jazon took off his cap and looked down into it in a way he had when about to say something final.

"Ventrebleu! I did not shoot at Long-Hair at all," he said, speaking slowly, "because the scoundrel was unarmed. He didn't have on even a knife, and he was havin' enough to do dodgin' the bullets that the rest of 'em were plumpin' at 'im without any compliments from me to bother 'im more."

"Well," Rene replied, turning away with a laugh, "if I'd been scalped by the Indians, as you have, I don't think there would be any particular reason why I should wait for an Indian thief to go and arm himself before I accepted him as a target."

Oncle Jazon lifted a hand involuntarily and rubbed his scalpless crown; then he chuckled with a grotesque grimace as if the recollection of having his head skinned were the funniest thing imaginable.

"When you've killed as many of 'em as Oncle Jazon has," remarked a bystander to Rene, "you'll not be so hungry for blood, maybe."

"Especially after ye've took fifty-nine scalps to pay for yer one," added Oncle Jazon, replacing his cap over the hairless area of his crown.

The men who had been chasing Long-Hair, presently came straggling back with their stories—each had a distinct one—of how the fugitive escaped. They were wild looking fellows, most of them somewhat intoxicated, all profusely liberal with their stock of picturesque profanity. They represented the roughest element of the well-nigh lawless post.

"I'm positive that he's wounded," said one. "Jacques and I shot at him together, so that our pistols sounded just as if only one had been fired—bang! that way—and he leaped sideways for all the world like a bird with a broken leg. I thought he'd fall; but ve! he ran faster'n ever, and all at once he was gone; just disappeared."

"Well, to-morrow we'll get him," said another. "You and I and Jacques, we'll take up his trail, the thief, and follow him till we find him. He can't get off so easy."

"I don't know so well about that," said another; "it's Long-Hair, you must remember, and Long-Hair is no common buck that just anybody can find asleep. You know what Long-Hair is. Nobody's ever got even with 'im yet. That's so, ain't it? Just ask Oncle Jazon, if you don't believe it!"

The next morning Long-Hair was tracked to the edge. He had been wounded, but whether seriously or not could only be conjectured. A sprinkle of blood, here and there quite a dash of it, reddened the grass and clumps of weeds he had run through, and ended close to the water into which it looked as if he had plunged with a view to baffling pursuit. Indeed pursuit was baffled. No further trace could be found, by which to follow the cunning fugitive. Some of the men consoled themselves by saying, without believing, that Long-Hair was probably lying drowned at the bottom of the river.

"Pas du tout," observed Oncle Jazon, his short pipe askew far over in the corner of his mouth, "not a bit of it is that Indian drowned. He's jes' as live as a fat cat this minute, and as drunk as the devil. He'll get some o' yer scalps yet after he's guzzled all that brandy and slep' a week."

It finally transpired that Oncle Jazon was partly right and partly wrong. Long-Hair was alive, even as a fat cat, perhaps; but not drunk, for in trying to swim with the rotund little dame jeanne under his arm he lost hold of it and it went to the bottom of the Wabash, where it may be lying at this moment patiently waiting for some one to fish it out of its bed deep in the sand and mud, and break the ancient wax from its neck!

Rene de Ronville, after the chase of Long-Hair had been given over, went to tell Father Beret what had happened, and finding the priest's hut empty turned into the path leading to the Roussillon place, which was at the head of a narrow street laid out in a direction at right angles to the river's course. He passed two or three diminutive cabins, all as much alike as bee-hives. Each had its squat veranda and thatched or clapboarded roof held in place by weight-poles ranged in roughly parallel rows, and each had the face of the wall under its veranda neatly daubed with a grayish stucco made of mud and lime. You may see such houses today in some remote parts of the creole country of Louisiana.

As Rene passed along he spoke with a gay French freedom to the dames and lasses who chanced to be visible. His air would be regarded as violently brigandish in our day; we might even go so far as to think his whole appearance comical. His jaunty cap with a tail that wagged as he walked, his short trousers and leggins of buckskin, and his loose shirt-like tunic, drawn in at the waist with a broad belt, gave his strong figure just the dash of wildness suited to the armament with which it was weighted. A heavy gun lay in the hollow of his shoulder under which hung an otter-skin bullet-pouch with its clear powder-horn and white bone charger. In his belt were two huge flint-lock pistols and a long case-knife.

"Bon jour, Ma'm'selle Adrienne," he cheerily called, waving his free hand in greeting to a small, dark lass standing on the step of a veranda and indolently swinging a broom. "Comment allez-vous auj ourd'hui?"

"J'm'porte tres bien, merci, Mo'sieu Rene," was the quick response; "et vous?"

"Oh, I'm as lively as a cricket."

"Going a hunting?"

"No, just up here a little way—just on business—up to Mo'sieu Roussillon's for a moment."

"Yes," the girl responded in a tone indicative of something very like spleen, "yes, undoubtedly, Mo'sieu de Ronville; your business there seems quite pressing of late. I have noticed your industrious application to that business."

"Ta-ta, little one," he wheedled, lowering his voice; "you mustn't go to making bug-bears out of nothing."

"Bug-bears!" she retorted, "you go on about your business and I'll attend to mine," and she flirted into the house.

Rene laughed under his breath, standing a moment as if expecting her to come out again; but she did not, and he resumed his walk singing softly—

"Elle a les joues vermeilles, vermeilles, Ma belle, ma belle petite."

But ten to one he was not thinking of Madamoiselle Adrienne Bourcier. His mind, however, must have been absorbingly occupied; for in the straight, open way he met Father Beret and did not see him until he came near bumping against the old man, who stepped aside with astonishing agility and said—

"Dieu vous benisse, mon fils; but what is your great hurry—where can you be going in such happy haste?" Rene did not stop to parley with the priest. He flung some phrase of pleasant greeting back over his shoulder as he trudged on, his heart beginning a tattoo against his ribs when the Roussillon place came in sight, and he took hold of his mustache to pull it, as some men must do in moments of nervousness and bashfulness. If sounds ever have color, the humming in his ears was of a rosy hue; if thoughts ever exhale fragrance, his brain overflowed with the sweets of violet and heliotrope.

13

He had in mind what he was going to say when Alice and he should be alone together. It was a pretty speech, he thought; indeed a very thrilling little speech, by the way it stirred his own nerve-centers as he conned it over.

Madame Roussillon met him at the door in not a very good humor.

"Is Mademoiselle Alice here?" he ventured to demand.

"Alice? no, she's not here; she's never here just when I want her most. V'la le picbois et la grive—see the woodpecker and the robin—eating the cherries, eating every one of them, and that girl running off somewhere instead of staying here and picking them," she railed in answer to the young man's polite inquiry. "I haven't seen her these four hours, neither her nor that rascally hunchback, Jean. They're up to some mischief, I'll be bound!"

Madame Roussillon puffed audibly between phrases; but she suddenly became very mild when relieved of her tirade.

"Mais entrez," she added in a pleasant tone, "come in and tell me the news."

Rene's disappointment rushed into his face, but he managed to laugh it aside.

"Father Beret has just been telling me," said Madame Roussillon, "that our friend Long-Hair made some trouble last night. How about it?"

Rene told her what he knew and added that Long-Hair would probably never be seen again.

"He was shot, no doubt of it," he went on, "and is now being nibbled by fish and turtles. We tracked him by his blood to where he jumped into the Wabash. He never came out."

Strangely enough it happened that, at the very time of this chat between Madame Roussillon and Rene Alice was bandaging Long-Hair's wounded leg with strips of her apron. It was under some willows which overhung the bank of a narrow and shallow lagoon or slough, which in those days extended a mile or two back into the country on the farther side of the river. Alice and Jean went over in a pirogue to see if the water lilies, haunting a pond there, were yet beginning to bloom. They landed at a convenient spot some distance up the little lagoon, made the boat fast by dragging its prow high ashore, and were on the point of setting out across a neck of wet, grassy land to the pond, when a deep grunt, not unlike that of a self-satisfied pig, attracted them to the willows, where they discovered Long-Hair, badly wounded, weltering in some black mud.

His hiding-place was cunningly chosen, save that the mire troubled him, letting him down by slow degrees, and threatening to engulf him bodily; and he was now too weak to extricate himself. He lifted his head and glared. His face was grimy, his hair matted with mud. Alice, although brave enough and quite accustomed to startling experiences, uttered a cry when she saw those snaky eyes glistening so savagely amid the shadows. But Jean was quick to recognize Long-Hair; he had often seen him about town, a figure not to be forgotten.

"They've been hunting him everywhere," he said in a half whisper to Alice, clutching the skirt of her dress. "It's Long-Hair, the Indian who stole the brandy; I know him."

Alice recoiled a pace or two.

"Let's go back and tell 'em," Jean added, still whispering, "they want to kill him; Oncle Jazon said so. Come on!"

He gave her dress a jerk; but she did not move any farther back; she was looking at the blood oozing from a wound in the Indian's leg.

"He is shot, he is hurt, Jean, we must help him," she presently said, recovering her self-control, yet still pale. "We must get him out of that bad place."

Jean caught Alice's merciful spirit with sympathetic readiness, and showed immediate willingness to aid her.

It was a difficult thing to do; but there was a will and of course a way. They had knives with which they cut willows to make a standing place on the mud. While they were doing this they spoke friendly words to Long-Hair, who understood French a little, and at last they got hold of his arms, tugged, rested, tugged again, and finally managed to help him to a dry place, still under the willows, where he could lie more at ease. Jean carried water in his cap with which they washed the wound and the stolid savage face. Then Alice tore up her cotton apron, in which she had hoped to bear home a load of lilies, and with the strips bound the wound very neatly. It took a long time, during which the Indian remained silent and apparently quite indifferent.

Long-Hair was a man of superior physique, tall, straight, with the muscles of a Vulcan; and while he lay stretched on the ground half clad and motionless, he would have been a grand model for an heroic figure in bronze. Yet from every lineament there came a strange repelling influence, like that from a snake. Alice felt almost unbearable disgust while doing her merciful task; but she bravely persevered until it was finished.

It was now late in the afternoon, and the sun would be setting before they could reach home.

14

"We must hurry back, Jean," Alice said, turning to depart. "It will be all we can do to reach the other side in daylight. I'm thinking that they'll be out hunting for us too, if we don't move right lively. Come."

She gave the Indian another glance when she had taken but a step. He grunted and held up something in his hand—something that shone with a dull yellow light. It was a small, oval, gold locket which she had always worn in her bosom. She sprang and snatched it from his palm.

"Thank you," she exclaimed, smiling gratefully. "I am so glad you found it."

The chain by which the locket had hung was broken, doubtless by some movement while dragging Long-Hair out of the mud, and the lid had sprung open, exposing a miniature portrait of Alice, painted when she was a little child, probably not two years old. It was a sweet baby face, archly bright, almost surrounded with a fluff of golden hair. The neck and the upper line of the plump shoulders, with a trace of richly delicate lace and a string of pearls, gave somehow a suggestion of patrician daintiness.

Long-Hair looked keenly into Alice's eyes, when she stooped to take the locket from his hand, but said nothing.

She and Jean now hurried away, and, so vigorously did they paddle the pirogue, that the sky was yet red in the west when they reached home and duly received their expected scolding from Madame Roussillon.

Alice sealed Jean's lips as to their adventure; for she had made up her mind to save Long-Hair if possible, and she felt sure that the only way to do it would be to trust no one but Father Beret.

It turned out that Long-Hair's wound was neither a broken bone nor a cut artery. The flesh of his leg, midway between the hip and the knee, was pierced; the bullet had bored a neat hole clean through. Father Beret took the case in hand, and with no little surgical skill proceeded to set the big Indian upon his feet again. The affair had to be cleverly managed. Food, medicines and clothing were surreptitiously borne across the river; a bed of grass was kept fresh under Long-Hair's back; his wound was regularly dressed; and finally his weapons—a tomahawk, a knife, a strong bow and a quiver of arrows—which he had hidden on the night of his bold theft, were brought to him.

"Now go and sin no more," said good Father Beret; but he well knew that his words were mere puffs of articulate wind in the ear of the grim and silent savage, who limped away with an air of stately dignity into the wilderness.

A load fell from Alice's mind when Father Beret informed her of Long-Hair's recovery and departure. Day and night the dread lest some of the men should find out his hiding place and kill him had depressed and worried her. And now, when it was all over, there still hovered like an elusive shadow in her consciousness a vague haunting impression of the incident's immense significance as an influence in her life. To feel that she had saved a man from death was a new sensation of itself; but the man and the circumstances were picturesque; they invited imagination; they furnished an atmosphere of romance dear to all young and healthy natures, and somehow stirred her soul with a strange appeal.

Long-Hair's imperturbable calmness, his stolid, immobile countenance, the mysterious reptilian gleam of his shifty black eyes, and the soulless expression always lurking in them, kept a fascinating hold on the girl's memory. They blended curiously with the impressions left by the romances she had read in M. Roussillon's mildewed books.

Long-Hair was not a young man; but it would have been impossible to guess near his age. His form and face simply showed long experience and immeasurable vigor. Alice remembered with a shuddering sensation the look he gave her when she took the locket from his hand. It was of but a second's duration, yet it seemed to search every nook of her being with its subtle power.

Romancers have made much of their Indian heroes, picturing them as models of manly beauty and nobility; but all fiction must be taken with liberal pinches of salt. The plain truth is that dark savages of the pure blood often do possess the magnetism of perfect physical development and unfathomable mental strangeness; but real beauty they never have. Their innate repulsiveness is so great that, like the snake's charm, it may fascinate; yet an indescribable, haunting disgust goes with it. And, after all, if Alice had been asked to tell just how she felt toward the Indian she had labored so hard to save, she would promptly have said:

"I loathe him as I do a toad!"

Nor would Father Beret, put to the same test, have made a substantially different confession. His work, to do which his life went as fuel to fire, was training the souls of Indians for the reception of divine grace; but experience had not changed his first impression of savage character. When he traveled in the wilderness he carried the Word and the Cross; but he was also armed with a gun and two good pistols, not to mention a dangerous knife. The rumor prevailed that Father Beret could drive a nail at sixty yards with his rifle, and at twenty snuff a candle with either one of his pistols.

CHAPTER IV
THE FIRST MAYOR OF VINCENNES

Governor Abbott probably never so much as heard of the dame jeanne of French brandy sent to him by his creole friend in New Orleans. He had been gone from Vincennes several months when the batteau arrived, having been recalled to Detroit by the British authorities; and he never returned. Meantime the little post with its quaint cabins and its dilapidated block-house, called Fort Sackville, lay sunning drowsily by the river in a blissful state of helplessness from the military point of view. There was no garrison; the two or three pieces of artillery, abandoned and exposed, gathered rust and cobwebs, while the pickets of the stockade, decaying and loosened in the ground by winter freezes and summer rains, leaned in all directions, a picture of decay and inefficiency.

The inhabitants of the town, numbering about six hundred, lived very much as pleased them, without any regular municipal government, each family its own tribe, each man a law unto himself; yet for mutual protection, they all kept in touch and had certain common rights which were religiously respected and defended faithfully. A large pasturing ground was fenced in where the goats and little black cows of the villagers browsed as one herd, while the patches of wheat, corn and vegetables were not inclosed at all. A few of the thriftier and more important citizens, however, had separate estates of some magnitude, surrounding their residences, kept up with care and, if the time and place be taken into account, with considerable show of taste.

Monsieur Gaspard Roussillon was looked upon as the aristocrat par excellence of Vincennes, notwithstanding the fact that his name bore no suggestion of noble or titled ancestry. He was rich and in a measure educated; moreover the successful man's patent of leadership, a commanding figure and a suave manner, came always to his assistance when a crisis presented itself. He traded shrewdly, much to his own profit, but invariably with the excellent result that the man, white or Indian, with whom he did business felt himself especially favored in the transaction. By the exercise of firmness, prudence, vast assumption, florid eloquence and a kindly liberality he had greatly endeared himself to the people; so that in the absence of a military commander he came naturally to be regarded as the chief of the town, Mo'sieu' le maire.

He returned from his extended trading expedition about the middle of July, bringing, as was his invariable rule, a gift for Alice. This time it was a small, thin disc of white flint, with a hole in the center through which a beaded cord of sinew was looped. The edge of the disc was beautifully notched and the whole surface polished so that it shone like glass, while the beads, made of very small segments of porcupine quills, were variously dyed, making a curiously gaudy show of bright colors.

"There now, ma cherie, is something worth fifty times its weight in gold," said M. Roussillon when he presented the necklace to his foster daughter with pardonable self-satisfaction. "It is a sacred charm-string given me by an old heathen who would sell his soul for a pint of cheap rum. He solemnly informed me that whoever wore it could not by any possibility be killed by an enemy."

Alice kissed M. Roussillon.

"It's so curious and beautiful," she said, holding it up and drawing the variegated string through her fingers. Then, with her mischievous laugh, she added; "and I'm glad it is so powerful against one's enemy; I'll wear it whenever I go where Adrienne Bourcier is, see if I don't!"

"Is she your enemy? What's up between you and la petite Adrienne, eh?" M. Roussillon lightly demanded. "You were always the best of good friends, I thought. What's happened?"

"Oh, we are good friends," said Alice, quickly, "very good friends, indeed; I was but chaffing."

"Good friends, but enemies; that's how it is with women. Who's the young man that's caused the coolness? I could guess, maybe!" He laughed and winked knowingly. "May I be so bold as to name him at a venture?"

"Yes, if you'll be sure to mention Monsieur Rene de Ronville," she gayly answered. "Who but he could work Adrienne up into a perfect green mist of jealousy?"

"He would need an accomplice, I should imagine; a young lady of some beauty and a good deal of heartlessness."

"Like whom, for example?" and she tossed her bright head. "Not me, I am sure."

16

"Poh! like every pretty maiden in the whole world, ma petite coquette; they're all alike as peas, cruel as blue jays and as sweet as apple-blossoms." He stroked her hair clumsily with his large hand, as a heavy and roughly fond man is apt to do, adding in an almost serious tone:

"But my little girl is better than most of them, not a foolish mischief-maker, I hope."

Alice was putting her head through the string of beads and letting the translucent white disc fall into her bosom.

"It's time to change the subject," she said; "tell me what you have seen while away. I wish I could go far off and see things. Have you been to Detroit, Quebec, Montreal?"

"Yes, I've been to all, a long, hard journey, but reasonably profitable. You shall have a goodly dot when you get married, my child."

"And did you attend any parties and balls?" she inquired quickly, ignoring his concluding remark. "Tell me about them. How do the fine ladies dress, and do they wear their hair high with great big combs? Do they have long skirts and—"

"Hold up, you double-tongued chatterbox!" he interrupted; "I can't answer forty questions at once. Yes, I danced till my legs ached with women old and girls young; but how could I remember how they were dressed and what their style of coiffure was? I know that silk rustled and there was a perfume of eau de Cologne and mignonette and my heart expanded and blazed while I whirled like a top with a sweet lady in my arms."

"Yes, you must have cut a ravishing figure!" interpolated Madame Roussillon with emphatic disapproval, her eyes snapping. "A bull in a lace shop. How delighted the ladies must have been!"

"Never saw such blushing faces and burning glances—such fluttering breasts, such—"

"Big braggart," Madame Roussillon broke in contemptuously, "it's a piastre to a sou that you stood gawping in through a window while gentlemen and ladies did the dancing. I can imagine how you looked—I can!" and with this she took her prodigious bulk at a waddling gait out of the room. "I remember how you danced even when you were not clumsy as a pig on ice!" she shrieked back over her shoulder.

"Parbleu! true enough, my dear," he called after her, "I should think you could—you mind how we used trip it together. You were the prettiest dancer them all, and the young fellows all went to the swords about you!"

"But tell me more," Alice insisted; "I want to know about what you saw in the great towns—in the fine houses—how the ladies looked, how they acted—what they said—the dresses they wore—how—"

"Ciel! you will split my ears, child; can't you fill my pipe and bring it to me with a coal on it? Then I'll try to tell you what I can," he cried, assuming a humorously resigned air. "Perhaps if I smoke I can remember everything."

Alice gladly ran to do what he asked. Meantime Jean was out on the gallery blowing a flute that M. Roussillon had brought him from Quebec.

The pipe well filled and lighted apparently did have the effect to steady and encourage M. Roussillon's memory; or if not his memory, then his imagination, which was of that fervid and liberal sort common to natives of the Midi, and which has been exquisitely depicted by the late Alphonse Daudet in Tartarin and Bombard. He leaned far back in a strong chair, with his massive legs stretched at full length, and gazed at the roof-poles while he talked.

He sympathized fully, in his crude way, with Alice's lively curiosity, and his affection for her made him anxious to appease her longing after news from the great outside world. If the sheer truth must come out, however, he knew precious little about that world, especially the polite part of it in which thrived those femininities so dear to the heart of an isolated and imaginative girl. Still, as he, too, lived in Arcadia, there was no great effort involved when he undertook to blow a dreamer's flute.

In the first place he had not been in Quebec or Montreal during his absence from home. Most of the time he had spent disposing of pelts and furs at Detroit and in extending his trading relations with other posts; but what mattered a trifling want of facts when his meridional fancy once began to warm up? A smattering of social knowledge gained at first hand in his youthful days in France while he was a student whose parents fondly expected him to conquer the world, came to his aid, and besides he had saturated himself all his life with poetry and romance. Scudery, Scarron, Prevost, Madame La Fayette and Calprenede were the chief sources of his information touching the life and manners, morals and gayeties of people who, as he supposed, stirred the surface of that resplendent and far-off ocean called society. Nothing suited him better than to smoke a pipe and talk about what he had seen and done; and the less he had really seen and done the more he had to tell.

His broad, almost over-virile, kindly and contented face beamed with the warmth of wholly imaginary recollections while he recounted with minute circumstantiality to the delighted

Alice his gallant adventures in the crowded and brilliant ball-rooms of the French-Canadian towns. The rolling burr of his bass voice, deep and resonant, gave force to the improvised descriptions.

Madame Roussillon heard the heavy booming and presently came softly back into the door from the kitchen to listen. She leaned against the facing in an attitude of ponderous attention, a hand, on her bulging hip. She could not suppress her unbounded admiration of her liege lord's manly physique, and jealous to fierceness as she was of his experiences so eloquently and picturesquely related, her woman's nature took fire with enjoyment of the scenes described.

This is the mission of the poet and the romancer—to sponge out of existence, for a time, the stiff, refractory, and unlovely realities and give in their place a scene of ideal mobility and charm. The two women reveled in Gaspard Roussillon's revelations. They saw the brilliant companies, the luxurious surroundings, heard the rustle of brocade and the fine flutter of laces, the hum of sweet voices, breathed in the wafts of costly perfumeries, looked on while the dancers whirled and flickered in the confusion of lights; and over all and through all poured and vibrated such ravishing music as only the southern imagination could have conjured up out of nothing.

Alice was absolutely charmed. She sat on a low wooden stool and gazed into Gaspard Roussillon's face with dilating eyes in which burned that rich and radiant something we call a passionate soul. She drank in his flamboyant stream of words with a thirst which nothing but experience could ever quench. He felt her silent applause and the admiring involuntary absorption that possessed his wife; the consciousness of his elementary magnetism augmented the flow of his fine descriptions, and he went on and on, until the arrival of Father Beret put an end to it all.

The priest, hearing of M. Roussillon's return, had come to inquire about some friends living at Detroit. He took luncheon with the family, enjoying the downright refreshing collation of broiled birds, onions, meal-cakes and claret, ending with a dish of blackberries and cream.

M. Roussillon seized the first opportunity to resume his successful romancing, and presently in the midst of the meal began to tell Father Beret about what he had seen in Quebec.

"By the way," he said, with expansive casualness in his voice, "I called upon your old-time friend and co-adjutor, Father Sebastien, while up there. A noble old man. He sent you a thousand good messages. Was mightily delighted when I told him how happy and hale you have always been here. Ah, you should have seen his dear old eyes full of loving tears. He would walk a hundred miles to see you, he said, but never expected to in this world. Blessings, blessings upon dear Father Beret, was what he murmured in my ear when we were parting. He says that he will never leave Quebec until he goes to his home above—ah!"

The way in which M. Roussillon closed his little speech, his large eyes upturned, his huge hands clasped in front of him, was very effective.

"I am under many obligations, my son," said Father Beret, "for what you tell me. It was good of you to remember my dear old friend and go to him for his loving messages to me. I am very, very thankful. Help me to another drop of wine, please."

Now the extraordinary feature of the situation was that Father Beret had known positively for nearly five years that Father Sebastien was dead and buried.

"Ah, yes," M. Roussillon continued, pouring the claret with one hand and making a pious gesture with the other; "the dear old man loves you and prays for you; his voice quavers whenever he speaks of you."

"Doubtless he made his old joke to you about the birth-mark on my shoulder," said Father Beret after a moment of apparently thoughtful silence. "He may have said something about it in a playful way, eh?"

"True, true, why yes, he surely mentioned the same," assented M. Roussillon, his face assuming an expression of confused memory; "it was something sly and humorous, I mind; but it just escapes my recollection. A right jolly old boy is Father Sebastien; indeed very amusing at times."

"At times, yes," said Father Beret, who had no birth-mark on his shoulder, and had never had one there, or on any other part of his person.

"How strange!" Alice remarked, "I, too, have a mark on my shoulder—a pink spot, just like a small, five-petaled flower. We must be of kin to each other, Father Beret."

The priest laughed.

"If our marks are alike, that would be some evidence of kinship," he said.

"But what shape is yours, Father?"

"I've never seen it," he responded.

"Never seen it! Why?"

"Well, it's absolutely invisible," and he chuckled heartily, meantime glancing shrewdly at M. Roussillon out of the tail of his eye.

"It's on the back part of his shoulder," quickly spoke up M. Roussillon, "and you know priests never use looking-glasses. The mark is quite invisible therefore, so far as Father Beret is concerned!"

"You never told me of your birth-mark before, my daughter," said Father Beret, turning to Alice with sudden interest. "It may some day be good fortune to you."

"Why so, Father?"

"If your family name is really Tarleton, as you suppose from the inscription on your locket, the birth-mark, being of such singular shape, would probably identify you. It is said that these marks run regularly in families. With the miniature and the distinguishing birth-mark you have enough to make a strong case should you once find the right Tarleton family."

"You talk as they write in novels," said Alice. "I've read about just such things in them. Wouldn't it be grand if I should turn out to be some great personage in disguise!"

The mention of novels reminded Father Beret of that terrible book, Manon Lescaut, which he last saw in Alice's possession, and he could not refrain from mentioning it in a voice that shuddered.

"Rest easy, Father Beret," said Alice; "that is one novel I have found wholly distasteful to me. I tried to read it, but could not do it, I flung it aside in utter disgust. You and mother Roussillon are welcome to hide it deep as a well, for all I care. I don't enjoy reading about low, vile people and hopeless unfortunates; I like sweet and lovely heroines and strong, high-souled, brave heroes."

"Read about the blessed saints, then, my daughter; you will find in them the true heroes and heroines of this world," said Father Beret.

M. Roussillon changed the subject, for he always somehow dreaded to have the good priest fall into the strain of argument he was about to begin. A stray sheep, no matter how refractory, feels a touch of longing when it hears the shepherd's voice. M. Roussillon was a Catholic, but a straying one, who avoided the confessional and often forgot mass. Still, with all his reckless independence, and with all his outward show of large and breezy self-sufficiency, he was not altogether free from the hold that the church had laid upon him in childhood and youth. Moreover, he was fond of Father Beret and had done a great deal for the little church of St. Xavier and the mission it represented; but he distinctly desired to be let alone while he pursued his own course; and he had promised the dying woman who gave Alice to him that the child should be left as she was, a Protestant, without undue influence to change her from the faith of her parents. This promise he had kept with stubborn persistence and he meant to keep it as long as he lived. Perhaps the very fact that his innermost conscience smote him with vague yet telling blows at times for this departure from the strict religion of his fathers, may have intensified his resistance of the influence constantly exerted upon Alice by Father Beret and Madame Roussillon, to bring her gently but surely to the church. Perverseness is a force to be reckoned with in all original characters.

A few weeks had passed after M. Roussillon's return, when that big-hearted man took it into his head to celebrate his successful trading ventures with a moonlight dance given without reserve to all the inhabitants of Vincennes. It was certainly a democratic function that he contemplated, and motley to a most picturesque extent.

Rene de Ronville called upon Alice a day or two previous to the occasion and duly engaged her as his partenaire; but she insisted upon having the engagement guarded in her behalf by a condition so obviously fanciful that he accepted it without argument.

"If my wandering knight should arrive during the dance, you promise to stand aside and give place to him," she stipulated. "You promise that? You see I'm expecting him all the time. I dreamed last night that he came on a great bay horse and, stooping, whirled me up behind the saddle, and away we went!"

There was a childish, half bantering air in her look; but her voice sounded earnest and serious, notwithstanding its delicious timbre of suppressed playfulness.

"You promise me?" she insisted.

"Oh, I promise to slink away into a corner and chew my thumb, the moment he comes," Rene eagerly assented. "Of course I'm taking a great risk, I know; for lords and barons and knights are very apt to appear Suddenly in a place like this."

"You may banter and make light if you want to," she said, pouting admirably. "I don't care. All the same the laugh will jump to the other corner of your mouth, see if it doesn't. They say that what a person dreams about and wishes for and waits for and believes in, will come true sooner or later."

"If that's so," said Rene, "you and I will get married; for I've dreamed it every night of the year, wished for it, waited for it and believed in it, and—"

It was a madly sudden rush. He made it on an impulse quite irresistible, as hypnotized persons are said to do in response to the suggestion of the hypnotist, and his heart was choking his throat before he could end his speech. Alice interrupted him with a hearty burst of laughter.

"A very pretty twist you give to my words, I must declare," she said; "but not new by any means. Little Adrienne Bourcier could tell you that. She says that you have vowed to her over and over that you dream about her, and wish for her, and wait for her, precisely as you have just said to me."

Rene's brown face flushed to the temples, partly with anger, partly with the shock of mingled surprise and fear. He was guilty, and the guilt showed in his eyes and paralyzed his tongue, so that he sat there before Alice with his under jaw sagging ludicrously.

"Don't you rather think, Monsieur Rene de Ronville," she presently added in a calmly advisory tone, "that you had better quit trying to say such foolish things to me, and just be my very good friend? If you don't, I do, which comes to the same thing. What's more, I won't be your partenaire at the dance unless you promise me on your word of honor that you will dance two dances with Adrienne to every one that you have with me. Do you promise?"

He dared not oppose her outwardly, although in his heart resistance amounted to furious revolt and riot.

"I promise anything you ask me to," he said resignedly, almost sullenly; "anything for you."

"Well, I ask nothing whatever on my own account," Alice quickly replied; "but I do tell you firmly that you shall not maltreat little Adrienne Bourcier and remain a friend of mine. She loves you, Rene de Ronville, and you have told her that you love her. If you are a man worthy of respect you will not desert her. Don't you think I am right?"

Like a singed and crippled moth vainly trying to rise once again to the alluring yet deadly flame, Rene de Ronville essayed to break out of his embarrassment and resume equal footing with the girl so suddenly become his commanding superior; but the effort disclosed to him as well as to her that he had fallen to rise no more. In his abject defeat he accepted the terms dictated by Alice and was glad when she adroitly changed her manner and tone in going on to discuss the approaching dance.

"Now let me make one request of you," he demanded after a while. "It's a small favor; may I ask it?"

"Yes, but I don't grant it in advance."

"I want you to wear, for my sake, the buff gown which they say was your grandmother's."

"No, I won't wear it."

"But why, Alice?"

"None of the other girls have anything like such a dress; it would not be right for me to put it on and make them all feel that I had taken the advantage of them, just because I could; that's why."

"But then none of them is beautiful and educated like you," he said; "you'll outshine them anyway."

"Save your compliments for poor pretty little Adrienne," she firmly responded, "I positively do not wish to hear them. I have agreed to be your partenaire at this dance of Papa Roussillon's, but it is understood between us that Adrienne is your sweet-heart. I am not, and I'm not going to be, either. So for your sake and Adrienne's, as well as out of consideration for the rest of the girls who have no fine dresses, I am not going to wear the buff brocade gown that belonged to Papa Roussillon's mother long ago. I shall dress just as the rest do."

It is safe to say that Rene de Ronville went home with a troublesome bee in his bonnet. He was not a bad-hearted fellow. Many a right good young man, before him and since, has loved an Adrienne and been dazzled by an Alice. A violet is sweet, but a rose is the garden's queen. The poor youthful frontiersman ought to have been stronger; but he was not, and what have we to say?

As for Alice, since having a confidential talk with Adrienne Bourcier recently, she had come to realize what M. Roussillon meant when he said; "But my little girl is better than most of them, not a foolish mischief-maker, I hope." She saw through the situation with a quick understanding of what Adrienne might suffer should Rene prove permanently fickle. The thought of it aroused all her natural honesty and serious nobleness of character, which lay deep under the almost hoydenish levity usually observable in her manner. Crude as her sense of life's larger significance was, and meager as had been her experience in the things which count for most in the sum of a young girl's existence under fair circumstances, she grasped intuitively the gist of it all.

The dance did not come off; it had to be postponed indefinitely on account of a grave change in the political relations of the little post. A day or two before the time set for that function a rumor ran through the town that something of importance was about to happen. Father Gibault, at the head of a small party, had arrived from Kaskaskia, far away on the Mississippi, with the news that France and the American Colonies had made common cause against the English in the great war of which the people of Vincennes neither knew the cause nor cared a straw about the outcome.

It was Oncle Jazon who came to the Roussillon place to tell M. Roussillon that he was wanted at the river house. Alice met him at the door.

"Come in, Oncle Jazon," she cheerily said, "you are getting to be a stranger at our house lately. Come in; what news do you bring? Take off your cap and rest your hair, Oncle Jazon."

The scalpless old fighter chuckled raucously and bowed to the best of his ability. He not only took off his queer cap, but looked into it with a startled gaze, as if he expected something infinitely dangerous to jump out and seize his nose.

"A thousand thanks, Ma'm'selle," he presently said, "will ye please tell Mo'sieu' Roussillon that I would wish to see 'im?"

"Yes, Oncle Jazon; but first be seated, and let me offer you just a drop of eau de vie; some that Papa Roussillon brought back with him from Quebec. He says it's old and fine."

She poured him a full glass, then setting the bottle on a little stand, went to find M. Roussillon. While she was absent Oncle Jazon improved his opportunity to the fullest extent. At least three additional glasses of the brandy went the way of the first. He grinned atrociously and smacked his corrugated lips; but when Gaspard Roussillon came in, the old man was sitting at some distance from the bottle and glass gazing indifferently out across the veranda. He told his story curtly. Father Gibault, he said, had sent him to ask M. Roussillon to come to the river house, as he had news of great importance to communicate.

"Ah, well, Oncle Jazon, we'll have a nip of brandy together before we go," said the host.

"Why, yes, jes' one agin' the broilin' weather," assented Oncle Jazon; "I don't mind jes' one."

"A very rich friend of mine in Quebec gave me this brandy, Oncle Jazon," said M. Roussillon, pouring the liquor with a grand flourish; "and I thought of you as soon as I got it. Now, says I to myself, if any man knows good brandy when he tastes it, it's Oncle Jazon, and I'll give him a good chance at this bottle just the first of all my friends."

"It surely is delicious," said Oncle Jazon, "very delicious." He spoke French with a curious accent, having spent long years with English-speaking frontiersmen in the Carolinas and Kentucky, so that their lingo had become his own.

As they walked side by side down the way to the river house they looked like typical extremes of rough, sun-burned and weather-tanned manhood; Oncle Jazon a wizened, diminutive scrap, wrinkled and odd in every respect; Gaspard Roussillon towering six feet two, wide shouldered, massive, lumbering, muscular, a giant with long curling hair and a superb beard. They did not know that they were going down to help dedicate the great Northwest to freedom.

CHAPTER V
FATHER GIBAULT

Great movements in the affairs of men are like tides of the seas which reach and affect the remotest and quietest nooks and inlets, imparting a thrill and a swell of the general motion. Father Gibault brought the wave of the American Revolution to Vincennes. He was a simple missionary; but he was, besides, a man of great worldly knowledge and personal force. Colonel George Rogers Clark made Father Gibault's acquaintance at Kaskaskia, when the fort and its garrison surrendered to his command, and, quickly discerning the fine qualities of the priest's character, sent him to the post on the Wabash to win over its people to the cause of freedom and independence. Nor was the task assumed a hard one, as Father Gibault probably well knew before he undertook it.

A few of the leading men of Vincennes, presided over by Gaspard Roussillon, held a consultation at the river house, and it was agreed that a mass meeting should be called bringing all of the inhabitants together in the church for the purpose of considering the course to be taken under the circumstances made known by Father Gibault. Oncle Jazon constituted himself an executive committee of one to stir up a noise for the occasion.

It was a great day for Vincennes. The volatile temperament of the French frontiersmen bubbled over with enthusiasm at the first hint of something new, and revolutionary in which they might be expected to take part. Without knowing in the least what it was that Father Gibault and Oncle Jazon wanted of them, they were all in favor of it at a venture.

Rene de Ronville, being an active and intelligent young man, was sent about through the town to let everybody know of the meeting. In passing he stepped into the cabin of Father Beret, who was sitting on the loose puncheon floor, with his back turned toward the entrance and so absorbed in trying to put together a great number of small paper fragments that he did not hear or look up.

"Are you not going to the meeting, Father?" Rene bluntly demanded. In the hurry that was on him he did not remember to be formally polite, as was his habit.

The old priest looked up with a startled face. At the same time he swept the fragments of paper together and clutched them hard in his right hand. "Yes, yes, my son—yes I am going, but the time has not yet come for it, has it?" he stammered. "Is it late?"

He sprang to his feet and appeared confused, as if caught in doing something very improper.

Rene wondered at this unusual behavior, but merely said:

"I beg pardon, Father Beret, I did not mean to disturb you," and went his way.

Father Beret stood for some minutes as if dazed, then squeezed the paper fragments into a tight ball, just as they were when he took them from under the floor some time before Rene came in, and put it in his pocket. A little later he was kneeling, as we have seen him once before, in silent yet fervent prayer, his clasped hands lifted toward the crucifix on the wall.

"Jesus, give me strength to hold on and do my work," he murmured beseechingly, "and oh, free thy poor servant from bitter temptation."

Father Gibault had come prepared to use his eloquence upon the excitable Creoles, and with considerable cunning he addressed a motley audience at the church, telling them that an American force had taken Kaskaskia and would henceforth hold it; that France had joined hands with the Americans against the British, and that it was the duty of all Frenchmen to help uphold the cause of freedom and independence.

"I come," said he, "directly from Colonel George Rogers Clark, a noble and brave officer of the American army, who told me the news that I have brought to you. He sent me here to say to you that if you will give allegiance to his government you shall be protected against all enemies and have the full freedom of citizens. I think you should do this without a moment's hesitation, as I and my people at Kaskaskia have already done. But perhaps you would like to have a word from your distinguished fellow-citizen, Monsieur Gaspard Roussillon. Speak to your friends, my son, they will be glad to take counsel of your wisdom."

There was a stir and a craning of necks. M. Roussillon presently appeared near the little chancel, his great form towering majestically. He bowed and waved his hand with the air of one who accepts distinction as a matter of course; then he took his big silver watch and looked at it. He was the only man in Vincennes who owned a watch, and so the incident was impressive. Father Gibault looked pleased, and already a murmur of applause went through the audience. M. Roussillon stroked the bulging crystal of the time-piece with a circular motion of his thumb and bowed again, clearing his throat resonantly, his face growing purplish above his beard.

"Good friends," he said, "what France does all high-class Frenchmen applaud." He paused for a shout of approbation, and was not disappointed. "The other name for France is glory," he added, "and all true Frenchmen love both names. I am a true Frenchman!" and he struck his breast a resounding blow with the hand that still held the watch. A huge horn button on his buckskin jerkin came in contact with the crystal, and there was a smash, followed by a scattered tinkling of glass fragments.

All Vincennes stood breathless, contemplating the irreparable accident. M. Roussillon had lost the effect of a great period in his speech, but he was quick. Lifting the watch to his ear, he listened a moment with superb dignity, then slowly elevating his head and spreading his free hand over his heart he said:

"The faithful time-piece still tells off the seconds, and the loyal heart of its owner still throbs with patriotism."

Oncle Jazon, who stood in front of the speaker, swung his shapeless cap as high as he could and yelled like a savage. Then the crowd went wild for a time.

"Vive la France! A bas l' Angleterre!" Everybody shouted at the top of his voice.

"What France does we all do," continued M. Roussillon, when the noise subsided. "France has clasped hands with George Washington and his brave compatriots; so do we."

"Vive Zhorzh Vasinton!" shrieked Oncle Jazon in a piercing treble, tiptoeing and shaking his cap recklessly under M. Roussillon's nose.

The orator winced and jerked his head back, but nobody saw it, save perhaps Father Gibault, who laughed heartily.

Great sayings come suddenly, unannounced and unexpected. They have the mysterious force of prophetic accident combined with happy economy of phrasing. The southern blood in

M. Roussillon's veins was effervescing upon his brain; his tongue had caught the fine freedom and abandon of inspired oratory. He towered and glowed; words fell melodiously from his lips; his gestures were compelling, his visage magnetic. In conclusion he said:

"Frenchmen, America is the garden-spot of the world and will one day rule it, as did Rome of old. Where freedom makes her home, there is the centre of power!"

It was in a little log church on the verge of a hummock overlooking a marshy wild meadow. Westward for two thousand miles stretched the unbroken prairies, woods, mountains, deserts reaching to the Pacific; southward for a thousand miles rolled the green billows of the wilderness to the warm Gulf shore; northward to the pole and eastward to the thin fringe of settlements beyond the mountains, all was houseless solitude.

If the reader should go to Vincennes to-day and walk southward along Second Street to its intersection with Church Street, the spot then under foot would be probably very near where M. Roussillon stood while uttering his great sentence. Mind you, the present writer does not pretend to know the exact site of old Saint Xavier church. If it could be fixed beyond doubt the spot should have an imperishable monument of Indiana stone.

When M. Roussillon ceased speaking the audience again exhausted its vocal resources; and then Father Gibault called upon each man to come forward and solemnly pledge his loyalty to the American cause. Not one of them hesitated.

Meantime a woman was doing her part in the transformation of Post Vincennes from a French-English picket to a full-fledged American fort and town. Madame Godere, finding out what was about to happen, fell to work making a flag in imitation of that under which George Washington was fighting. Alice chanced to be in the Godere home at the time and joined enthusiastically in the sewing. It was an exciting task. Their fingers trembled while they worked, and the thread, heavily coated with beeswax, squeaked as they drew it through the cloth.

"We shall not be in time," said Madame Godere; "I know we shall not. Everything hinders me. My thread breaks or gets tangled and my needle's so rusty I can hardly stick it through the cloth. O dear!"

Alice encouraged her with both words and work, and they had almost finished when Rene came with a staff which he had brought from the fort.

"Mon dieu, but we have had a great meeting!" he cried. He was perspiring with excitement and fast walking; leaning on the staff he mopped his face with a blue handkerchief.

"We heard much shouting and noise," said Madame Godere, "M. Roussillon's voice rose loud above the rest. He roared like a lion."

"Ah, he was speaking to us; he was very eloquent," Rene replied "But now they are waiting at the fort for the new flag. I have come for it."

"It is ready," said Madame Godere.

With flying fingers Alice sewed it to the staff.

"Voici!" she cried, "vive la republique Americaine!" She lifted the staff and let the flag droop over her from head to foot.

"Give it to me," said Rene, holding forth a hand for it, "and I'll run to the fort with it."

"No," said Alice, her face suddenly lighting up with resolve. "No, I am going to take it myself," and without a moment's delay off she went.

Rene was so caught by surprise that he stood gazing after her until she passed behind a house, where the way turned, the shining flag rippling around her, and her moccasins twinkling as she ran.

At the blockhouse, awaiting the moment when the symbol of freedom should rise like a star over old Vincennes the crowd had picturesquely broken into scattered groups. Alice entered through a rent in the stockade, as that happened to be a shorter route than through the gate, and appeared suddenly almost in their midst.

It was a happy surprise, a pretty and catching spectacular apparition of a sort to be thoroughly appreciated by the lively French fancy of the audience. The caught the girl's spirit, or it caught them, and they made haste to be noisy.

"V'la! V'la! I'p'tite Alice et la bannlere de Zhorzh Vasinton! (Look, look, little Alice and George Washington's flag!)" shouted Oncle Jazon. He put his wiry little legs through a sort of pas de zephyr and winked at himself with concentrated approval.

All the men danced around and yelled till they were hoarse.

By this time Rene had reached Alice's side; but she did not see him; she ran into the blockhouse and climbed up a rude ladder-way; then she appeared on the roof, still accompanied by Rene, and planted the staff in a crack of the slabs, where it stood bravely up, the colors floating free.

She looked down and saw M. Roussillon, Father Gibault and Father Beret grouped in the centre of the area. They were waving their hands aloft at her, while a bedlam of voices sent up applause which went through her blood like strong wine. She smiled radiantly, and a sweet flush glowed in her cheeks.

No one of all that wild crowd could ever forget the picture sketched so boldly at that moment when, after planting the staff, Alice stepped back a space and stood strong and beautiful against the soft blue sky. She glanced down first, then looked up, her arms folded across her bosom. It was a pose as unconsciously taken as that of a bird, and the grace of it went straight to the hearts of those below.

She turned about to descend, and for the first time saw that Rene had followed her. His face was beaming.

"What a girl you are!" he exclaimed, in a tone of exultant admiration. "Never was there another like you!"

Alice walked quickly past him without speaking; for down in the space where some women were huddled aside from the crowd, looking on, she had seen little Adrienne Bourcier. She made haste to descend. Now that her impulsively chosen enterprise was completed her boldness deserted her and she slipped out through a dilapidated postern opposite the crowd. On her right was the river, while southward before her lay a great flat plain, beyond which rose some hillocks covered with forest. The sun blazed between masses of slowly drifting clouds that trailed creeping fantastic shadows across the marshy waste.

Alice walked along under cover of the slight landswell which then, more plainly marked than it is now, formed the contour line of hummock upon which the fort and village stood. A watery swale grown full of tall aquatic weeds meandered parallel with the bluff, so to call it, and there was a soft melancholy whispering of wind among the long blades and stems. She passed the church and Father Beret's hut and continued for some distance in the direction of that pretty knoll upon which the cemetery is at present so tastefully kept. She felt shy now, as if to run away and hide would be a great relief. Indeed, so relaxed were her nerves that a slight movement in the grass and cat-tail flags near by startled her painfully, making her jump like a fawn.

"Little friend not be 'fraid," said a guttural voice in broken French. "Little friend not make noise."

At a glance she recognized Long-Hair, the Indian, rising out of the matted marsh growth. It was a hideous vision of embodied cunning, soullessness and murderous cruelty.

"Not tell white man you see me?" he grunted interrogatively, stepping close to her. He looked so wicked that she recoiled and lifted her hands defensively.

She trembled from head to foot, and her voice failed her; but she made a negative sign and smiled at him, turning as white as her tanned face could become.

In his left hand he held his bow, while in his right he half lifted a murderous looking tomahawk.

"What new flag mean?" he demanded, waving the bow's end toward the fort and bending his head down close to hers. "Who yonder?"

"The great American Father has taken us under his protection," she explained. "We are big-knives now." It almost choked her to speak.

"Ugh! heap damn fools," he said with a dark scowl. "Little friend much damn fool."

He straightened up his tall form and stood leering at her for some seconds, then added:

"Little friend get killed, scalped, maybe."

The indescribable nobility of animal largeness, symmetry and strength showed in his form and attitude, but the expression of his countenance was absolutely repulsive—cold, hard, beastly.

He did not speak again, but turned quickly, and stooping low, disappeared like a great brownish red serpent in the high grass, which scarcely stirred as he moved through it.

Somehow that day made itself strangely memorable to Alice. She had been accustomed to stirring scenes and sudden changes of conditions; but this was the first time that she had ever joined actively in a public movement of importance. Then, too, Long-Hair's picturesque and rudely dramatic reappearance affected her imagination with an indescribable force. Moreover, the pathetic situation in the love affair between Rene and Adrienne had taken hold of her conscience with a disturbing grip. But the shadowy sense of impending events, of which she could form no idea, was behind it all. She had not heard of Brandywine, or Bunker Hill, or Lexington, or Concord; but something like a waft of their significance had blown through her mind. A great change was coming into her idyllic life. She was indistinctly aware of it, as we sometimes are of an approaching storm, while yet the sky is sweetly blue and serene. When she reached home the house was full of people to whom M. Roussillon, in the gayest of moods, was dispensing wine and brandy.

"Vive Zhorzh Vasinton!" shouted Oncle Jazon as soon as he saw her.

And then they all talked at once, saying flattering things about her. Madame Roussillon tried to scold as usual; but the lively chattering of the guests drowned her voice.

24

"I suppose the American commander will send a garrison here," some one said to Father Gibault, "and repair the fort."

"Probably," the priest replied, "in a very few weeks. Meantime we will garrison it ourselves."

"And we will have M. Roussillon for commander," spoke up Rene de Ronville, who was standing by.

"A good suggestion," assented Father Gibault; "let us organize at once."

Immediately the word was passed that there would be a meeting at the fort that evening for the purpose of choosing a garrison and a commander. Everybody went promptly at the hour set. M. Roussillon was elected Captain by acclamation, with Rene de Ronville as his Lieutenant. It was observed that Oncle Jazon had resumed his dignity, and that he looked into his cap several times without speaking.

Meantime certain citizens, who had been in close relations with Governor Abbott during his stay, quietly slipped out of town, manned a batteau and went up the river, probably to Ouiatenon first and then to Detroit. Doubtless they suspected that things might soon grow too warm for their comfort.

It was thus that Vincennes and Fort Sackville first acknowledged the American Government and hoisted the flag which, as long as it floated over the blockhouse, was lightly and lovingly called by everyone la banniere d'Alice Roussillon.

Father Gibault returned to Fort Kaskaskia and a little later Captain Leonard Helm, a jovial man, but past the prime of life, arrived at Vincennes with a commission from Col. Clark authorizing him to supersede M. Roussillon as commander, and to act as Indian agent for the American Government in the Department of the Wabash. He was welcomed by the villagers, and at once made himself very pleasing to them by adapting himself to their ways and entering heartily into their social activities.

M. Roussillon was absent when Captain Helm and his party came. Rene de Ronville, nominally in command of the fort, but actually enjoying some excellent grouse shooting with a bell-mouthed old fowling piece on a distant prairie, could not be present to deliver up the post; and as there was no garrison just then visible, Helm took possession, without any formalities.

"I think, Lieutenant, that you'd better look around through the village and see if you can scare up this Captain what's-his-name," said the new commander to a stalwart young officer who had come with him. "I can't think of these French names without getting my brain in a twist. Do you happen to recollect the Captain's name, Lieutenant?"

"Yes, sir; Gaspard Roussillon it reads in Colonel Clark's order; but I am told that he's away on a trading tour," said the young man.

"You may be told anything by these hair-tongued parlyvoos," Helm remarked. "It won't hurt, anyway, to find out where he lives and make a formal call, just for appearance sake, and to enquire about his health. I wish you would try it, sir, and let me know the result."

The Lieutenant felt that this was a peremptory order and turned about to obey promptly.

"And I say, Beverley, come back sober, if you possibly can," Helm added in his most genial tone, thinking it a great piece of humor to suggest sobriety to a man whose marked difference from men generally, of that time, was his total abstinence from intoxicating drinks.

Lieutenant Fitzhugh Beverley was a Virginian of Virginians. His family had long been prominent in colonial affairs and boasted a record of great achievements both in peace and in war. He was the only son of his parents and heir to a fine estate consisting of lands and slaves; but, like many another of the restless young cavaliers of the Old Dominion, he had come in search of adventure over into Kentucky, along the path blazed by Daniel Boone; and when Clark organized his little army, the young man's patriotic and chivalrous nature leaped at the opportunity to serve his country under so gallant a commander.

Beverley was not a mere youth, although yet somewhat under thirty. Educated abroad and naturally of a thoughtful and studious turn, he had enriched his mind far beyond the usual limit among young Americans of the very best class in that time; and so he appeared older than he really was: an effect helped out by his large and powerful form and grave dignity of bearing. Clark, who found him useful in emergencies, cool, intrepid, daring to a fault and possessed of excellent judgement, sent him with Helm, hoping that he would offset with his orderly attention to details the somewhat go-as-you-please disposition of that excellent officer.

Beverley set out in search of the French commander's house, impressed with no particular respect for him or his office. Somehow Americans of Anglo-Saxon blood were slow to recognize any good qualities whatever in the Latin Creoles of the West and South. It seemed to them that the Frenchman and the Spaniard were much too apt to equalize themselves socially and matrimonially with Indians and negroes. The very fact that for a century, while Anglo-Americans had been in constant bloody warfare with savages, Frenchmen had managed to keep on easy and highly profitable trading terms with them, tended to confirm the worst implication. "Eat frogs and save your scalp," was a bit of contemptuous frontier humor indicative of what sober judgement held in reserve on the subject.

Intent upon his formal mission, Lieutenant Beverley stalked boldly into the inclosure at Roussillon place and was met on the gallery by Madame Roussillon in one of her worst moods. She glared at him with her hands on her hips, her mouth set irritably aslant upward, her eyebrows gathered into a dark knot over her nose. It would be hard to imagine a more forbidding countenance; and for supplementary effect out popped hunchback Jean to stand behind her, with his big head lying back in the hollow of his shoulders and his long chin elevated, while he gawped intently up into Beverley's face.

"Bon jour, Madame," said the Lieutenant, lifting his hat and speaking with a pleasant accent. "Would it be agreeable to Captain Roussillon for me to see him a moment?"

Despite Beverley's cleverness in using the French language, he had a decided brusqueness of manner and a curt turn of voice not in the least Gallic. True, the soft Virginian intonation marked every word, and his obeisance was as low as if Madame Roussillon had been a queen; but the light French grace was wholly lacking.

"What do you want of my husband?" Madame Roussillon demanded.

"Nothing unpleasant, I assure you, Madame," said Beverley.

"Well, he's not at home, Mo'sieu; he's up the river for a few days."

She relaxed her stare, untied her eyebrows, and even let fall her hands from her shelf-like hips.

"Thank you, Madame," said Beverley, bowing again, "I am sorry not to have seen him."

As he was turning to go a shimmer of brown hair streaked with gold struck upon his vision from just within the door. He paused, as if in response to a military command, while a pair of gray eyes met his with a flash. The cabin room was ill lighted; but the crepuscular dimness did not seem to hinder his sight. Beyond the girl's figure, a pair of slender swords hung crossed aslant on the wall opposite the low door.

Beverley had seen, in the old world galleries, pictures in which the shadowy and somewhat uncertain background thus forced into strongest projection the main figure, yet without clearly defining it. The rough frame of the doorway gave just the rustic setting suited to Alice's costume, the most striking part of which was a grayish short gown ending just above her fringed buckskin moccasins. Around her head she had bound a blue kerchief, a wide corner of which lay over her crown like a loose cap. Her bright hair hung free upon her shoulders in tumbled half curls. As a picture, the figure and its entourage might have been artistically effective; but as Beverley saw it in actual life the first impression was rather embarrassing. Somehow he felt almost irresistibly invited to laugh, though he had never been much given to risibility. The blending, or rather the juxtaposition, of extremes—a face, a form immediately witching, and a costume odd to grotesquery—had made an assault upon his comprehension at once so sudden and so direct that his dignity came near being disastrously broken up. A splendidly beautiful child comically clad would have made much the same half delightful, half displeasing impression.

Beverley could not stare at the girl, and no sooner had he turned his back upon her than the picture in his mind changed like a scene in a kaleidoscope. He now saw a tall, finely developed figure and a face delicately oval, with a low, wide forehead, arched brows, a straight, slightly tip-tilted nose, a mouth sweet and full, dimpled cheeks, and a strong chin set above a faultless throat. His imagination, in casting off its first impression, was inclined to exaggerate Alice's beauty and to dwell upon its picturesqueness. He smiled as he walked back to the fort, and even found himself whistling gayly a snatch from a rollicking fiddle-tune that he had heard when a boy.

CHAPTER VI
A FENCING BOUT

A few days after Helm's arrival, M. Roussillon returned to Vincennes, and if he was sorely touched in his amour propre by seeing his suddenly acquired military rank and title drop away, he did not let it be known to his fellow citizens. He promptly called upon the new commander and made acquaintance with Lieutenant Fitzhugh Beverley, who just then was superintending the work of cleaning up an old cannon in the fort and mending some breaks in the stockade.

Helm formed a great liking for the big Frenchman, whose breezy freedom of manner and expansive good humor struck him favorably from the beginning. M. Roussillon's ability to speak English with considerable ease helped the friendship along, no doubt; at all events their first interview ended with a hearty show of good fellowship, and as time passed they became almost inseparable companions during M. Roussillon's periods of rest from his trading excursions among the Indians. They played cards and brewed hot drinks over which they told marvelous stories, the latest one invariably surpassing all its predecessors.

Helm had an eye to business, and turned M. Roussillon's knowledge of the Indians to valuable account, so that he soon had very pleasant relations with most of the tribes within reach of his agents. This gave a feeling of great security to the people of Vincennes. They pursued their narrow agricultural activities with excellent results and redoubled those social gayeties which, even in hut and cabin under all the adverse conditions of extreme frontier life, were dear to the volatile and genial French temperament.

Lieutenant Beverley found much to interest him in the quaint town; but the piece de resistance was Oncle Jazon, who proved to be both fascinating and unmanageable; a hard nut to crack, yet possessing a kernel absolutely original in flavor. Beverley visited him one evening in his hut—it might better be called den—a curiously built thing, with walls of vertical poles set in a quadrangular trench dug in the ground, and roofed with grass. Inside and out it was plastered with clay, and the floor of dried mud was as smooth and hard as concrete paving. In one end there was a wide fireplace grimy with soot, in the other a mere peep-hole for a window: a wooden bench, a bed of skins and two or three stools were barely visible in the gloom. In the doorway Oncle Jazon sat whittling a slender billet of hickory into a ramrod for his long flint-lock American rifle.

"Maybe ye know Simon Kenton," said the old man, after he and Beverley had conversed for a while, "seeing that you are from Kentucky—eh?"

"Yes, I do know him well; he's a warm personal friend of mine," said Beverley with quick interest, for it surprised him that Oncle Jazon should know anything about Kenton. "Do you know him, Monsieur Jazon?"

Oncle Jazon winked conceitedly and sighted along his rudimentary ramrod to see if it was straight; then puckering his lips, as if on the point of whistling, made an affirmative noise quite impossible to spell.

"Well, I'm glad you are acquainted with Kenton," said Beverley. "Where did you and he come together?"

Oncle Jazon chuckled reminiscently and scratched the skinless, cicatrized spot where his scalp had once flourished.

"Oh, several places," he answered. "Ye see thet hair a hangin' there on the wall?" He pointed at a dry wisp dangling under a peg in a log barely visible by the bad light. "Well, thet's my scalp, he! he! he!" He snickered as if the fact were a most enjoyable joke. "Simon Kenton can tell ye about thet little affair! The Indians thought I was dead, and they took my hair; but I wasn't dead; I was just a givin' 'em a 'possum act. When they was gone I got up from where I was a layin' and trotted off. My head was sore and ventrebleu! but I was mad, he! he! he!"

All this time he spoke in French, and the English but poorly paraphrases his odd turns of expression. His grimaces and grunts cannot even be hinted.

It was a long story, as Beverley received it, told scrappily, but with certain rude art. In the end Oncle Jazon said with unctuous self-satisfaction:

"Accidents will happen. I got my chance at that damned Indian who skinned my head, and I jes took a bead on 'im with my old rifle. I can't shoot much, never could, but I happened to hit 'im square in the lef' eye, what I shot at, and it was a hundred yards. Down he tumbles, and I runs to 'im and finds my same old scalp a hangin' to his belt. Well, I lifted off his hair with my knife, and untied mine from the belt, and then I had both scalps, he! he! he! You ask Simon Kenton when ye see 'im. He was along at the same time, and they made 'im run the ga'ntlet and pretty nigh beat the life out o' 'im. Ventrebleu!"

Beverley now recollected hearing Kenton tell the same grim story by a camp-fire in the hills of Kentucky. Somehow it had caught a new spirit in the French rendering, which linked it with the old tales of adventure that he had read in his boyhood, and it suddenly endeared Oncle Jazon to him. The rough old scrap of a man and the powerful youth chatted together until sundown, smoking their pipes, each feeling for what was best in the other, half aware that in the future they would be tested together in the fire of wild adventure. Every man is more or less a prophet at certain points in his life.

Twilight and moonlight were blending softly when Beverley, on his way back to the fort, departing from a direct course, went along the river's side southward to have a few moments of reflective strolling within reach of the water's pleasant murmur and the town's indefinite evening stir. Rich sweetness, the gift of early autumn, was on the air blowing softly out of a lilac west and singing in the willow fringe that hung here and there over the bank.

27

On the farther side of the river's wide flow, swollen by recent heavy rains, Beverley saw a pirogue, in one end of which a dark figure swayed to the strokes of a paddle. The slender and shallow little craft was bobbing on the choppy waves and taking a zig-zag course among floating logs and masses of lighter driftwood, while making slow but certain headway toward the hither bank.

Beverley took a bit of punk and a flint and steel from his pocket, relit his pipe and stood watching the skilful boatman conduct his somewhat dangerous voyage diagonally against the rolling current. It was a shifting, hide-and-seek scene, its features appearing and disappearing with the action of the waves and the doubtful light reflected from fading clouds and sky. Now and again the man stood up in his skittish pirogue, balancing himself with care, to use a short pole in shoving driftwood out of his way; and more than once he looked to Beverley as if he had plunged head-long into the dark water.

The spot, as nearly as it can be fixed, was about two hundred yards below where the public road-bridge at present spans the Wabash. The bluff was then far different from what it is now, steeper and higher, with less silt and sand between it and the water's edge. Indeed, swollen as the current was, a man could stand on the top of the bank and easily leap into the deep water. At a point near the middle of the river a great mass of drift-logs and sand had long ago formed a barrier which split the stream so that one current came heavily shoreward on the side next the town and swashed with its muddy foam, making a swirl and eddy just below where Beverley stood.

The pirogue rounded the upper angle of this obstruction, not without difficulty to its crew of one, and swung into the rapid shoreward rush, as was evidently planned for by the steersman, who now paddled against the tide with all his might to keep from being borne too far down stream for a safe landing place.

Beverley stood at ease idly and half dreamily looking on, when suddenly something caused a catastrophe, which for a moment he did not comprehend. In fact the man in the pirogue came to grief, as a man in a pirogue is very apt to do, and fairly somersaulted overboard into the water. Nothing serious would have threatened (for the man could swim like an otter) had not a floating, half submerged log thrust up some short, stiff stumps of boughs, upon the points of which the man struck heavily and was not only hurt, but had his clothes impaled securely by one of the ugly spears, so that he hung in a helpless position, while the water's motion alternately lifted and submerged him, his arms beating about wildly.

When Beverley heard a strangling cry for help, he pulled himself promptly together, flung off his coat, as if by a single motion, and leaped down the bank into the water. He was a swimmer whose strokes counted for all that prodigious strength and excellent training could afford; he rushed through the water with long sweeps, making a semicircle, rounding against the current, so as to swing down upon the drowning man.

Less than a half-hour later a rumor by some means spread throughout the town that Father Beret and Lieutenant Beverley were drowned in the Wabash. But when a crowd gathered to verify the terrible news it turned out to be untrue. Gaspard Roussillon had once more distinguished himself by an exhibition of heroic nerve and muscle.

"Ventrebleu! Quel homme!" exclaimed Oncle Jazon, when told that M. Roussillon had come up the bank of the Wabash with Lieutenant Beverley under one arm and Father Beret under the other, both men apparently dead.

"Bring them to my house immediately," M. Roussillon ordered, as soon as they were restored to consciousness; and he shook himself, as a big wet animal sometimes does, covering everybody near him with muddy water. Then he led the way with melodramatic strides.

In justice to historical accuracy there must be a trifling reform of what appeared on the face of things to be grandly true. Gaspard Roussillon actually dragged Father Beret and Lieutenant Beverley one at a time out of the eddy water and up the steep river bank. That was truly a great feat; but the hero never explained. When men arrived he was standing between the collapsed forms, panting and dripping. Doubtless he looked just as if he had dropped them from under his arms, and why shouldn't he have the benefit of a great implication?

"I've saved them both," he roared; from which, of course, the ready creole imagination inferred the extreme of possible heroic performance.

"Bring them to my house immediately," and it was accordingly done.

The procession, headed by M. Roussillon, moved noisily, for the French tongue must shake off what comes to it on the thrill of every exciting moment. The only silent Frenchman is the dead one.

Father Beret was not only well-nigh drowned, but seriously hurt. He lay for a week on a bed in M. Roussillon's house before he could sit up. Alice hung over him night and day, scarcely sleeping or eating until he was past all danger. As for Beverley, he shook off all the effects of his struggle in a little while. Next day he was out, as well and strong as ever, busy with the affairs of his office. Nor was he less happy on account of what the little adventure had cast into his experience. It is good to feel that one has done an unselfish deed, and no young man's heart repels the freshness of what comes to him when a beautiful girl first enters his life.

Naturally enough Alice had some thoughts of Beverley while she was so attentively caring for Father Beret. She had never before seen a man like him, nor had she read of one. Compared with Rene de Ronville, the best youth of her acquaintance, he was in every way superior; this was too evident for analysis; but referred to the romantic standard taken out of the novels she had read, he somehow failed; and yet he loomed bravely in her vision, not exactly a knight of the class she had most admired, still unquestionably a hero of large proportions.

Beverley stepped in for a few minutes every day to see Father Beret, involuntarily lengthening his visit by a sliding ratio as he became better acquainted. He began to enjoy the priest's conversation, with its sly worldly wisdom cropping up through fervid religious sentiments and quaint humor. Alice must have interested him more than he was fully aware of; for his eyes followed her, as she came and went, with a curious criticism of her half-savage costume and her springy, Dryad-like suppleness, which reminded him of the shyest and gracefulest wild birds; and yet a touch of refinement, the subtlest and best, showed in all her ways. He studied her, as he would have studied a strange, showy and originally fragrant flower, or a bird of oddly attractive plumage. While she said little to him or to anyone else in his presence, he became aware of the willfulness and joyous lightness which played on her nature's changeable surface. He wondered at her influence over Father Beret, whom she controlled apparently without effort. But in due time he began to feel a deeper character, a broader intelligence, behind her superficial sauvagerie; and he found that she really had no mean smattering of books in the lighter vein.

A little thing happened which further opened his eyes and increased the interest that her beauty and elementary charm of style aroused in him gradually, apace with their advancing acquaintanceship.

Father Beret had got well and returned to his hut and his round of spiritual duties; but Beverley came to Roussillon place every day all the same. For a wonder Madame Roussillon liked him, and at most times held the scolding side of her tongue when he was present. Jean, too, made friendly advances whenever opportunity afforded. Of course Alice gave him just the frank cordiality of hospitable welcome demanded by frontier conditions. She scarcely knew whether she liked him or not; but he had a treasury of information from which he was enriching her with liberal carelessness day by day. The hungriest part of her mind was being sumptuously banqueted at his expense. Mere intellectual greediness drew her to him.

Naturally they soon threw off such troubling formalities as at first rose between them, and began to disclose to each other their true characteristics. Alice found in Beverley a large target for the missiles of her clever and tantalizing perversity. He in turn practiced a native dignity and an acquired superiority of manner to excellent effect. It was a meeting of Greek with Greek in a new Arcadia. To him here was Diana, strong, strange, simple, even crude almost to naturalness, yet admirably pure in spirit and imbued with highest womanly aspirations. To her Beverley represented the great outside area of life. He came to her from wonderland, beyond the wide circle of houseless woods and prairies. He represented gorgeous cities, teeming parks of fashion, boulevards, salons, halls of social splendor, the theater, the world of woman's dreams.

Now, there is an antagonism, vague yet powerful, generated between natures thus cast together from the opposite poles of experience and education: an antagonism practically equivalent to the most vigorous attraction. What one knows the other is but half aware of; neither knowledge nor ignorance being mutual, there is a scintillation of exchange, from opposing vantage grounds, followed by harmless snaps of thunder. Culture and refinement take on airs—it is the deepest artificial instinct of enlightenment to pose—in the presence of naturalness; and there is a certain style of ignorance which attitudinizes before the gate of knowledge. The return to nature has always been the dream of the conventionalized soul, while the simple Arcadian is forever longing for the maddening honey of sophistication.

Innate jealousies strike together like flint and steel dashing off sparks by which nearly everything that life can warm its core withal is kindled and kept burning. What I envy in my friend I store for my best use. I thrust and parry, not to kill, but to learn my adversary's superior feints and guards. And this hint of sword play leads back to what so greatly surprised and puzzled Beverley one day when he chanced to be examining the pair of colechemardes on the wall.

He took one down, and handling it with the indescribable facility possible to none save a practical swordsman, remarked:

"There's a world of fascination in these things; I like nothing better than a bout at fencing. Does your father practice the art?"

"I have no father, no mother," she quickly said; "but good Papa Roussillon does like a little exercise with the colechemarde."

"Well, I'm glad to hear it, I shall ask to teach him a trick or two," Beverley responded in the lightest mood. "When will he return from the woods?"

"I can't tell you; he's very irregular in such matters," she said. Then, with a smile half banter and half challenge, she added; "if you are really dying for some exercise, you shall not have to wait for him to come home, I assure you, Monsieur Beverley."

"Oh, it's Monsieur de Ronville, perhaps, that you will offer up as a victim to my skill and address," he slyly returned; for he was suspecting that a love affair in some stage of progress lay between her and Rene.

She blushed violently, but quickly overcoming a combined rush of surprise and anger, added with an emphasis as charming as it was unexpected.

"I myself am, perhaps, swordsman enough to satisfy the impudence and vanity of Monsieur Beverley, Lieutenant in the American army."

"Pardon me, Mademoiselle; forgive me, I beg of you," he exclaimed, earnestly modulating his voice to sincerest beseechment; "I really did not mean to be impudent, nor—"

Her vivacity cleared with a merry laugh.

"No apologies, I command you," she interposed. "We will have them after I have taught you a fencing lesson."

From a shelf she drew down a pair of foils and presenting the hilts, bade him take his choice.

"There isn't any difference between them that I know of," she said, and then added archly; "but you will feel better at last, when all is over and the sting of defeat tingles through you, if you are conscious of having used every sensible precaution."

He looked straight into her eyes, trying to catch what was in her mind, but there was a bewildering glamour playing across those gray, opal-tinted wells of mystery, from which he could draw only a mischievous smile-glint, direct, daring, irresistible.

"Well," he said, taking one of the foils, "what do you really mean? Is it a challenge without room for honorable retreat?"

"The time for parley is past," she replied, "follow me to the battle-ground."

She led the way to a pleasant little court in the rear of the cabin's yard, a space between two wings and a vine-covered trellis, beyond which lay a well kept vineyard and vegetable garden. Here she turned about and faced him, poising her foil with a fine grace.

"Are you ready?" she inquired.

He tried again to force a way into the depths of her eyes with his; but he might as well have attacked the sun; so he stood in a confusion of not very well defined feelings, undecided, hesitating, half expecting that there would be some laughable turn to end the affair.

"Are you afraid, Monsieur Beverley?" she demanded after a short waiting in silence.

He laughed now and whipped the air with his foil.

"You certainly are not in earnest?" he said interrogatively. "Do you really mean that you want to fence with me?"

"If you think because I'm only a girl you can easily beat me, try it," she tauntingly replied making a level thrust toward his breast.

Quick as a flash he parried, and then a merry clinking and twinkling of steel blades kept time to their swift movements. Instantly, by the sure sense which is half sight, half feeling—the sense that guides the expert fencer's hand and wrist—Beverley knew that he had probably more than his match, and in ten seconds his attack was met by a time thrust in opposition which touched him sharply.

Alice sprang far back, lowered her point and laughed.

"Je vous salue, Monsieur Beverley!" she cried, with childlike show of delight. "Did you feel the button?"

"Yes, I felt it," he said with frank acknowledgment in his voice, "it was cleverly done. Now give me a chance to redeem myself."

He began more carefully and found that she, too, was on her best mettle; but it was a short bout, as before. Alice seemed to give him an easy opening and he accepted it with a thrust; then something happened that he did not understand. The point of his foil was somehow caught under his opponent's hilt-guard while her blade seemed to twist around his; at the same time there was a wring and a jerk, the like of which he had never before felt, and he was disarmed, his wrist and fingers aching with the wrench they had received.

Of course the thing was not new; he had been disarmed before; but her trick of doing it was quite a mystery to him, altogether different from any that he had ever seen.

30

"Vous me pardonnerez, Monsieur," she mockingly exclaimed, picking up his weapon and offering the hilt to him. "Here is your sword!"

"Keep it," he said, folding his arms and trying to look unconcerned, "you have captured it fairly. I am at your mercy; be kind to me."

Madame Roussillon and Jean, the hunchback, hearing the racket of the foils had come out to see and were standing agape.

"You ought to be ashamed, Alice," said the dame in scolding approval of what she had done; "girls do not fence with gentlemen."

"This girl does," said Alice.

"And with extreme disaster to this gentleman," said Beverley, laughing in a tone of discomfiture and resignation.

"Ah, Mo'sieu', there's nothing but disaster where she goes," complained Madame Roussillon, "she is a destroyer of everything. Only yesterday she dropped my pink bowl and broke it, the only one I had."

"And just to think," said Beverley, "what would have been the condition of my heart had we been using rapiers instead of leather-buttoned foils! She would have spitted it through the very center."

"Like enough," replied the dame indifferently. "She wouldn't wince, either,—not she."

Alice ran into the house with the foils and Beverley followed.

"We must try it over again some day soon," he said; "I find that you can show me a few points. Where did you learn to fence so admirably? Is Monsieur Roussillon your master?"

"Indeed he isn't," she quickly replied, "he is but a bungling swordsman. My master—but I am not at liberty to tell you who has taught me the little I know."

"Well, whoever he is I should be glad to have lessons from him."

"But you'll never get them."

"Why?"

"Because."

"A woman's ultimatum."

"As good as a man's!" she bridled prettily; "and sometimes better—at the foils for example. Vous—comprenez, n'est ce pas?"

He laughed heartily.

"Yes, your point reaches me," he said, "but sperat et in saeva victus gladiatur arena, as the old Latin poet wisely remarks." The quotation was meant to tease her.

"Yes, Montaigne translated that or something in his book," she commented with prompt erudition. "I understand it."

Beverley looked amazed.

"What do you know about Montaigne?" he demanded with a blunt brevity amounting to something like gruffness.

"Sh', Monsieur, not too loud," she softly protested, looking around to see that neither Madame Roussillon nor Jean had followed them into the main room. "It is not permitted that I read that old book; but they do not hide it from me, because they think I can't make out its dreadful spelling."

She smiled so that her cheeks drew their dimples deep into the delicately tinted pink-and-brown, where wind and sun and wholesome exercise had set the seal of absolute health, and took from a niche in the logs of the wall a stained and dog-eared volume. He looked, and it was, indeed, the old saint and sinner, Montaigne.

Involuntarily he ran his eyes over the girl from head to foot, comparing her show of knowledge with the outward badges of abject rusticity, and even wildness, with which she was covered.

"Well," he said, "you are a mystery."

"You think it surprising that I can read a book! Frankly I can't understand half of this one. I read it because—well just because they want me to read about nothing but sickly old saints and woe-begone penitents. I like something lively. What do I care for all that uninteresting religious stuff?"

"Montaigne IS decidedly lively in spots," Beverley remarked. "I shouldn't think a girl—I shouldn't think you'd particularly enjoy his humors."

"I don't care for the book at all," she said, flushing quickly, "only I seem to learn about the world from it. Sometimes it seems as if it lifted me up high above all this wild, lonely and tiresome country, so that I can see far off where things are different and beautiful. It is the same with the novels; and they don't permit me to read them either; but all the same I do."

31

When Beverley, taking his leave, passed through the gate at Roussillon place, he met Rene de Ronville going in. It was a notable coincidence that each young man felt something troublesome rise in his throat as he looked into the other's eyes.

A week of dreamy autumn weather came on, during which Beverley managed to be with Alice a great deal, mostly sitting on the Roussillon gallery, where the fading vine leaves made fairy whispering, and where the tempered breeze blew deliciously cool from over the distant multi-colored woods. The men of Vincennes were gathering their Indian corn early to dry it on the cob for grating into winter meal. Many women made wine from the native grapes and from the sweeter and richer fruit of imported vines. Madame Roussillon and Alice stained their hands a deep purple during the pressing season, and Beverley found himself engaged in helping them handle the juicy crop, while around the overflowing earthen pots the wild bees, wasps and hornets hummed with an incessant, jarring monotony.

Jean, the hunchback, gathered ample stores of hickory nuts, walnuts, hazel-nuts and pin-oak acorns. Indeed, the whole population of the village made a great spurt of industry just before the falling of winter; and presently, when every preparation had been completed for the dreaded cold season, M. Roussillon carried out his long-cherished plan, and gave a great party at the river house. After the most successful trading experience of all his life he felt irrepressibly liberal.

"Let's have one more roaring good time," he said, "that's what life is for."

CHAPTER VII
THE MAYOR'S PARTY

Beverley was so surprised and confused in his mind by the ease with which he had been mastered at swordplay by a mere girl, that he felt as if just coming out of a dream. In fact the whole affair seemed unreal, yet so vivid and impressive in all its main features, that he could not emerge from it and look it calmly over from without. His experience with women had not prepared him for a ready understanding and acceptance of a girl like Alice. While he was fully aware of her beauty, freshness, vivacity and grace, this Amazonian strength of hers, this boldness of spirit, this curious mixture of frontier crudeness and a certain adumbration—so to call it—of patrician sensibilities and aspirations, affected him both pleasantly and unpleasantly. He did not sympathize promptly with her semi-barbaric costume; she seemed not gently feminine, as compared with the girls of Virginia and Maryland. He resented her muscular development and her independent disposition. She was far from coarseness, however, and, indeed, a trace of subtle refinement, although not conventional, imbued her whole character.

But why was he thinking so critically about her? Had his selfishness received an incurable shock from the button of her foil? A healthy young man of the right sort is apt to be jealous of his physical prowess—touch him there and he will turn the world over to right himself in, his own admiration and yours. But to be beaten on his highest ground of virility by a dimple-faced maiden just leaving her teens could not offer Beverley any open way to recoupment of damages.

He tried to shake her out of his mind, as a bit of pretty and troublesome rubbish, what time he pursued his not very exacting military duties. But the more he shook the tighter she clung, and the oftener he went to see her.

Helm was a good officer in many respects, and his patriotism was of the best; but he liked jolly company, a glass of something strong and a large share of ease. Detroit lay many miles northeastward across the wilderness, and the English, he thought, would scarcely come so far to attack his little post, especially now that most of the Indians in the intervening country had declared in favor of the Americans. Recently, too, the weather had been favoring him by changing from wet to dry, so that the upper Wabash and its tributaries were falling low and would soon be very difficult to navigate with large batteaux.

Very little was done to repair the stockade and dilapidated remnant of a blockhouse. There were no sufficient barracks, a mere shed in one angle serving for quarters, and the old cannon could not have been used to any effect in case of attack. As for the garrison, it was a nominal quantity, made up mostly of men who preferred hunting and fishing to the merest pretense of military duty.

Gaspard Roussillon assumed to know everything about Indian affairs and the condition of the English at Detroit. His optimistic eloquence lulled Helm to a very pleasant sense of security. Beverley was not so easy to satisfy; but his suggestions regarding military discipline and a vigorous prosecution of repairs to the blockhouse and stockade were treated with dilatory geniality by his superior officer. The soft wonder of a perfect Indian summer glorified land, river and sky. Why not dream and bask? Why not drink exhilarating toddies?

Meantime the entertainment to be given by Gaspard Roussillon occupied everybody's imagination to an unusual extent. Rene de Ronville, remembering but not heeding the doubtful success of his former attempt, went long beforehand to claim Alice as his partenaire; but she flatly refused him, once more reminding him of his obligations to little Adrienne Bourcier. He would not be convinced.

"You are bound to me," he said, "you promised before, you know, and the party was but put off. I hold you to it; you are my partenaire, and I am yours, you can't deny that."

"No you are not my partenaire," she firmly said; then added lightly, "Feu mon partenaire, you are dead and buried as my partner at that dance."

He glowered in silence for a few moments, then said:

"It is Lieutenant Beverley, I suppose."

She gave him a quick contemptuous look, but turned it instantly into one of her tantalising smiles.

"Do you imagine that?" she demanded.

"Imagine it! I know it," he said with a hot flush. "Have I no sense?"

"Precious little," she replied with a merry laugh.

"You think so."

"Go to Father Beret, tell him everything, and then ask him what he thinks," she said in a calm, even tone, her face growing serious.

There was an awkward silence.

She had touched Rene's vulnerable spot; he was nothing if not a devout Catholic, and his conscience rooted itself in what good Father Beret had taught him.

The church, no matter by what name it goes, Catholic or Protestant, has a saving hold on the deepest inner being of its adherents. No grip is so hard to shake off as that of early religious convictions. The still, small voice coming down from the times "When shepherds watched their flocks by night," in old Judea, passes through the priest, the minister, the preacher; it echoes in cathedral, church, open-air meeting; it gently and mysteriously imparts to human life the distinctive quality which is the exponent of Christian civilization. Upon the receptive nature of children it makes an impress that forever afterward exhales a fragrance and irradiates a glory for the saving of the nations.

Father Beret was the humble, self-effacing, never-tiring agent of good in his community. He preached in a tender sing-song voice the sweet monotonies of his creed and the sublime truths of Christ's code. He was indeed the spiritual father of his people. No wonder Rene's scowling expression changed to one of abject self-concern when the priest's name was suddenly connected with his mood. The confessional loomed up before the eyes of his conscience, and his knees smote together, spiritually if not physically.

"Now," said Alice, brusquely, but with sweet and gentle firmness, "go to your fiancee, go to pretty and good Adrienne, and ask her to be your partenaire. Refresh your conscience with a noble draught of duty and make that dear little girl overflow with joy. Go, Rene de Ronville."

In making over what she said into English, the translation turns out to be but a sonorous paraphrase. Her French was of that mixed creole sort, a blending of linguistic elegance and patois, impossible to imitate. Like herself it was beautiful, crude, fascinating, and something in it impressed itself as unimpeachable, despite the broken and incongruous diction. Rene felt his soul cowering, even slinking; but he fairly maintained a good face, and went away without saying another word.

"Ciel, ciel, how beautiful she is!" he thought, as he walked along the narrow street in the dreamy sunshine. "But she is not for me, not for me."

He shook himself and tried to be cheerful. In fact he hummed a Creole ditty, something about

"La belle Jeanette, qu' a brise mon coeur."

Days passed, and at last the time of the great event arrived. It was a frosty night, clear, sparkling with stars, a keen breath cutting down from the northwest. M. Roussillon, Madame Roussillon, Alice and Lieutenant Beverley went together to the river house, whither they had been preceded by almost the entire population of Vincennes. Some fires had been built outside; the crowd proving too great for the building's capacity, as there had to be ample space for the dancers. Merry groups hovered around the flaming logs, while within the house a fiddle sang its simple and ravishing tunes. Everybody talked and laughed; it was a lively racket of clashing voices and rhythmical feet.

You would have been surprised to find that Oncle Jazon was the fiddler; but there he sat, perched on a high stool in one corner of the large room, sawing away as if for dear life, his head wagging, his elbow leaping back and forth, while his scalpless crown shone like the side of a peeled onion and his puckered mouth wagged grotesquely from side to side keeping time to his tuneful scraping.

When the Roussillon party arrived it attracted condensed attention. Its importance, naturally of the greatest in the assembled popular mind, was enhanced—as mathematicians would say, to the nth power—by the gown of Alice. It was resplendent indeed in the simple, unaccustomed eyes upon which it flashed with a buff silken glory. Matrons stared at it; maidens gazed with fascinated and jealous vision; men young and old let their eyes take full liberty. It was as if a queen, arrayed in a robe of state, had entered that dingy log edifice, an apparition of dazzling and awe-inspiring beauty. Oncle Jazon caught sight of her, and snapped his tune short off. The dancers swung together and stopped in confusion. But she, fortified by a woman's strongest bulwark, the sense of resplendency, appeared quite unconscious of herself.

Little Adrienne, hanging in blissful delight upon Rene's strong arm, felt the stir of excitement and wondered what was the matter, being too short to see over the heads of those around her.

"What is it? what is it?" she cried, tiptoeing and tugging at her companion's sleeve. "Tell me, Rene, tell me, I say."

Rene was gazing in dumb admiration into which there swept a powerful anger, like a breath of flame. He recollected how Alice had refused to wear that dress when he had asked her, and now she had it on. Moreover, there she stood beside Lieutenant Beverley, holding his arm, looking up into his face, smiling, speaking to him.

"I think you might tell me what has happened," said Adrienne, pouting and still plucking at his arm. "I can't see a thing, and you won't tell me."

"Oh, it's nothing," he presently answered, rather fretfully. Then he stooped, lowered his voice and added; "it's Mademoiselle Roussillon all dressed up like a bride or something. She's got on a buff silk dress that Mo'sieu' Roussillon's mother had in France."

"How beautiful she must look!" cried the girl. "I wish I could see her."

Rene put a hand on each side of her slender waist and lifted her high, so that her pretty head rose above the crowding people. Alice chanced to turn her face that way just then and saw the unconventional performance. Her eyes met those of Adrienne and she gave a nod of smiling recognition. It was a rose beaming upon a gilliflower.

M. Roussillon naturally understood that all this stir and crowding to see was but another demonstration of his personal popularity. He bowed and waved a vast hand.

But the master of ceremonies called loudly for the dancers to take their places. Oncle Jazon attacked his fiddle again with startling energy. Those who were not to dance formed a compact double line around the wall, the shorter ones in front, the taller in the rear. And what a scene it was! but no person present regarded it as in any way strange or especially picturesque, save as to the gown of Alice, which was now floating and whirling in time to Oncle Jazon's mad music. The people outside the house cheerfully awaited their turn to go in while an equal number went forth to chat and sing around the fires.

Beverley was in a young man's seventh heaven. The angels formed a choir circling around his heart, and their song brimmed his universe from horizon to horizon.

When he called at Roussillon place, and Alice appeared so beautifully and becomingly robed, it was another memorable surprise. She flashed a new and subtly stimulating light upon him. The old gown, rich in subdued splendor of lace and brocade, was ornamented at the throat with a heavy band of pearls, just above which could be seen a trace of the gold chain that supported her portrait locket. There, too, with a not unbecoming gleam of barbaric colors, shone the string of porcupine beads to which the Indian charmstone hidden in her bosom was attached. It all harmonized with the time, the place, the atmosphere. Anywhere else it would have been preposterous as a decorative presentment, but here, in this little nook where the coureurs de bois, the half-breeds, the traders and the missionaries had founded a centre of assembly, it was the best possible expression in the life so formed at hap-hazard, and so controlled by the coarsest and narrowest influences. To Fitzhugh Beverley, of Beverley Hall, the picture conveyed immediately a sweet and pervading influence.

Alice looked superbly tall, stately and self-possessed in her transforming costume, a woman of full stature, her countenance gravely demure yet reserving near the surface the playful dimples and mischievous smiles so characteristic of her more usual manner. A sudden mood of the varium et mutabile semper femina had led her to wear the dress, and the mood still illuminated her.

Beverley stood before her frankly looking and admiring. The underglow in her cheeks deepened and spread over her perfect throat; her eyes met his a second, then shyly avoided him. He hardly could have been sure which was master, her serenity or her girlish delight in being attractively dressed; but there could be no doubt as to her self-possession; for, saving the pretty blush under his almost rude gaze of admiration, she bore herself as firmly as any fine lady he remembered.

They walked together to the river house, she daintily holding up her skirts, under the insistent verbal direction of Madame Roussillon, and at the same time keeping a light, strangely satisfying touch on his arm. When they entered the room there was no way for Beverley to escape full consciousness of the excitement they aroused; but M. Roussillon's assumption broke the force of what would have otherwise been extremely embarrassing.

"It is encouraging, very encouraging," murmured the big man to Beverley in the midst of the staring and scrambling and craning of necks, "to have my people admire and love me so; it goes to the middle of my heart." And again he bowed and waved his hand with an all-including gesture, while he swept his eyes over the crowd.

Alice and Beverley were soon in the whirl of the dance, forgetful of everything but an exhilaration stirred to its utmost by Oncle Jazon's music.

A side remark here may be of interest to those readers who enjoy the dream that on some fortunate day they will invade a lonely nook, where amid dust and cobwebs, neglected because unrecognized, reposes a masterpiece of Stradivari or some other great fiddle-maker. Oncle Jazon knew nothing whatever about old violins. He was a natural musician, that was all, and flung himself upon his fiddle with the same passionate abandon that characterizes a healthy boy's assault when a plum pudding is at his mercy. But his fiddle was a Carlo Bergonzi; and now let the search be renewed, for the precious instrument was certainly still in Vincennes as late as 1819, and there is a vague tradition that Governor Whitcomb played on it not long before he died. The mark by which it may be identified is the single word "Jazon" cut in the back of its neck by Oncle Jazon himself.

When their dance was ended Alice and Beverley followed the others of their set out into the open air while a fresh stream of eager dancers poured in. Beverley insisted upon wrapping Alice in her mantle of unlined beaver skin against the searching winter breath. They did not go to the fire, but walked back and forth, chatting until their turn to dance should come again, pausing frequently to exchange pleasantries with some of the people. Curiously enough both of them had forgotten the fact that other young men would be sure to ask Alice for a dance, and that more than one pretty creole lass was rightfully expecting a giddy turn with the stalwart and handsome Lieutenant Beverley.

Rene de Ronville before long broke rudely into their selfish dream and led Alice into the house. This reminded Beverley of his social duty, wherefore seeing little Adrienne Bourcier he made a rush and secured her at a swoop from the midst of a scrambling circle of mutually hindered young men.

"Allons, ma petite!" he cried, quite in the gay tone of the occasion, and swung her lightly along with him.

It was like an eagle dancing with a linnet, or a giant with a fairy, when the big Lieutenant led out la petite Adrienne, as everybody called her. The honor of Beverley's attention sat unappreciated on Adrienne's mind, for all her thoughts went with her eyes toward Rene and Alice. Nor was Beverley so absorbed in his partner's behalf that he ever for a moment willingly lost sight of the floating buff gown, the shining brown hair and the beautiful face, which formed, indeed, the center of attraction for all eyes.

Father Beret was present, sharing heartily in the merriment of his flock. Voices greeted him on all sides with intonations of tender respect. The rudest man there was loyal to the kind-hearted priest, and would as soon have thought of shooting him as of giving him any but the most reverent attention. It is to be noted, however, that their understanding of reverence included great freedom and levity not especially ecclesiastical in its nature. Father Beret understood the conditions around him and had the genius to know what not to hear, what not to see; but he never failed when a good word or a fatherly touch with his hand seemed worth trying on a sheep that appeared to be straying dangerously far from the fold. Upon an occasion like this dance at the river house, he was no less the faithful priest because of his genial sympathy with the happiness of the young people who looked to him for spiritual guidance.

It was some time before Beverley could again secure Alice for a dance, and he found it annoying him atrociously to see her smile sweetly on some buckskin-clad lout who looked like an Indian and danced like a Parisian. He did not greatly enjoy most of his partners; they could not appeal to any side of his nature just then. Not that he at all times stood too much on his aristocratic traditions, or lacked the virile traits common to vigorous and worldly-minded men; but the contrast between Alice and the other girls present was somehow an absolute bar to a democratic freedom of the sort demanded by the occasion. He met Father Beret and passed a few pleasant words with him.

"They have honored your flag, my son, I am glad to see," the priest said, pointing with a smile to where, in one corner, the banner that bore Alice's name was effectively draped.

Beverley had not noticed it before, and when he presently got possession of Alice he asked her to tell him the story of how she planted it on the fort, although he had heard it to the last detail from Father Beret just a moment ago. They stood together under its folds while she naively sketched the scene for him, even down to her picturesquely disagreeable interview with Long-Hair, mention of whom led up to the story of the Indian's race with the stolen dame jeanne of brandy under his arm on that memorable night, and the subsequent services performed for him by Father Beret and her, after she and Jean had found him in the mud beyond the river.

The dancing went on at a furious pace while they stood there. Now and again a youth came to claim her, but she said she was tired and begged to rest awhile, smiling so graciously upon each one that his rebuff thrilled him as if it had been the most flattering gift of tender partiality, while at the same time he suspected that it was all for Beverley.

Helm in his most jovial mood was circulating freely among those who formed the periphery of the dancing-area; he even ventured a few clumsy capers in a cotillion with Madame Godere for partner. She danced well; but he, as someone remarked, stumbled all over himself.

There was but one thing to mar the evening's pleasure: some of the men drank too much and grew boisterous. A quarrel ended in a noisy but harmless fight near one of the fires. M. Roussillon rushed to the spot, seized the combatants, tousled them playfully, as if they had been children, rubbed their heads together, laughed stormily and so restored the equilibrium of temper.

It was late when fathers and mothers in the company began to suggest adjournment. Oncle Jazon's elbow was tired and the enthusiasm generated by his unrecognized Bergonzi became fitful, while the relaxing crowd rapidly encroached upon the space set apart for the dancers. In the open lamps suspended here and there the oil was running low, and the rag wicks sputtered and winked with their yellow flames.

"Well," said M. Roussillon, coming to where Alice and Beverley stood insulated and isolated by their great delight in each other's company, "it's time to go home."

Beverley looked at his watch; it was a quarter to three!

Alice also looked at the watch, and saw engraved and enameled on its massive case the Beverley crest, but she did not know what it meant. There was something of the sort in the back of her locket, she remembered with satisfaction.

Just then there was a peculiar stir in the flagging crowd. Someone had arrived, a coureur de bois from the north. Where was the commandant? the coureur had something important for him.

Beverley heard a remark in a startled voice about the English getting ready for a descent upon the Wabash valley. This broke the charm which thralled him and sent through his nerves the bracing shock that only a soldier can feel when a hint of coming battle reaches him.

Alice saw the flash in his face.

"Where is Captain Helm? I must see him immediately. Excuse me," he said, abruptly turning away and looking over the heads of the people; "yonder he is, I must go to him."

The coureur de bois, Adolphe Dutremble by name, was just from the head waters of the Wabash. He was speaking to Helm when Beverley came up. M. Roussillon followed close upon the Lieutenant's heels, as eager as he to know what the message amounted to; but Helm took the coureur aside, motioning Beverley to join them. M. Roussillon included himself in the conference.

After all it was but the gossip of savages that Dutremble communicated; still the purport was startling in the extreme. Governor Hamilton, so the story ran, had been organizing a large force; he was probably now on his way to the portage of the Wabash with a flotilla of batteaux, some companies of disciplined soldiers, artillery and a strong body of Indians.

Helm listened attentively to Dutremble's lively sketch, then cross-questioned him with laconic directness.

"Send Mr. Jazon to me," he said to M. Roussillon, as if speaking to a servant.

The master Frenchman went promptly, recognizing Captain Helm's right to command, and sympathizing with his unpleasant military predicament if the news should prove true.

Oncle Jazon came in a minute, his fiddle and bow clamped under his arm, to receive a verbal commission, which sent him with some scouts of his own choosing forthwith to the Wabash portage, or far enough to ascertain what the English commander was doing.

After the conference Beverley made haste to join Alice; but he found that she had gone home.

"One hell of a fix we'll be in if Hamilton comes down here with a good force," said Helm.

Beverley felt like retorting that a little forethought, zeal and preparation might have lessened the prospective gloom. He had been troubled all the time about Helm's utter lack of military precaution. True, there was very little material out of which that optimistic officer could have formed a body of resistance against the army probably at Hamilton's command; but Beverley was young, energetic, bellicose, and to him everything seemed possible; he believed in vigilance, discipline, activity, dash; he had a great faith in the efficacy of enthusiasm.

"We must organize these Frenchmen," he said; "they will make good fighters if we can once get them to act as a body. There's no time to be lost; but we have time enough in which to do a great deal before Hamilton can arrive, if we go at it in earnest."

"Your theory is excellent, Lieutenant, but the practice of it won't be worth a damn," Helm replied with perfect good nature. "I'd like to see you organize these parly-voos. There ain't a dozen of 'em that wouldn't accept the English with open arms. I know 'em. They're good hearted, polite and all that; they'll hurrah for the flag; that's easy enough; but put 'em to the test and they'll join in with the strongest side, see if they don't. Of course there are a few exceptions. There's Jazon, he's all right, and I have faith in Bosseron, and Legrace, and young Ronville."

"Roussillon—" Beverley began.

"Is much of a blow-hard," Helm interrupted with a laugh. "Barks loud, but his biting disposition is probably not vicious."

"He and Father Beret control the whole population at all events," said Beverley.

"Yes, and such a population!"

While joining in Captain Helm's laugh at the expense of Vincennes, Beverley took leave to indulge a mental reservation in favor of Alice. He could not bear to class her with the crowd of noisy, thoughtless, mercurial beings whom he heard still singing gay snatches and calling to one another from distance to distance, as they strolled homeward in groups and pairs. Nor could the impending danger of an enforced surrender to the English and Indians drive from his mind her beautiful image, while he lay for the rest of the night between sleeping and waking on his primitive bed, alternately hearing over again her every phrase and laugh, and striving to formulate some definite plan for defending the town and fort. His heart was full of her. She had surprised his nature and filled it, as with a wonderful, haunting song. His youth, his imagination, all that was fresh and spontaneously gentle and natural in him, was flooded with the magnetic splendor of her beauty. And yet, in his pride (and it was not a false pride, but rather a noble regard for his birthright) he vaguely realized how far she was from him, how impossible.

CHAPTER VIII
THE DILEMMA OF CAPTAIN HELM

Oncle Jazon, feeling like a fish returned to the water after a long and torturing captivity in the open air, plunged into the forest with anticipations of lively adventure and made his way toward the Wea plains. It was his purpose to get a boat at the village of Ouiatenon and pull thence up the Wabash until he could find out what the English were doing. He chose for his companions on this dangerous expedition two expert coureurs de bois, Dutremble and Jacques Bailoup. Fifty miles up the river they fell in with some friendly Indians, well known to them all, who were returning from the portage.

The savages informed them that there were no signs of an English advance in that quarter. Some of them had been as far as the St. Joseph river and to within a short distance of Detroit without seeing a white man or hearing of any suspicious movements on the part of Hamilton. So back came Oncle Jazon with his pleasing report, much disappointed that he had not been able to stir up some sort of trouble.

It was Helm's turn to laugh.

"What did I tell you?" he cried, in a jolly mood, slapping Beverley on the shoulder. "I knew mighty well that it was all a big story with nothing in it. What on earth would the English be thinking about to march an army away off down here only to capture a rotten stockade and a lot of gabbling parly-voos?"

Beverley, while he did not feel quite as confident as his chief, was not sorry that things looked a little brighter than he had feared they would turn out to be. Secretly, and without acknowledging it to himself, he was delighted with the life he was living. The Arcadian atmosphere of Vincennes clothed him in its mists and dreams. No matter what way the weather blew its breath, cold or warm, cloudy or fair, rain or snow, the peace in his soul changed not. His nature seemed to hold all of its sterner and fiercer traits in abeyance while he domiciled himself absolutely within his narrow and monotonous environment. Since the dance at the river house a new content, like a soft and diffused sweetness, had crept through his blood with a vague, tingling sense of joy.

He began to like walking about rather aimlessly in the town's narrow streets, with the mud-daubed cabins on either hand. This simple life under low, thatched roofs had a charm. When a door was opened he could see a fire of logs on the ample hearth shooting its yellow tongues up the sooty chimney-throat. Soft creole voices murmured and sang, or jangled their petty domestic discords. Women in scant petticoats, leggings and moccasins swept snow from the squat verandas, or fed the pigs in little sties behind the cabins. Everybody cried cheerily: "Bon jour, Monsieur, comment allez-vous?" as he went by, always accompanying the verbal salute with a graceful wave of the hand.

When he walked early in the morning a waft of broiling game and browning corn scones was abroad. Pots and kettles occupied the hearths with glowing coals heaped around and under. Shaggy dogs whined at the doors until the mensal remnants were tossed out to them in the front yard.

But it was always a glimpse of Alice that must count for everything in Beverley's reckonings, albeit he would have strenuously denied it. True he went to Roussillon place almost every day, it being a fixed part of his well ordered habit, and had a talk with her. Sometimes, when Dame Roussillon was very busy and so quite off her guard, they read together in a novel, or in certain parts of the odd volume of Montaigne. This was done more for the sweetness of disobedience than to enjoy the already familiar pages.

Now and again they repeated their fencing bout; but never with the result which followed the first. Beverley soon mastered Alice's tricks and showed her that, after all, masculine muscle is not to be discounted at its own game by even the most wonderful womanly strength and suppleness. She struggled bravely to hold her vantage ground once gained so easily, but the inevitable was not to be avoided. At last, one howling winter day, he disarmed her by the very trick that she had shown him. That ended the play and they ran shivering into the house.

"Ah," she cried, "it isn't fair. You are so much bigger than I; you have so much longer arms; so much more weight and power. It all counts against me! You ought to be ashamed of yourself!" She was rosy with the exhilarating exercise and the biting of the frosty breeze. Her beauty gave forth a new ray.

Deep in her heart she was pleased to have him master her so superbly; but as the days passed she never said so, never gave over trying to make him feel the touch of her foil. She did not know that her eyes were getting through his guard, that her dimples were stabbing his heart to its middle.

"You have other advantages," he replied, "which far overbalance my greater stature and stronger muscles." Then after a pause he added: "After all a girl must be a girl."

Something in his face, something in her heart, startled her so that she made a quick little move like that of a restless bird.

"You are beautiful and that makes my eyes and my hand uncertain," he went on. "Were I fencing with a man there would be no glamour."

He spoke in English, which he did not often do in conversation with her. It was a sign that he was somewhat wrought upon. She followed his rapid words with difficulty; but she caught from them a new note of feeling. He saw a little pale flare shoot across her face and thought she was angry.

"You should not use your dimples to distract my vision," he quickly added, with a light laugh. "It would be no worse for me to throw my hat in your face!"

His attempt at levity was obviously weak; she looked straight into his eyes, with the steady gaze of a simple, earnest nature shocked by a current quite strange to it. She did not understand him, and she did. Her fine intuition gathered swiftly together a hundred shreds of impression received from him during their recent growing intimacy. He was a patrician, as she vaguely made him out, a man of wealth, whose family was great. He belonged among people of gentle birth and high attainments. She magnified him so that he was diffused in her imagination, as difficult to comprehend as a mist in the morning air—and as beautiful.

"You make fun of me," she said, very deliberately, letting her eyes droop; then she looked up again suddenly and continued, with a certain naive expression of disappointment gathering in her face. "I have been too free with you. Father Beret told me not to forget my dignity when in your company. He told me you might misunderstand me. I don't care; I shall not fence with you again." She laughed, but there was no joyous freedom in the sound.

"Why, Alice—my dear Miss Roussillon, you do me a wrong; I beg a thousand pardons if I've hurt you," he cried, stepping nearer to her, "and I can never forgive myself. You have somehow misunderstood me, I know you have!"

On his part it was exaggerating a mere contact of mutual feelings into a dangerous collision. He was as much self-deceived as was she, and he made more noise about it.

"It is you who have misunderstood me," she replied, smiling brightly now, but with just a faint, pitiful touch of regret, or self-blame lingering in her voice. "Father Beret said you would. I did not believe him; but—"

"And you shall not believe him," said Beverley. "I have not misunderstood you. There has been nothing. You have treated me kindly and with beautiful friendliness. You have not done or said a thing that Father Beret or anybody else could criticise. And if I have said or done the least thing to trouble you I repudiate it—I did not mean it. Now you believe me, don't you, Miss Roussillon?"

He seemed to be falling into the habit of speaking to her in English. She understood it somewhat imperfectly, especially when in an earnest moment he rushed his words together as if they had been soldiers he was leading at the charge-step against an enemy. His manner convinced her, even though his diction fell short.

"Then we'll talk about something else," she said, laughing naturally now, and retreating to a chair by the hearthside. "I want you to tell me all about yourself and your family, your home and everything."

She seated herself with an air of conscious aplomb and motioned him to take a distant stool.

There was a great heap of dry logs in the fireplace, with pointed flames shooting out of its crevices and leaping into the gloomy, cave-like throat of the flue. Outside a wind passed heavily across the roof and bellowed in the chimney-top.

Beverley drew the stool near Alice, who, with a charred stick, used as a poker, was thrusting at the glowing crevices and sending showers of sparks aloft.

"Why, there wouldn't be much to tell," he said, glad to feel secure again. "Our home is a big old mansion named Beverley Hall on a hill among trees, and half surrounded with slave cabins. It overlooks the plantation in the valley where a little river goes wandering on its way." He was speaking French and she followed him easily now, her eyes beginning to fling out again their natural sunny beams of interest. "I was born there twenty-six years ago and haven't done much of anything since. You see before you, Mademoiselle, a very undistinguished young man, who has signally failed to accomplish the dream of his boyhood, which was to be a great artist like Raphael or Angelo. Instead of being famous I am but a poor Lieutenant in the forces of Virginia."

"You have a mother, father, brothers and sisters?" she interrogated. She did not understand his allusion to the great artists of whom she knew nothing. She had never before heard of them. She leaned the poker against the chimney jamb and turned her face toward him.

"Mother, father, and one sister," he said, "no brothers. We were a happy little group. But my sister married and lives in Baltimore. I am here. Father and mother are alone in the old house. Sometimes I am terribly homesick." He was silent a moment, then added: "But you are selfish, you make me do all the telling. Now I want you to give me a little of your story, Mademoiselle, beginning as I did, at the first."

"But I can't," she replied with childlike frankness, "for I don't know where I was born, nor my parents' names, nor who I am. You see how different it is with me. I am called Alice Roussillon, but I suppose that my name is Alice Tarleton; it is not certain, however. There is very little to help out the theory. Here is all the proof there is. I don't know that it is worth anything."

She took off her locket and handed it to him.

He handled it rather indifferently, for he was just then studying the fine lines of her face. But in a moment he was interested.

"Tarleton, Tarleton," he repeated. Then he turned the little disc of gold over and saw the enameled drawing on the back,—a crest clearly outlined.

He started. The crest was quite familiar.

"Where did you get this?" he demanded in English, and with such blunt suddenness that she was startled. "Where did it come from?"

"I have always had it."

"Always? It's the Tarleton crest. Do you belong to that family?"

"Indeed I do not know. Papa Roussillon says he thinks I do."

"Well, this is strange and interesting," said Beverley, rather to himself than addressing her. He looked from the miniature to the crest and back to the miniature again, then at Alice. "I tell you this is strange," he repeated with emphasis. "It is exceedingly strange."

Her cheeks flushed quickly under their soft brown and her eyes flashed with excitement.

"Yes, I know." Her voice fluttered; her hands were clasped in her lap. She leaned toward him eagerly. "It is strange. I've thought about it a great deal."

"Alice Tarleton; that is right; Alice is a name of the family. Lady Alice Tarleton was the mother of the first Sir Garnett Tarleton who came over in the time of Yardley. It's a great family. One of the oldest and best in Virginia." He looked at her now with a gaze of concentrated interest, under which her eyes fell. "Why, this is romantic!" he exclaimed, "absolutely romantic. And you don't know how you came by this locket? You don't know who was your father, your mother?"

"I do not know anything."

"And what does Monsieur Roussillon know?"

"Just as little."

"But how came he to be taking you and caring for you? He must know how he got you, where he got you, of whom he got you? Surely he knows—"

"Oh, I know all that. I was twelve years old when Papa Roussillon took me, eight years ago. I had been having a hard life, and but for him I must have died. I was a captive among the Indians. He took me and has cared for me and taught me. He has been very, very good to me. I love him dearly."

"And don't you remember anything at all about when, where, how the Indians got you?"

"No." She shook her head and seemed to be trying to recollect something. "No, I just can't remember; and yet there has always been something like a dream in my mind, which I could not quite get hold of. I know that I am not a Catholic. I vaguely remember a sweet woman who taught me to pray like this: 'Our Father who art in heaven, hallowed be Thy name.'"

And Alice went on through the beautiful and perfect prayer, which she repeated in English with infinite sweetness and solemnity, her eyes uplifted, her hands clasped before her. Beverley could have sworn that she was a shining saint, and that he saw an aureole.

"I know," she continued, "that sometime, somewhere, to a very dear person I promised that I never, never, never would pray any prayer but that. And I remember almost nothing else about that other life, which is far off back yonder in the past, I don't know where,—sweet, peaceful, shadowy; a dream that I have all but lost from my mind."

Beverley's sympathy was deeply moved. He sat for some minutes looking at her without speaking. She, too, was pensive and silent, while the fire sputtered and sang, the great logs slowly melting, the flames tossing wisps of smoke into the chimney still booming to the wind.

"I know, too, that I am not French," she presently resumed, "but I don't know just how I know it. My first words must have been English, for I have always dreamed of talking in that language, and my dimmest half recollections of the old days are of a large, white house, and a soft-voiced black woman, who sang to me in that language the very sweetest songs in the world."

It must be borne in mind that all this was told by Alice in her creole French, half bookish, half patois, of which no translation can give any fair impression.

Beverley listened, as one who hears a clever reader intoning a strange and captivating poem. He was charmed. His imagination welcomed the story and furnished it with all that it lacked of picturesque completeness. In those days it was no uncommon thing for a white child to be found among the Indians with not a trace left by which to restore it to its people. He had often heard of such a case. But here was Alice right before him, the most beautiful girl that he had ever seen, telling him the strangest story of all. To his mind it was clear that she belonged to the Tarleton family of Virginia. Youth always concludes a matter at once. He knew some of the Tarletons; but it was a widely scattered family, its members living in almost every colony in America. The crest he recognized at a glance by the dragon on the helmet with three stars. It was not for a woman to bear; but doubtless it had been enameled on the locket merely as a family mark, as was often done in America.

"The black woman was your nurse, your mammy," he said. "I know by that and by your prayer in English, as well as by your locket, that you are of a good old family."

Like most Southerners, he had strong faith in genealogy, and he held at his tongue's tip the names of all the old families. The Carters, the Blairs, the Fitzhughs, the Hansons, the Randolphs, the Lees, the Ludwells, the Joneses, the Beverleys, the Tarletons—a whole catalogue of them stretched back in his memory. He knew the coat of arms displayed by each house. He could repeat their legends.

"I wish you could tell me more," he went on. "Can't you recollect anything further about your early childhood, your first impressions—the house, the woman who taught you to pray, the old black mammy? Any little thing might be of priceless value as evidence."

Alice shrugged her shoulders after the creole fashion with something of her habitual levity of manner, and laughed. His earnestness seemed disproportioned to the subject, as she fancied he must view it, although to her it had always been something to dream over. It was impossible for her to realize, as he did, the importance of details in solving a problem like that involved in her past history. Nor could she feel the pathos and almost tragic fascination with which her story had touched him.

"There is absolutely nothing more to tell," she said. "All my life I have tried to remember more, but it's impossible; I can't get any further back or call up another thing. There's no use trying. It's all like a dream—probably it is one. I do have such dreams. In my sleep I can lift myself into the air, just as easy, and fly back to the same big white house that I seem to remember. When you told me about your home it was like something that I had often seen before. I shall be dreaming about it next!"

Beverley cross-questioned her from every possible point of view; he was fascinated with the mystery; but she gave him nothing out of which the least further light could be drawn. A half-breed woman, it seemed, had been her Indian foster-mother; a silent, grave, watchful guardian from whom not a hint of disclosure ever fell. She was, moreover, a Christian woman, had received her conversion from an English-speaking Protestant missionary. She prayed with Alice, thus keeping in the child's mind a perfect memory of the Lord's prayer.

"Well," said Beverley at last, "you are more of a mystery to me, the longer I know you."

"Then I must grow every day more distasteful to you."

"No, I love mystery."

He went away feeling a new web of interest binding him to this inscrutable maiden whose life seemed to him at once so full of idyllic happiness and so enshrouded in tantalizing doubt. At the first opportunity he frankly questioned M. Roussillon, with no helpful result. The big Frenchman told the same meager story. The woman was dying in the time of a great epidemic, which killed most of her tribe. She gave Alice to M. Roussillon, but told him not a word about her ancestry or previous life. That was all.

A wise old man, when he finds himself in a blind alley, no sooner touches the terminal wall than he faces about and goes back the way he came. Under like circumstances a young man must needs try to batter the wall down with his head. Beverley endeavored to break through the web of mystery by sheer force. It seemed to him that a vigorous attempt could not fail to succeed; but, like the fly in the spider's lines, he became more hopelessly bound at every move he made. Moreover against his will he was realizing that he could no longer deceive himself about Alice. He loved her, and the love was mastering him body and soul. Such a confession carries with it into an honest masculine heart a sense of contending responsibilities. In Beverley's case the clash was profoundly disturbing. And now he clutched the thought that Alice was not a mere child of the woods, but a daughter of an old family of cavaliers!

With coat buttoned close against the driving wind, he strode toward the fort in one of those melodramatic moods to which youth in all climes and times is subject. It was like a slap in the face when Captain Helm met him at the stockade gate and said:

"Well, sir, you are good at hiding."

"Hiding! what do you mean, Captain Helm?" he demanded, not in the mildest tone.

"I mean, sir, that I've been hunting you for an hour and more, over the whole of this damned town. The English and Indians are upon us, and there's no time for fooling. Where are all the men?"

Beverley comprehended the situation in a second. Helm's face was congested with excitement. Some scouts had come in with the news that Governor Hamilton, at the head of five or six hundred soldiers and Indians, was only three or four miles up the river.

"Where are all the men?" Helm repeated.

"Buffalo hunting, most of them," said Beverley.

"What in hell are they off hunting buffaloes for?" raged the excited captain.

"You might go to hell and see," Beverley suggested, and they both laughed in sheer masculine contempt of a predicament too grave for anything but grim mirth.

What could they do? Even Oncle Jazon and Rene de Ronville were off with the hunters. Helm sent for M. Roussillon in the desperate hope that he could suggest something; but he lost his head and hustled off to hide his money and valuables. Indeed the French people all felt that, so far as they were concerned, the chief thing was to save what they had. They well knew that it mattered little which of the two masters held over them—they must shift for themselves. In their hearts they were true to France and America; but France and America could not now protect them against Hamilton; therefore it would be like suicide to magnify patriotism or any other sentiment objectionable to the English. So they acted upon M. Roussillon's advice and offered no resistance when the new army approached.

"My poor people are not disloyal to your flag and your cause," said good Father Beret next morning to Captain Helm, "but they are powerless. Winter is upon us. What would you have us do? This rickety fort is not available for defense; the men are nearly all far away on the plains. Isn't it the part of prudence and common sense to make the best of a desperate situation? Should we resist, the British and their savage allies would destroy the town and commit outrages too horrible to think about. In this case diplomacy promises much more than a hopeless fight against an overwhelming force."

"I'll fight 'em," Helm ground out between his teeth, "if I have to do it single-handed and alone! I'll fight 'em till hell freezes over!"

Father Beret smiled grimly, as if he, too, would enjoy a lively skirmish on the ice of Tophet, and said:

"I admire your courage, my son. Fighting is perfectly proper upon fair occasion. But think of the poor women and children. These old eyes of mine have seen some terrible things done by enraged savages. Men can die fighting; but their poor wives and daughters—ah, I have seen, I have seen!"

Beverley felt a pang of terror shoot through his heart as Father Beret's simple words made him think of Alice in connection with an Indian massacre.

"Of course, of course it's horrible to think of," said Helm; "but my duty is clear, and that flag," he pointed to where la banniere d'Alice Roussillon was almost blowing away in the cold wind, "that flag shall not come down save in full honor."

His speech sounded preposterously boastful and hollow; but he was manfully in earnest; every word came from his brave heart.

Father Beret's grim smile returned, lighting up his strongly marked face with the strangest expression imaginable.

"We will get all the women inside the fort," Helm began to say.

"Where the Indians will find them ready penned up and at their mercy," quickly interpolated the priest "That will not do."

"Well, then, what can be done?" Beverley demanded, turning with a fierce stare upon Father Beret. "Don't stand there objecting to everything, with not a suggestion of your own to offer."

"I know what is best for my people," the old man replied softly, still smiling, "I have advised them to stay inside their houses and take no part in the military event. It is the only hope of averting an indiscriminate massacre, and things worse."

The curt phrase, "things worse," went like a bullet-stroke through Beverley's heart. It flashed an awful picture upon his vision. Father Beret saw his face whiten and his lips set themselves to resist a great emotion.

"Do not be angry with me, my son," he said, laying a hand on the young man's arm. "I may be wrong, but I act upon long and convincing experience."

"Experience or no experience," Helm exclaimed with an oath, "this fort must be manned and defended. I am commanding here!"

"Yes, I recognize your authority," responded the priest in a firm yet deferential tone, "and I heartily wish you had a garrison; but where is your command, Captain Helm?" Then it was that the doughty Captain let loose the accumulated profanity with which he had been for some time well-nigh bursting. He tiptoed in order to curse with extremest violence. His gestures were threatening. He shook his fists at Father Beret, without really meaning offence.

"Where is my garrison, you ask! Yes, and I can tell you. It's where you might expect a gang of dad blasted jabbering French good-for-nothings to be, off high-gannicking around shooting buffaloes instead of staying here and defending their wives, children, homes and country, damn their everlasting souls! The few I have in the fort will sneak off, I suppose."

"The French gave you this post on easy terms, Captain," blandly retorted Father Beret.

"Yes, and they'll hand it over to Hamilton, you think, on the same basis," cried Helm, "but I'll show you! I'll show you, Mr. Priest!"

"Pardon me, Captain, the French are loyal to you and to the flag yonder. They have sworn it. Time will prove it. But in the present desperate dilemma we must choose the safer horn."

Saying this Father Beret turned about and went his way. He was chuckling heartily as he passed out of the gate.

"He is right," said Beverley after a few moments of reflection, during which he was wholly occupied with Alice, whose terrified face in his anticipation appealed to him from the midst of howling savages, smoking cabins and mangled victims of lust and massacre. His imagination painted the scene with a merciless realism that chilled his blood. All the sweet romance fell away from Vincennes.

"Well, sir, right or wrong, your, duty is to obey orders," said Helm with brutal severity.

"We had better not quarrel, Captain," Beverley replied. "I have not signified any unwillingness to obey your commands. Give them, and you will have no cause to grumble."

"Forgive me, old fellow," cried the impulsive commander. "I know you are true as steel. I s'pose I'm wound up too tight to be polite. But the time is come to do something. Here we are with but five or six men—"

He was interrupted by the arrival of two more half-breed scouts.

Only three miles away was a large flotilla of boats and canoes with cannon, a force of Indians on land and the British flag flying,—that was the report.

"They are moving rapidly," said the spokesman, "and will be here very soon. They are at least six hundred strong, all well armed."

"Push that gun to the gate, and load it to the muzzle, Lieutenant Beverley," Helm ordered with admirable firmness, the purple flush in his face giving way to a grayish pallor. "We are going to die right here, or have the honors of war."

Beverley obeyed without a word. He even loaded two guns instead of one—charging each so heavily that the last wad looked as if ready to leap from the grimy mouth.

Helm had already begun, on receiving the first report, a hasty letter to Colonel Clark at Kaskaskia. He now added a few words and at the last moment sent it out by a trusted man, who was promptly captured by Hamilton's advance guard. The missive, evidently written in installments during the slow approach of the British, is still in the Canadian archives, and runs thus:

"Dear Sir—At this time there is an army within three miles of this place; I heard of their coming several days beforehand. I sent spies to find the certainty—the spies being taken prisoner I never got intelligence till they got within three miles of town. As I had called the militia and had all assurances of their integrity I ordered at the firing of a cannon every man to appear, but I saw but few. Captain Buseron behaved much to his honor and credit, but I doubt the conduct of a certain gent. Excuse haste, as the army is in sight. My determination is to defend the garrison, (sic) though I have but twenty-one men but what has left me. I refer you to Mr. Wmes (sic) for the rest. The army is within three hundred yards of the village. You must think how I feel; not four men that I really depend upon; but am determined to act brave—think of my condition. I know it is out of my power to defend the town, as not one of the militia will take arms, though before sight of the army no braver men. There is a flag at a small distance, I must conclude.

"Your humble servant,

"Leo'd Helm. Must stop."

"To Colonel Clark."

Having completed this task, the letter shows under what a nervous strain, Helm turned to his lieutenant and said:

"Fire a swivel with a blank charge. We'll give these weak-kneed parly-voos one more call to duty. Of course not a frog-eater of them all will come. But I said that a gun should be the signal. Possibly they didn't hear the first one, the damned, deaf, cowardly hounds!"

Beverley wheeled forth the swivel and rammed a charge of powder home. But when he fired it, the effect was far from what it should have been. Instead of calling in a fresh body of militia, it actually drove out the few who up to that moment had remained as a garrison; so that Captain Helm and his Lieutenant found themselves quite alone in the fort, while out before the gate, deployed in fine open order, a strong line of British soldiers approached with sturdy steps, led by a tall, erect, ruddy-faced young officer.

CHAPTER IX
THE HONORS OF WAR

Gaspard Roussillon was thoroughly acquainted with savage warfare, and he knew all the pacific means so successfully and so long used by French missionaries and traders to control savage character; but the emergency now upon him was startling. It confused him. The fact that he had taken a solemn oath of allegiance to the American government could have been pushed aside lightly enough upon pressing occasion, but he knew that certain confidential agents left in Vincennes by Governor Abbott had, upon the arrival of Helm, gone to Detroit, and of course they had carried thither a full report of all that happened in the church of St. Xavier, when Father Gibault called the people together, and at the fort, when the British flag was hauled down and la banniere d'Alice Roussillon run up in its place. His expansive imagination did full credit to itself in exaggerating the importance of his part in handing the post over to the rebels. And what would Hamilton think of this? Would he consider it treason? The question certainly bore a tragic suggestion.

M. Roussillon lacked everything of being a coward, and treachery had no rightful place in his nature. He was, however, so in the habit of fighting windmills and making mountains of molehills that he could not at first glance see any sudden presentment with a normal vision. He had no love for Englishmen and he did like Americans, but he naturally thought that Helm's talk of fighting Hamilton was, as his own would have been in a like case, talk and nothing more. The fort could not hold out an hour, he well knew. Then what? Ah, he but too well realized the result.

Resistance would inflame the English soldiers and madden the Indians. There would be a massacre, and the belts of savages would sag with bloody scalps. He shrugged his shoulders and felt a chill creep up his back.

The first thing M. Roussillon did was to see Father Beret and take counsel of him; then he hurried home to dig a great pit under his kitchen floor in which he buried many bales of fur and all his most valuable things. He worked like a giant beaver all night long. Meantime Father Beret went about over the town quietly notifying the inhabitants to remain in their houses until after the fort should surrender, which he was sure would happen the next day.

"You will be perfectly safe, my children," he said to them. "No harm can come to you if you follow my directions."

Relying implicitly upon him, they scrupulously obeyed in every particular.

He did not think it necessary to call at Roussillon place, having already given M. Roussillon the best advice he could command.

Just at the earliest break of day, while yet the gloom of night scarcely felt the sun's approach, a huge figure made haste along the narrow streets in the northern part of the town. If any person had been looking out through the little holes, called windows, in those silent and rayless huts, it would have been easy to recognize M. Roussillon by his stature and his gait, dimly outlined as he was. A thought, which seemed to him an inspiration of genius, had taken possession of him and was leading him, as if by the nose, straight away to Hamilton's lines. He was freighted with eloquence for the ear of that commander, and as he strode along facing the crisp morning air he was rehearsing under his breath, emphasizing his periods in tragic whispers with sweeping gestures and liberal facial contortions. So absorbed was he in his oratorical soliloquy that he forgot due military precaution and ran plump into the face of a savage picket guard who, without respect for the great M. Roussillon's dignity, sprang up before him, grunted cavernously, flourished a tomahawk and spoke in excellent and exceedingly guttural Indian:

"Wah, surrender!"

It is probable that no man ever complied with a modest request in a more docile spirit than did M. Roussillon upon that occasion. In fact his promptness must have been admirable, for the savage grunted approval and straightway conducted him to Hamilton's headquarters on a batteau in the river.

The British commander, a hale man of sandy complexion and probably under middle age, was in no very pleasant humor. Some of his orders had been misunderstood by the chief of his Indian allies, so that a premature exposure of his approach had been made to the enemy.

"Well, sir, who are you?" he gruffly demanded, when M. Roussillon loomed before him.

"I am Gaspard Roussillon, the Mayor of Vincennes," was the lofty reply. "I have come to announce to you officially that my people greet you loyally and that my town is freely at your command." He felt as important as if his statements had been true.

"Humph, that's it, is it? Well, Mr. Mayor, you have my congratulations, but I should prefer seeing the military commander and accepting his surrender. What account can you give me of the American forces, their numbers and condition?"

M. Roussillon winced, inwardly at least, under Hamilton's very undeferential air and style of address. It piqued him cruelly to be treated as a person without the slightest claim to respect. He somehow forgot the rolling and rhythmical eloquence prepared for the occasion.

"The American commander naturally would not confide in me, Monsieur le Gouverneur, not at all; we are not very friendly; he ousted me from office, he offended me—" he was coughing and stammering.

"Oh, the devil! what do I care? Answer my question, sir," Hamilton gruffly interrupted. "Tell me the number of American troops at the fort, sir."

"I don't know exactly. I have not had admittance to the fort. I might be deceived as to numbers; but they're strong, I believe, Monsieur le Gouverneur, at least they make a great show and much noise."

Hamilton eyed the huge bulk before him for a moment, then turning to a subaltern said:

"Place this fellow under guard and see that he doesn't get away. Send word immediately to Captain Farnsworth that I wish to see him at once."

The interview thereupon closed abruptly. Hamilton's emissaries had given him a detailed account of M. Roussillon's share in submitting Vincennes to rebel dominion, and he was not in the least inclined toward treating him graciously.

"I would suggest to you, Monsieur le Gouverneur, that my official position demands—" M. Roussillon began; but he was fastened upon by two guards, who roughly hustled him aft and bound him so rigidly that he could scarcely move finger or toe.

Hamilton smiled coldly and turned to give some orders to a stalwart, ruddy young officer who in a canoe had just rowed alongside the batteau.

"Captain Farnsworth," he said, acknowledging the military salute, "you will take fifty men and make everything ready for a reconnaissance in the direction of the fort. We will move down the river immediately and choose a place to land. Move lively, we have no time to lose."

In the meantime Beverley slipped away from the fort and made a hurried call upon Alice at Roussillon place. There was not much they could say to each other during the few moments at command. Alice showed very little excitement; her past experience had fortified her against the alarms of frontier life; but she understood and perfectly appreciated the situation.

"What are you going to do?" Beverley demanded in sheer despair. He was not able to see any gleam of hope out of the blackness which had fallen around him and into his soul.

"What shall you do?" he repeated.

"Take the chances of war," she said, smiling gravely. "It will all come out well, no doubt."

"I hope so, but—but I fear not."

His face was gray with trouble. "Helm is determined to fight, and that means—"

"Good!" she interrupted with spirit. "I am so glad of that. I wish I could go to help him! If I were a man I'd love to fight! I think it's just delightful."

"But it is reckless bravado; it is worse than foolishness," said Beverley, not feeling her mood. "What can two or three men do against an army?"

"Fight and die like men," she replied, her whole countenance lighting up. "Be heroic!"

"We will do that, of course; we—I do not fear death; but you—you—" His voice choked him.

A gun shot rang out clear in the distance, and he did not finish speaking.

"That's probably the beginning," he added in a moment, extending both hands to her. "Good bye. I must hurry to the fort. Good bye."

She drew a quick breath and turned so white that her look struck him like a sudden and hard blow. He stood for a second, his arms at full reach, then:

"My God, Alice, I cannot, cannot leave you!" he cried, his voice again breaking huskily.

She made a little movement, as if to take hold of his hands: but in an instant she stepped back a pace and said:

"Don't fear about me. I can take care of myself. I'm all right. You'd better return to the fort as quickly as you can. It is your country, your flag, not me, that you must think of now."

She folded her arms and stood boldly erect.

Never before, in all his life, had he felt such a rebuke. He gave her a straight, strong look in the eyes.

"You are right, Alice." he cried, and rushed from the house to the fort.

She held her rigid attitude for a little while after she heard him shut the front gate of the yard so forcibly that it broke in pieces, then she flung her arms wide, as if to clasp something, and ran to the door; but Beverley was out of sight. She turned and dropped into a chair. Jean came to her out of the next room. His queer little face was pale and pinched; but his jaw was set with the expression of one who has known danger and can meet it somehow.

"Are they going to scalp us?" he half whispered presently, with a shuddering lift of his distorted shoulders.

Her face was buried in her hands and she did not answer. Childlike he turned from one question to another inconsequently.

"Where did Papa Roussillon go to?" he next inquired. "Is he going to fight?"

She shook her head.

"They'll tear down the fort, won't they?"

If she heard him she did not make any sign.

"They'll kill the Captain and Lieutenant and get the fine flag that you set so high on the fort, won't they, Alice?"

She lifted her head and gave the cowering hunchback such a stare that he shut his eyes and put up a hand, as if afraid of her. Then she impulsively took his little misshapen form in her arms and hugged it passionately. Her bright hair fell all over him, almost hiding him. Madame Roussillon was lying on a bed in an adjoining room moaning diligently, at intervals handling her rosary and repeating a prayer. The whole town was silent outside.

"Why don't you go get the pretty flag down and hide it before they come?" Jean murmured from within the silken meshes of Alice's hair.

In his small mind the gaudy banner was the most beautiful of all things. Every day since it was set up he had gone to gaze at it as it fluttered against the sky. The men had frequently said in his presence that the enemy would take it down if they captured the fort.

Alice heard his inquisitive voice; but it seemed to come from far off; his words were a part of the strange, wild swirl in her bosom. Beverley's look, as he turned and left her, now shook every chord of her being. He had gone to his death at her command. How strong and true and brave he was! In her imagination she saw the flag above him, saw him die like a panther at bay, saw the gay rag snatched down and torn to shreds by savage hands. It was the tragedy of a single moment, enacted in a flashlight of anticipation.

She released Jean so suddenly that he fell to the floor. She remembered what she had said to Beverley on the night of the dance when they were standing under the flag.

"You made it and set it up," he lightly remarked; "you must see that no enemy ever gets possession of it, especially the English."

"I'll take it down and hide it when there's danger of that," she said in the same spirit.

And now she stood there looking at Jean, without seeing him, and repeated the words under her breath.

"I'll take it down and hide it. They shan't have it."

Madame Roussillon began to call from the other room in a loud, complaining voice; but Alice gave no heed to her querulous demands.

"Stay here, Jean, and take care of Mama Roussillon," she presently said to the hunchback. "I am going out; I'll be back soon; don't you dare leave the house while I'm gone; do you hear?"

She did not wait for his answer; but snatching a hood-like fur cap from a peg on the wall, she put it on and hastily left the house.

Down at the fort Helm and Beverley were making ready to resist Hamilton's attack, which they knew would not be long deferred. The two heavily charged cannon were planted so as to cover the space in front of the gate, and some loaded muskets were ranged near by ready for use.

"We'll give them one hell of a blast," growled the Captain, "before they overpower us."

Beverley made no response in words; but he was preparing a bit of tinder on the end of a stick with which to fire the cannon. Not far away a little heap of logs was burning in the fort's area.

The British officer, already mentioned as at the head of the line advancing diagonally from the river's bank, halted his men at a distance of three hundred yards from the fort, and seemed to be taking a deliberately careful survey of what was before him.

"Let 'em come a little nearer, Lieutenant," said Helm, his jaw setting itself like a lion's. "When we shoot we want to hit."

He stooped and squinted along his gun.

"When they get to that weedy spot out yonder," he added, "just opposite the little rise in the river bank, we'll turn loose on 'em."

Beverley had arranged his primitive match to suit his fancy, and for probably the twentieth time looked critically to the powder in the beveled touch-hole of his old cannon. He and Helm were facing the enemy, with their backs to the main area of the stockade, when a well known voice attracted their attention to the rear.

"Any room for a feller o' my size in this here crowded place?" it demanded in a cracked but cheerful tenor. "I'm kind o' outen breath a runnin' to git here."

They turned about. It was Oncle Jazon with his long rifle on his shoulder and wearing a very important air. He spoke in English, using the backwoods lingo with the ease of long practice.

"As I's a comin' in f'om a huntin' I tuck notice 'at somepin' was up. I see a lot o' boats on the river an' some fellers wi' guns a scootin' around, so I jes' slipped by 'em all an' come in the back way. They's plenty of 'em, I tell you what! I can't shoot much, but I tuck one chance at a buck Indian out yander and jes' happened to hit 'im in the lef' eye. He was one of the gang 'at scalped me down yander in Kaintuck."

The greasy old sinner looked as if he had not been washed since he was born. He glanced about with furtive, shifty eyes, grimaced and winked, after the manner of an animal just waking from a lazy nap.

"Where's the rest o' the fighters?" he demanded quizzically, lolling out his tongue and peeping past Helm so as to get a glimpse of the English line. "Where's yer garrison? Have they all gone to breakfas'?"

The last question set Helm off again cursing and swearing in the most melodramatic rage.

Oncle Jazon turned to Beverley and said in rapid French: "Surely the man's not going to fight those fellows yonder?"

Beverley nodded rather gloomily.

"Well," added the old man, fingering his rifle's stock and taking another glance through the gate, "I can't shoot wo'th a cent, bein' sort o' nervous like; but I'll stan' by ye awhile, jes' for luck. I might accidentally hit one of 'em."

When a man is truly brave himself there is nothing that touches him like an exhibition of absolutely unselfish gameness in another. A rush of admiration for Oncle Jazon made Beverley feel like hugging him.

Meantime the young British officer showed a flag of truce, and, with a file of men, separated himself from the line, now stationary, and approached the stockade. At a hundred yards he halted the file and came on alone, waving the white clout. He boldly advanced to within easy speaking distance and shouted:

"I demand the surrender of this fort."

"Well, you'll not get it, young man," roared Helm, his profanity well mixed in with the words, "not while there's a man of us left!"

"Ye'd better use sof' soap on 'im, Cap'n," said Oncle Jazon in English, "cussin' won't do no good." While he spoke he rubbed the doughty Captain's arm and then patted it gently.

Helm, who was not half as excited as he pretended to be, knew that Oncle Jazon's remark was the very essence of wisdom; but he was not yet ready for the diplomatic language which the old trooper called "soft soap."

"Are you the British commander?" he demanded.

"No," said the officer, "but I speak for him."

"Not to me by a damned sight, sir. Tell your commander that I will hear what he has to say from his own mouth. No understrapper will be recognized by me."

That ended the conference. The young officer, evidently indignant, strode back to his line, and an hour later Hamilton himself demanded the unconditional surrender of the fort and garrison.

"Fight for it," Helm stormed forth. "We are soldiers."

Hamilton held a confab with his officers, while his forces, under cover of the town's cabins, were deploying so as to form a half circle about the stockade. Some artillery appeared and was planted directly opposite the gate, not three hundred yards distant. One blast of that battery would, as Helm well knew, level a large part of the stockade.

"S'posin' I hev' a cannon, too, seein' it's the fashion," said Oncle Jazon. "I can't shoot much, but I might skeer 'em. This little one'll do me."

He set his rifle against the wall and with Beverley's help rolled one of the swivels alongside the guns already in position.

In a few minutes Hamilton returned under the white flag and shouted:

"Upon what terms will you surrender?"

"All the honors of war," Helm firmly replied. "It's that or fight, and I don't care a damn which!"

Hamilton half turned away, as if done with the parley, then facing the fort again, said:

"Very well, sir, haul down your flag."

Helm was dumbounded at this prompt acceptance of his terms. Indeed the incident is unique in history.

As Hamilton spoke he very naturally glanced up to where la banniere d'Alice Roussillon waved brilliantly. Someone stood beside it on the dilapidated roof of the old blockhouse, and was already taking it from its place. His aid, Captain Farnsworth, saw this, and the vision made his heart draw in a strong, hot flood It was a girl in short skirts and moccasins, with a fur hood on her head, her face, thrillingly beautiful, set around with fluffs of wind-blown brown-gold hair. Farnsworth was too young to be critical and too old to let his eyes deceive him. Every detail of the fine sketch, with its steel-blue background of sky, flashed into his mind, sharp-cut as a cameo. Involuntarily he took off his hat.

Alice had come in by way of the postern. She mounted to the roof unobserved, and made her way to the flag, just at the moment when Helm, glad at heart to accept the easiest way out of a tight place, asked Oncle Jazon to lower it.

Beverley was thinking of Alice, and when he looked up he could scarcely realize that he saw her; but the whole situation was plain the instant she snatched the staff from its place; for he, too, recollected what she had said at the river house. The memory and the present scene blended perfectly during the fleeting instant that she was visible. He saw that Alice was smiling somewhat as in her most mischievous moods, and when she jerked the staff from its fastening she lifted it high and waved it once, twice, thrice defiantly toward the British lines, then fled down the ragged roof-slope with it and disappeared. The vision remained in Beverley's eyes forever afterward. The English troops, thinking that the flag was taken down in token of surrender, broke into a wild tumult of shouting.

Oncle Jazon intuitively understood just what Alice was doing, for he knew her nature and could read her face. His blood effervesced in an instant.

"Vive Zhorzh Vasinton! Vive la banniere d'Alice Roussillon!" he screamed, waving his disreputable cap round his scalpless head. "Hurrah for George Washington! Hurrah for Alice Roussillon's flag!"

It was all over soon. Helm surrendered himself and Beverley with full honors. As for Oncle Jazon, he disappeared at the critical moment. It was not just to his mind to be a prisoner of war, especially under existing conditions; for Hamilton's Indian allies had some old warpath scores to settle with him dating back to the days when he and Simon Kenton were comrades in Kentucky.

When Alice snatched the banner and descended with it to the ground, she ran swiftly out through the postern, as she had once before done, and sped along under cover of the low bluff or swell, which, terrace-like, bounded the flat "bottom" lands southward of the stockade. She kept on until she reached a point opposite Father Beret's hut, to which she then ran, the flag streaming bravely behind her in the wind, her heart beating time to her steps.

It was plainly a great surprise to Father Beret, who looked up from his prayer when she rushed in, making a startling clatter, the loose puncheons shaking together under her reckless feet.

"Oh, Father, here it is! Hide it, hide it, quick!"

She thrust the flag toward him.

"They shall not have it! They shall never have it!"

He opened wide his shrewd, kindly eyes; but did not fairly comprehend her meaning.

She was panting, half laughing, half crying. Her hair, wildly disheveled, hung in glorious masses over her shoulders. Her face beamed triumphantly.

"They are taking the fort," she breathlessly added, again urging the flag upon him, "they're going in, but I got this and ran away with it. Hide it, Father, hide it, quick, quick, before they come!"

The daring light in her eyes, the witching play of her dimples, the madcap air intensified by her attitude and the excitement of the violent exercise just ended—something compounded of all these and more—affected the good priest strangely. Involuntarily he crossed himself, as if against a dangerous charm.

"Mon Dieu, Father Beret," she exclaimed with impatience, "haven't you a grain of sense left? Take this flag and hide it, I tell you! Don't stay there gazing and blinking. Here, quick! They saw me take it, they may be following me. Hurry, hide it somewhere!"

He comprehended now, rising from his knees with a queer smile broadening on his face. She put the banner into his hands and gave him a gentle push.

"Hide it, I tell you, hide it, you dear old goose!"

Without sneaking he turned the staff over and over in his hand, until the flag was closely wrapped around it, then stooping he lifted a puncheon and with it covered the gay roll from sight.

Alice caught him in her arms and kissed him vigorously on the cheek. Her warm lips made the spot tingle.

"Don't you dare to let any person have it! It's the flag of George Washington."

She gave him a strong squeeze.

He pushed her from him with both hands and hastily crossed himself; but his eyes were laughing.

"You ought to have seen me; I waved the flag at them—at the English—and one young officer took off his hat to me! Oh, Father Beret, it was like what is in a novel. They'll get the fort, but not the banner! Not the banner! I've saved it, I've saved it!"

Her enthusiasm gave a splendor to her countenance, heightening its riches of color and somehow adding to its natural girlish expression an audacious sweetness. The triumphant success of her undertaking lent the dignity of conscious power to her look, a dignity which always sits well upon a young and somewhat immaturely beautiful face.

Father Beret could not resist her fervid eloquence, and he could not run away from her or stop up his ears while she went on. So he had to laugh when she said:

"Oh, if you had seen it all you would have enjoyed it. There was Oncle Jazon squatting behind the little swivel, and there were Captain Helm and Lieutenant Beverley holding their burning sticks over the big cannon ready to shoot—all of them so intent that they didn't see me—and yonder came the English officer and his army against the three. When they got close to the gate the officer called out: 'Surrender!' and then Captain Helm yelled back: 'Damned if I do! Come another step and I'll blow you all to hell in a second!' I was mightily in hopes that they'd come on; I wanted to see a cannon ball hit that English commander right in the face; he looked so arrogant."

Father Beret shook his head and tried to look disapproving and solemn.

Meantime down at the fort Hamilton was demanding the flag. He had seen Alice take it down, and supposed that it was lowered officially and would be turned over to him. Now he wanted to handle it as the best token of his bloodless but important victory.

"I didn't order the flag down until after I had accepted your terms," said Helm, "and when my man started to obey, we saw a young lady snatch it and run away with it."

"Who was the girl?"

"I do not inform on women," said Helm.

Hamilton smiled grimly, with a vexed look in his eyes, then turned to Captain Farnsworth and ordered him to bring up M. Roussillon, who, when he appeared, still had his hands tied together.

"Tell me the name of the young woman who carried away the flag from the fort. You saw her, you know every soul in this town. Who was it, sir?"

It was a hard question for M. Roussillon to answer. Although his humiliating captivity had somewhat cowed him, still his love for Alice made it impossible for him to give the information demanded by Hamilton. He choked and stammered, but finally managed to say:

"I assure you that I don't know—I didn't look—I didn't see—It was too far off for me to—I was some-what excited—I—"

"Take him away. Keep him securely bound," said Hamilton. "Confine him. We'll see how long it will take to refresh his mind. We'll puncture the big windbag."

While this curt scene was passing, the flag of Great Britain rose over the fort to the lusty cheering of the victorious soldiers.

Hamilton treated Helm and Beverley with extreme courtesy. He was a soldier, gruff, unscrupulous and cruel to a degree; but he could not help admiring the daring behavior of these two officers who had wrung from him the best terms of surrender. He gave them full liberty, on parole of honor not to attempt escape or to aid in any way an enemy against him while they were prisoners.

Nor was it long before Helm's genial and sociable disposition won the Englishman's respect and confidence to such an extent that the two became almost inseparable companions, playing cards, brewing toddies, telling stories, and even shooting deer in the woods together, as if they had always been the best of friends.

Hamilton did not permit his savage allies to enter the town, and he immediately required the French inhabitants to swear allegiance to Great Britain, which they did with apparent heartiness, all save M. Roussillon, who was kept in close confinement and bound like a felon, chafing lugubriously and wearing the air of a martyr. His prison was a little log pen in one corner of the stockade, much open to the weather, its gaping cracks giving him a dreary view of the frozen landscape through which the Wabash flowed in a broad steel-gray current. Helm, who really liked him, tried in vain to procure his release; but Hamilton was inexorable on account of what he regarded as duplicity in M. Roussillon's conduct.

"No, I'll let him reflect," he said; "there's nothing like a little tyranny to break up a bad case of self-importance. He'll soon find out that he has over-rated himself!"

CHAPTER X
M. ROUSSILLON ENTERTAINS COLONEL HAMILTON

A day or two after the arrival of Hamilton the absent garrison of buffalo hunters straggled back to Vincennes and were duly sworn to demean themselves as lawful subjects of Great Britain. Rene de Ronville was among the first to take the oath, and it promptly followed that Hamilton ordered him pressed into service as a wood-chopper and log-hauler during the erection of a new blockhouse, large barracks and the making of some extensive repairs of the stockade. Nothing could have been more humiliating to the proud young Frenchman. Every day he had to report bright and early to a burly Irish Corporal and be ordered about, as if he had been a slave, cursed at, threatened and forced to work until his hands were blistered and his muscles sore. The bitterest part of it all was that he had to trudge past both Roussillon place and the Bourcier cabin with the eyes of Alice and Adrienne upon him.

Hamilton did not forget M. Roussillon in this connection. The giant orator soon found himself face to face with a greater trial even than Rene's. He was calmly told by the English commander that he could choose between death and telling who it was that stole the flag.

"I'll have you shot, sir, to-morrow morning if you prevaricate about this thing any longer," said Hamilton, with a right deadly strain in his voice. "You told me that you knew every man, woman and child in Vincennes at sight. I know that you saw that girl take the flag—lying does not serve your turn. I give you until this evening to tell me who she is; if you fail, you die at sunrise to-morrow."

In fact, it may be that Hamilton did not really purpose to carry out this blood-thirsty threat; most probably he relied upon M. Roussillon's imagination to torture him successfully; but the effect, as time proved, could not be accurately foreseen.

Captain Farnsworth had energy enough for a dozen ordinary men. Before he had been in Vincennes twelve hours he had seen every nook and corner of its surface. Nor was his activity due altogether to military ardor, although he never let pass an opportunity to serve the best interests of his commander; all the while his mind was on the strikingly beautiful girl whose saucy countenance had so dazzled him from the roof-top of the fort, what time she wrenched away the rebel flag.

"I'll find her, high or low," he thought, "for I never could fail to recognize that face. She's a trump."

It was not in Alice's nature to hide from the English. They had held the town and fort before Helm came, and she had not found them troublesome under Abbott. She did not know that M. Roussillon was a prisoner, the family taking it for granted that he had gone away to avoid the English. Nor was she aware that Hamilton felt so keenly the disappearance of the flag. What she did know, and it gladdened her greatly, was that Beverley had been well treated by his captor. With this in her heart she went about Roussillon place singing merry snatches of Creole songs; and when at the gate, which still hung lop-sided on account of Beverley's force in shutting it, she came unexpectedly face to face with Captain Farnsworth, there was no great surprise on her part.

He lifted his hat and bowed very politely; but a bold smile broke over his somewhat ruddy face. He spoke in French, but in a drawling tone and with a bad accent:

"How do you do, Mademoiselle; I am right glad to see you again."

Alice drew back a pace or two. She was quick to understand his allusion, and she shrank from him, fearing that he was going to inquire about the flag.

"Don't be afraid," he laughed. "I am not so dangerous. I never did hurt a girl in all my life. In fact, I am fond of them when they're nice."

"I am not in the least afraid," she replied, assuming an air of absolute dismissal, "and you don't look a bit ferocious, Monsieur. You may pass on, if you please."

He flushed and bit his lip, probably to keep back some hasty retort, and thought rapidly for a moment. She looked straight at him with eyes that stirred and dazzled him. He was handsome in a coarse way, like a fine young animal, well groomed, well fed, magnetic, forceful; but his boldness, being of a sort to which she had not been accustomed, disturbed her vaguely and strangely.

"Suppose that I don't pass on?" he presently ventured, with just a suspicion of insolence in his attitude, but laughing until he showed teeth of remarkable beauty and whiteness. "Suppose that I should wish to have a little chat with you, Mademoiselle?"

"I have been told that there are men in the world who think themselves handsome, and clever, and brilliant, when in fact they are but conceited simpletons," she remarked, rather indifferently, muffling herself in her fur wrap. "You certainly would be a fairly good hitching-post for our horses if you never moved." Then she laughed out of the depth of her hood, a perfectly merry laugh, but not in the least flattering to Captain Farnsworth's vanity. He felt the scorn that it conveyed.

His face grew redder, while a flash from hers made him wish that he had been more gracious in his deportment. Here, to his surprise, was not a mere creole girl of the wild frontier. Her superiority struck him with the force of a captivating revelation, under the light of which he blinked and winced.

She laid a shapely hand on the broken gate and pushed it open.

"I beg your pardon, Mademoiselle;" his manner softened as he spoke; "I beg your pardon; but I came to speak to you about the flag—the flag you took away from the fort."

She had been half expecting this; but she was quite unprepared, and in spite of all she could do showed embarrassment.

"I have come to get the flag; if you will kindly bring it to me, or tell me where it is I—"

She quickly found words to interrupt him with, and at the same time by a great effort pulled herself together.

"You have come to the wrong place," she flung in. "I assure you that I haven't the flag."

"You took it down, Mademoiselle."

"Oh, did I?"

"With bewitching grace you did, Mademoiselle. I saw and admired. Will you fetch it, please?"

"Indeed I won't."

The finality in her voice belied her face, which beamed without a ray of stubbornness or perversity. He did not know how to interpret her; but he felt that he had begun wrong. He half regretted that he had begun at all.

"More depends upon returning that flag than you are probably aware of," he presently said in a more serious tone. "In fact, the life of one of your townsmen, and a person of some importance here I believe, will surely be saved by it. You'd better consider, Mademoiselle. You wouldn't like to cause the death of a man."

She did not fairly grasp the purport of his words; yet the change in his manner, and the fact that he turned from French to English in making the statement, aroused a sudden feeling of dread or dark apprehension in her breast. The first distinct thought was of Beverley—that some deadly danger threatened him.

"Who is it?" she frankly demanded.

"It's the Mayor, the big man of your town, Monsieur Roussillon, I think he calls himself. He's got himself into a tight place. He'll be shot to-morrow morning if that flag is not produced. Governor Hamilton has so ordered, and what he orders is done."

"You jest, Monsieur."

"I assure you that I speak the plain truth."

"You will probably catch Monsieur Roussillon before you shoot him." She tossed her head.

"He is already a prisoner in the fort."

Alice turned pale.

"Monsieur, is this true?" Her voice had lost its happy tone. "Are you telling me that to—"

"You can verify it, Mademoiselle, by calling upon the commander at the fort. I am sorry that you doubt my veracity. If you will go with me I will show you M. Roussillon a tightly bound prisoner."

Jean had crept out of the gate and was standing just behind Alice with his feet wide apart, his long chin elevated, his head resting far back between his upthrust shoulders, his hands in his pockets, his uncanny eyes gazing steadily at Farnsworth. He looked like a deformed frog ready to jump.

Alice unmistakably saw truth in the Captain's countenance and felt it in his voice. The reality came to her with unhindered effect. M. Roussillon's life depended upon the return of the flag. She put her hands together and for a moment covered her eyes with them.

"I will go now, Mademoiselle," said Farnsworth; "but I hope you will be in great haste about returning the flag."

He stood looking at her. He was profoundly touched and felt that to say more would be too brutal even for his coarse nature; so he simply lifted his hat and went away.

Jean took hold of Alice's dress as she turned to go back into the house.

"Is he going to take the flag? Can he find it? What does he want with it? What did you do with the flag, Alice?" he whined, in his peculiar, quavering voice. "Where is it?"

Her skirt dragged him along as she walked.

"Where did you put it, Alice?"

"Father Beret hid it under his floor," she answered, involuntarily, and almost unconsciously. "I shall have to take it back and give it up."

"No—no—I wouldn't," he quavered, dancing across the veranda as she quickened her pace and fairly spun him along. "I wouldn't let 'em have it at all."

Alice's mind was working with lightning speed. Her imagination took strong grip on the situation so briefly and effectively sketched by Captain Farnsworth. Her decision formed itself quickly.

"Stay here, Jean. I am going to the fort. Don't tell Mama Roussillon a thing. Be a good boy."

She was gone before Jean could say a word. She meant to face Hamilton at once and be sure what danger menaced M. Roussillon. Of course, the flag must be given up if that would save her foster father any pain; and if his life were in question there could not be too great haste on her part.

She ran directly to the stockade gate and breathlessly informed a sentinel that she must see Governor Hamilton, into whose presence she was soon led. Captain Farnsworth had preceded her but a minute or two, and was present when she entered the miserable shed room where the commander was having another talk with M. Roussillon.

The meeting was a tableau which would have been comical but for the pressure of its tragic possibilities. Hamilton, stern and sententious, stood frowning upon M. Roussillon, who sat upon the ground, his feet and hands tightly bound, a colossal statue of injured innocence.

Alice, as soon as she saw M. Roussillon, uttered a cry of sympathetic endearment and flung herself toward him with open arms. She could not reach around his great shoulders; but she did her best to include the whole bulk.

"Papa! Papa Roussillon!" she chirruped between the kisses that she showered upon his weather-beaten face.

Hamilton and Farnsworth regarded the scene with curious and surprised interest. M. Roussillon began speaking rapidly; but being a Frenchman he could not get on well with his tongue while his hands were tied. He could shrug his shoulders; that helped him some.

"I am to be shot, MA PETITE," he pathetically growled in his deep bass voice; "shot like a dog at sunrise to-morrow."

Alice kissed M. Roussillon's rough cheek once more and sprang to her feet facing Hamilton.

"You are not such a fiend and brute as to kill Papa Roussillon," she cried. "Why do you want to injure my poor, good papa?"

"I believe you are the young lady that stole the flag?" Hamilton remarked, smiling contemptuously.

She looked at him with a swift flash of indignation as he uttered these words.

"I am not a thief. I could not steal what was my own. I helped to make that flag. It was named after me. I took it because it was mine. You understand me, Monsieur."

"Tell where it is and your father's life will be spared."

She glanced at M. Roussillon.

"No, Alice," said he, with a pathetically futile effort to make a fine gesture, "don't do it. I am brave enough to die. You would not have me act the coward."

No onlooker would have even remotely suspected the fact that M. Roussillon had chanced to overhear a conversation between Hamilton and Farnsworth, in which Hamilton stated that he really did not intend to hurt M. Roussillon in any event; he merely purposed to humiliate the "big wind-bag!"

"Ah, no; let me die bravely for honor's sake—I fear death far less than dishonor! They can shoot me, my little one, but they cannot break my proud spirit." He tried to strike his breast over his heart.

"Perhaps it would be just as well to let him be shot," said Hamilton gruffly, and with dry indifference. "I don't fancy that he's of much value to the community at best. He'll make a good target for a squad, and we need an example."

"Do you mean it?—you ugly English brute—would you murder him?" she stamped her foot.

"Not if I get that flag between now and sundown. Otherwise I shall certainly have him shot. It is all in your hands, Mademoiselle. You can tell me where the flag is." Hamilton smiled again with exquisite cruelty.

Farnsworth stood by gazing upon Alice in open admiration. Her presence had power in it, to which he was very susceptible.

"You look like a low, dishonorable, soulless tyrant," she said to Hamilton, "and if you get my flag, how shall I know that you will keep your promise and let Papa Roussillon go free?"

"I am sorry to say that you will have to trust me, unless you'll take Captain Farnsworth for security. The Captain is a gentleman, I assure you. Will you stand good for my veracity and sincerity, Captain Farnsworth?"

The young man smiled and bowed.

Alice felt the irony; and her perfectly frank nature preferred to trust rather than distrust the sincerity of others. She looked at Farnsworth, who smiled encouragingly.

"The flag is under Father Beret's floor," she said.

"Under the church floor?"

"No, under the floor of his house."

"Where is his house?"

She gave full directions how to reach it.

"Untie the prisoner," Hamilton ordered, and it was quickly done. "Monsieur Roussillon, I congratulate you upon your narrow escape. Go to the priest's house, Monsieur, and bring me that flag. It would be well, I assure you, not to be very long about it. Captain Farnsworth, you will send a guard with Monsieur Roussillon, a guard of honor, fitting his official dignity, a Corporal and two men. The honorable Mayor of this important city should not go alone upon so important an errand. He must have his attendants."

"Permit me to go myself and get it," said Alice, "I can do it quickly. May I, please, Monsieur?"

Hamilton looked sharply at her.

"Why, certainly, Mademoiselle, certainly. Captain Farnsworth, you will escort the young lady."

"It is not necessary, Monsieur."

"Oh, yes, it is necessary, my dear young lady, very necessary; so let's not have further words. I'll try to entertain his honor, the Mayor, while you go and get the flag. I feel sure, Mademoiselle, that you'll return with it in a few minutes. But you must not go alone."

Alice set forth immediately, and Farnsworth, try as hard as he would, could never reach her side, so swift was her gait.

When they arrived at Father Beret's cabin, she turned and said with imperious severity:

"Don't you come in; you stay out here. I'll get it in a minute."

Farnsworth obeyed her command.

The door was wide open, but Father Beret was not inside; he had gone to see a sick child in the outskirts of the village. Alice looked about and hesitated. She knew the very puncheon that covered the flag; but she shrank from lifting it. There seemed nothing else to do, however; so, after some trouble with herself, she knelt upon the floor and turned the heavy slab over with a great thump. The flag did not appear. She peeped under the other puncheons. It was not there. The only thing visible was a little ball of paper fragments not larger than an egg.

Farnsworth heard her utter a low cry of surprise or dismay, and was on the point of going in when Father Beret, coming around the corner of the cabin, confronted him. The meeting was so sudden and unexpected that both men recoiled slightly, and then, with a mutual stare, saluted.

"I came with a young lady to get the flag," said Farnsworth. "She is inside. I hope there is no serious intrusion. She says the flag is hidden under your floor."

Father Beret said nothing, but frowning as if much annoyed, stepped through the doorway to Alice's side, and stooping where she knelt, laid a hand on her shoulder as she glanced up and recognized him.

"What are you doing, my child?"

"Oh, Father, where is the flag?" It was all that she could say. "Where is the flag?"

"Why, isn't it there?"

"No, you see it isn't there! Where is it?"

The priest stood as if dumfounded, gazing into the vacant space uncovered by the puncheon.

"Is it gone? Has some one taken it away?"

They turned up all the floor to no avail. La banniere d'Alice Roussillon had disappeared, and Captain Farnsworth went forthwith to report the fact to his commander. When he reached the shed at the angle of the fort he found Governor Hamilton sitting stupid and dazed on the ground. One jaw was inflamed and swollen and an eye was half closed and bloodshot. He turned his head with a painful, irregular motion and his chin sagged.

Farnsworth sprang to him and lifted him to his feet; but he could scarcely stand. He licked his lips clumsily.

"What is the matter? What hurt you?"

The Governor rubbed his forehead trying to recollect.

"He struck me," he presently said with difficulty. "He hit me with his fist Where—where is he?"

"Who?"

"That big French idiot—that Roussillon—go after him, take him, shoot him—quick! I have been stunned; I don't know how long he's been gone. Give the alarm—do something!"

Hamilton, as he gathered his wits together, began to foam with rage, and his passion gave his bruised and swollen face a terrible look.

The story was short, and may be quickly told. M. Roussillon had taken advantage of the first moment when he and Hamilton were left alone. One herculean buffet, a swinging smash of his enormous fist on the point of the Governors jaw, and then he walked out of the fort unchallenged, doubtless on account of his lordly and masterful air.

"Ziff!" he exclaimed, shaking himself and lifting his shoulders, when he had passed beyond hearing of the sentinel at the gate, "ziff! I can punch a good stiff stroke yet, Monsieur le Gouverneur. Ah, ziff!" and he blew like a porpoise.

Every effort was promptly made to recapture M. Roussillon; but his disappearance was absolute; even the reward offered for his scalp by Hamilton only gave the Indians great trouble—they could not find the man.

Such a beginning of his administration of affairs at Vincennes did not put Hamilton into a good humor. He was overbearing and irascible at best, and under the irritation of small but exceedingly unpleasant experiences he made life well-nigh unendurable to those upon whom his dislike chanced to fall. Beverley quickly felt that it was going to be very difficult for him and Hamilton to get along agreeably. With Helm it was quite different; smoking, drinking, playing cards, telling good stories—in a word, rude and not unfrequently boisterous conviviality drew him and the commandant together.

Under Captain Farnsworth's immediate supervision the fort was soon in excellent repair and a large blockhouse and comfortable quarters for the men were built. Every day added to the strength of the works and to the importance of the post as a strategic position for the advance guard of the British army.

Hamilton was ambitious to prove himself conspicuously valuable to his country. He was dreaming vast dreams and laying large plans. The Indians were soon anxious to gain his favor; and to bind them securely to him he offered liberal pay in rum and firearms, blankets, trinkets and ammunition for the scalps of rebels. He kept this as secret as possible from his prisoners; but Beverley soon suspected that a "traffic in hair," as the terrible business had been named, was going on. Savages came in from far away with scalps yet scarcely dry dangling at their belts. It made the young Virginian's blood chill in his heart, and he regretted that he had given Hamilton his parole of honor not to attempt to escape.

Among the Indians occasionally reporting to Hamilton with their ghastly but valuable trophies was Long-Hair, who slipped into the fort and out again rather warily, not having much confidence in those Frenchmen who had once upon a time given him a memorable run for his life.

Winter shut down, not cold, but damp, changeable, raw. The work on the fort was nearly completed, and Rene de Ronville would have soon been relieved of his servile and exasperating employment under the Irish Corporal; but just at the point of time when only a few days' work remained for him, he became furious, on account of an insulting remark, and struck the Corporal over the head with a handspike. This happened in a wood some miles from town, where he was loading logs upon a sled. There chanced to be no third person present when the deed was done, and some hours passed before they found the officer quite cold and stiff beside the sled. His head was crushed to a pulp.

Hamilton, now thoroughly exasperated, began to look upon the French inhabitants of Vincennes as all like M. Roussillon and Rene, but waiting for an opportunity to strike him unawares. He increased his military vigilance, ordered the town patrolled day and night, and forbade public gatherings of the citizens, while at the same time he forced them to furnish him a large amount of provisions.

When little Adrienne Bourcier heard of Renews terrible act, followed by his successful escape to the woods, and of the tempting reward offered by Hamilton for his scalp, she ran to Roussillon place well-nigh crazed with excitement. She had always depended upon Alice for advice, encouragement and comfort in her troubles; but in the present case there was not much that her friend could do to cheer her. With M. Roussillon and Rene both fugitives, tracked by wily savages, a price on their heads, while every day added new dangers to the French inhabitants of Vincennes, no rosy view could possibly be taken of the situation. Alice did her best, however, to strengthen her little friend's faith in a happy outcome. She quoted what she considered unimpeachable authority to support her optimistic argument.

"Lieutenant Beverley says that the Americans will be sure to drive Hamilton out of Vincennes, or capture him. Probably they are not so very far away now, and Rene may join them and come back to help punish these brutal Englishmen. Don't you wish he would, Adrienne? Wouldn't it be romantic?"

"He's armed, I know that," said Adrienne, brightening a little, "and he's brave, Alice, brave as can be. He came right back into town the other night and got his gun and pistols. He was at our house, too, and, oh!—"

She burst out crying again. "O Alice! It breaks my heart to think that the Indians will kill him. Do you think they will kill him, Alice?"

"He'll come nearer killing them," said Alice confidently, with her strong, warm arms around the tiny lass; "he's a good woodsman, a fine shot—he's not so easy to kill, my dear. If he and Papa Roussillon should get together by chance they would be a match for all the Indians in the country. Anyway, I feel that it's much better for them to take their chances in the woods than to be in the hands of Governor Hamilton. If I were a man I'd do just as Papa Roussillon and

Rene did; I'd break the bigoted head of every Englishman that mistreated me, I'll do it, girl as I am, if they annoy me, see if I don't!"

She was thinking of Captain Farnsworth, who had been from the first untiring in his efforts to gain something more than a passing acquaintance. As yet he had not made himself unbearable; but Alice's fine intuition led her to the conclusion that she must guard against him from the outset.

Adrienne's simple heart could not grasp the romantic criterion with which Alice was wont to measure action. Her mind was single, impulsive, narrow and direct in all its movements. She loved, hated, desired, caressed, repulsed, not for any assignable reason more solid or more luminous than "because." She adored Rene and wanted him near her. He was a hero in her imagination, no matter what he did. Little difference was it to her whether he hauled logs for the English or smoked his pipe in idleness by the winter fire—what could it matter which flag he served under, so that he was true to her? Or whom he served if she could always have him coming to see her and calling her his little pet? He might crush an Irish Corporal's head every day, if he would but stroke her hair and say: "My sweet little one."

"Why couldn't he be quiet and do as your man, Lieutenant Beverley, did?" she cried in a sudden change of mood, the tears streaming down her cheeks. "Lieutenant Beverley surrendered and took the consequences. He didn't kill somebody and run off to be hunted like a bear. No wonder you're happy, Alice; I'd be happy, too, if Rene were here and came to spend half of every day with me. I—"

"Why, what a silly girl you are!" Alice exclaimed, her face reddening prettily. "How foolishly you prattle! I'm sure I don't trouble myself about Lieutenant Beverley—what put such absurd nonsense into your head, Adrienne?"

"Because, that's what, and you know it's so, too. You love him just as much as I love Rene, and that's just all the love in the world, and you needn't deny it, Alice Roussillon!"

Alice laughed and hugged the wee, brown-faced mite of a girl until she almost smothered her.

It was growing dusk when Adrienne left Roussillon place to go home. The wind cut icily across the commons and moaned as it whirled around the cabins and cattle-sheds. She ran briskly, muffled in a wrap, partly through fear and partly to keep warm, and had gone two-thirds of her way when she was brought to an abrupt stop by the arms of a man. She screamed sharply, and Father Beret, who was coming out of a cabin not far away, heard and knew the voice.

"Ho-ho, my little lady!" cried Adrienne's captor in a breezy, jocund tone, "you wouldn't run over a fellow, would you?" The words were French, but the voice was that of Captain Farnsworth, who laughed while he spoke. "You jump like a rabbit, my darling! Why, what a lively little chick of a girl it is!"

Adrienne screamed and struggled recklessly.

"Now don't rouse up the town," coaxed the Captain. He was just drunk enough to be quite a fool, yet sufficiently sober to imagine himself the most proper person in the world. "I don't mean you any harm, Mademoiselle; I'll just see you safe home, you know; 'scort you to your residence; come on, now—that's a good girl."

Father Beret hurried to the spot, and when in the deepening gloom he saw Adrienne flinging herself violently this way and that, helplessly trying to escape from the clasp of a man, he did to perfection what a priest is supposed to be the least fitted to do. Indeed, considering his age and leaving his vocation out of the reckoning, his performance was amazing. It is not certain that the blow dealt upon Governor Hamilton's jaw by M. Roussillon was a stiffer one than that sent straight from the priest's shoulder right into the short ribs of Captain Farnsworth, who thereupon released a mighty grunt and doubled himself up.

Adrienne recognized her assailant at the first and used his name freely during the struggle. When Father Beret appeared she cried out to him—

"Oh, Father—Father Beret! help me! help me!"

When Farnsworth recovered from the breath-expelling shock of the jab in his side and got himself once more in a vertical position, both girl and priest were gone. He looked this way and that, rapidly becoming sober, and beginning to wonder how the thing could have happened so easily. His ribs felt as if they had been hit with a heavy hammer.

"By Jove!" he muttered all to himself, "the old prayer-singing heathen! By Jove!" And with this very brilliant and relevant observation he rubbed his sore side and went his way to the fort.

CHAPTER XI

A SWORD AND A HORSE PISTOL

We hear much about the "days that tried men's souls"; but what about the souls of women in those same days? Sitting in the liberal geniality of the nineteenth century's sunset glow, we insist upon having our grumble at the times and the manners of our generation; but if we had to exchange places, periods and experiences with the people who lived in America through the last quarter of the eighteenth century, there would be good ground for despairing ululations. And if our men could not bear it, if it would try their souls too poignantly, let us imagine the effect upon our women. No, let us not imagine it; but rather let us give full credit to the heroic souls of the mothers and the maidens who did actually bear up in the center of that terrible struggle and unflinchingly help win for us not only freedom, but the vast empire which at this moment is at once the master of the world and the model toward which all the nations of the earth are slowly but surely tending.

If Alice was an extraordinary girl, she was not aware of it; nor had she ever understood that her life was being shaped by extraordinary conditions. Of course it could not but be plain to her that she knew more and felt more than the girls of her narrow acquaintance; that her accomplishments were greater; that she nursed splendid dreams of which they could have no proper comprehension, but until now she had never even dimly realized that she was probably capable of being something more than a mere creole lass, the foster daughter of Gaspard Roussillon, trader in pelts and furs. Even her most romantic visions had never taken the form of personal desire, or ambition in its most nebulous stage; they had simply pleased her fresh and natural fancy and served to gild the hardness and crudeness of her life,—that was all.

Her experiences had been almost too terrible for belief, viewed at our distance from them; she had passed through scenes of incredible horror and suffering, but her nature had not been chilled, stunted or hardened. In body and in temper her development had been sound and beautiful. It was even thus that our great-grandmothers triumphed over adversity, hardship, indescribable danger. We cannot say that the strong, lithe, happy-hearted Alice of old Vincennes was the only one of her kind. Few of us who have inherited the faded portraits of our revolutionary forbears can doubt that beauty, wit and great lovableness flourished in the cabins of pioneers all the way from the Edisto to the Licking, from the Connecticut to the Wabash.

Beverley's advent could not fail to mean a great deal in the life of a girl like Alice; a new era, as it were, would naturally begin for her the moment that his personal influence touched her imagination; but it is well not to measure her too strictly by the standard of our present taste and the specialized forms of our social and moral code. She was a true child of the wilderness, a girl who grew, as the wild prairie rose grew, not on account of innumerable exigencies, accidents and hardships, but in spite of them. She had blushed unseen, and had wasted divine sweets upon a more than desert air. But when Beverley came near her, at first carelessly droning his masculine monotonies, as the wandering bee to the lonely and lovely rose, and presently striking her soul as with the wings of Love, there fell a change into her heart of hearts, and lo! her haunting and elusive dreams began to condense and take on forms that startled her with their wonderful splendor and beauty. These she saw all the time, sleeping or waking; they made bright summer of the frozen stream and snapping gale, the snowdrifts and the sleet. In her brave young heart, swelled the ineffable song—the music never yet caught by syrinx or flute or violin, the words no tongue can speak.

Ah, here may be the secret of that vigorous, brave, sweet life of our pioneer maids, wives, and mothers. It was love that gave those tender hearts the iron strength and heroic persistence at which the world must forever wonder. And do we appreciate those women? Let the Old World boast its crowned kings, its mailed knights, its ladies of the court and castle; but we of the New World, we of the powerful West, let us brim our cups with the wine of undying devotion, and drink to the memory of the Women of the Revolution,—to the humble but good and marvelously brave and faithful women like those of old Vincennes.

But if Alice was being radically influenced by Beverley, he in turn found a new light suffusing his nature, and he was not unaware that it came out of her eyes, her face, her smiles, her voice, her soul. It was the old, well-known, inexplicable, mutual magnetism, which from the first has been the same on the highest mountain-top and in the lowest valley. The queen and the milkmaid, the king and the hind may come together only to find the king walking off with the lowly beauty and her fragrant pail, while away stalks the lusty rustic, to be lord and master of the queen. Love is love, and it thrives in all climes, under all conditions.

There is an inevitable and curious protest that comes up unbidden between lovers; it takes many forms in accordance with particular circumstances. It is the demand for equality and perfection. Love itself is without degrees—it is perfect—but when shall it see the perfect object? It does see it, and it does not see it, in every beloved being. Beverley found his mind turning, as on a pivot, round and round upon the thought that Alice might be impossible to him. The mystery of her life seemed to force her below the line of his aristocratic vision, so that he could not fairly consider her, and yet with all his heart he loved her. Alice, on the other hand, had her bookish ideal to reckon with, despite the fact that she daily dashed it contemptuously down. She was different from Adrienne Bourcier, who bewailed the absence of her un-tamable lover; she wished that Beverley had not, as she somehow viewed it, weakly surrendered to Hamilton. His apparently complacent acceptance of idle captivity did not comport with her dream of knighthood and heroism. She had been all the time half expecting him to do something that would stamp him a hero.

Counter protests of this sort are never sufficiently vigorous to take a fall out of Love; they merely serve to worry his temper by lightly hindering his feet. And it is surprising how Love does delight himself with being entangled.

Both Beverley and Alice day by day felt the cord tightening which drew their hearts together—each acknowledged it secretly, but strove not to evince it openly. Meantime both were as happy and as restlessly dissatisfied as love and uncertainty could make them.

Amid the activities in which Hamilton was engaged—his dealings with the Indians and the work of reconstructing the fort—he found time to worry his temper about the purloined flag. Like every other man in the world, he was superstitious, and it had come into his head that to insure himself and his plans against disaster, he must have the banner of his captives as a badge of his victory. It was a small matter; but it magnified itself as he dwelt upon it. He suspected that Alice had deceived him. He sharply questioned Father Beret, only to be half convinced that the good priest told the truth when he said that he knew nothing whatever on the subject beyond the fact that the banner had mysteriously disappeared from under his floor.

Captain Farnsworth scarcely sympathized with his chief about the flag, but he was nothing if not anxious to gain Hamilton's highest confidence. His military zeal knew no bounds, and he never let pass even the slightest opportunity to show it. Hence his persistent search for a clue to the missing banner. He was no respecter of persons. He frankly suspected both Alice and Father Beret of lying. He would himself have lied under the existing circumstances, and he considered himself as truthful and trustworthy as priest or maiden.

"I'll get that flag for you," he said to Hamilton, "if I have to put every man, woman and child in this town on the rack. It lies, I think, between Miss Roussillon and the priest, although both insistently deny it. I've thought it over in every way, and I can't see how they can both be ignorant of where it is, or at least who got it."

Hamilton, since being treated to that wonderful blow on the jaw, was apt to fall into a spasm of anger whenever the name Roussillon was spoken in his hearing. Involuntarily he would put his hand to his cheek, and grimace reminiscently.

"If it's that girl, make her tell," he savagely commanded. "Let's have no trifling about it. If it's the priest, then make him tell, or tie him up by the thumbs. Get that flag, or show some good reason for your failure. I'm not going to be baffled."

The Captain's adventure with Father Beret came just in time to make it count against that courageous and bellicose missionary in more ways than one. Farnsworth did not tell Hamilton or any other person about what the priest had done to him, but nursed his sore ribs and his wrath, waiting patiently for the revenge that he meant soon to take.

Alice heard from Adrienne the story of Farnsworth's conduct and his humiliating discomfiture at the hands of Father Beret. She was both indignant and delighted, sympathizing with Adrienne and glorying in the priest's vigorous pugilistic achievement.

"Well," she remarked, with one of her infectious trills of laughter, "so far the French have the best of it, anyway! Papa Roussillon knocked the Governor's cheek nearly off, then Rene cracked the Irish Corporal's head, and now Father Beret has taught Captain Farnsworth a lesson in fisticuffs that he'll not soon forget! If the good work can only go on a little longer we shall see every English soldier in Vincennes wearing the mark of a Frenchman's blow." Then her mood suddenly changed from smiling lightness to almost fierce gravity, and she added:

"Adrienne Bourcier, if Captain Farnsworth ever offers to treat me as he did you, mark my words, I'll kill him—kill him, indeed I will! You ought to see me!"

"But he won't dare touch you," said Adrienne, looking at her friend with round, admiring eyes. "He knows very well that you are not little and timid like me. He'd be afraid of you."

"I wish he would try it. How I would love to shoot him into pieces, the hateful wretch! I wish he would."

The French inhabitants all, or nearly all, felt as Alice did; but at present they were helpless and dared not say or do anything against the English. Nor was this feeling confined to the Creoles of Vincennes; it had spread to most of the points where trading posts existed. Hamilton found this out too late to mend some of his mistakes; but he set himself on the alert and organized scouting bodies of Indians under white officers to keep him informed as to the

57

American movements in Kentucky and along the Ohio. One of these bands brought in as captive Colonel Francis Vigo, of St. Louis, a Spaniard by birth, an American by adoption, a patriot to the core, who had large influence over both Indians and Creoles in the Illinois country.

Colonel Vigo was not long held a prisoner. Hamilton dared not exasperate the Creoles beyond their endurance, for he knew that the savages would closely sympathize with their friends of long standing, and this might lead to revolt and coalition against him,—a very dangerous possibility. Indeed, at least one of the great Indian chieftains had already frankly informed him that he and his tribe were loyal to the Americans. Here was a dilemma requiring consummate diplomacy. Hamilton saw it, but he was not of a diplomatic temper or character. With the Indians he used a demoralizing system of bribery, while toward the whites he was too often gruff, imperious, repellant. Helm understood the whole situation and was quick to take advantage of it. His personal relations with Hamilton were easy and familiar, so that he did not hesitate to give advice upon all occasions. Here his jovial disposition helped him.

"You'd better let Vigo return to St. Louis," he said. They had a bowl of something hot steaming between them. "I know him. He's harmless if you don't rub him too hard the wrong way. He'll go back, if you treat him well, and tell Clark how strong you are here and how foolish it would be to think of attacking you. Clark has but a handful of men, poorly supplied and tired with long, hard marches. If you'll think a moment you cannot fail to understand that you'd better be friends with this man Vigo. He and Father Gibault and this old priest here, Beret, carry these Frenchmen in their pockets. I'm not on your side, understand, I'm an American, and I'd blow the whole of you to kingdom come in a minute, if I could; but common sense is common sense all the same. There's no good to you and no harm to Clark in mistreating, or even holding this prisoner. What harm can he do you by going back to Clark and telling him the whole truth? Clark knew everything long before Vigo reached here. Old Jazon, my best scout, left here the day you took possession, and you may bet he got to Kaskaskia in short order. He never fails. But he'll tell Clark to stay where he is, and Vigo can do no more."

What effect Helm's bold and apparently artless talk had upon Hamilton's mind is not recorded; but the meager historical facts at command show that Vigo was released and permitted to return under promise that he would give no information to the enemy ON HIS WAY to Kaskaskia.

Doubtless this bit of careless diplomacy on the Governor's part did have a somewhat soothing effect upon a large class of Frenchmen at Vincennes; but Farnsworth quickly neutralized it to a serious extent by a foolish act while slightly under the influence of liquor.

He met Father Beret near Roussillon place, and feeling his ribs squirm at sight of the priest, he accosted him insolently, demanding information as to the whereabouts of the missing flag.

A priest may be good and true—Father Beret certainly was—and yet have the strongest characteristics of a worldly man. This thing of being bullied day after day, as had recently been the rule, generated nothing to aid in removing a refractory desire from the priest's heart—the worldly desire to repeat with great increment of force the punch against Farnsworth's lower ribs.

"I order you, sir, to produce that rebel flag," said Farnsworth. "You will obey forthwith or take the consequences. I am no longer in the humor to be trifled with. Do you understand?"

"I might be forced to obey you, if I could," said the priest, drawing his robe about him; "but, as I have often told you, my son, I do not know where the flag is or who took it. I do not even suspect any person of taking it. All that I know about it is the simple fact that it is gone."

Father Beret's manner and voice were very mild, but there must have been a hint of sturdy defiance somewhere in them. At all events Farnsworth was exasperated and fell into a white rage. Perhaps it was the liquor he had been drinking that made him suddenly desperate.

"You canting old fool!" he cried, "don't lie to me any longer; I won't have it. Don't stand there grinning at me. Get that flag, or I'll make you."

"What is impossible, my son, is possible to God alone. Apud homines hoc impossible est, apud Deum autem omnia possibilia sunt."

"None of your Jesuit Latin or logic to me—I am not here to argue, but to command. Get that flag. Be in a hurry about it, sir."

He whipped out his sword, and in his half drunken eyes there gathered the dull film of murderous passion.

"Put up your weapon, Captain; you will not attack an unarmed priest. You are a soldier, and will not dare strike an old, defenceless man."

"But I will strike a black-robed and black-hearted French rebel. Get that flag, you grinning fool!"

The two men stood facing each other. Father Beret's eyes did not stir from their direct, fearless gaze. What Farnsworth had called a grin was a peculiar smile, not of merriment, a grayish flicker and a slight backward wrinkling of the cheeks. The old man's arms were loosely crossed upon his sturdy breast.

"Strike if you must," he said very gently, very firmly. "I never yet have seen the man that could make me afraid." His speech was slightly sing-song in tone, as it would have been during a prayer or a blessing.

"Get the flag then!" raged Farnsworth, in whose veins the heat of liquor was aided by an unreasoning choler.

"I cannot," said Father Beret.

"Then take the consequences!"

Farnsworth lifted his sword, not to thrust, but to strike with its flat side, and down it flashed with a noisy whack. Father Beret flung out an arm and deftly turned the blow aside. It was done so easily that Farnsworth sprang back glaring and surprised.

"You old fool!" he cried, leveling his weapon for a direct lunge. "You devilish hypocrite!"

It was then that Father Beret turned deadly pale and swiftly crossed himself. His face looked as if he saw something startling just beyond his adversary. Possibly this sudden change of expression caused Farnsworth to hesitate for a mere point of time. Then there was the swish of a woman's skirts; a light step pattered on the frozen ground, and Alice sprang between the men, facing Farnsworth. As she did this something small and yellow,—the locket at her throat,—fell and rolled under her feet. Nobody saw it.

In her hand she held an immense horse pistol, which she leveled in the Captain's face, its flaring, bugle-shaped muzzle gaping not a yard from his nose. The heavy tube was as steady as if in a vise.

"Drop that sword!"

That was all she said; but her finger was pressing the trigger, and the flint in the backward slanting hammer was ready to click against the steel. The leaden slugs were on the point of leaping forth.

"Drop that sword!"

The repetition seemed to close the opportunity for delay.

Farnsworth was on his guard in a twinkling. He set his jaw and uttered an ugly oath; then quick as lightning he struck sidewise at the pistol with his blade. It was a move which might have taken a less alert person than Alice unawares; but her training in sword-play was ready in her wrist and hand. An involuntary turn, the slightest imaginable, set the heavy barrel of her weapon strongly against the blow, partly stopping it, and then the gaping muzzle spat its load of balls and slugs with a bellow that awoke the drowsy old village.

Farnsworth staggered backward, letting fall his sword. There was a rent in the clothing of his left shoulder. He reeled; the blood spun out; but he did not fall, although he grew white.

Alice stood gazing at him with a look on her face he would never forget. It was a look that changed by wonderful swift gradations from terrible hate to something like sweet pity. The instant she saw him hurt and bleeding, his countenance relaxing and pale, her heart failed her. She took a step toward him, her hand opened, and with a thud the heavy old pistol fell upon the ground beside her.

Father Beret sprang nimbly to sustain Farnsworth, snatching up the pistol as he passed around Alice.

"You are hurt, my son," he gently said, "let me help you." He passed his arm firmly under that of Farnsworth, seeing that the Captain was unsteady on his feet.

"Lean upon me. Come with me, Alice, my child, I will take him into the house."

Alice picked up the Captain's sword and led the way.

It was all done so quickly that Farnsworth, in his half dazed condition, scarcely realized what was going on until he found himself on a couch in the Roussillon home, his wound (a jagged furrow plowed out by slugs that the sword's blade had first intercepted) neatly dressed and bandaged, while Alice and the priest hovered over him busy with their careful ministrations.

Hamilton and Helm were, as usual, playing cards at the former's quarters when a guard announced that Mademoiselle Roussillon wished an audience with the Governor.

"Bring the girl in," said Hamilton, throwing down his cards and scowling darkly.

"Now you'd better be wise as a serpent and gentle as a dove," remarked Helm. "There is something up, and that gun-shot we heard awhile ago may have a good deal to do with it. At any rate, you'll find kindness your best card to play with Alice Roussillon just at the present stage of the game."

Of course they knew nothing of what had happened to Farnsworth; but they had been discussing the strained relations between the garrison and the French inhabitants when the roar of Alice's big-mouthed pistol startled them. Helm was slyly beating about to try to make Hamilton lose sight of the danger from Clark's direction. To do this he artfully magnified the insidious work that might be done by the French and their Indian friends should they be driven to desperation by oppressive or exasperating action on the part of the English.

Hamilton felt the dangerous uncertainty upon which the situation rested; but, like many another vigorously self-reliant man, he could not subordinate his passions to the dictates of policy. When Alice was conducted into his presence he instantly swelled with anger. It was her father who had struck him and escaped, it was she who had carried off the rebel flag at the moment of victory.

"Well, Miss, to what do I owe the honor of this visit?" he demanded with a supercilious air, bending a card between his thumb and finger on the rude table.

She stood before him tall and straight, well bundled in furs. She was not pale; her blood was too rich and brilliant for that; but despite a half-smile and the inextinguishable dimples, there was a touch of something appealingly pathetic in the lines of her mouth. She did not waver or hesitate, however, but spoke promptly and distinctly.

"I have come, Monsieur, to tell you that I have hurt Captain Farnsworth. He was about to kill Father Beret, and I shot him. He is in our house and well cared for. I don't think his wound is bad. And—" here she hesitated at last and let her gaze fall,—"so here I am." Then she lifted her eyes again and made an inimitable French gesture with her shoulders and arms. "You will do as you please, Monsieur, I am at your mercy."

Hamilton was astounded. Helm sat staring phlegmatically. Meantime Beverley entered the room and stopped hat in hand behind Alice. He was flushed and evidently excited; in fact, he had heard of the trouble with Farnsworth, and seeing Alice enter the floor of Hamilton's quarters he followed her in, his heart stirred by no slight emotion. He met the Governor's glare and parried it with one of equal haughtiness. The veins on his forehead swelled and turned dark. He was in a mood to do whatever desperate act should suggest itself.

When Hamilton fairly comprehended the message so graphically presented by Alice, he rose from his seat by the fire.

"What's this you tell me?" he blurted. "You say you've shot Captain Farnsworth?"

"Oui, Monsieur."

He stared a moment, then his features beamed with hate.

"And I'll have you shot for it, Miss, as sure as you stand there in your silly impudence ogling me so brazenly!"

He leaned toward her as he spoke and sent with the words a shock of coarse, passionate energy from which she recoiled as if expecting a blow to follow it.

An irresistible impulse swept Beverley to Alice's side, and his attitude was that of a protector. Helm sprang up.

A Lieutenant came in and respectfully, but with evident over-haste, reported that Captain Farnsworth had been shot and was at Roussillon place in care of the surgeon.

"Take this girl into custody. Confine her and put a strong guard over her."

In giving the order Hamilton jerked his thumb contemptuously toward Alice, and at the same time gave Beverley a look of supreme defiance and hatred. When Helm began to speak he turned fiercely upon him and stopped him with:

"None of your advice, sir. I have had all I want of it. Keep your place or I'll make you."

Then to Beverley:

"Retire, sir. When I wish to see you I'll send for you. At present you are not needed here."

The English Lieutenant saluted his commander, bowed respectfully to Alice and said:

"Come with me, Miss, please."

Helm and Beverley exchanged a look of helpless and enquiring rage. It was as if they had said: "What can we do? Must we bear it?" Certainly they could do nothing. Any interference on their part would be sure to increase Alice's danger, and at the same time add to the weight of their own humiliation.

Alice silently followed the officer out of the room. She did not even glance toward Beverley, who moved as if to interfere and was promptly motioned back by the guard. His better judgement returning held him from a rash and futile act, until Hamilton spoke again, saying loudly as Alice passed through the door:

"I'll see who's master of this town if I have to shoot every French hoyden in it!"

"Women and children may well fear you, Colonel Hamilton," said Beverley. "That young lady is your superior."

"You say that to me, sir!"

"It is the best I could possibly say of you."

"I will send you along with the wench if you do not guard your language. A prisoner on parole has no license to be a blackguard."

"I return you my parole, sir, I shall no longer regard it as binding," said Beverley, by a great effort, holding back a blow; "I will not keep faith with a scoundrel who does not know how to be decent in the presence of a young girl. You had better have me arrested and confined. I will escape at the first opportunity and bring a force here to reckon with you for your villainy. And if you dare hurt Alice Roussillon I will have you hanged like a dog!"

Hamilton looked at him scornfully, smiling as one who feels safe in his authority and means to have his own way with his victim. Naturally he regarded Beverley's words as the merest vaporings of a helpless and exasperated young man. He saw very clearly that love was having a hand in the affair, and he chuckled inwardly, thinking what a fool Beverley was.

"I thought I ordered you to leave this room," he said with an air and tone of lofty superiority, "and I certainly mean to be obeyed. Go, sir, and if you attempt to escape, or in any way break your parole, I'll have you shot."

"I have already broken it. From this moment I shall not regard it. You have heard my statement. I shall not repeat it. Govern yourself accordingly."

With these words Beverley turned and strode out of the house, quite beside himself, his whole frame quivering.

Hamilton laughed derisively, then looked at Helm and said:

"Helm, I like you; I don't wish to be unkind to you; but positively you must quit breaking in upon my affairs with your ready-made advice. I've given you and Lieutenant Beverley too much latitude, perhaps. If that young fool don't look sharp he'll get himself into a beastly lot of trouble. You'd better give him a talk. He's in a way to need it just now."

"I think so myself," said Helm, glad to get back upon fair footing with the irascible Governor. "I'll wait until he cools off somewhat, and then I can manage him. Leave him to me."

"Well, come walk with me to see what has really happened to Farnsworth. He's probably not much hurt, and deserves what he's got. That girl has turned his head. I think I understand the whole affair. A little love, a little wine, some foolishness, and the wench shot him."

Helm genially assented; but they were delayed for some time by an officer who came in to consult with Hamilton on some pressing Indian affairs. When they reached Roussillon place they met Beverley coming out; but he did not look at them. He was scarcely aware of them. A little way outside the gate, on going in, he had picked up Alice's locket and broken chain, which he mechanically put into his pocket. It was all like a dream to him, and yet he had a clear purpose. He was going away from Vincennes, or at least he would try, and woe be to Hamilton on his coming back. It was so easy for an excited young mind to plan great things and to expect success under apparently impossible conditions. Beverley gave Jean a note for Alice; it was this that took him to Roussillon place; and no sooner fell the night than he shouldered a gun furnished him by Madame Godere, and guided by the woodsman's fine craft, stole away southward, thinking to swim the icy Wabash some miles below, and then strike across the plains of Illinois to Kaskaskia.

It was a desperate undertaking; but in those days desperate undertakings were rather the rule than the exception. Moreover, love was the leader and Beverley the blind follower. Nothing could daunt him or turn him back, until he found an army to lead against Hamilton. It seems but a romantic burst of indignation, as we look back at it, hopelessly foolish, with no possible end but death in the wilderness. Still there was a method in love's madness, and Beverley, with his superb physique, his knowledge of the wilderness and his indomitable self-reliance, was by no means without his fighting chance for success.

CHAPTER XII
MANON LESCAUT. AND A RAPIER-THRUST

Beverley's absence was not noticed by Hamilton until late on the following day, and even then he scouted Helm's suggestion that the young man was possibly carrying out his threat to disregard his parole.

"He would be quite justified in doing it; you know that very well," said Helm with a laugh, "and he's just the man to undertake what is impossible. Of course, however, he'll get scalped for his trouble, and that will cost you something, I'm happy to say."

"It's a matter of small importance," Hamilton replied; "but I'll wager you the next toddy that he's not at the present moment a half-mile from this spot. He may be a fool, I readily grant that he is, but even a fool is not going to set out alone in this kind of weather to go to where your rebel friends are probably toasting their shins by a fire of green logs and half starving over yonder on the Mississippi."

"Joking aside, you are doubtless right. Beverley is hot-headed, and if he could he'd get even with you devilish quick; but he hasn't left Vincennes, I think. Miss Roussillon would keep him here if the place were on fire!"

Hamilton laughed dryly. He had thought just what Helm was saying. Beverley's attentions to Alice had not escaped his notice.

"Speaking of that girl," he remarked after a moment's silence, "what am I do to do with her? There's no place to keep her, and Farnsworth insists that she wasn't to blame." He chuckled again and added:

"It's true as gospel. He's in love with her, too. Seems to be glad she shot him. Says he's ashamed of himself for ever suspecting her of anything but being a genuine angel. Why, he's got as flabby as a rabbit and mumbles like a fool!"

"Same as you or I at his age," said Helm, taking a chew of tobacco. "She IS a pretty thing. Beverley don't know his foot from his shoulder-blade when she's anywhere near him. Boys are boys. I'm a sort of a boy myself."

"If she'd give up that flag he'd let her go," said Hamilton. "I hate like the devil to confine her; it looks brutal, and makes me feel like a tyrant."

"Have you ever happened to notice the obvious fact, Governor Hamilton, that Alice Roussillon and Father Beret are not all the French in Vincennes?"

"What do you mean?"

"I mean that I don't for a moment believe that either the girl or the priest knows a thing about where that flag is. They are both as truthful and honorable as people ever get to be. I know them. Somebody else got that flag from under the priest's floor. You may depend upon that. If Miss Roussillon knew where it is she'd say so, and then dare you to make her tell where it's hidden."

"Oh, the whole devilish town is rotten with treason; that's very clear. There's not a loyal soul in it outside of my forces."

"Thank you for not including me among the loyalists."

"Humph, I spoke of these French people; they pretend to be true; but I believe they are all traitors."

"You can manage them if you try. A little jolly kindness goes a long way with 'em. *I* had no trouble while *I* held the town."

Hamilton bit his lip and was silent. Helm was exasperatingly good tempered, and his jocularity was irresistible. While he was yet speaking a guard came up followed by Jean, the hunchback, and saluting said to Hamilton:

"The lad wants to see the young lady, sir."

Hamilton gazed quizzically at Jean, who planted himself in his habitual attitude before him and stared up into his face with the grotesque expression which seems to be characteristic of hunchbacks and unfledged birds—the look of an embodied and hideous joke.

"Well, sir, what will you have?" the Governor demanded.

"I want to see Alice, if you please."

"What for?"

"I want to give her a book to read."

"Ah, indeed. Where is it? Let me see it."

Jean took from the breast of his loose jerkin a small volume, dog-eared and mildewed, and handed it to Hamilton. Meantime he stood first on one foot, then the other, gnawing his thumb-nail and blinking rapidly.

"Well, Helm, just look here!"

"What?"

"Manon Lescaut."

"And what's that?"

"Haven't you ever read it?"

"Read what?"

"This novel—Manon Lescaut."

"Never read a novel in my life. Never expect to."

Hamilton laughed freely at Helm's expense, then turned to Jean and gave him back the book.

It would have been quite military, had he taken the precaution to examine between the pages for something hidden there, but he did not.

"Go, give it to her," he said, "and tell her I send my compliments, with great admiration of her taste in literature." He motioned the soldier to show Jean to Alice. "It's a beastly French story," he added, addressing Helm; "immoral enough to make a pirate blush. That's the sort of girl Mademoiselle Roussillon is!"

"I don't care what kind of a book she reads," blurted Helm, "she's a fine, pure, good girl. Everybody likes her. She's the good angel of this miserable frog-hole of a town. You'd like her yourself, if you'd straighten up and quit burning tow in your brain all the time. You're always so furious about something that you never have a chance to be just to yourself, or pleasant to anybody else."

Hamilton turned fiercely on Helm, but a glimpse of the Captain's broad good-humored face heartily smiling, dispelled his anger. There was no ground upon which to maintain a quarrel with a person so persistently genial and so absurdly frank. And in fact Hamilton was not half so bad as his choleric manifestations seemed to make him out. Besides, Helm knew just how far to go, just when to stop.

"If I had got furious at you every time there was overwhelming provocation for it," Hamilton said, "you'd have been long since hanged or shot. I fancy that I have shown angelic forbearance. I've given you somewhat more than a prisoner's freedom."

"So you have, so you have," assented Helm. "I've often been surprised at your generous partiality in my case. Let's have some hot water with something else in it, what do you say? I won't give you any more advice for five minutes by your watch."

"But I want some advice at once."

"What about?"

"That girl."

"Turn her loose. That's easy and reputable."

"I'll have to, I presume; but she ought to be punished."

"If you'll think less about punishment, revenge and getting even with everybody and everything, you'll soon begin to prosper."

Hamilton winced, but smiled as one quite sure of himself.

Jean followed the soldier to a rickety log pen on the farther side of the stockade, where he found the prisoner restlessly moving about like a bird in a rustic cage. It had no comforts, that gloomy little room. There was no fireplace, the roof leaked, and the only furniture consisted of a bench to sit on and a pile of skins for bed. Alice looked charmingly forlorn peeping out of the wraps in which she was bundled against the cold, her hair fluffed and rimpled in shining disorder around her face.

The guard let Jean in and closed the door, himself staying outside.

Alice was as glad to see the poor lad as if they had been parted for a year. She hugged him and kissed his drawn little face.

"You dear, good Jean!" she murmured, "you did not forget me."

"I brought you something," he whispered, producing the book.

Alice snatched it, looked at it, and then at Jean.

"Why, what did you bring this for? you silly Jean! I didn't want this. I don't like this book at all. It's hateful. I despise it. Take it back."

"There's something in it for you, a paper with writing on it; Lieutenant Beverley wrote it on there. It's shut up between the leaves about the middle."

"Sh-s-sh! not so loud, the guard'll hear you," Alice breathlessly whispered, her whole manner changing instantly. She was trembling, and the color had been whisked from her face, as the flame from a candle in a sudden draught.

She found the note and read it a dozen times without a pause, her eyes leaping along the lines back and forth with pathetic eagerness and concentration. Presently she sat down on the bench and covered her face with her hands. A tremor first, then a convulsive sobbing, shook her collapsed form. Jean regarded her with a drolly sympathetic grimace, elevating his long chin and letting his head settle back between his shoulders.

"Oh, Jean, Jean!" she cried at last, looking up and reaching out her arms; "O Jean, he is gone, gone, gone!"

Jean stepped closer to her while she sobbed again like a little child.

She pulled him to her and held him tightly against her breast while she once more read the note through blinding tears. The words were few, but to her they bore the message of desolation and despair. A great, haunting, hollow voice in her heart repeated them until they echoed from vague distance to distance.

It was written with a bit of lead on the half of a mildewed fly-leaf torn from the book:

"Dear Alice:

"I am going away. When you read this, think of me as hurrying through the wilderness to reach our army and bring it here. Be brave, as you always have been; be good, as you cannot help being; wait and watch for me; love me, as I love you. I will come. Do not doubt it, I will come, and I will crush Hamilton and his command. Courage, Alice dear; courage, and wait for me.

"Faithfully ever,
"Beverley."

She kissed the paper with passionate fervor, pouring her tears upon it in April showers between which the light of her eyes played almost fiercely, so poignant was her sense of a despair which bordered upon desperation. "Gone, gone!" It was all she could think or say. "Gone, gone."

Jean took the offending novel back home with him, hidden under his jerkin; but Beverley's note lay upon Alice's heart, a sweet comfort and a crushing weight, when an hour later Hamilton sent for her and she was taken before him. Her face was stained with tears and she looked pitifully distressed and disheveled; yet despite all this her beauty asserted itself with subtle force.

Hamilton felt ashamed looking at her, but put on sternness and spoke without apparent sympathy:

"Miss Roussillon, you came near committing a great crime. As it is, you have done badly enough; but I wish not to be unreasonably severe. I hope you are sorry for your act, and feel like doing better hereafter."

She was trembling, but her eyes looked steadily straight into his. They were eyes of baby innocence, yet they irradiated a strong womanly spirit just touched with the old perverse, mischievous light which she could neither banish nor control. When she did not make reply, Hamilton continued:

"You may go home now, and I shall expect to have no more trouble on your account." He made a gesture indicative of dismissal; then, as she turned from him, he added, somewhat raising his voice:

"And further, Miss Roussillon, that flag you took from here must positively be returned. See that it is done."

She lifted her head high and walked away, not deigning to give him a word.

"Humph! what do you think now of your fine young lady?" he demanded, turning to Helm with a sneering curl of his mouth. "She gives thanks copiously for a kindness, don't you think?"

"Poor girl, she was scared nearly out of her life," said Helm. "She got away from you, like a wounded bird from a snare. I never saw a face more pitiful than hers."

"Much pity she needs, and greatly like a wounded bird she acts, I must say; but good riddance if she'll keep her place hereafter. I despise myself when I have to be hard with a woman, especially a pretty one. That girl's a saucy and fascinating minx, and as dangerous as twenty men. I'll keep a watch on her movements from this on, and if she gets into mischief again I'll transport her to Detroit, or give her away to the Indians, She must stop her high-handed foolishness."

Helm saw that Hamilton was talking mere wind, VOX ET PRAETEREA NIHIL, and he furthermore felt that his babbling signified no harm to Alice; but Hamilton surprised him presently by saying:

"I have just learned that Lieutenant Beverley is actually gone. Did you know of his departure?"

"What are you saying, sir?"

Helm jumped to his feet, not angry, but excited.

"Keep cool, you need not answer if you prefer silence or evasion. You may want to go yourself soon."

Helm burst out laughing, but quickly growing serious said:

"Has Beverley been such a driveling fool as that? Are you in earnest?"

"He killed two of my scouts, wounded another, and crossed the Wabash in their canoe. He is going straight towards Kaskaskia."

"The idiot! Hurrah for him! If you catch your hare you may roast him, but catch him first, Governor!"

"You'll joke out of the other corner of your mouth, Captain Helm, if I find out that you gave him aid or countenance in breaking his parole."

"Aid or countenance! I never saw him after he walked out of this room. You gave him a devil of a sight more aid and countenance than I did. What are you talking about! Broke his parole! He did no such thing. He returned it to you fairly, as you well know. He told you he was going."

"Well, I've sent twenty of my swiftest Indians after him to bring him back. I'll let you see him shot. That ought to please you."

64

"They'll never get him, Governor. I'll bet high on him against your twenty scalp-lifters any day. Fitzhugh Beverley is the best Indian fighter, Daniel Boone and Simon Kenton excepted, in the American colonies."

On her way home Alice met Father Beret, who turned and walked beside her. He was so overjoyed at her release that he could scarcely speak; but held her hand and stroked it gently while she told him her story. It was beginning to rain, a steady, cold shower, when they reached the house, and for many days and nights thereafter the downfall continued almost incessantly.

"Dear child," said Father Beret, stopping at the gate and looking beseechingly into Alice's face, "you must stay at home now—stay in the house—it will be horribly dangerous for you to pass about in the village after your—after what has happened."

"Do not fear, Father, I will be careful. Aren't you coming in? I'll find you a cake and a glass of wine."

"No, child, not now."

"Then good-bye, good-bye," she said, turning from him to run into the house. "Come soon, I shall be so lonesome."

On the veranda she suddenly stopped, running her fingers about her neck and into her bosom.

"Oh, Father, Father Beret, I've lost my locket!" she cried. "See if I dropped it there."

She went back to the gate, searching the ground with her eyes. Of course she did not find the locket. It was miles and miles away close to the heart of her lover. If she could but have known this, it would have comforted her. Beverley had intended to leave it with Jean, but in his haste and excitement he forgot; writing the note distracted his attention; and so he bore Alice's picture on his breast and in his heart while pursuing his long and perilous journey.

Four of Hamilton's scouts came upon Beverley twenty miles south of Vincennes, but having the advantage of them, he killed two almost immediately, and after a running fight, the other two attempted escape in a canoe on the Wabash. Here, firing from a bluff, he wounded a third. Both then plunged head-foremost into the water, and by keeping below the surface, got away. The adventure gave Beverley new spirit and self-reliance; he felt that he could accomplish anything necessary to his undertaking. In the captured pirogue he crossed the river, and, to make his trail hard to find, sent the little craft adrift down the current.

Then alone, in the dead of winter, he took his bearings and struck across the dreary, houseless plain toward St. Louis.

As soon as Hamilton's discomfited scouts reported to him, he sent Long-Hair with twenty picked savages, armed and supplied for continuous and rapid marching, in pursuit of Beverley. There was a large reward for bringing him in alive, a smaller one for his scalp.

When Alice heard of all this, her buoyant and happy nature seemed entirely to desert her for a time. She was proud to find out that Beverley had shown himself brave and capable; it touched her love of heroism; but she knew too much about Indian warfare to hope that he could hold his own against Long-Hair, the wiliest and boldest of scalp-hunters, and twenty of the most experienced braves in Hamilton's forces. He would almost certainly be killed and scalped, or captured and brought back to be shot or hanged in Vincennes. The thought chilled and curdled her blood.

Both Helm and Father Beret tried to encourage and comfort her by representing the probabilities in the fairest light.

"It's like hunting for a needle in a haystack, going out to find a man in that wilderness," said Helm with optimistic cheerfulness; "and besides Beverley is no easy dose for twenty red niggers to take. I've seen him tried at worse odds than that, and he got out with a whole skin, too. Don't you fret about him, Miss Roussillon."

Little help came to her from attempts of this sort. She might brighten up for a while, but the dark dread, and the terrible gnawing at her heart, the sinking and despairing in her soul, could not be cured.

What added immeasurably to her distress was the attention of Farnsworth, whose wound troubled him but a short time. He seemed to have had a revelation and a change of spirit since the unfortunate rencounter and the subsequent nursing at Alice's hands. He was grave, earnest, kindly, evidently striving to play a gentle and honorable part. She could feel that he carried a load of regret, that he wanted to pay a full price in good for the evil that he had done; his sturdy English heart was righting itself nobly, yet she but half understood him, until his actions and words began to betray his love; and then she hated him unreasonably. Realizing this, Farnsworth bore himself more like a faithful dog than in the manner hitherto habitual to him. He simply shadowed Alice and would not be rebuffed.

There can be nothing more painful to a finely sympathetic nature than regret for having done a kindness. Alice experienced this to the fullest degree. She had nursed Farnsworth but a little while, yet it was a while of sweet influence. Her tender woman nature felt the blessedness of doing good to her enemy lying helpless in her house and hurt by her own hand. But now she hated the man, and with all her soul she was sorry that she had been kind to him; for out of her kindness he had drawn the spell of a love under which he lived a new life, and all for her. Yet deep down in her consciousness the pity and the pathos of the thing hovered gloomily and would not be driven out.

The rain in mid-winter gave every prospect a sad, cold, sodden gray appearance. The ground was soaked, little rills ran in the narrow streets, the small streams became great rivers, the Wabash overflowed its banks and made a sea of all the lowlands on either side. It was hard on the poor dwellers in the thatched and mostly floorless cabins, for the grass roofs gradually let the water through and puddles formed on the ground inside. Fuel was distant and had to be hauled in the pouring rain; provisions were scarce and hunting almost impossible. Many people, especially children, were taken ill with colds and fever. Alice found some relief from her trouble in going from cabin to cabin and waiting upon the sufferers; but even here Farnsworth could not be got rid of; he followed her night and day. Never was a good soldier, for he was that from head to foot, more lovelorn and love-docile. The maiden had completely subdued the man.

About this time, deep in a rainy and pitch-black night, Gaspard Roussillon came home. He tapped on the door again and again. Alice heard, but she hesitated to speak or move. Was she growing cowardly? Her heart beat like a drum. There was but one person in all the world that she could think of—it was not M. Roussillon. Ah, no, she had well-nigh forgotten her gigantic foster father.

"It is I, ma cherie, it is Gaspard, my love, open the door," came in a booming half-whisper from without. "Alice, Jean, it is your Papa Roussillon, my dears. Let me in."

Alice was at the door in a minute, unbarring it. M. Roussillon entered, armed to the teeth, the water dribbling from his buckskin clothes.

"Pouf!" he exclaimed, "my throat is like dust." His thoughts were diving into the stores under the floor. "I am famished. Dear children, dear little ones! They are glad to see papa! Where is your mama?"

He had Alice in his arms and Jean clung to his legs. Madame Roussillon, to be sure of no mistake, lighted a lamp with a brand that smoldered on the hearth and held it up, then, satisfied as to her husband's identity, set it on a shelf and flung herself into the affectionate group with clumsy abandon, making a great noise.

"Oh, my dear Gaspard!" she cried as she lunged forward. "Gaspard, Gaspard!" Her voice fairly lifted the roof; her great weight, hurled with such force, overturned everybody, and all of them tumbled in a heap, the rotund and solid dame sitting on top.

"Ouf! not so impetuous, my dear," puffed M. Roussillon, freeing himself from her unpleasant pressure and scrambling to his feet. "Really you must have fared well in my absence, Madame, you are much heavier." He laughed and lifted her up as if she had been a child, kissing her resonantly.

His gun had fallen with a great clatter. He took it from the floor and examined it to see if it had been injured, then set it in a corner.

"I am afraid we have been making too much noise," said Alice, speaking very low. "There is a patrol guard every night now. If they should hear you—"

"Shh!" whispered M. Roussillon, "we will be very still. Alice, is there something to eat and a drop of wine handy? I have come many miles; I am tired, hungry, thirsty,—ziff!"

Alice brought some cold roast venison, a loaf, and a bottle of claret. These she set before him on a little table.

"Ah, this is comfort," he said after he had gulped a full cup. "Have you all been well?"

Then he began to tell where he had been, what he had seen, and the many things he had done. A Frenchman must babble while he eats and drinks. A little wine makes him eloquent. He talks with his hands, shoulders, eyes. Madame Roussillon, Alice and Jean, wrapped in furs, huddled around him to hear. He was very entertaining, and they forgot the patrol until a noise startled them. It was the low of a cow. They laughed and the master of the house softened his voice.

M. Roussillon had been the guest of a great Indian chieftain, who was called the "Gate of the Wabash," because he controlled the river. The chief was an old acquaintance and treated him well.

"But I wanted to see you all," Gaspard said. "I was afraid something might have happened to you. So I came back just to peep in. I can't stay, of course; Hamilton would kill me as if I were a wolf. I can remain but an hour and then slip out of town again before daylight conies. The rain and darkness are my friends."

He had seen Simon Kenton, who said he had been in the neighborhood of Vincennes acting as a scout and spy for Clark. Presently and quite casually he added:

"And I saw Lieutenant Beverley, too. I suppose you know that he has escaped from Hamilton, and—" Here a big mouthful of venison interfered.

Alice leaned toward him white and breathless, her heart standing still.

Then the door, which had been left unbarred, was flung open and, along with a great rush of wind and rain, the patrol guard, five in number, sprang in.

M. Roussillon reached his gun with one hand, with the other swung a tremendous blow as he leaped against the intruders. Madame Roussillon blew out the light. No cave in the depth of earth was ever darker than that room. The patrolmen could not see one another or know what to do; but M. Roussillon laid about him with the strength of a giant. His blows sounded as if they smashed bones. Men fell heavily thumping on the floor where he rushed along. Some one fired a pistol and by its flash they all saw him; but instantly the darkness closed again, and before they could get their bearings he was out and gone, his great hulking form making its way easily over familiar ground where his would be captors could have proceeded but slowly, even with a light to guide them. There was furious cursing among the patrolmen as they tumbled about in the room, the unhurt ones trampling their prostrate companions and striking wildly at each other in their blindness and confusion. At last one of them bethought him to open a dark lantern with which the night guards were furnished. Its flame was fluttering and gave forth a pale red light that danced weirdly on the floors and walls.

Alice had snatched down one of her rapiers when the guards first entered. They now saw her facing them with her slender blade leveled, her back to the wall, her eyes shining dangerously. Madame Roussillon had fled into the adjoining room. Jean had also disappeared. The officer, a subaltern, in charge of the guard, seeing Alice, and not quickly able to make out that it was a woman thus defying him, crossed swords with her. There was small space for action; moreover the officer being not in the least a swordsman, played awkwardly, and quick as a flash his point was down. The rapier entered just below his thread with a dull chucking stab. He leaped backward, feeling at the same time a pair of arms clasp his legs. It was Jean, and the Lieutenant, thus unexpectedly tangled, fell to the floor, breaking but not extinguishing the guard's lantern as he went down. The little remaining oil spread and flamed up brilliantly, as if eager for conflagration, sputtering along the uneven boards.

"Kill that devil!" cried the Lieutenant, in a strangling voice, while trying to regain his feet. "Shoot! Bayonet!"

In his pain, rage and haste, he inadvertently set his hand in the midst of the blazing oil, which clung to the flesh with a seething grip.

"Hell!" he screamed, "fire, fire!"

Two or three bayonets were leveled upon Alice. Some one kicked Jean clean across the room, and he lay there curled up in his hairy night-wrap looking like an enormous porcupine.

At this point a new performer came upon the stage, a dark-robed thing, so active that its outlines changed elusively, giving it no recognizable features. It might have been the devil himself, or some terrible unknown wild animal clad somewhat to resemble a man, so far as the startled guards could make out. It clawed right and left, hurled one of them against the wall, dashed another through the door into Madame Roussillon's room, where the good woman was wailing at the top of her voice, and felled a third with a stroke like that of a bear's paw.

Consternation was at high tide when Farnsworth, who always slept with an ear open, reached Roussillon place and quickly quieted things. He was troubled beyond expression when he found out the true state of the affair, for there was nothing that he could do but arrest Alice and take her to Hamilton. It made his heart sink. He would have thought little of ordering a file of soldiers to shoot a man under the same conditions; but to subject her again to the Governor's stern cruelty—how could he do it? This time there would be no hope for her.

Alice stood before him flushed, disheveled, defiant, sword in hand, beautiful and terrible as an angel. The black figure, man or devil, had disappeared as strangely as it had come. The sub-Lieutenant was having his slight wound bandaged. Men were raging and cursing under their breath, rubbing their bruised heads and limbs.

"Alice—Mademoiselle Roussillon, I am so sorry for this," said Captain Farnsworth. "It is painful, terrible—"

He could not go on, but stood before her unmanned. In the feeble light his face was wan and his hurt shoulder, still in bandages, drooped perceptibly.

"I surrender to you," she presently said in French, extending the hilt of her rapier to him. "I had to defend myself when attacked by your Lieutenant there. If an officer finds it necessary to set upon a girl with his sword, may not the girl guard her life if she can?"

She was short of breath, so that her voice palpitated with a touching plangency that shook the man's heart.

Farnsworth accepted the sword; he could do nothing less. His duty admitted of no doubtful consideration; yet he hesitated, feeling around in his mind for a phrase with which to evade the inevitable.

"It will be safer for you at the fort, Mademoiselle; let me take you there."

CHAPTER XIII
A MEETING IN THE WILDERNESS

Beverley set out on his mid-winter journey to Kaskaskia with a tempest in his heart, and it was, perhaps, the storm's energy that gave him the courage to face undaunted and undoubting what his experience must have told him lay in his path. He was young and strong; that meant a great deal; he had taken the desperate chances of Indian warfare many times before this, and the danger counted as nothing, save that it offered the possibility of preventing him from doing the one thing in life he now cared to do. What meant suffering to him, if he could but rescue Alice? And what were life should he fail to rescue her? The old, old song hummed in his heart, every phrase of it distinct above the tumult of the storm. Could cold and hunger, swollen streams, ravenous wild beasts and scalp-hunting savages baffle him? No, there is no barrier that can hinder love. He said this over and over to himself after his rencounter with the four Indian scouts on the Wabash. He repeated it with every heart-beat until he fell in with some friendly red men, who took him to their camp, where to his great surprise he met M. Roussillon. It was his song when again he strode off toward the west on his lonely way.

We need not follow him step by step; the monotony of the woods and prairies, the cold rains, alternating with northerly winds and blinding snow, the constant watchfulness necessary to guard against a meeting with hostile savages, the tiresome tramping, wading and swimming, the hunger, the broken and wretched sleep in frozen and scant wraps,—why detail it all?

There was but one beautiful thing about it—the beauty of Alice as she seemed to walk beside him and hover near him in his dreams. He did not know that Long-Hair and his band were fast on his track; but the knowledge could not have urged him to greater haste. He strained every muscle to its utmost, kept every nerve to the highest tension. Yonder towards the west was help for Alice; that was all he cared for.

But if Long-Hair was pursuing him with relentless greed for the reward offered by Hamilton, there were friendly footsteps still nearer behind him; and one day at high noon, while he was bending over a little fire, broiling some liberal cuts of venison, a finger tapped him on the shoulder. He sprang up and grappled Oncle Jazon; at the same time, standing near by, he saw Simon Kenton, his old-time Kentucky friend. The pungled features of one and the fine, rugged face of the other swam as in a mist before Beverley's eyes. Kenton was laughing quietly, his strong, upright form shaking to the force of his pleasure. He was in the early prime of a vigorous life, not handsome, but strikingly attractive by reason of a certain glow in his face and a kindly flash in his deep-set eyes.

"Well, well, my boy!" he exclaimed, laying his left hand on Beverley's shoulder, while in the other he held a long, heavy rifle. "I'm glad to see ye, glad to see ye."

"Thought we was Injuns, eh?" said Oncle Jazon. "An' ef we had 'a' been we'd 'a' been shore o' your scalp!" The wizzened old creole cackled gleefully.

"And where are ye goin'?" demanded Kenton. "Ye're making what lacks a heap o' bein' a bee-line for some place or other."

Beverley was dazed and vacant-minded; things seemed wavering and dim. He pushed the two men from him and gazed at them without speaking. Their presence and voices did not convince him.

"Yer meat's a burnin'," said Oncle Jazon, stooping to turn it on the smouldering coals. "Ye must be hungry. Cookin' enough for a regiment."

Kenton shook Beverley with rough familiarity, as if to rouse his faculties.

"What's the matter? Fitz, my lad, don't ye know Si Kenton? It's not so long since we were like brothers, and now ye don't speak to me! Ye've not forgot me, Fitz!"

"Mebby he don't like ye as well as ye thought he did," drawled Oncle Jazon. "I HEV known o' fellers a bein' mistaken jes' thet way."

Beverley got his wits together as best he could, taking in the situation by such degrees as seemed at the time unduly slow, but which were really mere momentary falterings.

"Why, Kenton! Jazon!" he presently exclaimed, a cordial gladness blending with his surprise. "How did you get here? Where did you come from?"

He looked from one to the other back and forth with a wondering smile breaking over his bronzed and determined face.

"We've been hot on yer trail for thirty hours," said Kenton. "Roussillon put us on it back yonder. But what are ye up to? Where are ye goin'?"

"I'm going to Clark at Kaskaskia to bring him yonder." He waved his hand eastward. "I am going to take Vincennes and kill Hamilton."

"Well, ye're taking a mighty queer course, my boy, if ye ever expect to find Kaskaskia. Ye're already twenty miles too far south."

"Carryin' his gun on the same shoulder all the time," said Oncle Jazon, "has made 'im kind o' swing in a curve like. 'Tain't good luck no how to carry yer gun on yer lef' shoulder. When you do it meks yer take a longer step with yer right foot than ye do with yer lef' an' ye can't walk a straight line to save yer liver. Ventreblue! La venaison brule encore! Look at that dasted meat burnin' agin!"

He jumped back to the fire to turn the scorching cuts.

Beverley wrung Kenton's hand and looked into his eyes, as a man does when an old friend comes suddenly out of the past, so to say, and brings the freshness and comfort of a strong, true soul to brace him in his hour of greatest need.

"Of all men in the world, Simon Kenton, you were the least expected; but how glad I am! How thankful! Now I know I shall succeed. We are going to capture Vincennes, Kenton, are we not? We shall, sha'n't we, Jazon? Nothing, nothing can prevent us, can it?"

Kenton heartily returned the pressure of the young man's hand, while Oncle Jazon looked up quizzically and said:

"We're a tol'ble 'spectable lot to prevent; but then we might git pervented. I've seed better men an' us purty consid'ble pervented lots o' times in my life."

In speaking the colloquial dialect of the American backwoodsmen, Oncle Jazon, despite years of practice among them, gave to it a creole lisp and some turns of pronunciation not to be indicated by any form of spelling. It added to his talk a peculiar soft drollery. When he spoke French it was mostly that of the COUREURS DE BOIS, a PATOIS which still lingers in out-of-the-way nooks of Louisiana.

"For my part," said Kenton, "I am with ye, old boy, in anything ye want to do. But now ye've got to tell me everything. I see that ye're keeping something back. What is it?" He glanced sidewise slyly at Oncle Jazon.

Beverley was frank to a fault; but somehow his heart tried to keep Alice all to itself. He hesitated; then—

"I broke my parole with Governor Hamilton," he said. "He forced me to do it. I feel altogether justified. I told him beforehand that I should certainly leave Vincennes and go get a force to capture and kill him; and I'll do it, Simon Kenton, I'll do it!"

"I see, I see," Kenton assented, "but what was the row about? What did he do to excite ye—to make ye feel justified in breakin' over yer parole in that high-handed way? Fitz, I know ye too well to be fooled by ye—you've got somethin' in mind that ye don't want to tell. Well, then don't tell it. Oncle Jazon and I will go it blind, won't we, Jazon?"

"Blind as two moles," said the old man; "but as for thet secret," he added, winking both eyes at once, "I don't know as it's so mighty hard to guess. It's always safe to 'magine a woman in the case. It's mostly women 'at sends men a trottin' off 'bout nothin', sort o' crazy like."

Beverley looked guilty and Oncle Jazon continued: "They's a poo'ty gal at Vincennes, an' I see the young man a steppin' into her house about fifteen times a day 'fore I lef' the place. Mebbe she's tuck up wi' one o' them English officers. Gals is slippery an' onsartin'."

"Jazon!" cried Beverley, "stop that instantly, or I'll wring your old neck." His anger was real and he meant what he said. He clenched his hands and glowered.

Oncle Jazon, who was still squatting by the little fire, tumbled over backwards, as if Beverley had kicked him; and there he lay on the ground with his slender legs quivering akimbo in the air, while he laughed in a strained treble that sounded like the whining of a screech-owl.

The old scamp did not know all the facts in Beverley's case, nor did he even suspect what had happened; but he was aware of the young man's tender feeling for Alice, and he did shrewdly conjecture that she was a factor in the problem.

The rude jest at her expense did not seem to his withered and toughened taste in the least out of the way. Indeed it was a delectable bit of humor from Oncle Jazon's point of view.

"Don't get mad at the old man," said Kenton, plucking Beverley aside. "He's yer friend from his heels to his old scalped crown. Let him have his fun." Then lowering his voice almost to a whisper he continued:

"I was in Vincennes for two days and nights spyin' around. Madame Godere hid me in her house when there was need of it. I know how it is with ye; I got all the gossip about ye and the young lady, as well as all the information about Hamilton and his forces that Colonel Clark wants. I'm goin' to Kaskaskia; but I think it quite possible that Clark will be on his march to Vincennes before we get there; for Vigo has taken him full particulars as to the fort and its garrison, and I know that he's determined to capture the whole thing or die tryin'."

Beverley felt his heart swell and his blood leap strong in his veins at these words.

"I saw ye while I was in Vincennes," Kenton added, "but I never let ye see me. Ye were a prisoner, and I had no business with ye while your parole held. I felt that it was best not to tempt ye to give me aid, or to let ye have knowledge of me while I was a spy. I left two days before ye did, and should have been at Kaskaskia by this time if I hadn't run across Jazon, who detained me. He wanted to go with me, and I waited for him to repair the stock of his old gun. He tinkered at it 'tween meals and showers for half a week at the Indian village back yonder before he got it just to suit him. But I tell ye he's wo'th waiting for any length of time, and I was glad to let him have his way."

Kenton, who was still a young man in his early thirties, respected Beverley's reticence on the subject uppermost in his mind. Madame Godere had told the whole story with flamboyant embellishments; Kenton tiad seen Alice, and, inspired with the gossip and a surreptitious glimpse of her beauty, he felt perfectly familiar with Beverley's condition. He was himself a victim of the tender passion to the extent of being an exile from his Virginia home, which he had left on account of dangerously wounding a rival. But he was well touched with the backwoodsman's taste for joke and banter. He and Oncle Jazon, therefore, knowing the main feature of Beverley's predicament, enjoyed making the most of their opportunity in their rude but perfectly generous and kindly way.

By indirection and impersonal details, as regarded his feelings toward Alice, Beverley in due time made his friends understand that his whole ambition was centered in rescuing her. Nor did the motive fail to enlist their sympathy to the utmost. If all the world loves a lover, all men having the best virile instinct will fight for a lover's cause. Both Kenton and Oncle Jazon were enthusiastic; they wanted nothing better than an opportunity to aid in rescuing any girl who had shown so much patriotism and pluck. But Oncle Jazon was fond of Alice, and Beverley's story affected him peculiarly on her account.

"They's one question I'm a goin' to put to ye, young man," he said, after he had heard everything and they had talked it all over, "an' I want ye to answer it straight as a bullet f'om yer gun."

"Of course, Jazon, go ahead," said Beverley. "I shall be glad to answer." But his mind was far away with the gold-haired maiden in Hamilton's prison. He scarcely knew what he was saying.

"Air ye expectin' to marry Alice Roussillon?"

The three men were at the moment eating the well broiled venison. Oncle Jazon's puckered lips and chin were dripping with the fragrant grease and juice, which also flowed down his sinewy, claw-like fingers. Overhead in the bare tops of the scrub oaks that covered the prairie oasis, the February wind sang a shrill and doleful song.

Beverley started as if a blow had been aimed at him. Oncle Jazon's question, indeed, was a blow as unexpected as it was direct and powerful.

"I know it's poo'ty p'inted," the old man added after a short pause, "an' ye may think 'at I ain't got no business askin' it; but I have. That leetle gal's a pet o' mine, an' I'm a lookin' after her, an' expectin' to see 'at she's not bothered by nobody who's not goin' to do right by her. Marryin' is a mighty good thing, but—"

"What do ye know about matrimony, ye old raw-headed bachelor?" demanded Kenton, who felt impelled to relieve Beverley of the embarrassment of an answer. "Ye wouldn't know a wife from a sack o' meal!"

"Now don't git too peart an' fast, Si Kenton," cried Oncle Jazon, glaring truculently at his friend, but at the same time showing a dry smile that seemed to be hopelessly entangled in criss-cross wrinkles. "Who told ye I was a bach'lor? Not by a big jump. I've been married mighty nigh on to twenty times in my day. Mos'ly Injuns, o' course; but a squaw's a wife w'en ye marries her, an' I know how it hurts a gal to be dis'p'inted in sich a matter. That's w'y I put the question I did. I'm not goin' to let no man give sorry to that little Roussillon gal; an' so ye've got my say. Ye seed her raise thet flag on the fort, Lieutenant Beverley, an' ye seed her take it down an' git away wi' it. You know 'at she deserves nothin' but the best; an' by the Holy Virgin, she's got to have it, or I'm a goin' to know several reasons why. Thet's what made me put the question straight to ye, young man, an' I expects a straight answer."

Beverley's face paled; but not with anger. He grasped one of Oncle Jazon's greasy hands and gave it such a squeeze that the old fellow grimaced painfully.

"Thank you, Oncle Jazon, thank you!" he said, with a peculiar husky burr in his voice. "Alice will never suffer if I can help it. Let the subject drop now, my friend, until we have saved her from the hands of Hamilton." In the power of his emotion he continued to grip the old man's hand with increasing severity of pressure.

"Ventrebleu! let go! Needn't smash a feller's fingers 'bout it!" screeched Oncle Jazon. "I can't shoot wo'th a cent, nohow, an' ef ye cripple up my trigger-finger—"

Kenton had been peeping under the low-hanging scrub-oak boughs while Oncle Jazon was speaking these last words; and now he suddenly interrupted:

"The devil! look yonder!" he growled out in startling tone. "Injuns!"

It was a sharp snap of the conversation's thread, and at the same time our three friends realized that they had been careless in not keeping a better look-out. They let fall the meat they had not yet finished eating and seized their guns.

Five or six dark forms were moving toward them across a little point of the prairie that cut into the wood a quarter of a mile distant.

"Yander's more of 'em," said Oncle Jazon, as if not in the least concerned, wagging his head in an opposite direction, from which another squad was approaching.

That he duly appreciated the situation appeared only in the celerity with which he acted.

Kenton at once assumed command, and his companions felt his perfect fitness. There was no doubt from the first as to what the Indians meant; but even if there had been it would have soon vanished; for in less than three minutes twenty-one savages were swiftly and silently forming a circle inclosing the spot where the three white men, who had covered themselves as best they could with trees, waited in grim steadiness for the worst.

Quite beyond gunshot range, but near enough for Oncle Jazon to recognize Long-Hair as their leader, the Indians halted and began making signs to one another all round the line. Evidently they dreaded to test the marksmanship of such riflemen as they knew most border men to be. Indeed, Long-Hair had personal knowledge of what might certainly be expected from both Kenton and Oncle Jazon; they were terrible when out for fight; the red warriors from Georgia to the great lakes had heard of them; their names smacked of tragedy. Nor was Beverley without fame among Long-Hair's followers, who had listened to the story of his fighting qualities, brought to Vincennes by the two survivors of the scouting party so cleverly defeated by him.

"The liver-colored cowards," said Kenton, "are afeared of us in a shootin'-match; they know that a lot of 'em would have to die if they should undertake an open fight with us. It's some sort of a sneakin' game they are studyin' about just now."

"I'm a gittin' mos' too ole to shoot wo'th a cent," said Oncle Jazon, "but I'd give half o' my scalp ef thet Long-Hair would come clost enough fo' me to git a bead onto his lef' eye. It's tol'ble plain 'at we're gone goslins this time, I'm thinkin'; still it'd be mighty satisfyin' if I could plug out a lef' eye or two 'fore I go."

Beverley was silent; the words of his companions were heard by him, but not noticed. Nothing interested him save the thought of escaping and making his way to Clark. To fail meant infinitely more than death, of which he had as small fear as most brave men, and to succeed meant everything that life could offer. So, in the unlimited selfishness of love, he did not take his companions into account.

The three stood in a close-set clump of four or five scrub oaks at the highest point of a thinly wooded knoll that sloped down in all directions to the prairie. Their view was wide, but in places obstructed by the trees.

"Men," said Kenton, after a thoughtful and watchful silence, "the thing looks kind o' squally for us. I don't see much of a chance to get out of this alive; but we've got to try."

He showed by the density of his voice and a certain gray film in his face that he felt the awful gravity of the situation; but he was calm and not a muscle quivered.

"They's jes' two chances for us," said Oncle Jazon, "an' them's as slim as a broom straw. We've got to stan' here an' fight it out, or wait till night an' sneak through atween 'em an' run for it."

"I don't see any hope o' sneakin' through the line," observed Kenton. "It's not goin' to be dark tonight."

"Wa-a-l," Oncle Jazon drawled nonchalantly while he took in a quid of tobacco, "I've been into tighter squeezes 'an this, many a time, an' I got out, too."

"Likely enough," said Kenton, still reflecting while his eyes roamed around the circle of savages.

"I fit the skunks in Ferginny 'fore you's thought of, Si Kenton, an' down in Car'lina in them hills. If ye think I'm a goin' to be scalped where they ain't no scalp, 'ithout tryin' a few dodges, yer a dad dasteder fool an' I used to think ye was, an' that's makin' a big compliment to ye."

71

"Well, we don't have to argy this question, Oncle Jazon; they're a gittin' ready to run in upon us, and we've got to fight. I say, Beverley, are ye ready for fast shootin'? Have ye got a plenty of bullets?"

"Yes, Roussillon gave me a hundred. Do you think—"

He was interrupted by a yell that leaped from savage mouth to mouth all round the circle, and then the charge began.

"Steady, now," growled Kenton, "let's not be in a hurry. Wait till they come nigh enough to hit 'em before we shoot."

The time was short; for the Indians came on at almost race-horse speed.

Oncle Jazon fired first, the long, keen crack of his small-bore rifle splitting the air with a suggestion of vicious energy, and a lithe young warrior, who was outstripping all his fellows, leaped high and fell paralyzed.

"Can't shoot wo'th a cent," muttered the old man, deftly beginning to reload his gun the while; "but I jes' happened to hit that buck. He'll never git my scalp, thet's sartin' sure."

Beverley and Kenton each likewise dropped an Indian; but the shots did not even check the rush. Long-Hair had planned to capture his prey, not kill it. Every savage had his orders to take the white men alive; Hamilton's larger reward depended on this.

Right on they came, as fast as their nimble legs could carry them, yelling like demons; and they reached the grove before the three white men could reload their guns. Then every warrior took cover behind a tree and began scrambling forward from bole to bole, thus approaching rapidly without much exposure.

"Our 'taters is roasted brown," muttered Oncle Jazon. He crossed himself. Possibly he prayed; but he was priming his old gun the next instant.

Kenton fired again, making a hurried and ineffectual attempt to stop the nearest warrior, who saved himself by quickly skipping behind a tree. Beverley's gun snapped, the flint failing to make fire; but Oncle Jazon bored a little hole through the head of the Indian nearest him; and then the final rush was made from every direction.

A struggle ensued, which for desperate energy has probably never been surpassed. Like three lions at bay, the white men met the shock, and lion-like they fought in the midst of seventeen stalwart and determined savages.

"Don't kill them, take them alive; throw them down and hold them!" was Long-Hair's order loudly shouted in the tongue of his tribe.

Both Kenton and Jazon understood every word and knew the significance of such a command from the leader. It naturally came into Kenton's mind that Hamilton had been informed of his visit to Vincennes and had offered a reward for his capture. This being true, death as a spy would be the certain result if he were taken back. He might as well die now. As for Beverley, he thought only of Alice, yonder as he had left her, a prisoner in Hamilton's hands, Oncle Jazon, if he thought at all, probably considered nothing but present escape, though he prayed audibly to the Blessed Virgin, even while he lay helpless upon the ground, pinned down by the weight of an enormous Indian. He could not move any part of himself, save his lips, and these mechanically put forth the wheezing supplication.

Beverley and Kenton, being young and powerful, were not so easily mastered. For a while, indeed, they appeared to be more than holding their own. They time and time again scattered the entire crowd by the violence of their muscular efforts; and after it had finally closed in upon them in a solid body they swayed and swung it back and forth and round and round until the writhing, savage mass looked as if caught in the vortex of a whirlwind. But such tremendous exertion could not last long. Eight to one made too great a difference between the contending parties, and the only possible conclusion of the struggle soon came. Seized upon by desperate, clinging, wolf-like assailants, the white men felt their arms, legs and bodies weighted down and their strength fast going.

Kenton fell next after Oncle Jazon, and was soon tightly bound with rawhide thongs. He lay on his back panting and utterly exhausted, while Beverley still kept up the unequal fight.

Long-Hair sprang in at the last moment to make doubly certain the securing of his most important captive. He flung his long and powerful arms around Beverley from behind and made a great effort to throw him upon the ground. The young man, feeling this fresh and vigorous clasp, turned himself about to put forth one more mighty spurt of power. He lifted the stalwart Indian bodily and dashed him headlong against the buttressed root of a tree half a rod distant, breaking the smaller bone of his left fore-arm and well-nigh knocking him senseless.

It was a fine exhibition of manly strength; but there could be nothing gained by it. A blow on the back of his head the next instant stretched Beverley face downward and unconscious on the ground. The savages turned him over and looked satisfied when they found that he was not dead. They bound him with even greater care than they had shown in securing the others, while Long-Hair stood by stolidly looking on, meantime supporting his broken fore-arm in his hand.

"Ugh! dog!" he grunted, and gave Beverley a kick in the side. Then turning a fiendish stare upon Oncle Jazon he proceeded to deliver against his old, dry ribs three or four like contributions with resounding effect. "Polecat! Little old greasy woman!" he snarled, "make good fire for warrior to dance by!" Kenton also received his full share of the kicks and verbal abuse, after which Long-Hair gave orders for fires to be built. Then he looked to his hurt arm and had the bone set and bandaged, never so much as wincing the while.

It was soon apparent that the Indians purposed to celebrate their successful enterprise with a feast. They cooked a large amount of buffalo steak; then, each with his hands full of the savory meat, they began to dance around the fires, droning meantime an atrociously repellant chant.

"They're a 'spectin' to hev a leetle bit o' fun outen us," muttered Oncle Jazon to Beverley, who lay near him. "I onderstan' what they're up to, dad dast 'em! More'n forty years ago, in Ca'lina, they put me an' Jim Hipes through the ga'ntlct, an' arter thct, in Kaintuck, me an' Si Kenton tuck the run. Hi, there, Si! where air ye?"

"Shut yer fool mouth," Kenton growled under his breath. "Ye'll have that Injun a kickin' our lights out of us again."

Oncle Jazon winked at the gray sky and puckered his mouth so that it looked like a nutgall on an old, dry leaf.

"What's the diff'ence?" he demanded. "I'd jest as soon be kicked now as arter while; it's got to come anyhow."

Kenton made no response. The thongs were torturing his arms and legs. Beverley was silent, but consciousness had returned, and with it a sense of despair. All three of the prisoners lay face upward quite unable to move, knowing full well that a terrible ordeal awaited them. Oncle Jazon's grim humor could not be quenched, even by the galling agony of the thongs that buried themselves in the flesh, and the anticipation of torture beside which death would seem a luxury.

"Yap! Long-Hair, how's yer arm?" he called jeeringly. "Feels pooty good, hay?"

Long-Hair, who was not joining in the dance and song, turned when he heard these taunting words, and mistaking whence they came, went to Beverley's side and kicked him again and again.

Oncle Jazon heard the loud blows, and considered the incident a remarkably good joke.

"He, he, he!" he snickered, as soon as Long-Hair walked away again. "I does the talkin' an' somebody else gits the thumpin'! He, he, he! I always was devilish lucky. Them kicks was good solid jolts, wasn't they, Lieutenant? Sounded like they was. He, he, he!"

Beverley gave no heed to Oncle Jazon's exasperating pleasantry; but Kenton, sorely chafing under the pressure of his bonds, could not refrain from making retort in kind.

"I'd give ye one poundin' that ye'd remember, Emile Jazon, if I could get to ye, ye old twisted-face, peeled-headed, crooked-mouthed, aggravatin' scamp!" he exclaimed, not thinking how high his naturally strong voice was lifted. "I can stand any fool but a damn fool!"

Long-Hair heard the concluding epithet and understood its meaning. Moreover, he thought himself the target at which it was so energetically launched. Wherefore he promptly turned back and gave Kenton a kicking that made his body resound not unlike a drum.

And here it was that Oncle Jazon overreached himself. He was so delighted at Kenton's luck that he broke forth giggling and thereby drew against his own ribs a considerable improvement of Long-Hair's pedal applications.

"Ventrebleu!" whined the old man, when the Indian had gone away again. "Holy Mary! Jee-ru-sa-lem! They's nary bone o' me left 'at's not splintered as fine as toothpickers! S'pose yer satisfied now, ain't ye, Si Kenton? Ef ye ain't I'm shore to satisfy ye the fust time I git a chance at ye, ye blab-mouthed eejit!"

Before this conversation was ended a rain began to fall, and it rapidly thickened from a desultory shower to a roaring downpour that effectually quenched not only the fires around which the savages were dancing, but the enthusiasm of the dancers as well. During the rest of the afternoon and all night long the fall was incessant, accompanied by a cold, panting, wailing southwest wind.

Beverley lay on the ground, face upward, the rawhide strings torturing his limbs, the chill of cold water searching his bones. He could see nothing but the dim, strange canopy of flying rain, against which the bare boughs of the scrub oaks were vaguely outlined; he could hear nothing but the cry of the wind and the swash of the water which fell upon him and ran under him, bubbling and gurgling as if fiendishly exultant.

The night dragged on through its terrible length, dealing out its indescribable horrors, and at last morning arrived, with a stingy and uncertain gift of light slowly increasing until the dripping trees appeared forlornly gray and brown against clouds now breaking into masses that gave but little rain.

Beverley lived through the awful trial and even had the hardihood to brighten inwardly with the first flash of sunlight that shot through a cloud-crack on the eastern horizon. He thought of Alice, as he had done all night; but now the thought partook somehow of the glow yonder above old Vincennes, although he could only see its reflection.

There was great stir among the Indians. Long-Hair stalked about scrutinizing the ground. Beverley saw him come near time and again with a hideous, inquiring scowl on his face. Grunts and laconic exclamations passed from mouth to mouth, and presently the import of it all could not be mistaken. Kenton and Jazon were gone—had escaped during the night—and the rain had completely obliterated their tracks.

The Indians were furious. Long-Hair sent out picked parties of his best scouts with orders to scour the country in all directions, keeping with himself a few of the older warriors. Beverley was fed what he would eat of venison, and Long-Hair made him understand that he would have to suffer some terrible punishment on account of the action of his companions.

Late in the day the scouts straggled back with the report that no track or sign of the fugitives had been discovered, and immediately a consultation was held. Most of the warriors, including all of the young bucks, demanded a torture entertainment as compensation for their exertions and the unexpected loss of their own prisoners; for it had been agreed that Beverley belonged exclusively to Long-Hair, who objected to anything which might deprive him of the great reward offered by Hamilton for the prisoner if brought to him alive.

In the end it was agreed that Beverley should be made to run the gauntlet, provided that no deadly weapons were used upon him during the ordeal.

CHAPTER XIV
A PRISONER OF LOVE

Alice put on her warmest clothes and followed Captain Farnsworth to the fort, realizing that no pleasant experience awaited her. The wind and rain still prevailed when they were ready to set forth, and, although it was not extremely cold, a searching chill went with every throb that marked the storm's waves. No lights shone in the village houses. Overhead a gray gloom covered stars and sky, making the darkness in the watery streets seem densely black. Farnsworth offered Alice his arm, but she did not accept it.

"I know the way better than you do," she said. "Come on, and don't be afraid that I am going to run. I shall not play any trick on you."

"Very well, Mademoiselle, as you like. I trust you."

He followed her from the house. He was so filled with the bitterness of what he was doing that he carried her sword in his hand all the way to the fort, quite unaware that its point often touched her dress so that she plainly felt it. Indeed, she thought he was using that ruffianly and dangerous means of keeping pace with her. He had sent the patrol on its rounds, taking upon himself the responsibility of delivering her to Hamilton. She almost ran, urged by the strange excitement that burned in her heart, and he followed somewhat awkwardly, stumbling over the unfamiliar way in the rain and darkness.

At every step he was wishing that she would escape from him. Coarse as his nature was and distorted by hardening experiences, it was rooted in good English honesty and imbued with a chivalric spirit. When, as happened too often, he fell under the influence of liquor, the bad in him promptly came uppermost; but at all other times his better traits made him a good fellow to meet, genial, polite, generous, and inclined to recognize the finer sentiments of manliness. To march into his commander's presence with Alice as his prisoner lacked everything of agreeing with his taste; yet he had not been willing to give her over into the hands of the patrol. If his regard for military obligation had not been exceptionally strong, even for an English soldier, he would have given way to the temptation of taking her to some place of hiding and safety, instead of brutally subjecting her to Hamilton's harsh judgment. He anticipated a trying experience for her on account of this new transgression.

They hastened along until a lantern in the fort shot a hazy gleam upon them.

"Stop a moment, Mademoiselle," Farnsworth called. "I say, Miss Roussillon, stop a moment, please."

Alice halted and turned facing him so short and so suddenly that the rapier in his hand pricked through her wraps and slightly scratched her arm.

"What do you mean, sir?" she demanded, thinking that he had thrust purposely. "Do I deserve this brutality?"

"You mistake me, Miss Roussillon. I cannot be brutal to you now. Do not fear me; I only had a word to say."

"Oh, you deem it very polite and gentle to jab me with your sword, do you? If I had one in my hand you would not dare try such a thing, and you know it very well."

He was amazed, not knowing that the sword-point had touched her. He could not see her face, but there was a flash in her voice that startled him with its indignant contempt and resentment.

"What are you saying, Miss Roussillon? I don't understand you. When did I ever—when did I jab you with my sword? I never thought of such a thing."

"This moment, sir, you did, and you know you did. My arm is bleeding now."

She spoke rapidly in French; but he caught her meaning, and for the first became aware of the rapier in his hand. Even then its point was toward her and very near her breast. He lowered it instantly while the truth rushed into his mind.

"Forgive me," he murmured, his words barely audible in the tumult of wind and rain, but charged with the intensest feeling.

"Forgive me; I did not know—it was an accident—I could not do such a thing purposely. Believe me, believe me, Miss Roussillon. I did not mean it."

She stood facing him, trying to look right into his eyes. A quality in his voice had checked her hot anger. She could only see his dim outlines in the dull gleam from the fort's lantern. He seemed to be forlornly wretched.

"I should like to believe you," she presently said, "but I cannot. You English are all, all despicable, mean, vile!"

She was remembering the young officer who had assaulted her with his sword in the house a while ago. And (what a strange thing the human brain is!) she at the same time comforted herself with the further thought that Beverley would never, never, be guilty of rudeness to a woman.

"Some time you shall not say that," Farnsworth responded. "I asked you to stop a moment that I might beg you to believe how wretchedly sorry I am for what I am doing. But you cannot understand me now. Are you really hurt, Miss Roussillon? I assure you that it was purely accidental."

"My hurt is nothing," she said.

"I am very glad."

"Well, then, shall we go on to the fort?"

"You may go where you please, Mademoiselle."

She turned her back upon him and without an answering word walked straight to the lantern that hung by the gate of the stockade, where a sentinel tramped to and fro. A few moments later Captain Farnsworth presented her to Hamilton, who had been called from his bed when the news of the trouble at Roussillon place reached the fort.

"So you've been raising hell again, have you, Miss?" he growled, with an ugly frown darkening his face.

"I beg your pardon," said Farnsworth, "Miss Roussillon was not to blame for—"

"In your eyes she'd not be to blame, sir, if she burned up the fort and all of us in it," Hamilton gruffly interrupted. "Miss, what have you been doing? What are you here for? Captain Farnsworth, you will please state the particulars of the trouble that I have just heard about. And I may as well notify you that I wish to hear no special lover's pleading in this girl's behalf."

Farnsworth's face whitened with anger; he bit his lip and a shiver ran through his frame; but he had to conquer the passion. In a few words, blunt and direct as musket-balls, he told all the circumstances of what had taken place, making no concealments to favor Alice, but boldly blaming the officer of the patrol, Lieutenant Barlow, for losing his head and attacking a young girl in her own home.

"I will hear from Barlow," said Hamilton, after listening attentively to the story. "But take this girl and confine her. Show her no favors. I hold you responsible for her until to-morrow morning. You can retire."

There was no room for discussion. Farnsworth saluted and turned to Alice.

"Come with me," he gently said.

Hamilton looked after them as they went out of his room, a curious smile playing around his firmly set lips.

"She's the most beautiful vixen that I ever saw," he thought. "She doesn't look to be a French girl, either—decidedly English." He shrugged his shoulders, then laughed dryly. "Farnsworth's as crazy as can be, the beggar; in love with her so deep that he can't see out. By Jove, she IS a beauty! Never saw such eyes. And plucky to beat the devil. I'll bet my head Barlow'll be daft about her next!"

Still, notwithstanding the lightness of his inward comments, Hamilton regarded the incident as rather serious. He knew that the French inhabitants were secretly his bitter enemies, yet probably willing, if he would humor their peculiar social, domestic and commercial prejudices, to refrain from active hostilities, and even to aid him in furnishing his garrison with a large amount of needed supplies. The danger just now was twofold; his Indian allies were deserting him, and a flotilla loaded with provisions and ammunition from Detroit had failed to arrive. He might, if the French rose against him and were joined by the Indians, have great difficulty defending the fort. It was clear that M. Roussillon had more influence with both creoles and savages than any other person save Father Beret. Urgent policy dictated that these two men should somehow be won over. But to do this it would be necessary to treat Alice in such a way that her arrest would aid, instead of operating against the desired result,—a thing not easy to manage.

Hamilton was not a man of fine scruples, but he may have been, probably was, better than our American historians have made him appear. His besetting weakness, which, as a matter of course, he regarded as the highest flower of efficiency, was an uncontrollable temper, a lack of fine human sympathy and an inability to forgive. In his calmest moments, when prudence appealed to him, he would resolve to use diplomatic means; but no sooner was his opinion questioned or his purpose opposed than anger and the thirst for revenge overpowered every gentler consideration. He returned to his bed that night fully resolved upon a pleasant and successful interview with Alice next morning.

Captain Farnsworth took his fair prisoner straight-way from Hamilton's presence to a small room connected with a considerable structure in a distant angle of the stockade. Neither he nor Alice spoke on the way. With a huge wooden key he unlocked the door and stepped aside for her to enter. A dim lamp was burning within, its yellowish light flickering over the scant furniture, which consisted of a comfortable bed, a table with some books on it, three chairs, a small looking-glass on the wall, a guitar and some articles of men's clothing hanging here and there. A heap of dull embers smouldered in the fireplace. Alice did not falter at the threshold, but promptly entered her prison.

"I hope you can be comfortable," said Farnsworth in a low tone. "It's the best I can give you."

"Thank you," was the answer spoken quite as if he had handed her a glass of water or picked up her handkerchief.

He held the door a moment, while she stopped, with her back toward him, in the middle of the room; then she heard him close and lock it. The air was almost too warm after her exposure to the biting wind and cold dashes of rain. She cast off her outer wraps and stood by the fireplace. At a glance she comprehended that the place was not the one she had formerly occupied as a prisoner, and that it belonged to a man. A long rifle stood in a corner, a bullet-pouch and powder-horn hanging on a projecting hickory ramrod; a heavy fur top-coat lay across one of the chairs.

Alice felt her situation bitterly enough; but she was not of the stuff that turns to water at the touch of misfortune. Pioneer women took hardships as a matter of course, and met calamity with admirable fortitude. There was no wringing of hands, no frantic wailing, no hollow, despairing groan. While life lasted hope flourished, even in most tragic surroundings; and not unfrequently succor came, at the last verge of destruction, as the fitting reward of unconquerable courage. A girl like Alice must be accepted in the spirit of her time and surroundings. She was born amid experiences scarcely credible now, and bred in an area and an atmosphere of incomparable dangers. Naturally she accepted conditions of terrible import with a sang froid scarcely possible to a girl of our day. She did not cry, she did not sink down helpless when she found herself once more imprisoned with some uncertain trial before her; but simply knelt and repeated the Lord's prayer, then went to bed and slept; even dreamed the dream of a maid's first love.

Meantime Farnsworth, who had given Alice his own apartment, took what rest he could on the cold ground under a leaky shed hard by. His wound, not yet altogether healed, was not benefited by the exposure.

In due time next morning Hamilton ordered Alice brought to his office, and when she appeared he was smiling with as near an approach to affability as his disposition would permit. He rose and bowed like a courtier.

76

"I hope you rested well, Mademoiselle," he said in his best French. He imagined that the use of her language would be agreeable to begin with.

The moment that Alice saw him wearing that shallow veneering of pleasantness on his never prepossessing visage, she felt a mood of perversity come over her. She, too, smiled, and he mistook her expression for one of reciprocal amenity. She noticed that her sword was on his table.

"I am sorry, Monsieur, that I cannot say as much to you," she glibly responded. "If you lay upon a bed of needles the whole night through, your rest was better than you deserved. My own sleep was quite refreshing, thank you."

Instantly Hamilton's choler rose. He tried to suppress it at first; but when he saw Alice actually laughing, and Farnsworth (who had brought her in) biting his lip furiously to keep from adding an uproarious guffaw, he lost all hold of himself. He unconsciously picked up the rapier and shook it till its blade swished.

"I might have known better than to expect decency from a wench of your character," he said. "I hoped to do you a favor; but I see that you are not capable of accepting kindness politely."

"I am sure, Monsieur, that I have but spoken the truth plainly to you. You would not have me do otherwise, I hope."

Her voice, absolutely witching in its softness, freshness and suavity, helped the assault of her eyes, while her dimples twinkled and her hair shone. Hamilton felt his heart move strangely; but he could not forbear saying in English:

"If you are so devilish truthful, Miss, you will probably tell me where the flag is that you stole and hid."

It was always the missing banner that came to mind when he saw her.

"Indeed I will do nothing of the sort," she promptly replied. "When you see that flag again you will be a prisoner and I will wave it high over your head."

She lifted a hand as she spoke and made the motion of shaking a banner above him. It was exasperation sweetened almost to delight that took hold of the sturdy Briton. He liked pluck, especially in a woman; all the more if she was beautiful. Yet the very fact that he felt her charm falling upon him set him hard against her, not as Hamilton the man, but as Hamilton the commander at Vincennes.

"You think to fling yourself upon me as you have upon Captain Farnsworth," he said, with an insulting leer and in a tone of prurient innuendo. "I am not susceptible, my dear." This more for Farnsworth's benefit than to insult her, albeit he was not in a mood to care.

"You are a coward and a liar!" she exclaimed, her face flushing with hot shame. "You stand here," she quickly added, turning fiercely upon Farnsworth, "and quietly listen to such words! You, too, are a coward if you do not make him retract! Oh, you English are low brutes!"

Hamilton laughed; but Farnsworth looked dark and troubled, his glance going back and forth from Alice to his commander, as if another word would cause him to do something terrible.

"I rather think I've heard all that I care to hear from you, Miss," Hamilton presently said. "Captain Farnsworth, you will see that the prisoner is confined in the proper place, which, I suggest to you, is not your sleeping quarters, sir."

"Colonel Hamilton," said Farnsworth in a husky voice, "I slept on the ground under a shed last night in order that Miss Roussillon might be somewhat comfortable."

"Humph! Well, see that you do not do it again. This girl is guilty of harboring a spy and resisting a lawful attempt of my guards to capture him. Confine her in the place prepared for prisoners and see that she stays there until I am ready to fix her punishment."

"There is no place fit for a young girl to stay in," Farnsworth ventured. "She can have no comfort or—"

"Take her along, sir; any place is good enough for her so long as she behaves like a—"

"Very well," Farnsworth bluntly interrupted, thus saving Alice the stroke of a vile comparison. "Come with me, please, Miss Roussillon."

He pulled her toward the door, then dropped the arm he had grasped and murmured an apology.

She followed him out, holding her head high. No one looking on would have suspected that a sinking sensation in her heart made it difficult for her to walk, or that her eyes, shining like stars, were so inwardly clouded with distress that she saw her way but dimly.

It was a relief to Hamilton when Helm a few minutes later entered the room with something breezy to say.

"What's up now, if I may ask?" the jolly American demanded. "What's this I hear about trouble with the French women? Have they begun a revolution?"

"That elephant, Gaspard Roussillon, came back into town last night," said Hamilton sulkily.

"Well, he went out again, didn't he?"

"Yes, but—"

"Stepped on somebody's toe first, eh?"

"The guard tried to capture him, and that girl of his wounded Lieutenant Barlow in the neck with a sword. Roussillon fought like a tiger and the men swear that the devil himself appeared on the scene to help the Frenchman out."

"Moral: Be generous in your dealings with Frenchmen and Frenchwomen and so get the devil on your side."

"I've got the girl a prisoner, and I swear to you that I'll have her shot this time if—"

"Why not shoot her yourself? You oughtn't to shirk a dirty job like that and force it upon your men."

Hamilton laughed and elevated his shoulders as if to shake off an annoying load. Just then a young officer with a white bandage around his neck entered and saluted. He was a small, soft-haired, blue-eyed man of reckless bearing, with marks of dissipation sharply cut into his face. He saluted, smiling self-consciously.

"Well, Barlow," said Hamilton, "the kitten scratched you, did she?"

"Yes, slightly, and I don't think I've been treated fairly in the matter, sir."

"How so?"

"I stood the brunt and now Captain Farnsworth gets the prize." He twisted his mouth in mock expression of maudlin disappointment. "I'm always cheated out of the sweets. I never get anything for gallant conduct on the field."

"Poor boy! It is a shame. But I say, Lieutenant, has Roussillon really escaped, or is he hidden somewhere in town? Have you been careful?"

"Oh, it's the Indians. They all swear by these Frenchmen. You can't get any help from them against a fellow like Roussillon. In fact they aid him; he's among them now."

"Moral again," Helm interposed; "keep on the good side of the French!"

"That's sensible talk, sir," assented Barlow.

"Bah!" exclaimed Hamilton. "You might as well talk of keeping on the good side of the American traitors—a bloody murrain seize the whole race!"

"That's what I say," chimed in the Lieutenant, with a sly look at Helm.

"They have been telling me a cock-and-bull story concerning the affair at the Roussillon cabin," Hamilton said, changing his manner. "What is this about a disguised and wonderful man who rushed in and upset the whole of you. I want no romancing; give me the facts."

Barlow's dissolute countenance became troubled.

"The facts," he said, speaking with serious deliberation, "are not clear. It was like a clap of thunder, the way that man performed. As you say, he did fling the whole squad all of a heap, and it was done that quickly," he snapped his thumb and finger demonstratively with a sharp report; "nobody could understand it."

Hamilton looked at his subaltern with a smile of unlimited contempt and said:

"A pretty officer of His Majesty's army, you are, Lieutenant Barlow! First a slip of a girl shows herself your superior with the sword and wounds you, then a single man wipes up the floor of a house with you and your guard, depriving you at the same time of both vision and memory, so that you cannot even describe your assailant!"

"He was dressed like a priest," muttered Barlow, evidently frightened at his commander's scathing comment. "That was all there was to see."

"A priest! Some of the men say the devil. I wonder—" Hamilton hesitated and looked at the floor.

"This Father Beret, he is too old for such a thing, isn't he?"

"I have thought of him—it was like him—but he is, as you say, very old to be so tremendously strong and active. Why, I tell you that men went from his hands against the walls and floor as if shot out of a mortar. It was the strangest and most astounding thing I ever heard of."

A little later Barlow seized a favorable opportunity and withdrew. The conversation was not to his liking.

Hamilton sent for Father Beret and had a long talk with him, but the old man looked so childishly inoffensive in spirit and so collapsed physically that it seemed worse than foolishness to accuse him of the exploit over which the entire garrison was wondering. Farnsworth sat by during the interview. He looked the good priest curiously and critically over from head to foot, remembering, but not mentioning, the most unclerical punch in the side received from that energetic right arm now lying so flabbily across the old man's lap.

When the talk ended and Father Beret humbly took his leave, Hamilton turned to Farnsworth and said:

"What do you think of this affair? I have cross-questioned all the men who took part in it, and every one of them says simply priest or devil. I think old Beret is both; but plainly he couldn't hurt a chicken, you can see that at a glance."

Farnsworth smiled, rubbing his side reminiscently; but he shook his head.

"I'm sure it's puzzling, indeed."

Hamilton sat in thoughtful silence for a while, then abruptly changed the subject.

"I think, Captain, that you had better send out Lieutenant Barlow and some of the best woodsmen to kill some game. We need fresh venison, and, by George! I'm not going to depend upon these French traitors any longer. I have set my foot down; they've got to do better or take the consequences." He paused for a breath, then added: "That girl has done too much to escape severest punishment. The garrison will be demoralized if this thing goes on without an example of authority rigidly enforced. I am resolved that there shall be a startling and effective public display of my power to punish. She shot you; you seem to be glad of it, but it was a grave offence. She has stabbed Barlow; that is another serious crime; but worst of all she aided a spy and resisted arrest. She must be punished."

Farnsworth knew Hamilton's nature, and he now saw that Alice was in dreadful danger of death or something even worse. Whenever his chief talked of discipline and the need of maintaining his authority, there was little hope of softening his decisions. Moreover, the provocation to apply extreme measures really seemed sufficient, regarded from a military point of view, and Captain Farnsworth was himself, under ordinary circumstances, a disciplinarian of the strictest class. The fascination, however, by which Alice held him overbore every other influence, and his devotion to her loosened every other tie and obligation to a most dangerous extent. No sooner had he left headquarters and given Barlow his instructions touching the hunting expedition, than his mind began to wander amid visions and schemes by no means consistent with his military obligations. In order to reflect undisturbed he went forth into the dreary, lane-like streets of Vincennes and walked aimlessly here and there until he met Father Beret.

Farnsworth saluted the old man, and was passing him by, when seeing a sword in his hand, half hidden in the folds of his worn and faded cassock, he turned and addressed him.

"Why are you armed this morning, Father?" he demanded very pleasantly. "Who is to suffer now?"

"I am not on the war-path, my son," replied the priest. "It is but a rapier that I am going to clean of rust spots that are gathering on its blade."

"Is it yours, Father? Let me see it." He held out his hand.

"No, not mine."

Father Beret seemed not to notice Farnsworth's desire to handle the weapon, and the young man, instead of repeating his words, reached farther, nearly grasping the scabbard.

"I cannot let you take it, my son," said Father Beret "You have its mate, that should satisfy you."

"No, Colonel Hamilton took it," Farnsworth quickly replied. "If I could I would gladly return it to its owner. I am not a thief, Father, and I am ashamed of—of—what I did when I was drunk."

The priest looked sharply into Farnsworth's eyes and read there something that reassured him. His long experience had rendered him adept at taking a man's value at a glance. He slightly lifted his face and said: "Ah, but the poor little girl! why do you persecute her? She really does not deserve it. She is a noble child. Give her back to her home and her people. Do not soil and spoil her sweet life."

It was the sing-song voice used by Father Beret in his sermons and prayers; but something went with it indescribably touching. Farnsworth felt a lump rise in his throat and his eyes were ready to show tears. "Father," he said, with difficulty making his words distinct, "I would not harm Miss Roussillon to save my own life, and I would do anything—" he paused slightly, then added with passionate force; "I would do anything, no matter what, to save her from the terrible thing that now threatens her."

Father Beret's countenance changed curiously as he gazed at the young man and said:

"If you really mean what you say, you can easily save her, my son."

"Father, by all that is holy, I mean just what I say."

"Swear not at all, my son, but give me your hand."

The two men stood with a tight grip between them and exchanged a long, steady, searching gaze.

A drizzling rain had begun to fall again, with a raw wind creeping from the west.

79

"Come with me to my house, my son," Father Beret presently added; and together they went, the priest covering Alice's sword from the rain with the folds of his cassock.

CHAPTER XV
VIRTUE IN A LOCKET

Long-Hair stood not upon ceremony in conveying to Beverley the information that he was to run the gauntlet, which, otherwise stated, meant that the Indians would form themselves in two parallel lines facing each other about six feet apart, and that the prisoner would be expected to run down the length of the space between, thus affording the warriors an opportunity, greatly coveted and relished by their fiendish natures, to beat him cruelly during his flight. This sort of thing was to the Indians, indeed, an exquisite amusement, as fascinating to them as the theater is to more enlightened people. No sooner was it agreed upon that the entertainment should again be undertaken than all the younger men began to scurry around getting everything ready for it. Their faces glowed with a droll cruelty strange to see, and they further expressed their lively expectations by playful yet curiously solemn antics.

The preparations were simple and quickly made. Each man armed himself with a stick three feet long and about three-quarters of an inch in diameter. Rough weapons they were, cut from boughs of scrub-oak, knotty and tough as horn. Long-Hair unbound Beverley and stripped his clothes from his body down to the waist. Then the lines formed, the Indians in each row standing about as far apart as the width of the space in which the prisoner was to run. This arrangement gave them free use of their sticks and plenty of room for full swing of their lithe bodies.

In removing Beverley's clothes Long-Hair found Alice's locket hanging over the young man's heart. He tore it rudely off and grunted, glaring viciously, first at it, then at Beverley. He seemed to be mightily wrought upon.

"White man damn thief," he growled deep in his throat; "stole from little girl!"

He put the locket in his pouch and resumed his stupidly indifferent expression.

When everything was ready for the delightful entertainment to begin, Long-Hair waved his tomahawk three times over Beverley's head, and pointing down between the waiting lines said:

"Ugh, run!"

But Beverley did not budge. He was standing erect, with his arms, deeply creased where the thongs had sunk, folded across his breast. A rush of thoughts and feelings had taken tumultuous possession of him and he could not move or decide what to do. A mad desire to escape arose in his heart the moment that he saw Long-Hair take the locket. It was as if Alice had cried to him and bidden him make a dash for liberty.

"Ugh, run!"

The order was accompanied with a push of such violence from Long-Hair's left elbow that Beverley plunged and fell, for his limbs, after their long and painful confinement in the raw-hide bonds, were stiff and almost useless. Long-Hair in no gentle voice bade him get up. The shock of falling seemed to awaken his dormant forces; a sudden resolve leaped into his brain. He saw that the Indians had put aside their bows and guns, most of which were leaning against the boles of trees here and yonder. What if he could knock Long-Hair down and run away? This might possibly be easy, considering the Indian's broken arm. His heart jumped at the possibility. But the shrewd savage was alert and saw the thought come into his face.

"You try git 'way, kill dead!" he snarled, lifting his tomahawk ready for a stroke. "Brains out, damn!"

Beverley glanced down the waiting and eager lines. Swiftly he speculated, wondering what would be his chance for escape were he to break through. But he did not take his own condition into account.

"Ugh, run!"

Again the elbow of Long-Hair's hurt arm pushed him toward the expectant rows of Indians, who flourished their clubs and uttered impatient grunts.

This time he did not fall; but in trying to run he limped stiffly at first, his legs but slowly and imperfectly regaining their strength and suppleness from the action. Just before reaching the lines, however, he stopped short. Long-Hair, who was close behind him, took hold of his shoulder and led him back to the starting place. The big Indian's arm must have given him pain when he thus used it, but he did not wince. "Fool—kill dead!" he repeated two or three times, holding his tomahawk on high with threatening motions and frequent repetitions of his one echo from the profanity of civilization. He was beginning to draw his mouth down at the corners, and his eyes were narrowed to mere slits.

Beverley understood now that he could not longer put off the trial. He must choose between certain death and the torture of the gauntlet, as frontiersmen named this savage ordeal. An old man might have preferred the stroke of the hatchet to such an infliction as the clubs must afford, considering that, even after all the agony, his captivity and suffering would be only a little nearer its end. Youth, however, has faith in the turn of fortune's wheel, and faith in itself, no matter how dark the prospect. Hope blows her horn just over the horizon, and the strain bids the young heart take courage and beat strong. Moreover, men were men, who led the van in those days on the outmost lines of our march to the summit of the world. Beverley was not more a hero than any other young, brave, unconquerable patriot of the frontier army. His situation simply tried him a trifle harder than was common. But it must be remembered that he had Love with him, and where Love is there can be no cowardice, no surrender.

Long-Hair once again pushed him and said

"Ugh, run!"

Beverley made a direct dash for the narrow lane between the braced and watchful lines. Every warrior lifted his club; every copper face gleamed stolidly, a mask behind which burned a strangely atrocious spirit. The two savages standing at the end nearest Beverley struck at him the instant he reached than, but they taken quite by surprise when he checked himself between them and, leaping this way and that, swung out two powerful blows, left and right, stretching one of them flat and sending the other reeling and staggering half a dozen paces backward with the blood streaming from his nose.

This done, Beverley turned to run away, but his breath was already short and his strength rapidly going.

Long-Hair, who was at his heels, leaped before him when he had gone but a few steps and once more flourished the tomahawk. To struggle was useless, save to insist upon being brained outright, which just then had no part in Beverley's considerations. Long-Hair kicked his victim heavily, uttering laconic curses meanwhile, and led him back again to the starting-point.

A genuine sense of humor seems almost entirely lacking in the mind of the American Indian. He smiles at things not in the least amusing to us and when he laughs, which is very seldom, the cause of his merriment usually lies in something repellantly cruel and inhuman. When Beverley struck his two assailants, hurting them so that one lay half stunned, while the other spun away from his fist with a smashed nose, all the rest of the Indians grunted and laughed raucously in high delight. They shook their clubs, danced, pointed at their discomfited fellows and twisted their painted faces into knotted wrinkles, their eyes twinkling with devilish expression of glee quite indescribable.

"Ugh, damn, run!" said Long-Half, this time adding a hard kick to the elbow-shove he gave Beverley.

The young man, who had borne all he could, now turned upon him furiously and struck straight from the shoulder, setting the whole weight of his body into the blow. Long-Hair stepped out of the way and quick as a flash brought the flat side of his tomahawk with great force against Beverley's head. This gave the amusement a sudden and disappointing end, for the prisoner fell limp and senseless to the ground. No more running the gauntlet for him that day. Indeed it required protracted application of the best Indian skill to revive him so that he could fairly be called a living man. There had been no dangerous concussion, however, and on the following morning camp was broken.

Beverley, sore, haggard, forlornly disheveled, had his arms bound again and was made to march apace with his nimble enemies, who set out swiftly eastward, their disappointment at having their sport cut short, although bitter enough, not in the least indicated by any facial expression or spiteful act.

Was it really a strange thing, or was it not, that Beverley's mind now busied itself unceasingly with the thought that Long-Hair had Alice's picture in his pouch? One might find room for discussion of a cerebral problem like this; but our history cannot be delayed with analyses and speculations; it must run its direct course unhindered to the end. Suffice it to record that, while tramping at Long-Hair's side and growing more and more desirous of seeing the picture again, Beverley began trying to converse with his taciturn captor. He had a considerable smattering of several Indian dialects, which he turned upon Long-Hair to the best of his ability, but apparently without effect. Nevertheless he babbled at intervals, always upon the same subject and always endeavoring to influence that huge, stolid, heartless savage in the direction of letting him see again the child face of the miniature.

A stone, one of our travel-scarred and mysterious western granite bowlders brought from the far north by the ancient ice, would show as much sympathy as did the face of Long-Hair.

Once in a while he gave Beverley a soulless glance and said "damn" with utter indifference. Nothing, however, could quench or even in the slightest sense allay the lover's desire. He talked of Alice and the locket with constantly increasing volubility, saying over and over phrases of endearment in a half-delirious way, not aware that fever was fermenting his blood and heating his brain. Probably he would have been very ill but for the tremendous physical exercise forced upon him. The exertion kept him in a profuse perspiration and his robust constitution cast off the malarial poison. Meantime he used every word and phrase, every grunt and gesture of Indian dialect that he could recall, in the iterated and reiterated attempt to make Long-Hair understand what he wanted.

When night came on again the band camped under some trees beside a swollen stream. There was no rain falling, but almost the entire country lay under a flood of water. Fires of logs were soon burning brightly on the comparatively dry bluff chosen by the Indians. The weather was chill, but not cold. Long-Hair took great pains, however, to dry Beverley's clothes and see that he had warm wraps and plenty to eat. Hamilton's large reward would not be forthcoming should the prisoner die, Beverley was good property, well worth careful attention. To be sure his scalp, in the worst event, would command a sufficient honorarium, but not the greatest. Beverley thought of all this while the big Indian was wrapping him snugly in skins and blankets for the night, and there was no comfort in it, save that possibly if he were returned to Hamilton he might see Alice again before he died.

A fitful wind cried dolefully in the leafless treetops, the stream hard by gave forth a rushing sound, and far away some wolves howled like lost souls. Worn out, sore from head to foot, Beverley, deep buried in the blankets and skins, soon fell into a profound sleep. The fires slowly crumbled and faded; no sentinel was posted, for the Indians did not fear an attack, there being no enemies that they knew of nearer than Kaskaskia. The camp slumbered as one man.

At about the mid-hour of the night Long-Hair gently awoke his prisoner by drawing a hand across his face, then whispered in his ear:

"Damn, still!"

Beverley tried to rise, uttering a sleepy ejaculation under his breath. "No talk," hissed Long-Hair. "Still!"

There was something in his voice that not only swept the last film of sleep out of Beverley's brain, but made it perfectly clear to him that a very important bit of craftiness was being performed; just what its nature was, however, he could not surmise. One thing was obvious, Long-Hair did not wish the other Indians to know of the move he was making. Deftly he slipped the blankets from around Beverley, and cut the thongs at his ankles.

"Still!" he whispered. "Come 'long."

Under such circumstances a competent mind acts with lightning celerity. Beverley now understood that Long-Hair was stealing him away from the other savages and that the big villain meant to cheat them out of their part of the reward. Along with this discovery came a fresh gleam of hope. It would be far easier to escape from one Indian than from nearly a score. Ah, he would follow Long-Hair, indeed he would! The needed courage came with the thought, and so with immense labor he crept at the heels of that crawling monster. It was a painful process, for his arms were still fast bound at the wrists with the raw-hide strings; but what was pain to him? He shivered with joy, thinking of what might happen. The voice of the wind overhead and the noisy bubbling of the stream near by were cheerful and cheering sounds to him now. So much can a mere shadow of hope do for a human soul on the verge of despair! Already he was planning or trying to plan some way by which he could kill Long-Hair when they should reach a safe distance from the sleeping camp.

But how could the thing be done? A man with his hands tied, though they are in front of him, is in no excellent condition to cope with a free and stalwart savage armed to the teeth. Still Beverley's spirits rose with every rod of distance that was added to their slow progress.

Their course was nearly parallel with that of the stream, but slightly converging toward it, and after they had gone about a furlong they reached the bank. Here Long-Hair stopped and, without a word, cut the thongs from Beverley's wrists. This was astounding; the young man could scarcely realize it, nor was he ready to act.

"Swim water," Long-Hair said in a guttural murmur barely audible. "Swim, damn!"

Again it was necessary for Beverley's mind to act swiftly and with prudence. The camp was yet within hailing distance. A false move now would bring the whole pack howling to the rescue. Something told him to do as Long-Hair ordered, so with scarcely a perceptible hesitation he scrambled down the bushy bank and slipped into the water, followed by Long-Hair, who seized him by one arm when he began to swim, and struck out with him into the boiling and tumbling current.

Beverley had always thought himself a master swimmer, but Long-Hair showed him his mistake. The giant Indian, with but one hand free to use, fairly rushed through that deadly cold and turbulent water, bearing his prisoner with him despite the wounded arm, as easily as if towing him at the stern of a pirogue. True, his course was down stream for a considerable distance, but even when presently he struck out boldly for the other bank, breasting a current in which few swimmers could have lived, much less made headway, he still swung forward rapidly, splitting the waves and scarcely giving Beverley freedom enough so that he could help in the progress. It was a long, cold struggle, and when at last they touched the sloping low bank on the other side, Long-Hair had fairly to lift his chilled and exhausted prisoner to the top.

"Ugh, cold," he grunted, beginning to pound and rub Beverley's arms, legs and body. "Make warm, damn heap!"

All this he did with his right hand, holding the tomahawk in his left.

It was a strange, bewildering experience out of which the young man could not see in any direction far enough to give him a hint upon which to act. In a few minutes Long-Hair jerked him to his feet and said:

"Go."

It was just light enough to see that the order had a tomahawk to enforce it withal. Long-Hair indicated the direction and drove Beverley onward as fast as he could.

"Try run 'way, kill, damn!" he kept repeating, while with his left hand on the young man's shoulder he guided him from behind dexterously through the wood for some distance. Then he stopped and grunted, adding his favorite expletive, which he used with not the least knowledge of its meaning. To him the syllable "damn" was but a mouthful of forcible wind.

They had just emerged from a thicket into an open space, where the ground was comparatively dry. Overhead the stars were shining in great clusters of silver and gold against a dark, cavernous looking sky, here and there overrun with careering black clouds. Beverley shivered, not so much with cold as on account of the stress of excitement which amounted to nervous rigor. Long-Hair faced him and leaned toward him, until his breathing was audible and his massive features were dimly outlined. A dragon of the darkest age could not have been more repulsive.

"Ugh, friend, damn!"

Beverley started when these words were followed by a sentence in an Indian dialect somewhat familiar to him, a dialect in which he had tried to talk with Long-Hair during the day's march. The sentence, literally translated, was:

"Long-Hair is friendly now."

A blow in the face could not have been so surprising. Beverley not only started, but recoiled as if from a sudden and deadly apparition. The step between supreme exhilaration and utter collapse is now and then infinitesimal. There are times, moreover, when an expression on the face of Hope makes her look like the twin sister of Despair. The moment falling just after Long-Hair spoke was a century condensed in a breath.

"Long-Hair is friendly now; will white man be friendly?"

Beverley heard, but the speech seemed to come out of vastness and hollow distance; he could not realize it fairly. He felt as if in a dream, far off somewhere in loneliness, with a big, shadowy form looming before him. He heard the chill wind in the thickets round about, and beyond Long-Hair rose a wall of giant trees.

"Ugh, not understand?" the savage presently demanded in his broken English.

"Yes, yes," said Beverley, "I understand."

"Is the white man friendly now?" Long-Hair then repeated in his own tongue, with a certain insistence of manner and voice.

"Yes, friendly."

Beverley said this absently in a tone of perfunctory dryness. His throat was parched, his head seemed to waver. But he was beginning to comprehend that Long-Hair, for some inscrutable reason of his own, was desirous of making a friendship between them. The thought was bewildering.

Long-Hair fumbled in his pouch and took out Alice's locket, which he handed to Beverley. "White man love little girl?" he inquired in a tone that bordered upon tenderness, again speaking in Indian.

Beverley clutched the disk as soon as he saw it gleam in the star-light.

"White man going to have little girl for his squaw—eh?"

"Yes, yes," cried Beverley without hearing his own voice. He was trying to open the locket but his hands were numb and trembling. When at last he did open it he could not see the child face within, for now even the star-light was shut off by a scudding black cloud.

"Little girl saved Long-Hair's life. Long-Hair save white warrior for little girl."

83

A dignity which was almost noble accompanied these simple sentences. Long-Hair stood proudly erect, like a colossal dark statue in the dimness.

The great truth dawned upon Beverley that here was a characteristic act. He knew that an Indian rarely failed to repay a kindness or an injury, stroke for stroke, when opportunity offered. Long-Hair was a typical Indian. That is to say, a type of inhumanity raised to the last power; but under his hideous atrocity of nature lay the indestructible sense of gratitude so fixed and perfect that it did its work almost automatically.

It must be said, and it may or may not be to the white man's shame, that Beverley did not respond with absolute promptness and sincerity to Long-Hair's generosity. He had suffered terribly at the hands of this savage. His arms and legs were raw from the biting of the thongs; his body ached from the effect of blows and kicks laid upon him while bound and helpless. Perhaps he was not a very emotional man. At all events there was no sudden recognition of the favor he was receiving. And this pleased Long-Hair, for the taste of the American Indian delights in immobility of countenance and reserve of feeling under great strain.

"Wait here a little while," Long-Hair presently said, and without lingering for reply, turned away and disappeared in the wood. Beverley was free to run if he wished to, and the thought did surge across his mind; but a restraining something, like a hand laid upon him, would not let his limbs move. Down deep in his heart a calm voice seemed to be repeating Long-Hair's Indian sentence—"Wait here a little while."

A few minutes later Long-Hair returned bearing two guns, Beverley's and his own, the latter, a superb weapon given him by Hamilton. He afterward explained that he had brought these, with their bullet-pouches and powder-horns, to a place of concealment near by before he awoke Beverley. This meant that he had swum the cold river three times since night-fall; once over with the guns and accouterments; once back to camp, then over again with Beverley! All this with a broken arm, and to repay Alice for her kindness to him.

Beverley may have been slow, but at last his appreciation was, perhaps, all the more profound. As best he could he expressed it to Long-Hair, who showed no interest whatever in the statement. Instead of responding in Indian, he said "damn" without emphasis. It was rather as if he had yawned absently, being bored.

Delay could not be thought of. Long-Hair explained briefly that he thought. Beverley must go to Kaskaskia. He had come across the stream in the direction of Vincennes in order to set his warriors at fault. The stream must be recrossed, he said, farther down, and he would help Beverley a certain distance on his way, then leave him to shift for himself. He had a meager amount of parched corn and buffalo meat in his pouch, which would stay hunger until they could kill some game. Now they must go.

The resilience of a youthful and powerful physique offers many a problem to the biologist. Vital force seems to find some mysterious reservoir of nourishment hidden away in the nerve-centers. Beverley set out upon that seemingly impossible undertaking with renewed energy. It could not have been the ounce of parched corn and bit of jerked venison from which he drew so much strength; but on the other hand, could it have been the miniature of Alice, which he felt pressing over his heart once more, that afforded a subtle stimulus to both mind and body? They flung miles behind them before day-dawn, Long-Hair leading, Beverley pressing close at his heels. Most of the way led over flat prairies covered with water, and they therefore left no track by which they could be followed.

Late in the forenoon Long-Hair killed a deer at the edge of a wood. Here they made a fire and cooked a supply which would last them for a day or two, and then on they went again. But we cannot follow them step by step. When Long-Hair at last took leave of Beverley, the occasion had no ceremony. It was an abrupt, unemotional parting. The stalwart Indian simply said in his own dialect, pointing westward:

"Go that way two days. You will find your friends."

Then, without another look or word, he turned about and stalked eastward at a marvelously rapid gait. In his mind he had a good tale to tell his warrior companions when he should find them again: how Beverley escaped that night and how he followed him a long, long chase, only to lose him at last under the very guns of the fort at Kaskaskia. But before he reached his band an incident of some importance changed his story to a considerable degree. It chanced that he came upon Lieutenant Barlow, who, in pursuit of game, had lost his bearings and, far from his companions, was beating around quite bewildered in a watery solitude. Long-Hair promptly murdered the poor fellow and scalped him with as little compunction as he would have skinned a rabbit; for he had a clever scheme in his head, a very audacious and outrageous scheme, by which he purposed to recoup, to some extent, the damages sustained by letting Beverley go.

84

Therefore, when he rejoined his somewhat disheartened and demoralized band he showed them the scalp and gave them an eloquent account of how he tore it from Beverley's head after a long chase and a bloody hand to hand fight. They listened, believed, and were satisfied.

CHAPTER XVI
FATHER BERET'S OLD BATTLE

The room in which Alice was now imprisoned formed part of the upper story of a building erected by Hamilton in one of the four angles of the stockade. It had no windows and but two oblong port-holes made to accommodate a small swivel, which stood darkly scowling near the middle of the floor. From one of these apertures Alice could see the straggling roofs and fences of the dreary little town, while from the other a long reach of watery prairie, almost a lake, lay under view with the rolling, muddy Wabash gleaming beyond. There seemed to be no activity of garrison or townspeople. Few sounds broke the silence of which the cheerless prison room seemed to be the center.

Alice felt all her courage and cheerfulness leaving her. She was alone in the midst of enemies. No father or mother, no friend—a young girl at the mercy of soldiers, who could not be expected to regard her with any sympathy beyond that which is accompanied with repulsive leers and hints. Day after day her loneliness and helplessness became more agonizing. Farnsworth, it is true, did all he could to relieve the strain of her situation; but Hamilton had an eye upon what passed and soon interfered. He administered a bitter reprimand, under which his subordinate writhed in speechless anger and resentment.

"Finally, Captain Farnsworth," he said in conclusion, "you will distinctly understand that this girl is my prisoner, not yours; that I, not you, will direct how she is to be held and treated, and that hereafter I will suffer no interference on your part. I hope you fully understand me, sir, and will govern yourself accordingly."

Smarting, or rather smothering, under the outrageous insult of these remarks, Farnsworth at first determined to fling his resignation at the Governor's feet and then do whatever desperate thing seemed most to his mood. But a soldier's training is apt to call a halt before the worst befalls in such a case. Moreover, in the present temptation, Farnsworth had a special check and hindrance. He had had a conference with Father Beret, in which the good priest had played the part of wisdom in slippers, and of gentleness more dove like than the dove's. A very subtle impression, illuminated with the "hope that withers hope," had come of that interview; and now Farnsworth felt its restraint. He therefore saluted Hamilton formally and walked away.

Father Beret's paternal love for Alice,—we cannot characterize it more nicely than to call it paternal,—was his justification for a certain mild sort of corruption insinuated by him into the heart of Farnsworth. He was a crafty priest, but his craft was always used for a good end. Unquestionably Jesuitic was his mode of circumventing the young man's military scruples by offering him a puff of fair weather with which to sail toward what appeared to be the shore of delight. He saw at a glance that Farnsworth's love for Alice was a consuming passion in a very ardent yet decidedly weak heart. Here was the worldly lever with which Father Beret hoped to raze Alice's prison and free her from the terrible doom with which she was threatened.

The first interview was at Father Beret's cabin, to which, as will be remembered, the priest and Farnsworth went after their meeting in the street. It actually came to nothing, save an indirect understanding but half suggested by Father Beret and never openly sanctioned by Captain Farnsworth. The talk was insinuating on the part of the former, while the latter slipped evasively from every proposition, as if not able to consider it on account of a curious obtuseness of perception. Still, when they separated they shook hands and exchanged a searching look perfectly satisfactory to both.

The memory of that interview with the priest was in Farnsworth's mind when, boiling with rage, he left Hamilton's presence and went forth into the chill February air. He passed out through the postern and along the sodden and queachy aedge of the prairie, involuntarily making his way to Father Beret's cabin. His indignation was so great that he trembled from head to foot at every step. The door of the place was open and Father Beret was eating a frugal meal of scones and sour wine (of his own make, he said), which he hospitably begged to share with his visitor. A fire smouldered on the hearth, and a flat stone showed, by the grease smoking over its hot surface, where the cakes had been baked.

"Come in, my son," said the priest, "and try the fare of a poor old man. It is plain, very plain, but good." He smacked his lips sincerely and fingered another scone. "Take some, take some."

Farnsworth was not tempted. The acid bouquet of the wine filled the room with a smack of vinegar, and the smoke from rank scorching fat and wheat meal did not suggest an agreeable feast.

"Well, well, if you are not hungry, my son, sit down on the stool there and tell me the news."

Farnsworth took the low seat without a word, letting his eyes wander over the walls. Alice's rapier, the mate to that now worn by Hamilton, hung in its curiously engraved scabbard near one corner. The sight of it inflamed Farnsworth.

"It's an outrage," he broke forth. "Governor Hamilton sent a man to Roussillon place with orders to bring him the scabbard of Miss Roussillon's sword, and he now wears the beautiful weapon as if he had come by it honestly. Damn him!"

"My dear, dear son, you must not soil your lips with such language!" Father Beret let fall the half of a well bitten cake and held up both hands.

"I beg your pardon, Father; I know I ought to be more careful in your presence; but— but—the beastly, hellish scoundrel—"

"Bah! doucement, mon fils, doucement." The old man shook his head and his finger while speaking. "Easy, my son, easy. You would be a fine target for bullets were your words to reach Hamilton's ears. You are not permitted to revile your commander."

"Yes, I know; but how can a man restrain himself under such abominable conditions?"

Father Beret shrewdly guessed that Hamilton had been giving the Captain fresh reason for bitter resentment. Moreover, he was sure that the moving cause had been Alice. So, in order to draw out what he wished to hear, he said very gently:

"How is the little prisoner getting along?"

Farnsworth ground his teeth and swore; but Father Beret appeared not to hear; he bit deep into a scone, took a liberal sip of the muddy red wine and added:

"Has she a comfortable place? Do you think Governor Hamilton would let me visit her?"

"It is horrible!" Farnsworth blurted. "She's penned up as if she were a dangerous beast, the poor girl. And that damned scoundrel—"

"Son, son!"

"Oh, it's no use to try, I can't help it, Father. The whelp—"

"We can converse more safely and intelligently if we avoid profanity, and undue emotion, my son. Now, if you will quit swearing, I will, and if you will be calm, so will I."

Farnsworth felt the sly irony of this absurdly vicarious proposition. Father Beret smiled with a kindly twinkle in his deep-set eyes.

"Well, if you don't use profane language, Father, there's no telling how much you think in expletives. What is your opinion of a man who tumbles a poor, defenseless girl into prison and then refuses to let her be decently cared for? How do you express yourself about him?"

"My son, men often do things of which they ought to be ashamed. I heard of a young officer once who maltreated a little girl that he met at night in the street. What evil he would have done, had not a passing kind-hearted man reminded him of his honor by a friendly punch in the ribs, I dare not surmise."

"True, and your sarcasm goes home as hard as your fist did, Father. I know that I've been a sad dog all my life. Miss Roussillon saved you by shooting me, and I love her for it. Lay on, Father, I deserve more than you can give me."

"Surely you do, my son, surely you do; but my love for you will not let me give you pain. Ah, we priests have to carry all men's loads. Our backs are broad, however, very broad, my son."

"And your fists devilish heavy, Father, devilish heavy."

The gentle smile again flickered over the priest's weather-beaten face as he glanced sidewise at Farnsworth and said:

"Sometimes, sometimes, my son, a carnal weapon must break the way for a spiritual one. But we priests rarely have much physical strength; our dependence is upon—"

"To be sure; certainly," Farnsworth interrupted, rubbing his side, "your dependence is upon the first thing that offers. I've had many a blow; but yours was the solidest that ever jarred thy mortal frame, Father Beret."

The twain began to laugh. There is nothing like a reminiscence to stir up fresh mutual sympathy.

"If your intercostals were somewhat sore for a time, on account of a contact with priestly knuckles, doubtless there soon set in a corresponding uneasiness in the region of your conscience. Such shocks are often vigorously alterative and tonic—eh, my son?"

"You jolted me sober, Father, and then I was ashamed of myself. But where does all your tremendous strength lie? You don't look strong."

While speaking Farnsworth leaned near Father Beret and grasped his arm. The young man started, for his fingers, instead of closing around a flabby, shrunken old man's limb, spread themselves upon a huge, knotted mass of iron muscles. With a quick movement Father Beret shook off Farnsworth's hand, and said:

"I am no Samson, my son. Non sum qualis eram." Then, as if dismissing a light subject for a graver one, he sighed and added; "I suppose there is nothing that can be done for little Alice."

He called the tall, strong girl "little Alice," and so she seemed to him. He could not, without direct effort, think of her as a magnificently maturing woman. She had always been his spoiled pet child, perversely set against the Holy Church, but dear to him nevertheless.

"I came to you to ask that very question, Father," said Farnsworth.

"And what do I know? Surely, my son, you see how utterly helpless an old priest is against all you British. And besides—"

"Father Beret," Farnsworth huskily interrupted, "is there a place that you know of anywhere in which Miss Roussillon could be hidden, if—"

"My dear son."

"But, Father, I mean it."

"Mean what? Pardon an old man's slow understanding. What are you talking about, my son?"

Father Beret glanced furtively about, then quickly stepped through the doorway, walked entirely around the house and came in again before Farnsworth could respond. Once more seated on his stool he added interrogatively:

"Did you think you heard something moving outside?"

"No."

"You were saying something when I went out. Pardon my interruption."

Farnsworth gave the priest a searching and not wholly confiding look.

"You did not interrupt me, Father Beret. I was not speaking. Why are you so watchful? Are you afraid of eavesdroppers?"

"You were speaking recklessly. Your words were incendiary: ardentia verba. My son, you were suggesting a dangerous thing. Your life would scarcely satisfy the law were you convicted of insinuating such treason. What if one of your prowling guards had overheard you? Your neck and mine might feel the halter. Quod avertat dominus." He crossed himself and in a solemn voice added in English:

"May the Lord forbid! Ah, my son, we priests protect those we love."

"And I, who am not fit to tie a priest's shoe, do likewise. Father, I love Alice Roussillon."

"Love is a holy thing, my son. Amare divinum est et humanum."

"Father Beret, can you help me?"

"Spiritually speaking, my son?"

"I mean, can you hide Mademoiselle Roussillon in some safe place, if I take her out of the prison yonder? That's just what I mean. Can you do it?"

"Your question is a remarkable one. Have you thought upon it from all directions, my son? Think of your position, your duty as an officer."

A shrewd polemical expression beamed from Father Beret's eyes, and a very expert physiognomist might have suspected duplicity from certain lines about the old man's mouth.

"I simply know that I cannot stand by and see Alice—Mademoiselle Roussillon, forced to suffer treatment too beastly for an Indian thief. That's the only direction there is for me to look at it from, and you can understand my feelings if you will; you know that very well, Father Beret. When a man loves a girl, he loves her; that's the whole thing.".

The quiet, inscrutable half-smile flickered once more on Father Beret's face; but he sat silent some time with a sinewy forefinger lying alongside his nose. When at last he spoke it was in a tone of voice indicative of small interest in what he was saying. His words rambled to their goal with the effect of happy accident.

"There are places in this neighborhood in which a human being would be as hard to find as the flag that you and Governor Hamilton have so diligently and unsuccessfully been in quest of for the past month or two. Really, my son, this is a mysterious little town."

Farnsworth's eyes widened and a flush rose in his swarthy cheeks.

"Damn the flag!" he exclaimed. "Let it lie hidden forever; what do I care? I tell you, Father Beret, that Alice Roussillon is in extreme danger. Governor Hamilton means to put some terrible punishment on her. He has a devil's vindictiveness. He showed it to me clearly awhile ago."

"You showed something of the same sort to me, once upon a time, my son."

"Yes, I did, Father Beret, and I got a load of slugs in my shoulder for it from that brave girl's pistol. She saved your life. Now I ask you to help me save hers; or, if not her life, what is infinitely more, her honor."

"Her honor!" cried Father Beret, leaping to his feet so suddenly and with such energy that the cabin shook from base to roof. "What do you say, Captain Farnsworth? What do you mean?"

The old man was transformed. His face was terrible to see, with its narrow, burning eyes deep under the shaggy brows, its dark veins writhing snakelike on the temples and forehead, the projected mouth and chin, the hard lines of the jaws, the iron-gray gleam from all the features—he looked like an aged tiger stiffened for a spring.

Farnsworth was made of right soldierly stuff; but he felt a distinct shiver flit along his back. His past life had not lacked thrilling adventures and strangely varied experiences with desperate men. Usually he met sudden emergencies rather calmly, sometimes with phlegmatic indifference. This passionate outburst on the priest's part, however, surprised him and awed him, while it stirred his heart with a profound sympathy unlike anything he had ever felt before.

Father Beret mastered himself in a moment, and passing his hand over his face, as if to brush away the excitement, sat down again on his stool. He appeared to collapse inwardly.

"You must excuse the weakness of an old man, my son," he said, in a voice hoarse and shaking. "But tell me what is going to be done with Alice. Your words—what you said—I did not understand."

He rubbed his forehead slowly, as one who has difficulty in trying to collect his thoughts.

"I do not know what Governor Hamilton means to do, Father Beret. It will be something devilish, however,—something that must not happen," said Farnsworth.

Then he recounted all that Hamilton had done and said. He described the dreary and comfortless room in which Alice was confined, the miserable fare given her, and how she would be exposed to the leers and low remarks of the soldiers. She had already suffered these things, and now that she could no longer have any protection, what was to become of her? He did not attempt to overstate the case; but presented it with a blunt sincerity which made a powerfully realistic impression.

Father Beret, like most men of strong feeling who have been subjected to long years of trial, hardship, multitudinous dangers and all sorts of temptation, and who have learned the lessons of self-control, had an iron will, and also an abiding distrust of weak men. He saw Farnsworth's sincerity; but he had no faith in his constancy, although satisfied that while resentment of Hamilton's imperiousness lasted, he would doubtless remain firm in his purpose to aid Alice. Let that wear off, as in a short time it would, and then what? The old man studied his companion with eyes that slowly resumed their expression of smouldering and almost timid geniality. His priestly experience with desperate men was demanding of him a proper regard for that subtlety of procedure which had so often compassed most difficult ends.

He listened in silence to Farnsworth's story. When it came to an end he began to offer some but half relevant suggestions in the form of indirect cross-questions, by means of which he gradually drew out a minute description of Alice's prison, the best way to reach it, the nature of its door-fastenings, where the key was kept, and everything, indeed, likely to be helpful to one contemplating a jail delivery. Farnsworth was inwardly delighted. He felt Father Beret's cunning approach to the central object and his crafty method of gathering details.

The shades of evening thickened in the stuffy cabin room while the conversation went on. Father Beret presently lifted a puncheon in one corner of the floor and got out a large bottle, which bore a mildewed and faded French label, and with it a small iron cup. There was just light enough left to show a brownish sparkle when, after popping out the cork, he poured a draught in the fresh cup and in his own.

"We may think more clearly, my son, if we taste this old liquor. I have kept it a long while to offer upon a proper occasion. The occasion is here."

A ravishing bouquet quickly imbued the air. It was itself an intoxication.

"The Brothers of St. Martin distilled this liquor," Father Beret added, handing the cup to Farnsworth, "not for common social drinking, my son, but for times when a man needs extraordinary stimulation. It is said to be surpassingly good, because St. Martin blessed the vine."

The doughty Captain felt a sudden and imperious thirst seize his throat. The liquor flooded his veins before his lips touched the cup. He had been abstaining lately; now his besetting appetite rushed upon him. At one gulp he took in the fiery yet smooth and captivating draught. Nor did he notice that Father Beret, instead of joining him in the potation, merely lifted his cup and set it down again, smacking his lips gusto.

There followed a silence, during which the aromatic breath of the bottle increased its dangerous fascination. Then Father Beret again filled Farnsworth's cup and said:

"Ah, the blessed monks, little thought they that their matchless brew would ever be sipped in a poor missionary's hut on the Wabash! But, after all, my son, why not here as well as in sunny France? Our object justifies any impropriety of time and place."

"You are right, Father. I drink to our object. Yes, I say, to our object."

88

In fact, the drinking preceded his speech, and his tongue already had a loop in it The liquor stole through him, a mist of bewildering and enchanting influence. The third cup broke his sentences into unintelligible fragments; the fourth made his underjaw sag loosely, the fifth and sixth, taken in close succession, tumbled him limp on the floor, where he slept blissfully all night long, snugly covered with some of Father Beret's bed clothes.

"Per casum obliquum, et per indirectum," muttered the priest, when he had returned the bottle and cup to their hiding-place." The end justifies the means. Sleep well, my son. Ah, little Alice, little Alice, your old Father will try—will try!"

He fumbled along the wall in the dark until he found the rapier, which he took down; then he went out and sat for some time motionless beside the door, while the clouds thickened overhead. It was late when he arose and glided away shadow-like toward the fort, over which the night hung black, chill and drearily silent. The moon was still some hours high, smothered by the clouds; a fog slowly drifted from the river.

Meantime Hamilton and Helm had spent a part of the afternoon and evening, as usual, at cards. Helm broke off the game and went to his quarters rather early for him, leaving the Governor alone and in a bad temper, because Farnsworth, when he had sent for him, could not be found. Three times his orderly returned in as many hours with the same report; the Captain had not been seen or heard of. Naturally this sudden and complete disappearance, immediately after the reprimand, suggested to Hamilton an unpleasant possibility. What if Farnsworth had deserted him? Down deep in his heart he was conscious that the young man had good cause for almost any desperate action. To lose Captain Farnsworth, however, would be just now a calamity. The Indians were drifting over rapidly to the side of the Americans, and every day showed that the French could not long be kept quiet.

Hamilton sat for some time after Helm's departure, thinking over what he now feared was a foolish mistake. Presently he buckled on Alice's rapier, which he had lately been wearing as his own, and went out into the main area of the stockade. A sentinel was tramping to and fro at the gate, where a hazy lantern shone. The night was breathless and silent. Hamilton approached the soldier on duty and asked him if he had seen Captain Farnsworth, and receiving a negative reply, turned about puzzled and thoughtful to walk back and forth in the chill, foggy air.

Presently a faint yellow light attracted his attention. It shone through a porthole in an upper room of the block-house at the farther angle of the stockade. In fact, Alice was reading by a sputtering lamp a book Farnsworth had sent her, a volume of Ronsard that he had picked up in Canada. Hamilton made his way in that direction, at first merely curious to know who was burning oil so late; but after a few paces he recognized where the light came from, and instantly suspected that Captain Farnsworth was there. Indeed he felt sure of it. Somehow he could not regard Alice as other than a saucy hoyden, incapable of womanly virtue. His experience with the worst element of Canadian French life and his peculiar cast of mind and character colored his impression of her. He measured her by the women with whom the coureurs de bois and half-breed trappers consorted in Detroit and at the posts eastward to Quebec.

Alice, unable to sleep, had sought forgetfulness of her bitter captivity in the old poet's charming lyrics. She sat on the floor, some blankets and furs drawn around her, the book on her lap, the stupidly dull lamp hanging beside her on a part of the swivel. Her hair lay loose over her neck and shoulders and shimmered around her face with a cloud-like effect, giving to the features in their repose a setting that intensified their sweetness and sadness. In a very low but distinct voice was reading, with a slightly quavering emotion:

"Mignonne,   allons   voir   si   la   rose,
Que   ce   matin   avoit   desclose
Sa robe de pourpe au soleil."

When Hamilton, after stealthily mounting the rough stairway which led to her door, peeped in through a space between the slabs and felt a stroke of disappointment, seeing at a glance that Farnsworth was not there. He gazed for some time, not without a sense of villainy, while she continued her sweetly monotonous reading. If his heart had been as hard as the iron swivel-balls that lay beside Alice, he must still have felt a thrill of something like tender sympathy. She now showed no trace of the vivacious sauciness which had heretofore always marked her features when she was in his presence. A dainty gentleness, touched with melancholy, gave to her face an appealing look all the more powerful on account of its unconscious simplicity of expression.

The man felt an impulse pure and noble, which would have borne him back down the ladder and away from the building, had not a stronger one set boldly in the opposite direction. There was a short struggle with the seared remnant of his better nature, and then he tried to open the door; but it was locked.

Alice heard the slight noise and breaking off her reading turned to look. Hamilton made another effort to enter before he recollected that the wooden key, or notched lever, that controlled the cumbrous wooden lock, hung on a peg beside the door. He felt for it along the wall, and soon laid his hand on it. Then again he peeped through to see Alice, who was now standing upright near the swivel. She had thrown her hair back from her face and neck; the lamp's flickering light seemed suddenly to have magnified her stature and enhanced her beauty. Her book lay on the tumbled wraps at her feet, and in either hand she grasped a swivel-shot.

Hamilton's combative disposition came to the aid of his baser passion when he saw once more a defiant flash from his prisoner's face. It was easy for him to be fascinated by opposition. Helm had profited by this trait as much as others had suffered by it; but, in the case of Alice, Hamilton's mingled resentment and admiration were but a powerful irritant to the coarsest and most dangerous side of his nature.

After some fumbling and delay he fitted the key with a steady hand and moved the wooden bolt creaking and jolting from its slot. Then flinging the clumsy door wide open, he stepped in.

Alice started when she recognized the midnight intruder, and a second deeper look into his countenance made her brave heart recoil, while with a sinking sensation her breath almost stopped. It was but a momentary weakness, however, followed by vigorous reaction.

"What are you here for, sir?" she demanded. "What do you want?"

"I am neither a burglar nor a murderer, Mademoiselle," he responded, lifting his hat and bowing, with a smile not in the least reassuring.

"You look like both. Stop where you are!"

"Not so loud, my dear Miss Roussillon; I am not deaf. And besides the garrison needs to sleep."

"Stop, sir; not another step."

She poised herself, leaning slightly backward, and held the iron ball in her right hand ready to throw it at him.

He halted, still smiling villainously.

"Mademoiselle, I assure you that your excitement is quite unnecessary. I am not here to harm you."

"You cannot harm me, you cowardly wretch!"

"Humph! Pride goes before a fall, wench," he retorted, taking a half-step backward. Then a thought arose in his mind which added a new shade to the repellent darkness of his countenance.

"Miss Roussillon," he said in English and with a changed voice, which seemed to grow harder, each word deliberately emphasized, "I have come to break some bad news to you."

"You would scarcely bring me good news, sir, and I am not curious to hear the bad."

He was silent for a little while, gazing at her with the sort of admiration from which a true woman draws away appalled. He saw how she loathed him, saw how impossible it was for him to get a line nearer to her by any turn of force or fortune. Brave, high-headed, strong as a young leopard, pure and sweet as a rose, she stood before him fearless, even aggressive, showing him by every line of her face and form that she felt her infinite superiority and meant to maintain it. Her whole personal expression told him he was defeated; therefore he quickly seized upon a suggestion caught from a transaction with Long-Hair, who had returned a few hours before from his pursuit of Beverley.

"It pains me, I assure you, Miss Roussillon, to tell you what will probably grieve you deeply," he presently added; "but I have not been unaware of your tender interest in Lieutenant Beverley, and when I had bad news from him, I thought it my duty to inform you."

He paused, feeling with a devil's satisfaction the point of his statement go home to the girl's heart.

The wind was beginning to blow outside, shaking open the dark clouds and letting gleams of moonlight flicker on the thinning fog. A ghostly ray came through a crack between the logs and lit Alice's face with a pathetic wanness. She moved her lips as if speaking, but Hamilton heard no sound.

"The Indian, Long-Hair, whom I sent upon Lieutenant Beverley's trail, reported to me this afternoon that his pursuit had been quite successful. He caught his game."

Alice's voice came to her now. She drew in a quivering breath of relief.

"Then he is here—he is—you have him a prisoner again?"

"A part of him, Miss Roussillon. Enough to be quite sure that there is one traitor who will trouble his king no more. Mr. Long-Hair brought in the Lieutenant's scalp."

Alice received this horrible statement in silence; but her face blanched and she stood as if frozen by the shock. The shifty moon-glimmer and the yellow glow of the lamp showed

Hamilton to what an extent his devilish cruelty hurt her, and somehow it chilled him as if by reflection; but he could not forego another thrust.

"He deserved hanging, and would have got it had he been brought to me alive. So after all, you should be satisfied. He escaped my vengeance and Long-Hair got his pay. You see I am the chief sufferer."

These words, however, fell without effect upon the girl's ears, in which was booming the awful, storm-like roar of her excitement. She did not see her persecutor standing there; her vision, unhindered by walls and distance, went straight away to a place in the wilderness, where all mangled and disfigured Beverley lay dead. A low cry broke from her lips; she dropped the heavy swivel-balls; and then, like a bird, swiftly, with a rustling swoop, she went past Hamilton and down the stair.

For perhaps a full minute the man stood there motionless, stupefied, amazed; and when at length he recovered himself, it was with difficulty that he followed her. Everything seemed to hinder him. When he reached the open air, however, he quickly regained his activity of both mind and body, and looked in all directions. The clouds were breaking into parallel masses with streaks of sky between. The moon hanging aslant against the blue peeped forth just in time to show him a flying figure which, even while he looked, reached the postern, opened it and slipped through.

With but a breath of hesitation between giving the alarm and following Alice silently and alone, he chose the latter. He was a swift runner and light footed. With a few bounds he reached the little gate, which was still oscillating on its hinges, darted through and away, straining every muscle in desperate pursuit, gaining rapidly in the race, which bore eastward along the course twice before chosen by Alice in leaving the stockade.

CHAPTER XVII.
A MARCH THROUGH COLD WATER

On the fifth day of February, 1779, Colonel George Rogers Clark led an army across the Kaskaskia River and camped. This was the first step in his march towards the Wabash. An army! Do not smile. Fewer than two hundred men, it is true, answered the roll-call, when Father Gibault lifted the Cross and blessed them; but every name told off by the company sergeants belonged to a hero, and every voice making response struck a full note in the chorus of freedom's morning song.

It was an army, small indeed, but yet an army; even though so rudely equipped that, could we now see it before us, we might wonder of what use it could possibly be in a military way.

We should nevertheless hardly expect that a hundred and seventy of our best men, even if furnished with the latest and most deadly engines of destruction, could do what those pioneers cheerfully undertook and gloriously accomplished in the savage wilderness which was to be the great central area of the United States of America.

We look back with a shiver of awe at the three hundred Spartans for whom Simonides composed his matchless epitaph. They wrought and died gloriously; that was Greek. The one hundred and seventy men, who, led by the backwoodsman, Clark, made conquest of an empire's area for freedom in the west, wrought and lived gloriously; that was American. It is well to bear in mind this distinction by which our civilization separates itself from that of old times. Our heroism has always been of life—our heroes have conquered and lived to see the effect of conquest. We have fought all sorts of wars and have never yet felt defeat. Washington, Jackson, Taylor, Grant, all lived to enjoy, after successful war, a triumphant peace. "These Americans," said a witty Frenchman, "are either enormously lucky, or possessed of miraculous vitality. You rarely kill them in battle, and if you wound them their wounds are never mortal. Their history is but a chain of impossibilities easily accomplished. Their undertakings have been without preparation, their successes in the nature of stupendous accidents." Such a statement may appear critically sound from a Gallic point of view; but it leaves out the dominant element of American character, namely, heroic efficiency. From the first we have had the courage to undertake, the practical common sense which overcomes the lack of technical training, and the vital force which never flags under the stress of adversity.

Clark knew, when he set out on his march to Vincennes, that he was not indulging a visionary impulse. The enterprise was one that called for all that manhood could endure, but not more. With the genius of a born leader he measured his task by his means. He knew his own courage and fortitude, and understood the best capacity of his men. He had genius; that is, he possessed the secret of extracting from himself and from his followers the last refinement of devotion to purpose. There was a certainty, from first to last, that effort would not flag at any point short of the top-most possible strain.

The great star of America was no more than a nebulous splendor on the horizon in 1779. It was a new world forming by the law of youth. The men who bore the burdens of its exacting life were mostly stalwart striplings who, before the down of adolescence fairly sprouted on their chins, could swing the ax, drive a plow, close with a bear or kill an Indian. Clark was not yet twenty-seven when he made his famous campaign. A tall, brawny youth, whose frontier experience had enriched a native character of the best quality, he marched on foot at the head of his little column, and was first to test every opposing danger. Was there a stream to wade or swim? Clark enthusiastically shouted, "Come on!" and in he plunged. Was there a lack of food? "I'm not hungry," he cried. "Help yourselves, men!" Had some poor soldier lost his blanket? "Mine is in my way," said Clark. "Take it, I'm glad to get rid of it!" His men loved him, and would die rather than fall short of his expectations.

The march before them lay over a magnificent plain, mostly prairie, rich as the delta of the Nile, but extremely difficult to traverse. The distance, as the route led, was about a hundred and seventy miles. On account of an open and rainy winter all the basins and flat lands were inundated, often presenting leagues of water ranging in depth from a few inches to three of four feet. Cold winds blew, sometimes with spits of snow and dashes of sleet, while thin ice formed on the ponds and sluggish streams. By day progress meant wading ankle-deep, knee-deep, breast-deep, with an occasional spurt of swimming. By night the brave fellows had to sleep, if sleep they could, on the cold ground in soaked clothing under water-heavy blankets. They flung the leagues behind them, however, cheerfully stimulating one another by joke and challenge, defying all the bitterness of weather, all the bitings of hunger, all the toil, danger and deprivation of a trackless and houseless wilderness, looking only eastward, following their youthful and intrepid commander to one of the most valuable victories gained by American soldiers during the War of the Revolution.

Colonel Clark understood perfectly the strategic importance of Vincennes as a post commanding the Wabash, and as a base of communication with the many Indian tribes north of the Ohio and east of the Mississippi. Francis Vigo (may his name never fade!) had brought him a comprehensive and accurate report of Hamilton's strength and the condition of the fort and garrison. This information confirmed his belief that it would be possible not only to capture Vincennes, but Detroit as well.

Just seven days after the march began, the little army encamped for a night's rest at the edge of a wood; and here, just after nightfall, when the fires were burning merrily and the smell of broiling buffalo steaks burdened the damp air, a wizzened old man suddenly appeared, how or from where nobody had observed He was dirty and in every way disreputable in appearance, looking like an animated mummy, bearing a long rifle on his shoulder, and walking with the somewhat halting activity of a very old, yet vivacious and energetic simian. Of course it was Oncle Jason, "Oncle Jazon sui generis," as Father Beret had dubbed him.

"Well, here I am!" he cried, approaching the fire by which Colonel Clark and some of his officers were cooking supper, "but ye can't guess in a mile o' who I am to save yer livers and lights."

He danced a few stiff steps, which made the water gush out of his tattered moccasins, then doffed his nondescript cap and nodded his scalpless head in salutation to the commander.

Clark looked inquiringly at him, while the old fellow grimaced and rubbed his shrunken chin.

"I smelt yer fat a fryin' somepin like a mile away, an' it set my in'ards to grumblin' for a snack; so I jes thought I'd drap in on ye an' chaw wittles wi' ye."

"Your looks are decidedly against you," remarked the Colonel with a dry smile. He had recognized Oncle Jazon after a little sharp scrutiny. "I suppose, however, that we can let you gnaw the bones after we've got off the meat."

"Thank 'ee, thank 'ee, plenty good. A feller 'at's as hongry as I am kin go through a bone like a feesh through water."

Clark laughed and said:

"I don't see any teeth that you have worth mentioning, but your gums may be unusually sharp."

"Ya-a-s, 'bout as sharp as yer wit, Colonel Clark, an' sharper'n yer eyes, a long shot. Ye don't know me, do ye? Take ernother squint at me, an' see'f ye kin 'member a good lookin' man!"

"You have somewhat the appearance of an old scamp by the name of Jazon that formerly loafed around with a worthless gun on his shoulder, and used to run from every Indian he saw down yonder in Kentucky." Clark held out his hand and added cordially:

"How are you, Jazon, my old friend, and where upon earth have you come from?"

Oncle Jazon pounced upon the hand and gripped it in his own knotted fingers, gazing delightedly up into Clark's bronzed and laughing face.

"Where'd I come frum? I come frum ever'wheres. Fust time I ever got lost in all my born days. I've been a trompin' 'round in the water seems like a week, crazy as a pizened rat, not a knowin' north f'om south, ner my big toe f'om a turnip! Who's got some tobacker?"

Oncle Jazon's story, when presently he told it, interested Clark deeply. In the first place he was glad to hear that Simon Kenton had once more escaped from the Indians; and the news from Beverley, although bad enough, left room for hope. Frontiersmen always regarded the chances better than even, so long as there was life. Oncle Jazon, furthermore, had much to tell about the situation at Vincennes, the true feeling of the French inhabitants, the lukewarm friendship of the larger part of the Indians for Hamilton, and, indeed, everything that Clark wished to know regarding the possibilities of success in his arduous undertaking. The old man's advent cheered the whole camp. He soon found acquaintances and friends among the French volunteers from Kaskaskia, with whom he exchanged creole gestures and chatter with a vivacity apparently inexhaustible. He and Kenton had, with wise judgement, separated on escaping from the Indian camp, Kenton striking out for Kentucky, while Oncle Jazon went towards Kaskaskia.

The information that Beverley would be shot as soon as he was returned to Hamilton, caused Colonel Clark serious worry of mind. Not only the fact that Beverley, who had been a charming friend and a most gallant officer, was now in such imminent danger, but the impression (given by Oncle Jazon's account) that he had broken his parole, was deeply painful to the brave and scrupulously honorable commander. Still, friendship rose above regret, and Clark resolved to push his little column forward all the more rapidly, hoping to arrive in time to prevent the impending execution.

Next morning the march was resumed at the break of dawn; but a swollen stream caused some hours of delay, during which Beverley himself arrived from the rear, a haggard and weirdly unkempt apparition. He had been for three days following hard on the army's track, which he came to far westward. Oncle Jazon saw him first in the distance, and his old but educated eyes made no mistake.

"Yander's that youngster Beverley," he exclaimed. "Ef it ain't I'm a squaw!"

Nor did he parley further on the subject; but set off at a rickety trot to meet and assist the fagged and excited young man.

Clark had given Oncle Jazon his flask, which contained a few gills of whisky. This was the first thing offered to Beverley; who wisely took but a swallow. Oncle Jazon was so elated that he waved his cap on high, and unconsciously falling into French, yelled in a piercing voice:

"VIVE ZHORSH VASINTON! VIVE LA BANNIERE D'ALICE ROUSSILLON!"

Seeing Beverley reminded him of Alice and the flag. As for Beverley, the sentiment braced him, and the beloved name brimmed his heart with sweetness.

Clark went to meet them as they came in. He hugged the gaunt Lieutenant with genuine fervor of joy, while Oncle Jazon ran around them making a series of grotesque capers. The whole command, hearing Oncle Jazon's patriotic words, set up a wild shouting on the spur of a general impression that Beverley came as a messenger bearing glorious news from Washington's army in the east.

It was a great relief to Clark when he found out that his favorite Lieutenant had not broken his parole; but had instead boldly resurrendered himself, declaring the obligation no longer binding, and notifying Hamilton of his intention to go away with the purpose of returning and destroying him and his command. Clark laughed heartily when this explanation brought out Beverley's tender interest in Alice; but he sympathized cordially; for he himself knew what love is.

Although Beverley was half starved and still suffering from the kicks and blows given him by Long-Hair and his warriors, his exhausting run on the trail of Clark aad his band had not worked him serious harm. All of the officers and men did their utmost to serve him. He was feasted without stint and furnished with everything that the scant supply of clothing on the pack horses could afford for his comfort. He promptly asked for an assignment to duty in his company and took his place with such high enthusiasm that his companions regarded him with admiring wonder. None of them save Clark and Oncle Jazon suspected that love for a fair-haired girl yonder in Vincennes was the secret of his amazing zeal and intrepidity.

In one respect Clark's expedition was sadly lacking in its equipment for the march. It had absolutely no means of transporting adequate supplies. The pack-horses were not able to carry more than a little extra ammunition, a few articles of clothing, some simple cooking utensils and such tools as were needed in improvising rafts and canoes. Consequently, although buffalo and deer were sometimes plentiful, they furnished no lasting supply of meat, because it could not be transported; and as the army neared Vincennes wild animals became scarce, so that the men began to suffer from hunger when within but a few days of their journey's end.

Clark made almost superhuman efforts in urging forward his chilled, water-soaked, foot-sore command; and when hunger added its torture to the already disheartening conditions, his courage and energy seemed to burn stronger and brighter. Beverley was always at his side ready to undertake any task, accept any risk; his ardor made his face glow, and he seemed to thrive upon hardships. The two men were a source of inspiration—their followers could not flag and hesitate while under the influence of their example.

Toward the end of the long march a decided fall of temperature added ice to the water through which our dauntless patriots waded and swam for miles. The wind shifted northwesterly, taking on a searching chill. Each gust, indeed, seemed to shoot wintry splinters into the very marrow of the men's bones. The weaker ones began to show the approach of utter exhaustion just at the time when a final spurt of unflinching power was needed. True, they struggled heroically; but nature was nearing the inexorable limit of endurance. Without food, which there was no prospect of getting, collapse was sure to come.

Standing nearly waist-deep in freezing water and looking out upon the muddy, sea-like flood that stretched far away to the channel of the Wabash and beyond, Clark turned to Beverley and said, speaking low, so as not to be overheard by any other of his officers or men:

"Is it possible, Lieutenant Beverley, that we are to fail, with Vincennes almost in sight of us?"

"No, sir, it is not possible," was the firm reply. "Nothing must, nothing can stop us. Look at that brave child! He sets the heroic example."

Beverley pointed, as he spoke, at a boy but fourteen years old, who was using his drum as a float to bear him up while he courageously swam beside the men.

Clark's clouded face cleared once more. "You are right," he said, "come on! we must win or die."

"Sergeant Dewit," he added, turning to an enormously tall and athletic man near by, "take that little drummer and his drum on your shoulder and lead the way. And, sergeant, make him pound that drum like the devil beating tan-bark!"

The huge man caught the spirit of his commander's order. In a twinkling he had the boy astride of his neck with the kettle-drum resting on his head, and then the rattling music began. Clark followed, pointing onward with his sword. The half frozen and tottering soldiers sent up a shout that went back to where Captain Bowman was bringing up the rear under orders to shoot every man that straggled or shrank from duty.

Now came a time when not a mouthful of food was left. A whole day they floundered on, starving, growing fainter at every step, the temperature falling, the ice thickening. They camped on high land; and next morning they heard Hamilton's distant sunrise gun boom over the water.

"One half-ration for the men," said Clark, looking disconsolately in the direction whence the sound had come. "Just five mouthfuls apiece, even, and I'll have Hamilton and his fort within forty-eight hours."

"We will have the provisions, Colonel, or I will die trying to get them," Beverley responded "Depend upon me."

They had constructed some canoes in which to transport the weakest of the men.

"I will take a dugout and some picked fellows. We will pull to the wood yonder, and there we shall find some kind of game which has been forced to shelter from the high water."

It was a cheerful view of a forlorn hope. Clark grasped the hand extended by Beverley and they looked encouragement into each other's eyes.

Oncle Jazon volunteered to go in the pirogue. He was ready for anything, everything.

"I can't shoot wo'th a cent," he whined, as they took their places in the cranky pirogue; "but I might jes' happen to kill a squir'l or a elephant or somepin 'nother."

"Very well," shouted Clark in a loud, cheerful voice, when they had paddled away to a considerable distance, "bring the meat to the woods on the hill yonder," pointing to a distant island-like ridge far beyond the creeping flood. "We'll be there ready to eat it!"

He said this for the ears of his men. They heard and answered with a straggling but determined chorus of approval. They crossed the rolling current of the Wabash by a tedious process of ferrying, and at last found themselves once more wading in back-water up to their armpits, breaking ice an inch thick as they went. It was the closing struggle to reach the high wooded lands. Many of them fell exhausted; but their stronger comrades lifted them, holding their heads above water, and dragged them on.

Clark, always leading, always inspiring, was first to set foot on dry land. He shouted triumphantly, waved his sword, and then fell to helping the men out of the freezing flood. This accomplished, he ordered fires built; but there was not a soldier of them all whose hands could clasp an ax-handle, so weak and numbed with cold were they. He was not to be baffled, however. If fire could not be had, exercise must serve its purpose. Hastily pouring some powder into his hand he dampened it and blacked his face. "Victory, men, victory!" he shouted, taking off his hat and beginning to leap and dance. "Come on! We'll have a war dance and then a feast, as soon as the meat arrives that I have sent for. Dance! you brave lads, dance! Victory! victory!"

The strong men, understanding their Colonel's purpose, took hold of the delicate ones; and the leaping, the capering, the tumult of voices and the stamping of slushy moccasins with which they assaulted that stately forest must have frightened every wild thing thereabout into a deadly rigor, dark's irrepressible energy and optimism worked a veritable charm upon his faithful but almost dying companions in arms. Their trust in him made them feel sure that food would soon be forthcoming. The thought afforded a stimulus more potent than wine; it drove them into an ecstasy of frantic motion and shouting which soon warmed them thoroughly.

It is said that fortune favors the brave. The larger meaning of the sentence may be given thus: God guards those who deserve His protection. History tells us that just when Clark halted his command almost in sight of Vincennes—just when hunger was about to prevent the victory so close to his grasp—a party of his scouts brought in the haunch of a buffalo captured from some Indians. The scouts were Lieutenant Beverley and Oncle Jazon. And with the meat they brought Indian kettles in which to cook it.

With consummate forethought Clark arranged to prevent his men doing themselves injury by bolting their food or eating it half-cooked. Broth was first made and served hot; then small bits of well broiled steak were doled out, until by degrees the fine effect of nourishment set in, and all the command felt the fresh courage of healthy reaction.

"I ain't no gin'ral, nor corp'ral, nor nothin'," remarked Oncle Jazon to Colonel Clark, "but 'f I's you I'd h'ist up every dad dinged ole flag in the rig'ment, w'en I got ready to show myself to 'em, an' I'd make 'em think, over yander at the fort, 'at I had 'bout ninety thousan' men. Hit'd skeer that sandy faced Gov'nor over there till he'd think his back-bone was a comin' out'n 'im by the roots."

Clark laughed, but his face showed that the old man's suggestion struck him forcibly and seriously.

"We'll see about that presently, Oncle Jazon. Wait till we reach the hill yonder, from which the whole town can observe our manoeuvres, then we'll try it, maybe."

Once more the men were lined up, the roll-call gone through with satisfactorily, and the question put: "Are we ready for another plunge through the mud and water?"

The answer came in the affirmative, with a unanimity not to be mistaken. The weakest heart of them all beat to the time of the charge step. Again Clark and Beverley clasped hands and took the lead.

When they reached the next high ground they gazed in silence across a slushy prairie plot to where, on a slight elevation, old Vincennes and Fort Sackville lay in full view.

Beverley stood apart. A rush of sensations affected him so that he shook like one whose strength is gone. His vision was blurred. Fort and town swimming in a mist were silent and still. Save the British flag twinkling above Hamilton's headquarters, nothing indicated that the place was not deserted. And Alice? With the sweet name's echo Beverley's heart bounded high, then sank fluttering at the recollection that she was either yonder at the mercy of Hamilton, or already the victim of an unspeakable cruelty. Was it weakness for him to lift his clasped hands heavenward and send up a voiceless prayer?

While he stood thus Oncle Jazon came softly to his side and touched his arm. Beverley started.

"The nex' thing'll be to shoot the everlastin' gizzards outen 'em, won't it?" the old man inquired. "I'm jes' a eetchin' to git a grip onto that Gov'nor. Ef I don't scelp 'em I'm a squaw."

Beverley drew a deep breath and came promptly back from his dream. It was now Oncle Jazon's turn to assume a reflective, reminiscent mood. He looked about him with an expression of vague half tenderness on his shriveled features.

"I's jes' a thinkin' how time do run past a feller," he presently remarked. "Twenty-seven years ago I camped right here wi' my wife—ninth one, ef I 'member correct—jes' fresh married to 'r; sort o' honey-moon. 'Twus warm an' sunshiny an' nice. She wus a poorty squaw, mighty poorty, an' I wus as happy as a tomtit on a sugar-trough. We b'iled sap yander on them nobs under the maples. It wus glor'us. Had some several wives 'fore an' lots of 'm sence; but she wus sweetes' of 'm all. Strange how a feller 'members sich things an' feels sort o' lonesome like!"

The old man's mouth drooped at the corners and he hitched up his buckskin trousers with a ludicrous suggestion of pathos in every line of his attitude. Unconsciously he sidled closer to Beverley, remotely feeling that he was giving the young man very effective sympathy, well knowing that Alice was the sweet burden of his thoughts. It was thus Oncle Jazon honestly tried to fortify his friend against what probably lay in store for him.

95

But Beverley failed to catch the old man's crude comfort thus flung at him. The analogy was not apparent. Oncle Jazon probably felt that his kindness had been ineffectual, for he changed his tone and added:

"But I s'pose a young feller like ye can't onderstan' w'at it is to love a 'oman an' 'en hev 'er quit ye for 'nother feller, an' him a buck Injin. Wall, wall, wall, that's the way it do go! Of all the livin' things upon top o' this yere globe, the mos' onsartin', crinkety-crankety an' slippery thing is a young 'oman 'at knows she's poorty an' 'at every other man in the known world is blind stavin' crazy in love wi' 'er, same as you are. She'll drop ye like a hot tater 'fore ye know it, an' 'en look at ye jes' pine blank like she never knowed ye afore in her life. It's so, Lieutenant, shore's ye'r born. I know, for I've tried the odd number of 'em, an' they're all jes' the same."

By this time Beverley's ears were deaf to Oncle Jazon's querulous, whining voice, and his thoughts once more followed his wistful gaze across the watery plain to where the low roofs of the creole town appeared dimly wavering in the twilight of eventide, which was fast fading into night. The scene seemed unsubstantial; he felt a strange lethargy possessing his soul; he could not realize the situation. In trying to imagine Alice, she eluded him, so that a sort of cloudy void fell across his vision with the effect of baffling and benumbing it. He made vain efforts to recall her voice, things that she had said to him, her face, her smiles; all he could do was to evoke an elusive, tantalizing, ghostly something which made him shiver inwardly with a haunting fear that it meant the worst, whatever the worst might be. Where was she? Could she be dead, and this the shadowy message of her fate?

Darkness fell, and a thin fog began to drift in wan streaks above the water. Not a sound, save the suppressed stir of the camp, broke the wide, dreary silence. Oncle Jazon babbled until satisfied that Beverley was unappreciative, or at least unresponsive.

"Got to hev some terbacker," he remarked, and shambled away in search of it among his friends.

A little later Clark approached hastily and said:

"I have been looking for you. The march has begun. Bowman and Charleville are moving; come, there's no time to lose."

CHAPTER XVIII
A DUEL BY MOONLIGHT

When Hamilton, after running some distance, saw that he was gaining upon Alice and would soon overtake her, it added fresh energy to his limbs. He had quickly realized the foolishness of what he had done in visiting the room of his prisoner at so late an hour in the night. What would his officers and men think? To let Alice escape would be extremely embarrassing, and to be seen chasing her would give good ground for ridicule on the part of his entire command. Therefore his first thought, after passing through the postern and realizing fully what sort of predicament threatened him, was to recapture her and return her to the prison room in the block-house without attracting attention. This now promised to be an easier task than he had at first feared; for in the moonlight, which on account of the dispersing clouds, was fast growing stronger, he saw her seem to falter and weaken. Certainly her flight was checked and took an eccentric turn, as if some obstruction had barred her way. He rushed on, not seeing that, as Alice swerved, a man intervened. Indeed he was within a few strides of laying his hand on her when he saw her make the strange movement. It was as if, springing suddenly aside, she had become two persons instead of one. But instantly the figures coincided again, and in becoming taller faced about and confronted him.

Hamilton stopped short in his tracks. The dark figure was about five paces from him. It was not Alice, and a sword flashed dimly but unmistakably in a ray of the moon. The motion visible was that of an expert swordsman placing himself firmly on his legs, with his weapon at guard.

Alice saw the man in her path just in time to avoid running against him. Lightly as a flying bird, when it whisks itself in a short semicircle past a tree or a bough, she sprang aside and swung around to the rear of him, where she could continue her course toward the town. But in passing she recognized him. It was Father Beret, and how grim he looked! The discovery was made in the twinkling of an eye, and its effect was instantaneous, not only checking the force of her flight, but stopping her and turning her about to gaze before she had gone five paces farther.

Hamilton's nerve held, startled as he was, when he realized that an armed man stood before him. Naturally he fell into the error of thinking that he had been running after this fellow all the way from the little gate, where, he supposed, Alice had somehow given him the slip. It was a mere flash of brain-light, so to call it, struck out by the surprise of this curious discovery. He felt his bellicose temper leap up furiously at being balked in a way so unexpected and withal so inexplicable. Of course he did not stand there reasoning it all out. The rush of impressions came, and at the same time he acted with promptness. Changing the rapier, which he held in his right hand, over into his left, he drew a small pistol from the breast of his coat and fired. The report was sharp and loud; but it caused no uneasiness or inquiry in the fort, owing to the fact that Indians invariably emptied their guns when coming into the town.

Hamilton's aim, although hasty, was not bad. The bullet from his weapon cut through Father Beret's clothes between his left arm and his body, slightly creasing the flesh on a rib. Beyond him it struck heavily and audibly. Alice fell limp and motionless to the soft wet ground, where cold puddles of water were splintered over with ice. She lay pitifully crumpled, one arm outstretched in the moonlight. Father Beret heard the bullet hit her, and turned in time to see her stagger backward with a hand convulsively pressed over her heart. Her face, slightly upturned as she reeled, gave the moon a pallid target for its strengthening rays. Sweet, beautiful, its rigid features flashed for a second and then half turned away from the light and went down.

Father Beret uttered a short, thin cry and moved as if to go to the fallen girl, but just then he saw Hamilton's sword pass over again into his right hand, and knew that there was no time for anything but death or fight. The good priest did not shirk what might have made the readiest of soldiers nervous. Hamilton was known to be a great swordsman and proud of the distinction. Father Beret had seen him fence with Farnsworth in remarkable form, touching him at will, and in ministering to the men in the fort he had heard them talk of the Governor's incomparable skill.

A priest is, in perhaps all cases but the last out of a thousand, a man of peace, not to be forced into a fight; but the exceptional one out of the ten hundred it is well not to stir up if you are looking for an easy victim. Hamilton was in the habit of considering every antagonist immediately conquerable. His domineering spirit could not, when opposed, reckon with any possibility of disaster. As he sprang toward Father Beret there was a mutual recognition and, we speak guardedly, something that sounded exactly like an exchange of furious execrations. As for Father Beret's words, they may have been a mere priestly formula of objurgation.

The moon was accommodating. With a beautiful white splendor it entered a space of cloudless sky, where it seemed to slip along the dusky blue surface among the stars, far over in the west.

"It's you, is it?" Hamilton exclaimed between teeth that almost crushed one another. "You prowling hypocrite of hell!"

Father Beret said something. It was not complimentary, and it sounded sulphurous, if not profane. Remember, however, that a priest can scarcely hope to be better than Peter, and Peter did actually make the Simon pure remark when hard pressed. At all events Father Beret said something with vigorous emphasis, and met Hamilton half way.

Both men, stimulated to the finger-tips by a draught of imperious passion, fairly plunged to the inevitable conflict. Ah, if Alice could have seen her beautiful weapons cross, if she could have heard the fine, far-reaching clink, clink, clink, while sparks leaped forth, dazzling even in the moonlight; if she could have noted the admirable, nay, the amazing, play, as the men, regaining coolness to some extent, gathered their forces and fell cautiously to the deadly work, it would have been enough to change the cold shimmer of her face to a flash of warm delight. For she would have understood every feint, longe, parry, and seen at a glance how Father Beret set the pace and led the race at the beginning. She would have understood; for Father Beret had taught her all she knew about the art of fencing.

Hamilton quickly felt, and with a sense of its strangeness, the priest's masterly command of his weapon. The surprise called up all his caution and cleverness. Before he could adjust himself to such an unexpected condition he came near being spitted outright by a pretty pass under his guard. The narrow escape, while it put him on his best mettle, sent a wave of superstition through his brain. He recalled what Barlow had jocularly said about the doings of the devil-priest or priest-devil at Roussillon place on that night when the patrol guard attempted to take Gaspard Roussillon. Was this, indeed, Father Beret, that gentle old man, now before him, or was it an avenging demon from the shades?

The thought flitted electrically across his mind, while he deftly parried, feinted, longed, giving his dark antagonist all he could do to meet the play. Priest or devil, he thought, he cared not which, he would reach its vitals presently. Yet there lingered with him a haunting half-fear, or tenuous awe, which may have aided, rather than hindered his excellent swordsmanship.

Under foot it was slushy with mud, water and ice, the consistency varying from a somewhat solid crust to puddles that half inundated Hamilton's boots and quite overflowed Father Beret's moccasins. An execrable field for the little matter in hand. They gradually shifted position. Now it was the Governor, then the priest, who had advantage as to the light. For some time Father Beret seemed quite the shiftier and surer fighter, but (was it his age telling on him?) he lost perceptibly in suppleness. Still Hamilton failed to touch him. There was a baffling something in the old man's escape now and again from what ought to have been an inevitable stroke. Was it luck? It seemed to Hamilton more than that—a sort of uncanny evasion. Or was it supreme mastery, the last and subtlest reach of the fencer's craft?

Youth forced age slowly backward in the struggle, which at times took on spurts so furious that the slender blades, becoming mere glints of acicular steel, split the moonlight back and forth, up and down, so that their meetings, following one another in a well-nigh continuous stroke, sent a jarring noise through the air. Father Beret lost inch by inch, until the fighting was almost over the body of Alice; and now for the first time Hamilton became aware of that motionless something with the white, luminous face in profile against the ground; but he did not let even that unsettle his fencing gaze, which followed the sunken and dusky eyes of his adversary. A perspiration suddenly flooded his body, however, and began to drip across his face. His arm was tiring. A doubt crept like a chill into his heart. Then the priest appeared to add a cubit to his stature and waver strangely in the soft light. Behind him, low against the sky, a wide winged owl shot noiselessly across just above the prairie.

The soul of a true priest is double: it is the soul of a saint and the soul of a worldly man. What is most beautiful in this duality is the supreme courage with which the saintly spirit attacks the worldly and so often heroically masters it. In the beginning of the fight Father Beret let a passion of the earthly body take him by storm. It was well for Governor Henry Hamilton that the priest was so wrought upon as to unsettle his nerves, otherwise there would have been an evil heart impaled midway of Father Beret's rapier. A little later the saintly spirit began to assert itself, feebly indeed, but surely. Then it was that Father Beret seemed to be losing agility for a while as he backstepped away from Hamilton's increasing energy of assault. In his heart the priest was saying: "I will not murder him. I must not do that. He deserves death, but vengeance is not mine. I will disarm him." Step by step he retreated, playing erratically to make an opening for a trick he meant to use.

It was singularly loose play, a sort of wavering, shifty, incomprehensible show of carelessness, that caused Hamilton to entertain a doubt, which was really a fear, as to what was going to happen; for, notwithstanding all this neglect of due precaution on the priest's part, to touch him seemed impossible, miraculously so, and every plan of attack dissolved into futility in the most maddening way.

"Priest, devil or ghost!" raged Hamilton, with a froth gathering around his mouth; "I'll kill you, or—"

He made a longe, when his adversary left an opening which appeared absolutely beyond defence. It was a quick, dextrous, vicious thrust. The blade leaped toward Father Beret's heart with a twinkle like lightning.

At that moment, although warily alert and hopeful that his opportunity was at hand, Father Beret came near losing his life; for as he side-stepped and easily parried Hamilton's thrust, which he had invited, thinking to entangle his blade and disarm him, he caught his foot in Alice's skirt and stumbled, nearly falling across her. It would have been easy for Hamilton to run him through, had he instantly followed up the advantage. But the moonlight on Alice's face struck his eyes, and by that indirect ray of vision which is often strangely effective, he recognized her lying there. It was a disconcerting thing for him, but he rallied instantly and sprang aside, taking a new position just in time to face Father Beret again. A chill crept up his back. The horror which he could not shake off enraged him beyond measure. Gathering fresh energy, he renewed the assault with desperate steadiness the highest product of absolutely molten fury.

Father Beret felt the dangerous access of power in his antagonist's arm, and knew that a crisis had arrived. He could not be careless now. Here was a swordsman of the best school calling upon him for all the skill and strength and cunning that he could command. Again the saintly element was near being thrown aside by the worldly in the old man's breast. Alice lying there seemed mutely demanding that he avenge her. A riotous something in his blood clamored for a quick and certain act in this drama by moonlight—a tragic close by a stroke of terrible yet perfectly fitting justice.

There was but the space of a breath for the conflict in the priest's heart, yet during that little time he reasoned the case and quoted scripture to himself.

"Domine, percutimus in gladio?" rang through his mind. "Lord, shall we smite with the sword?"

Hamilton seemed to make answer to this with a dazzling display of skill. The rapiers sang a strange song above the sleeping girl, a lullaby with coruscations of death in every keen note.

Father Beret was thinking of Alice. His brain, playing double, calculated with lightning swiftness the chances and movements of that whirlwind rush of fight, while at the same time it swept through a retrospect of all the years since Alice came into his life. How he had watched her grow and bloom; how he had taught her, trained her mind and soul and body to high things, loved her with a fatherly passion unbounded, guarded her from the coarse and lawless influences of her surroundings. Like the tolling of an infinitely melancholy bell, all this went through his breast and brain, and, blending with a furious current of whatever passions were deadly dangerous in his nature, swept as a storm bearing its awful force into his sword-arm.

The Englishman was a lion, the priest a gladiator. The stars aloft in the vague, dark, yet splendid, amphitheater were the audience. It was a question. Would the thumbs go down or up? Life and death held the chances even; but it was at the will of Heaven, not of the stars. "Hoc habet" must follow the stroke ordered from beyond the astral clusters and the dusky blue.

Hamilton pressed, nay rushed, the fight with a weight and at a pace which could not last. But Father Beret withstood him so firmly that he made no farther headway; he even lost some ground a moment later.

"You damned Jesuit hypocrite!" he snarled; "you lowest of a vile brotherhood of liars!"

Then he rushed again, making a magnificent show of strength, quickness and accuracy. The sparks hissed and crackled from the rasping and ringing blades.

Father Beret was, in truth, a Jesuit, and as such a zealot; but he was not a liar or a hypocrite. Being human, he resented an insult. The saintly spirit in him was strong, yet not strong enough to breast the indignation which now dashed against it. For a moment it went down.

"Liar and scoundrel yourself!" he retorted, hoarsely forcing the words out of his throat. "Spawn of a beastly breed!"

Hamilton saw and felt a change pass over the spirit of the old priest's movements. Instantly the sword leaping against his own seemed endowed with subtle cunning and malignant treachery. Before this it had been difficult enough to meet the fine play and hold fairly even; now he was startled and confused; but he rose to the emergency with admirable will power and cleverness.

"Murderer of a poor orphan girl!" Father Beret added with a hot concentrated accent; "death is too good for you."

Hamilton felt nearer his grave than ever before in all his wild experience, for somehow doom, shadowy and formless, like the atmosphere of an awful dream, enmisted those words; but he was no weakling to quit at the height of desperate conflict. He was strong, expert, and game to the middle of his heart.

"I'll add a traitor Jesuit to my list of dead," he panted forth, rising yet again to the extremest tension of his power.

As he did this Father Beret settled himself as you have seen a mighty horse do in the home stretch of a race. Both men knew that the moment had arrived for the final act in their impromptu play. It was short, a duel condensed and crowded into fifteen seconds of time, and it was rapid beyond the power of words to describe. A bystander, had there been one, could not have seen what was finally done or how it was done. Father Beret's sword seemed to be revolving—it was a halo in front of Hamilton for a mere point of time. The old priest seemed to crouch and then make a quick motion as if about to leap backward. A wrench and a snip, as of something violently jerked from a fastening, were followed by a semicircular flight of Hamilton's rapier over Father Beret's head to stick in the ground ten feet behind him. The duel was over, and the whole terrible struggle had occupied less than three minutes.

With his wrist strained and his fingers almost broken, Hamilton stumbled forward and would have impaled himself had not Father Beret turned the point of his weapon aside as he lowered it.

"Surrender, or die!"

That was a strange order for a priest to make, but there could be no mistaking its authority or the power behind it. Hamilton regained his footing and looked dazed, wheezing and puffing like a porpoise, but he clearly understood what was demanded of him.

"If you call out I'll run you through," Father Beret added, seeing him move his lips as if to shout for help.

The level rapier now reinforced the words. Hamilton let the breath go noiselessly from his mouth and waved his hand in token of enforced submission.

"Well, what do you want me to do?" he demanded after a short pause. "You seem to have me at your mercy. What are your terms?"

Father Beret hesitated. It was a question difficult to answer.

"Give me your word as a British officer that you will never again try to harm any person, not an open, armed enemy, in this town."

Hamilton's gorge rose perversely. He erected himself with lofty reserve and folded his arms. The dignity of a Lieutenant Governor leaped into him and took control. Father Beret correctly interpreted what he saw.

"My people have borne much," he said, "and the killing of that poor child there will be awfully avenged if I but say the word. Besides, I can turn every Indian in this wilderness against you in a single day. You are indeed at my mercy, and I will be merciful if you will satisfy my demand."

He was trembling with emotion while he spoke and the desire to kill the man before him was making a frightful struggle with his priestly conscience; but conscience had the upper hand. Hamilton stood gazing fixedly, pale as a ghost, his thoughts becoming more and more clear and logical. He was in a bad situation. Every word that Father Beret had spoken was true and went home with force. There was no time for parley or subterfuge; the sword looked as if, eager to find his heart, it could not be held back another moment. But the wan, cold face of the girl had more power than the rapier's hungry point. It made an abject coward of him.

"I am willing to give you my word," he presently said. "And let me tell you," he went on more rapidly, "I did not shoot at her. She was behind you."

"Your word as a British officer?"

Hamilton again stiffened and hesitated, but only for the briefest space, then said:

"Yes, my word as a British officer."

Father Beret waved his hand with impatience.

"Go, then, back to your place in the fort and disturb, my people no more. The soul of this poor little girl will haunt you forever. Go!"

Hamilton stood a little while gazing at the face of Alice with the horrible wistfulness of remorse. What would he not have given to rub his eyes and find it all a dream?

He turned away; a cloud scudded across the moon; here and yonder in the dim town cocks crowed with a lonesome, desultory effect.

Father Beret plucked up the rapier that he had wrenched from Hamilton's hand. It suggested something.

"Hold!" he called out, "give me the scabbard of this sword." Hamilton, who was striding vigorously in the direction of the fort, turned about as the priest hastened to him.

"Give me the scabbard of this rapier; I want it. Take it off."

The command was not gently voiced. A hoarse, half-whisper winged every word with an imperious threat.

Hamilton obeyed. His hands were not firm; his fingers fumbled nervously; but he hurried, and Father Beret soon had the rapier sheathed and secured at his belt beside its mate.

A good and true priest is a burden-bearer. His motto is: Alter alterius onera portate; bear ye one another's burdens. His soul is enriched with the cast-off sorrows of those whom he relieves. Father Beret scarcely felt the weight of Alice's body when he lifted it from the ground, so heavy was the pressure of his grief. All that her death meant, not only to him, but to every person who knew her, came into his heart as the place of refuge consecrated for the indwelling of pain. He lifted her and bore her as far toward Roussillon place as he could; but his strength fell short just in front of the little Bourcier cottage, and half dead he staggered across the veranda to the door, where he sank exhausted.

After a breathing spell he knocked. The household, fast asleep, did not hear; but he persisted until the door was opened to him and his burden.

Captain Farnsworth unclosed his bloodshot eyes, at about eight o'clock in the morning, quite confused as to his place and surroundings. He looked about drowsily with a sheepish half-knowledge of having been very drunk. A purring in his head and a dull ache reminded him of an abused stomach. He yawned and stretched himself, then sat up, running a hand through his tousled hair. Father Beret was on his knees before the cross, still as a statue, his clasped hands extended upward.

Farnsworth's face lighted with recognition, and he smiled rather bitterly. He recalled everything and felt ashamed, humiliated, self-debased. He had outraged even a priest's hospitality with his brutish appetite, and he hated himself for it. Disgust nauseated his soul apace with the physical sinking and squirming that grew upon him.

"I'm a shabby, worthless dog!" he muttered, with petulant accent; "why don't you kick me out, Father?"

The priest turned a collapsed and bloodless gray face upon him, smiled in a tired, perfunctory way, crossed himself absently and said:

"You have rested well, my son. Hard as the bed is, you have done it a compliment in the way of sleeping. You young soldiers understand how to get the most out of things."

100

"You are too generous, Father, and I can't appreciate it. I know what I deserve, and you know it, too. Tell me what a brute and fool I am; it will do me good. Punch me a solid jolt in the ribs, like the one you gave me not long ago."

"Qui sine peccato est, primus lapidem mittat" said the priest. "Let him who is without sin cast the first stone."

He had gone to the hearth and was taking from the embers an earthen saucer, or shallow bowl, in which some fragrant broth simmered and steamed.

"A man who has slept as long as you have, my son, usually has a somewhat delicate appetite. Now, here is a soup, not especially satisfying to the taste of a gourmet like yourself, but possessing the soothing quality that is good for one just aroused from an unusual nap. I offer it, my son, propter stomachum tuum, et frequentes tuas infirmitates (on account of thy stomach, and thine often infirmities). This soup will go to the right spot."

While speaking he brought the hot bowl to Farnsworth and set it on the bedcover before him, then fetched a big horn spoon.

The fragrance of pungent roots and herbs, blent with a savory watt of buffalo meat, greeted the Captain's sense, and the anticipation itself cheered his aching throat. It made him feel greedy and in a hurry. The first spoonful, a trifle bitter, was not so pleasant at the beginning, but a moment after he swallowed it a hot prickling set in and seemed to dart through him from extremity to extremity.

Slowly, as he ate, the taste grew more agreeable, and all the effects of his debauch disappeared. It was like magic; his blood warmed and glowed, as if touched with mysterious fire.

"What is this in this soup, Father Beret, that makes it so searching and refreshing?" he demanded, when the bowl was empty.

Father Beret shook his head and smiled drolly.

"That I cannot divulge, my son, owing to a promise I had to make to the aged Indian who gave me the secret. It is the elixir of the Miamis. Only their consecrated medicine men hold the recipe. The stimulation is but temporary."

Just then someone knocked on the door. Father Beret opened it to one of Hamilton's aides.

"Your pardon, Father, but hearing Captain Farnsworth's voice I made bold to knock."

"What is it, Bobby?" Farnsworth called out.

"Nothing, only the Governor has been having you looked for in every nook and corner of the fort and town. You'd better report at once, or hell be having us drag the river for your body."

"All right, Lieutenant, go back and keep mum, that's a dear boy, and I'll shuffle into Colonel Hamilton's august presence before many minutes."

The aide laughed and went his way whistling a merry tune.

"Now I am sure to get what I deserve, with usury at forty per cent in advance," said Farnsworth dryly, shrugging his shoulders with undissembled dread of Hamilton's wrath. But the anticipation was not realized. The Governor received Farnsworth stiffly enough, yet in a way that suggested a suppressed desire to avoid explanations on the Captain's part and a reprimand on his own. In fact, Hamilton was hoping that something would turn up to shield him from the effect of his terrible midnight adventure, which seemed the darker the more he thought of it. He had a slow, numb conscience, lying deep where it was hard to reach, and when a qualm somehow entered it he endured in secret what most men would have cast off or confessed. He was haunted, if not with remorse, at least by a dread of something most disagreeable in connection with what he had done. Alice's white face had impressed itself indelibly on his memory, so that it met his inner vision at every turn. He was afraid to converse with Farnsworth lest she should come up for discussion; consequently their interview was curt and formal.

It was soon discovered that Alice had escaped from the stockade, and some show of search was made for her by Hamilton's order, but Farnsworth looked to it that the order was not carried out. He thought he saw at once that his chief knew where she was. The mystery perplexed and pained the young man, and caused him to fear all sorts of evil; but there was a chance that Alice had found a safe retreat and he knew that nothing but ill could befall her if she were discovered and brought back to the fort. Therefore his search for her became his own secret and for his own heart's ease. And doubtless he would have found her; for even handicapped and distorted love like his is lynx-eyed and sure on the track of its object; but a great event intervened and swept away his opportunity.

Hamilton's uneasiness, which was that of a strong, misguided nature trying to justify itself amid a confusion of unmanageable doubts and misgivings, now vented itself in a resumption of the repairs he had been making at certain points in the fort. These he completed just in time for the coming of Clark.

CHAPTER XIX
THE ATTACK

It has already been mentioned that Indians, arriving singly or in squads, to report at Hamilton's headquarters, were in the habit of firing their guns before entering the town or the fort, not only as a signal of their approach, but in order to rid their weapons of their charges preliminary to cleaning them before setting out upon another scalp-hunting expedition. A shot, therefore, or even a volley, heard on the outskirts of the village, was not a noticeable incident in the daily and nightly experience of the garrison. Still, for some reason, Governor Hamilton started violently when, just after nightfall, five or six rifles cracked sharply a short distance from the stockade.

He and Helm with two other officers were in the midst of a game of cards, while a kettle, swinging on a crane in the ample fire-place, sang a shrill promise of hot apple-jack toddy.

"By Jove!" exclaimed Farnsworth, who, although not in the game, was amusing himself with looking on; "you jump like a fine lady! I almost fancied I heard a bullet hit you."

"You may all jump while you can," remarked Helm. "That's Clark, and your time's short— He'll have this fort tumbling on your heads before daylight of to-morrow morning comes."

As he spoke he arose from his seat at the card table and went to look after the toddy, which, as an expert, he had under supervision.

Hamilton frowned. The mention of Clark was disturbing. Ever since the strange disappearance of Lieutenant Barlow he had nursed the fear that possibly Clark's scouts had captured him and that the American forces might be much nearer than Kaskaskia. Besides, his nerves were unruly, as they had been ever since the encounter with Father Beret; and his vision persisted in turning back upon the accusing cold face of Alice, lying in the moonlight. One little detail of that scene almost maddened him at times; it was a sheeny, crinkled wisp of warm looking hair looped across the cheek in which he had often seen a saucy dimple dance when Alice spoke or smiled. He was bad enough, but not wholly bad, and the thought of having darkened those merry eyes and stilled those sweet dimples tore through him with a cold, rasping pang.

"Just as soon as this toddy is properly mixed and tempered," said Helm, with a magnetic jocosity beaming from his genial face, "I'm going to propose a toast to the banner of Alice Roussillon, which a whole garrison of British braves has been unable to take!"

"If you do I'll blow a hole through you as big as the south door of hell," said Hamilton, in a voice fairly shaken to a husky quaver with rage. "You may do a great many insulting things; but not that."

Helm was in a half stooping attitude with a ladle in one hand, a cup in the other. He had met Hamilton's glowering look with a peculiarly innocent smile, as if to say: "What in the world is the matter now? I never felt in a better humor in all my life. Can't you take a joke, I wonder?" He did not speak, however, for a rattling volley of musket and rifle shots hit the top of the clay-daubed chimney, sending down into the toddy a shower of soot and dirt.

In a wink every man was on his feet and staring.

"Gentlemen," said Helm, with an impressive oath, "that is Clark's soldiers, and they will take your fort; but they ought not to have spoiled this apple toddy!"

"Oh, the devil!" said Hamilton, forcibly resuming a calm countenance, "it is only a squad of drunken Indians coming in. We'll forego excitement; there's no battle on hand, gentlemen."

"I'm glad you think so, Governor Hamilton," Helm responded, "but I should imagine that I ought to know the crack of a Kentucky rifle. I've heard one occasionally in my life. Besides, I got a whiff of freedom just now."

"Captain Helm is right," observed Farnsworth. "That is an attack."

Another volley, this time nearer and more concentrated, convinced Hamilton that he was, indeed, at the opening of a fight. Even while he was giving some hurried orders to his officers, a man was wounded at one of the port-holes. Then came a series of yells, answered by a ripple of sympathetic French shouting that ran throughout the town. The patrol guards came straggling in, breathless with excitement. They swore to having seen a thousand men marching across the water-covered meadows.

Hamilton was brave. The approach of danger stirred him like a trumpet-strain. His fighting blood rose to full tide, and he gave his orders with the steadiness and commanding force of a born soldier. The officers hastened to their respective positions. On all sides sounds indicative of rapid preparations for the fight mingled into a confused strain of military energy.

Men marched to their places; cannon were wheeled into position, and soon enough the firing began in good earnest.

Late in the afternoon a rumor of Clark's approach had gone abroad through the village; but not a French lip breathed it to a friend of the British. The creoles were loyal to the cause of freedom; moreover, they cordially hated Hamilton, and their hearts beat high at the prospect of a change in masters at the fort. Every cabin had its hidden gun and supply of ammunition, despite the order to disarm issued by Hamilton. There was a hustling to bring these forth, which was accompanied with a guarded yet irrepressible chattering, delightfully French and infinitely volatile.

"Tiens! je vais frotter mon fusil. J'ai vu un singe!" said Jaques Bourcier to his daughter, the pretty Adrienne, who was coming out of the room in which Alice lay.

"I saw a monkey just now; I must rub up my gun!" He could not be solemn; not he. The thought of an opportunity to get even with Hamilton was like wine in his blood.

If you had seen those hardy and sinewy Frenchmen gliding in the dusk of evening from cottage to cottage, passing the word that the Americans had arrived, saying airy things and pinching one another as they met and hurried on, you would have thought something very amusing and wholly jocund was in preparation for the people of Vincennes.

There was a current belief in the town that Gaspard Roussillon never missed a good thing and always somehow got the lion's share. He went out with the ebb to return on the flood. Nobody was surprised, therefore, when he suddenly appeared in the midst of his friends, armed to the teeth and emotionally warlike to suit the occasion. Of course he took charge of everybody and everything. You could have heard him whisper a bowshot away.

"Taisons!" he hissed, whenever he met an acquaintance. "We will surprise the fort and scalp the whole garrison. Aux armes! les Americains viennent d'arriver!"

At his own house he knocked and called in vain. He shook the door violently; for he was thinking of the stores under the floor, of the grimy bottles, of the fragrant Bordeaux—ah, his throat, how it throbbed! But where was Madame Roussillon? Where was Alice? "Jean! Jean!" he cried, forgetting all precaution, "come here, you scamp, and let me in this minute!"

A profoundly impressive silence gave him to understand that his home was deserted.

"Chiff! frightened and gone to stay with Madame Godere, I suppose—and I so thirsty! Bah! hum, hum, apres le vin la bataille, ziff!"

He kicked in the door and groped his way to the liquors. While he hastily swigged and smacked he heard the firing begin with a crackling, desultory volley. He laughed jovially, there in the dark, between draughts and deep sighs of enjoyment.

"Et moi aussi," he murmured, like the vast murmur of the sea, "I want to be in that dance! Pardonnez, messieurs. Moi, je veux danser, s'il vous plait."

And when he had filled himself he plunged out and rushed away, wrought up to the extreme fighting pitch of temper. Diable! if he could but come across that Lieutenant Barlow, how he would smash him and mangle him! In magnifying his prowess with the lens of imagination he swelled and puffed as he lumbered along.

The firing sounded as if it were between the fort and the river; but presently when one of Hamilton's cannon spoke, M. Roussillon saw the yellow spike of flame from its muzzle leap directly toward the church, and he thought it best to make a wide detour to avoid going between the firing lines. Once or twice he heard the whine of a stray bullet high overhead. Before he had gone very far he met a man hurrying toward the fort. It was Captain Francis Maisonville, one of Hamilton's chief scouts, who had been out on a reconnoissance, cut off from his party by some of Clark's forces, was trying to make his way to the main gate of the stockade.

M. Roussillon knew Maisonville as a somewhat desperate character, a leader of Indian forays and a trader in human scalps. Surely the fellow was legitimate prey.

"Ziff! diable de gredin!" he snarled, and leaping upon him choked him to the ground, "Je vais vous scalper immediatement!"

Clark's plan of approach showed masterly strategy. Lieutenant Bailey, with fourteen regulars, made a show of attack on the east, while Major Bowman led a company through the town, on a line near where Main street in Vincennes is now located, to a point north of the stockade. Charleville, a brave creole, who was at the head of some daring fellows, by a brilliant dash got position under cover of a natural terrace at the edge of the prairie, opposite the fort's southwestern angle. Lieutenant Beverley, in whom the commander placed highest confidence, was sent to look for a supply of ammunition, and to gather up all the Frenchmen in the town who wished to join in the attack. Oncle Jazon and ten other available men went with him.

They all made a great noise when they felt that the place was completely invested. Nor can we deny, much as we would like to, the strong desire for vengeance which raised those shouting voices and nerved those steady hearts to do or die in an undertaking which certainly had a desperate look. Patriotism of the purest strain those men had, and that alone would have borne them up; but the recollection of smouldering cabin homes in Kentucky, of women and children murdered and scalped, of men brave and true burned at the stake, and of all the indescribable outrages of Indian warfare incited and rewarded by the commander of the fort yonder, added to patriotism the terrible urge of that dark passion which clamors for blood to quench the fire of wrath. Not a few of those wet, half-frozen, emaciated soldiers of freedom had experienced the soul rending shock of returning from a day's hunting in the forest to find home in ashes and loved ones brutally murdered and scalped, or dragged away to unspeakable outrage under circumstances too harrowing for description, the bare thought of which turns our blood cold, even at this distance. Now the opportunity had arrived for a stroke of retaliation. The thought was tremendously stimulating.

Beverley, with the aid of Oncle Jazon, was able to lead his little company as far as the church before the enemy saw him. Here a volley from the nearest angle of the stockade had to be answered, and pretty soon a cannon began to play upon the position.

"We kin do better some'rs else," was Oncle Jazon's laconic remark flung back over his shoulder, as he moved briskly away from the spot just swept by a six-pounder. "Come this yer way, Lieutenant. I hyer some o' the fellers a talkin' loud jes' beyant Legrace's place. They ain't no sort o' sense a tryin' to hit anything a shootin' in the dark nohow."

When they reached the thick of the town there was a strange stir in the dusky streets. Men were slipping from house to house, arming themselves and joining their neighbors. Clark had sent an order earlier in the evening forbidding any street demonstration by the inhabitants; but he might as well have ordered the wind not to blow or the river to stand still. Oncle Jazon knew every man whose outlines he could see or whose voice he heard. He called each one by name:

"Here, Roger, fall in!—Come Louis, Alphonse, Victor, Octave—venez ici, here's the American army, come with me!" His rapid French phrases leaped forth as if shot from a pistol, and his shrill voice, familiar to every ear in Vincennes, drew the creole militiamen to him, and soon Beverley's company had doubled its numbers, while at the same time its enthusiasm and ability to make a noise had increased in a far greater proportion. In accordance with an order from Clark they now took position near the northeast corner of the stockade and began firing, although in the darkness there was but little opportunity for marksmanship.

Oncle Jazon had found citizens Legrace and Bosseron, and through them Clark's men were supplied with ammunition, of which they stood greatly in need, their powder having got wet during their long, watery march. By nine o'clock the fort was completely surrounded, and from every direction the riflemen and musketeers were pouring in volley after volley. Beverley with his men took the cover of a fence and some houses sixty yards from the stockade. Here to their surprise they found themselves below the line of Hamilton's cannon, which, being planted on the second floor of the fort, could not be sufficiently depressed to bear upon them. A well directed musket fire, however, fell from the loopholes of the blockhouses, the bullets rattling merrily against the cover behind which the attacking forces lay.

Beverley was thinking of Alice during every moment of all this stir and tumult He feared that she might still be a prisoner in the fort exposed to the very bullets that his men were discharging at every crack and cranny of those loosely constructed buildings. Should he ever see her again? Would she care for him? What would be the end of all this terrible suspense? Those remote forebodings of evils, formless, shadowy, ineffable, which have harried the lover's heart since time began, crowded all pleasant anticipations out of his mind.

Clark, in passing hurriedly from company to company around the line, stopped for a little while when he found Beverley.

"Have you plenty of ammunition?" was his first inquiry.

"A mighty sight more'n we kin see to shoot with," spoke up Oncle Jazon. "It's a right smart o' dad burn foolishness to be wastin' it on nothin'; seems like to me 'at we'd better set the dasted fort afire an' smoke the skunks out!"

"Speak when you are spoken to, my man," said the Colonel a trifle hotly, and trying by a sharp scrutiny to make him out in the gloom where he crouched.

"Ventrebleu! I'm not askin' YOU, Colonel Clark, nor no other man, when I shill speak. I talks whenever I gits ready, an' I shoots jes' the same way. So ye'd better go on 'bout yer business like a white man! Close up yer own whopper jawed mouth, ef ye want anything shet up!"

"Oho! is that you, Jazon? You're so little I didn't know you! Certainly, talk your whole damned under jaw off, for all I care," Clark replied, assuming a jocose tone. Then turning again to Beverley: "Keep up the firing and the noise; the fort will be ours in the morning."

"What's the use of waiting till morning?" Beverley demanded with impatience. "We can tear that stockade to pieces with our hands in half an hour."

"I don't think so, Lieutenant. It is better to play for the sure thing. Keep up the racket, and be ready for 'em if they rush out. We must not fail to capture the hair-buyer General."

He passed on, with something cheerful to say whenever he found a squad of his devoted men. He knew how to humor and manage those independent and undisciplined yet heroically brave fellows. What to see and hear, what to turn aside as a joke, what to insist upon with inflexible mastery, he knew by the fine instantaneous sense of genius. There were many men of Oncle Jazon's cast, true as steel, but refractory as flint, who could not be dominated by any person, no matter of what stamp or office. To them an order was an insult; but a suggestion pleased and captured them. Strange as it may seem, theirs was the conquering spirit of America— the spirit which has survived every turn of progress and built up the great body of our independence.

Beverley submitted to Clark's plan with what patience he could, and all night long fired shot for shot with the best riflemen in his squad. It was a fatiguing performance, with apparently little result beyond forcing the garrison now and again to close the embrasures, thus periodically silencing the cannon. Toward the close of the night a relaxation showed itself in the shouting and firing all round the line. Beverley's men, especially the creoles, held out bravely in the matter of noise; but even they flagged at length, their volatility simmering down to desultory bubbling and half sleepy chattering and chaffing.

Beverley leaned upon a rude fence, and for a time neglected to reload his hot rifle. Of course he was thinking of Alice,—he really could not think in any other direction; but it gave him a shock and a start when he presently heard her name mentioned by a little Frenchman near him on the left.

"There'll never be another such a girl in Post Vincennes as Alice Roussillon," the fellow said in the soft creole patois, "and to think of her being shot like a dog!"

"And by a man who calls himself a Governor, too!" said another. "Ah, as for myself, I'm in favor of burning him alive when we capture him. That's me!"

"Et moi aussi," chimed in a third voice. "That poor girl must be avenged. The man who shot her must die. Holy Virgin, but if Gaspard Roussillon were only here!"

"But he is here; I saw him just after dark. He was in great fighting temper, that terrible man. Ouf! but I should not like to be Colonel Hamilton and fall in the way of that Gaspard Roussillon!"

"Morbleu! I should say not. You may leave me out of a chance like that! I shouldn't mind seeing Gaspard handle the Governor, though. Ah, that would be too good! He'd pay him up for shooting Mademoiselle Alice."

Beverley could scarcely hold himself erect by the fence; the smoky, foggy landscape swam round him heavy and strange. He uttered a groan, which brought Oncle Jazon to his side in a hurry.

"Qu' avez-vous? What's the matter?" the old man demanded with quick sympathy. "Hev they hit ye? Lieutenant, air ye hurt much?"

Beverley did not hear the old man's words, did not feel his kindly touch.

"Alice! Alice!" he murmured, "dead, dead!"

"Ya-as," drawled Oncle Jazon, "I hearn about it soon as I got inter town. It's a sorry thing, a mighty sorry thing. But mebby I won't do a little somepin' to that—"

Beverley straightened himself and lifted his gun, forgetting that he had not reloaded it since firing last. He leveled it at the fort and touched the trigger. Simultaneously with his movement an embrasure opened and a cannon flashed, its roar flanked on either side by a crackling of British muskets. Some bullets struck the fence and flung splinters into Oncle Jazon's face. A cannon ball knocked a ridge pole from the roof of a house hard by, and sent it whirling through the air.

"Ventrebleu!—et apres? What the devil next? Better knock a feller's eyes out!" the old man cried. "I ain't a doin' nothin' to ye!"

He capered around rubbing his leathery face after the manner of a scalded monkey. Beverley was struck in the breast by a flattened and spent ball that glanced from a fence-picket. The shock caused him to stagger and drop his gun; but he quickly picked it up and turned to his companion.

"Are you hurt, Oncle Jazon?" he inquired. "Are you hurt?"

"Not a bit—jes' skeert mos' into a duck fit. Thought a cannon ball had knocked my whole dang face down my throat! Nothin' but a handful o' splinters in my poorty count'nance, makin' my head feel like a porc'-pine. But I sort o' thought I heard somepin' give you a diff."

"Something did hit me," said Beverley, laying a hand on his breast, "but I don't think it was a bullet. They seem to be getting our range at last. Tell the men to keep well under cover. They must not expose themselves until we are ready to charge."

The shock had brought him back to his duty as a leader of his little company, and with the funeral bell of all his life's happiness tolling in his agonized heart he turned afresh to directing the fire upon the block-house.

About this time a runner came from Clark with an order to cease firing and let a returning party of British scouts under Captain Lamothe re-enter the fort unharmed. A strange order it seemed to both officers and men; but it was implicitly obeyed. Clark's genius here made another fine strategic flash. He knew that unless he let the scouts go back into the stockade they would escape by running away, and might possibly organize an army of Indians with which to succor Hamilton. But if they were permitted to go inside they could be captured with the rest of the garrison; hence his order.

A few minutes passed in dead silence; then Captain Lamothe and his party marched close by where Beverley's squad was lying concealed. It was a difficult task to restrain the creoles, for some of them hated Lamothe. Oncle Jazon squirmed like a snake while they filed past all unaware that an enemy lurked so near. When they reached the fort, ladders were put down for them and they began to clamber over the wall, crowding and pushing one another in wild haste. Oncle Jazon could hold in no longer.

"Ya! ya! ya!" he yelled. "Look out! the ladder is a fallin' wi' ye!"

Then all the lurking crowd shouted as one man, and, sure enough, down came a ladder—men and all in a crashing heap.

"Silence! silence!" Beverley commanded; but he could not check the wild jeering and laughing, while the bruised and frightened scouts hastily erected their ladder again, fairly tumbling over one another in their haste to ascend, and so cleared the wall, falling into the stockade to join the garrison.

"Ventrebleu!" shrieked Oncle Jazon. "They've gone to bed; but we'll wake 'em up at the crack o' day an' give 'em a breakfas' o' hot lead!"

Now the fighting was resumed with redoubled spirit and noise, and when morning came, affording sufficient light to bring out the "bead sights" on the Kentucky rifles, the matchless marksmen in Clark's band forced the British to close the embrasures and entirely cease trying to use their cannon; but the fight with small arms went merrily on until the middle of the forenoon.

Meantime Gaspard Roussillon had tied Francis Maisonville's hands fast and hard with the strap of his bullet-pouch.

"Now, I'll scalp you," he said in a rumbling tone, terrible to hear. And with his words out came his hunting knife from its sheath.

"O have mercy, my dear Monsieur Roussillon!" cried the panting captive; "have mercy!"

"Mercy! yes, like your Colonel's, that's what you'll get. You stand by that forban, that scelerat, that bandit, and help him. Oh, yes, you'll get mercy! Yes, the same mercy that he showed to my poor little Alice! Your scalp, Monsieur, if you please! A small matter; it won't hurt much!"

"But, for the sake of old friendship, Gaspard, for the sake—"

"Ziff! poor little Alice!"

"But I swear to you that I—"

"Tout de meme, Monsieur, je vais vous scalper maintenant."

In fact he had taken off a part of Maisonville's scalp, when a party of soldiers, among whom was Maisonville's brother, a brave fellow and loyal to the American cause, were attracted by his cries and came to his rescue.

M. Roussillon struggled savagely, insisting upon completing his cruel performance; but he was at last overpowered, partly by brute force and partly by the pleading of Maisonville's brother, and made to desist. The big man wept with rage when he saw the bleeding prisoner protected. "Eh bien! I'll keep what I've got," he roared, "and I'll take the rest of it next time."

He shook the tuft of hair at Maisonville and glared like a mad bull.

Two or three other members of Lamothe's band were captured about the same time by some of the French militiamen; and Clark, when on his round cheering and directing his forces, discovered that these prisoners were being used as shields. Some young creoles, gay with drink and the stimulating effect of fight, had bound the poor fellows and were firing from behind them! Of course the commander promptly put an end to this cruelty; but they considered it exquisite fun while it lasted. It was in broad daylight, and they knew that the English in the fort could see what they were doing.

"It's shameful to treat prisoners in this way," said Clark. "I will not permit it. Shoot the next man that offers to do such a thing!"

One of the creole youths, a handsome, swarthy Adonis in buckskin, tossed his shapely head with a debonair smile and said:

"To be sure, mon Colonel! but what have they been doing to us? We have amused them all winter; it's but fair that they should give us a little fun now."

Clark shrugged his broad shoulders and passed on. He understood perfectly what the people of Vincennes had suffered under Hamilton's brutal administration.

At nine o'clock an order was passed to cease firing, and a flag of truce was seen going from Clark's headquarters to the fort. It was a peremptory demand for unconditional surrender. Hamilton refused, and fighting was fiercely resumed from behind rude breastworks meantime erected. Every loop-hole and opening of whatever sort was the focus into which the unerring backwoods rifles sent their deadly bullets. Men began to fall in the fort, and every moment Hamilton expected an assault in force on all sides of the stockade. This, if successful, would mean inevitable massacre. Clark had warned him of the terrible consequences of holding out until the worst should come. "For," said he in his note to the Governor, "if I am obliged to storm, you may depend upon such treatment as is justly due to a murderer."

Historians have wondered why Hamilton became so excited and acted so strangely after receiving the note. The phrase, "justly due to a murderer," is the key to the mystery. When he read it his heart sank and a terrible fear seized him. "Justly due to a murderer!" ah, that calm, white, beautiful girlish face, dead in the moonlight, with the wisp of shining hair across it! "Such treatment as is justly due to a murderer!" Cold drops of sweat broke out on his forehead and a shiver went through his body.

During the truce Clark's weary yet still enthusiastic besiegers enjoyed a good breakfast prepared for them by the loyal dames of Vincennes. Little Adrienne Bourcier was one of the handmaidens of the occasion. She brought to Beverley's squad a basket, almost as large as herself, heaped high with roasted duck and warm wheaten bread, while another girl bore two huge jugs of coffee, fragrant and steaming hot. The men cheered them lustily and complimented them without reserve, so that before their service was over their faces were glowing with delight.

And yet Adrienne's heart was uneasy, and full of longing to hear something of Rene de Ronville. Surely some one of her friends must know something about him. Ah, there was Oncle Jazon! Doubtless he could tell her all that she wanted to know. She lingered, after the food was distributed, and shyly inquired.

"Hain't seed the scamp," said Oncle Jazon, only he used the patois most familiar to the girl's ear. "Killed an' scelped long ago, I reckon."

His mouth was so full that he spoke mumblingly and with utmost difficulty. Nor did he glance at Adrienne, whose face took on as great pallor as her brown complexion could show.

Beverley ate but little of the food. He sat apart on a piece of timber that projected from the rough breastwork and gave himself over to infinite misery of spirit, which was trebled when he took Alice's locket from his bosom, only to discover that the bullet which struck him had almost entirely destroyed the face of the miniature.

He gripped the dinted and twisted case and gazed at it with the stare of a blind man. His heart almost ceased to beat and his breath had the rustling sound we hear when a strong man dies of a sudden wound. Somehow the defacement of the portrait was taken by his soul as the final touch of fate, signifying that Alice was forever and completely obliterated from his life. He felt a blur pass over his mind. He tried in vain to recall the face and form so dear to him; he tried to imagine her voice; but the whole universe was a vast hollow silence. For a long while he was cold, staring, rigid; then the inevitable collapse came, and he wept as only a strong man can who is hurt to death, yet cannot die.

Adrienne approached him, thinking to speak to him about Rene; but he did not notice her, and she went her way, leaving beside him a liberal supply of food.

CHAPTER XX
ALICE'S FLAG

Governor Hamilton received the note sent him by Colonel Clark and replied to it with curt dignity; but his heart was quaking. As a soldier he was true to the military tradition, and nothing could have induced him to surrender his command with dishonor.

"Lieutenant-Governor Hamilton," he wrote to Clark, "begs leave to acquaint Colonel Clark that he and his garrison are not disposed to be awed into any action unworthy of British subjects."

"Very brave words," said Helm, when Hamilton read the note to him, "but you'll sing a milder tune before many minutes, or you and your whole garrison will perish in a bloody heap. Listen to those wild yells! Clark has enough men to eat you all up for breakfast. You'd better be reasonable and prudent. It's not bravery to court massacre."

Hamilton turned away without a word and sent the message; but Helm saw that he was excited, and could be still further wrought up.

"You are playing into the hands of your bitterest enemies, the frog-eaters," he went on. "These creoles, over whom you've held a hot poker all winter, are crazy to be turned loose upon you; and you know that they've got good cause to feel like giving you the extreme penalty. They'll give it to you without a flinch if they get the chance. You've done enough."

Hamilton whirled about and glared ferociously.

"Helm, what do you mean?" he demanded in a voice as hollow as it was full of desperate passion.

The genial Captain laughed, as if he had heard a good joke.

"You won't catch any fish if you swear, and you look blasphemous," he said with the lightness of humor characteristic of him at all times. "You'd better say a prayer or two. Just reflect a moment upon the awful sins you have committed and—"

A crash of coalescing volleys from every direction broke off his levity. Clark was sending his response to Hamilton's lofty note. The guns of freedom rang out a prophecy of triumph, and the hissing bullets clucked sharply as they entered the solid logs of the walls or whisked through an aperture and bowled over a man. The British musketeers returned the fire as best they could, with a courage and a stubborn coolness which Helm openly admired, although he could not hide his satisfaction whenever one of them was disabled.

"Lamothe and his men are refusing to obey orders," said Farnsworth a little later, hastily approaching Hamilton, his face flushed and a gleam of hot anger in his eyes. "They're in a nasty mood; I can do nothing with them; they have not fired a shot."

"Mutiny?" Hamilton demanded.

"Not just that. They say they do not wish to fire on their kinsmen and friends. They are all French, you know, and they see their cousins, brothers, uncles and old acquaintances out there in Clark's rabble. I can do nothing with them."

"Shoot the scoundrels, then!"

"It will be a toss up which of us will come out on top if we try that. Besides, if we begin a fight inside, the Americans will make short work of us."

"Well, what in hell are we to do, then?"

"Oh, fight, that's all," said Farnsworth apathetically turning to a small loop-hole and leveling a field glass through it. "We might make a rush from the gates and stampede them," he presently added. Then he uttered an exclamation of great surprise.

"There's Lieutenant Beverley out there," he exclaimed.

"You're mistaken, you're excited," Hamilton half sneeringly remarked, yet not without a shade of uneasiness in his expression. "You forget, sir."

"Look for yourself, it's easily settled," and Farnsworth proffered the glass. "He's there, to a certainty, sir."

"I saw Beverley an hour ago," said Helm. "I knew all the time that he'd be on hand."

It was a white lie. Captain Helm was as much surprised as his captors at what he heard; but he could not resist the temptation to be annoying.

Hamilton looked as Farnsworth directed, and sure enough, there was the young Virginian Lieutenant, standing on a barricade, his hat off, cheering his men with a superb show of zeal. Not a hair of his head was missing, so far as the glass could be relied upon to show.

Oncle Jazon's quick old eyes saw the gleam of the telescope tube in the loop-hole.

"I never could shoot much," he muttered, and then a little bullet sped with absolute accuracy from his disreputable looking rifle and shattered the object-lens, just as Hamilton moved to withdraw the glass, uttering an ejaculation of intense excitement.

"Such devils of marksmen!" said he, and his face was haggard. "That infernal Indian lied."

"I could have told you all the time that the scalp Long-Hair brought to you was not Beverley's," said Helm indifferently. "I recognized Lieutenant Barlow's hair as soon as I saw it."

This was another piece of off-hand romance. Helm did not dream that he was accidentally sketching a horrible truth.

"Barlow's!" exclaimed Farnsworth.

"Yes, Barlow's, no mistake—"

Two more men reeled from a port-hole, the blood spinning far out of their wounds. Indeed, through every aperture in the walls the bullets were now humming like mad hornets.

"Close that port-hole!" stormed Hamilton; then turning to Farnsworth he added: "We cannot endure this long. Shut up every place large enough for a bullet to get through. Go all around, give strict orders to all. See that the men do not foolishly expose themselves. Those ruffians out there have located every crack."

His glimpse of Beverley and the sinister remark of Helm had completely unmanned him before his men fell. Now it rushed upon him that if he would escape the wrath of the maddened creoles and the vengeance of Alice's lover, he must quickly throw himself upon the mercy of Clark. It was his only hope. He chafed inwardly, but bore himself with stern coolness. He presently sought Farnsworth, pulled him aside and suggested that something must be done to prevent an assault and a massacre. The sounds outside seemed to forebode a gathering for a desperate rush, and in his heart he felt all the terrors of awful anticipation.

"We are completely at their mercy, that is plain," he said, shrugging his shoulders and gazing at the wounded men writhing in their agony. "What do you suggest?"

Captain Farnsworth was a shrewd officer. He recollected that Philip Dejean, justice of Detroit, was on his way down the Wabash from that post, and probably near at hand, with a flotilla of men and supplies. Why not ask for a few days of truce? It could do no harm, and if agreed to, might be their salvation. Hamilton jumped at the thought, and forthwith drew up a note which he sent out with a white flag. Never before in all his military career had he been so comforted by a sudden cessation of fighting. His soul would grovel in spite of him. Alice's cold face now had Beverley's beside it in his field of inner vision—a double assurance of impending doom, it seemed to him.

There was short delay in the arrival of Colonel Clark's reply, hastily scrawled on a bit of soiled paper. The request for a truce was flatly refused; but the note closed thus:

"If Mr. Hamilton is Desirous of a Conferance with Col. Clark he will meet him at the Church with Captn. Helms."

The spelling was not very good, and there was a redundancy of capital letters; yet Hamilton understood it all; and it was very difficult for him to conceal his haste to attend the proposed conference. But he was afraid to go to the church—the thought chilled him. He could not face Father Beret, who would probably be there. And what if there should be evidences of the funeral?—what if?—he shuddered and tried to break away from the vision in his tortured brain.

He sent a proposition to Clark to meet him on the esplanade before the main gate of the fort; but Clark declined, insisting upon the church. And thither he at last consented to go. It was an immense brace to his spirit to have Helm beside him during that walk, which, although but eighty yards in extent, seemed to him a matter of leagues. On the way he had to pass near the new position taken up by Beverley and his men. It was a fine test of nerve, when the Lieutenant's eyes met those of the Governor. Neither man permitted the slightest change of countenance to betray his feelings. In fact, Beverley's face was as rigid as marble; he could not have changed it.

But with Oncle Jazon it was a different affair. He had no dignity to preserve, no fine military bearing to sustain, no terrible tug of conscience, no paralyzing grip of despair on his heart. When he saw Hamilton going by, bearing himself so superbly, it affected the French volatility in his nature to such an extent that his tongue could not be controlled.

"Va t'en, bete, forban, meurtrier! Skin out f'om here! beast, robber, murderer!" he cried, in his keen screech-owl voice. "I'll git thet scelp o' your'n afore sundown, see 'f I don't! Ye onery gal-killer an' ha'r buyer!"

The blood in Hamilton's veins caught no warmth from these remarks; but he held his head high and passed stolidly on, as if he did not hear a word. Helm turned the tail of an eye upon Oncle Jazon and gave him a droll, quizzical wink of approval. In response the old man with grotesque solemnity drew his buckhorn handled knife, licked its blade and returned it to its sheath,—a bit of pantomime well understood and keenly enjoyed by the onlooking creoles.

"Putois! coquin!" they jeered, "goujat! poltron!"

Beverley heard the taunting racket, but did not realize it, which was well enough, for he could not have restrained the bitter effervescence. He stood like a statue, gazing fixedly at the now receding figure, the lofty, cold-faced man in whom centered his hate of hates. Clark had requested him to be present at the conference in the church; but he declined, feeling that he could not meet Hamilton and restrain himself. Now he regretted his refusal, half wishing that—no, he could not assassinate an enemy under a white flag. In his heart he prayed that there would be no surrender, that Hamilton would reject every offer. To storm the fort and revel in butchering its garrison seemed the only desirable thing left for him in life.

Father Beret was, indeed, present at the church, as Hamilton had dreaded; and the two duelists gave each other a rapier-like eye-thrust. Neither spoke, however, and Clark immediately demanded a settlement of the matter in hand. He was brusque and imperious to a degree, apparently rather anxious to repel every peaceful advance.

It was a laconic interview, crisp as autumn ice and bitter as gallberries. Colonel Clark had no respect whatever for Hamilton, to whom he had applied the imperishable adjective "hair-buyer General." On the other hand Governor Hamilton, who felt keenly the disgrace of having to equalize himself officially and discuss terms of surrender with a rough backwoodsman, could not conceal his contempt of Clark.

The five men of history, Hamilton, Helm, Hay, Clark and Bowman, were not distinguished diplomats. They went at their work rather after the hammer-and-tongs fashion. Clark bluntly demanded unconditional surrender. Hamilton refused. They argued the matter. Helm put in his oar, trying to soften the situation, as was his custom on all occasions, and received from Clark a stinging reprimand, with the reminder that he was nothing but a prisoner on parole, and had no voice at all in settling the terms of surrender.

"I release him, sir," said Hamilton. "He is no longer a prisoner. I am quite willing to have Captain Helm join freely in our conference."

"And I refuse to permit his acceptance of your favor," responded Clark. "Captain Helm, you will return with Mr. Hamilton to the fort and remain his captive until I free you by force. Meantime hold your tongue."

Father Beret, suave looking and quiet, occupied himself at the little altar, apparently altogether indifferent to what was being said; but he lost not a word of the talk.

"Qui habet aures audiendi, audiat," he inwardly repeated, smiling blandly. "Gaudete in illa die, et exultate!"

Hamilton rose to go; deep lines of worry creased his face; but when the party had passed outside, he suddenly turned upon Clark and said:

"Why do you demand impossible terms of me?"

"I will tell you, sir," was the stern answer, in a tone in which there was no mercy or compromise. "I would rather have you refuse. I desire nothing so much as an excuse to wreak full and bloody vengeance on every man in that fort who has engaged in the business of employing savages to scalp brave, patriotic men and defenseless women and children. The cries of the widows and the fatherless on our frontiers require the blood of the Indian partisans at my hands. If you choose to risk the massacre of your garrison to save those despicable red-handed partisans, have your pleasure. What you have done you know better than I do. I have a duty to perform. You may be able to soften its nature. I may take it into my head to send for some of our bereaved women to witness my terrible work and see that it is well done, if you insist upon the worst."

Major Hay, who was Hamilton's Indian agent, now, with some difficulty clearing his throat, spoke up.

"Pray, sir," said he, "who is it that you call Indian partisans?"

"Sir," replied Clark, seeing that his words had gone solidly home, "I take Major Hay to be one of the principals."

This seemed to strike Hay with deadly force. Clark's report says that he was "pale and trembling, scarcely able to stand," and that "Hamilton blushed, and, I observed, was much affected at his behavior. "Doubtless, if the doughty American commander had known more about the Governor's feelings just then, he would have added that an awful fear, even greater than the Indian agent's, did more than anything else to congest the veins in his face."

The parties separated without reaching an agreement; but the end had come. The terror in Hamilton's soul was doubled by a wild scene enacted under the walls of his fort; a scene which, having no proper place in this story, strong as its historical interest unquestionably is, must be but outlined. A party of Indians returning from a scalping expedition in Kentucky and along the Ohio, was captured on the outskirts of the town by some of Clark's men, who proceeded to kill and scalp them within full view of the beleaguered garrison, after which their mangled bodies were flung into the river.

If the British commander needed further wine of dread to fill his cup withal, it was furnished by ostentatious marshaling of the American forces for a general assault. His spirit broke completely, so that it looked like a godsend to him when Clark finally offered terms of honorable surrender, the consummation of which was to be postponed until the following morning. He accepted promptly, appending to the articles of capitulation the following reasons for his action: "The remoteness from succor; the state and quantity of provisions, etc.; unanimity of officers and men in its expediency; the honorable terms allowed; and, lastly, the confidence in a generous enemy."

Confidence in a generous enemy! Abject fear of the vengeance just wreaked upon his savage emissaries would have been the true statement. Beverley read the paper when Clark sent for him; but he could not join in the extravagant delight of his fellow officers and their brave men. What did all this victory mean to him? Hamilton to be treated as an honorable prisoner of war, permitted to strut forth from the feat with his sword at his side, his head up—the scalp-buyer, the murderer of Alice! What was patriotism to the crushed heart of a lover? Even if his vision had been able to pierce the future and realize the splendor of Anglo-Saxon civilization which was to follow that little triumph at Vincennes, what pleasure could it have afforded him? Alice, Alice, only Alice; no other thought had influence, save the recurring surge of desire for vengeance upon her murderer.

And yet that night Beverley slept, and so forgot his despair for many hours, even dreamed a pleasant dream of home, where his childhood was spent, of the stately old house on the breezy hill-top overlooking a sunny plantation, with a little river lapsing and shimmering through it. His mother's dear arms were around him, her loving breath stirred his hair; and his stalwart, gray-headed father sat on the veranda comfortably smoking his pipe, while away in the wide fields the negroes sang at the plow and the hoe. Sweeter and sweeter grew the scene, softer the air, tenderer the blending sounds of the water-murmur, leaf-rustle, bird-song, and slave-song, until hand in hand he wandered with Alice in greening groves, where the air was trembling with the ecstacy of spring.

A young officer awoke him with an order from Clark to go on duty at once with Captains Worthington and Williams, who, under Colonel Clark himself, were to take possession of the fort. Mechanically he obeyed. The sun was far up, shining between clouds of a leaden, watery hue, by the time everything was ready for the important ceremony. Beside the main gate of the stockade two companies of patriots under Bowman and McCarty were drawn up as guards, while the British garrison filed out and was taken in charge. This bit of formality ended, Governor Hamilton, attended by some of his officers, went back into the fort and the gate was closed.

Clark now gave orders that preparations be made for hauling down the British flag and hoisting the young banner of liberty in its place, when everything should be ready for a salute of thirteen guns from the captured battery.

Helm's round face was beaming. Plainly it showed that his happiness was supreme. He dared not say anything, however, for Clark was now all sternness and formality; it would be dangerous to take any liberties; but he could smile and roll his quid of tobacco from cheek to cheek.

Hamilton and Farnsworth, the latter slightly wounded in the left arm, which was bandaged, stood together somewhat apart from their fellow officers, while preliminary steps for celebrating their defeat and capture were in progress. They looked forlorn enough to have excited deep sympathy under fairer conditions.

Outside the fort the creoles were beginning a noise of jubilation. The rumor of what was going to be done had passed from mouth to mouth, until every soul in the town knew and thrilled with expectancy. Men, women and children came swarming to see the sight, and to hear at close range the crash of the cannon. They shouted, in a scattering way at first, then the tumult grew swiftly to a solid rolling tide that seemed beyond all comparison with the population of Vincennes. Hamilton heard it, and trembled inwardly, afraid lest the mob should prove too strong for the guard.

One leonine voice roared distinctly, high above the noise. It was a sound familiar to all the creoles,—that bellowing shout of Gaspard Roussillon's. He was roaming around the stockade, having been turned back by the guard when he tried to pass through the main gate.

"They shut me out!" he bellowed furiously. "I am Gaspard Roussillon, and they shut me out, me! Ziff! me voici! je vais entrer immediatement, moi!"

He attracted but little attention, however; the people and the soldiery were all too excited by the special interest of the occasion, and too busy with making a racket of their own, for any individual, even the great Roussillon, to gain their eyes or ears. He in turn scarcely heard the tumult they made, so self-centered were his burning thoughts and feelings. A great occasion in Vincennes and he, Gaspard Roussillon, not recognized as one of the large factors in it! Ah, no, never! And he strode along the wall of the stockade, turning the corners and heavily shambling over the inequalities till he reached the postern. It was not fastened, some one having passed through just before him.

"Ziff!" he ejaculated, stepping into the area and shaking himself after the manner of a dusty mastiff. "C'est moi! Gaspard Roussillon!" His massive under jaw was set like that of a vise, yet it quivered with rage, a rage which was more fiery condensation of self-approval than anger.

Outside the shouting, singing and huzzahs gathered strength and volume, until the sound became a hoarse roar. Clark was uneasy; he had overheard much of a threatening character during the siege. The creoles were, he knew, justly exasperated, and even his own men had been showing a spirit which might easily be fanned into a dangerous flame of vengeance. He was very anxious to have the formalities of taking possession of the fort over with, so that he could the better control his forces. Sending for Beverley he assigned him to the duty of hauling down the British flag and running up that of Virginia. It was an honor of no doubtful sort, which under different circumstances would have made the Lieutenant's heart glow. As it was, he proceeded without any sense of pride or pleasure, moving as a mere machine in performing an act significant beyond any other done west of the mountains, in the great struggle for American independence and the control of American territory.

Hamilton stood a little way from the foot of the tall flag-pole, his arms folded on his breast, his chin slightly drawn in, his brows contracted, gazing steadily at Beverley while he was untying the halyard, which had been wound around the pole's base about three feet above the ground. The American troops in the fort were disposed so as to form three sides of a hollow square, facing inward. Oncle Jazon, serving as the ornamental extreme of one line, was conspicuous for his outlandish garb and unmilitary bearing. The silence inside the stockade offered a strong contrast to the tremendous roar of voices outside. Clark made a signal, and at the tap of a drum, Beverley shook the ropes loose and began to lower the British colors. Slowly the bright emblem of earth's mightiest nation crept down in token of the fact that a handful of back-woodsmen had won an empire by a splendid stroke of pure heroism. Beverley detached the flag, and saluting, handed it to Colonel Clark. Hamilton's breast heaved and his iron jaws tightened their pressure until the lines of his cheeks were deep furrows of pain.

Father Beret, who had just been admitted, quietly took a place at one side near the wall. There was a fine, warm, benignant smile on his old face, yet his powerful shoulders drooped as if weighted down with a heavy load. Hamilton was aware when he entered, and instantly the scene of their conflict came into his memory with awful vividness, and he saw Alice lying outstretched, stark and, cold, the shining strand of hair fluttering across her pallid cheek. Her ghost overshadowed him.

Just then there was a bird-like movement, a wing-like rustle, and a light figure flitted swiftly across the area. All eyes were turned upon it. Hamilton recoiled, as pale as death, half lifting his hands, as if to ward off a deadly blow, and then a gay flag was flung out over his head. He saw before him the girl he had shot; but her beautiful face was not waxen now, nor was it cold or lifeless. The rich red blood was strong under the browned, yet delicate skin, the eyes were bright and brave, the cherry lips, slightly apart, gave a glimpse of pearl white teeth, and the dimples,—those roguish dimples,—twinkled sweetly.

Colonel Clark looked on in amazement, and in spite of himself, in admiration. He did not understand; the sudden incident bewildered him; but his virile nature was instantly and wholly charmed. Something like a breath of violets shook the tenderest chords of his heart.

Alice stood firmly, a statue of triumph, her right arm outstretched, holding the flag high above Hamilton's head; and close by her side the little hunchback Jean was posed in his most characteristic attitude, gazing at the banner which he himself had stolen and kept hidden for Alice's sake, and because he loved it.

There was a dead silence for some moments, during which Hamilton's face showed that he was ready to collapse; then the keen voice of Oncle Jazon broke forth:

"Vive Zhorzh Vasinton! Vim la banniere d'Alice Roussillon!"

He sprang to the middle of the area and flung his old cap high in air, with a shrill war-whoop.

"H'ist it! h'ist it! hissez la banniere de Mademoiselle Alice Roussillon! Voila, que c'est glorieuse, cette banniere la! H'ist it! h'ist it!"

He was dancing with a rickety liveliness, his goatish legs and shriveled body giving him the look of an emaciated satyr.

Clark had been told by some of his creole officers the story of how Alice raised the flag when Helm took the fort, and how she snatched it from Hamilton's hand, as it were, and would not give it up when he demanded it. The whole situation pretty soon began to explain itself, as he saw what Alice was doing. Then he heard her say to Hamilton, while she slowly swayed the rippling flag back and forth:

"I said, as you will remember, Monsieur le Gouverneur, that when you next should see this flag, I should wave it over your head. Well, look, I am waving it! Vive la republique! Vive George Washington! What do you think of it, Monsieur le Gouverneur?"

The poor little hunchback Jean took off his cap and tossed it in rhythmical emphasis, keeping time to her words.

And now from behind the hollow square came a mighty voice:

"C'est moi, Gaspard Roussillon; me voici, messieurs!"

There was a spirit in the air which caught from Alice a thrill of romantic energy. The men in the ranks and the officers in front of them felt a wave of irresistible sympathy sweep through their hearts. Her picturesque beauty, her fine temper, the fitness of the incident to the occasion, had an instantaneous power which moved all men alike.

"Raise her flag! Run up the young lady's flag!" some one shouted, and then every voice seemed to echo the words. Clark was a young man of noble type, in whose veins throbbed the warm chivalrous blood of the cavaliers. A waft of the suddenly prevailing influence bore him also quite off his feet. He turned to Beverley and said:

"Do it! It will have a great effect. It is a good idea; get the young lady's flag and her permission to run it up."

Before he finished speaking, indeed at the first glance, he saw that Beverley, like Hamilton, was white as a dead man; and at the same time it came to his memory that his young friend had confided to him during the awful march through the prairie wilderness, a love-story about this very Alice Roussillon. In the worry and stress of the subsequent struggle, he had forgotten the tender basis upon which Beverley had rested his excuse for leaving Vincennes. Now, it all reappeared in justification of what was going on. It touched the romantic core of his southern nature.

"I say, Lieutenant Beverley," he repeated, "beg the young lady's permission to use her flag upon this glorious occasion; or shall I do it for you?"

There were no miracles in those brave days, and the strain of life with its terrible realities braced all men and women to meet sudden explosions of surprise, whether of good or bad effect, with admirable equipoise; but Beverley's trial, it must be admitted, was extraordinary; still he braced himself quickly and his whole expression changed when Clark moved to go to Alice. For he realized now that it was, indeed, Alice in flesh and blood, standing there, the center of admiration, filling the air with her fine magnetism and crowning a great triumph with her beauty. He gave her a glad, flashing smile, as if he had just discovered her, and walked straight to her, his hands extended. She was not looking toward him; but she saw him and turned to face him. Hers was the advantage; for she had known, for some hours, of his presence in Vincennes, and had prepared herself to meet him courageously and with maidenly reserve.

There is no safety, however, where Love lurks. Neither Beverley nor Alice was as much agitated at Hamilton, yet they both forgot, what he remembered, that a hundred grim frontier soldiers were looking on. Hamilton had his personal and official dignity to sustain, and he fairly did it, under what a pressure of humiliating and surprising circumstances we can fully comprehend. Not so with the two young people, standing as it were in a suddenly bestowed and incomparable happiness, on the verge of a new life, each to the other an unexpected, unhoped-for resurrection from the dead. To them there was no universe save the illimitable expanse of their love. In that moment of meeting, all that they had suffered on account of love was transfused and poured forth,—a glowing libation for love's sake,—a flood before which all barriers broke.

Father Beret was looking on with a strange fire in his eyes, and what he feared would happen, did happen. Alice let the flag fall at Hamilton's feet, when Beverley came near her smiling that great, glad smile, and with a joyous cry leaped into his outstretched arms.

Jean snatched up the fallen banner and ran to Colonel Clark with it. Two minutes later it was made fast and the halyard began to squeak through the rude pulley at the top of the pole. Up, up, climbed the gay little emblem of glory, while the cannon crashed from the embrasures of the blockhouse hard by, and outside the roar of voices redoubled. Thirteen guns boomed the salute, though it should have been fourteen,—the additional one for the great Northwestern Territory, that day annexed to the domain of the young American Republic. The flag went up at old Vincennes never to come down again, and when it reached its place at the top of the staff, Beverley and Alice stood side by side looking at it, while the sun broke through the clouds and flashed on its shining folds, and love unabashed glorified the two strong young faces.

CHAPTER XXI
SOME TRANSACTIONS IN SCALPS

History would be a very orderly affair, could the dry-as-dust historians have their way, and doubtless it would be thrillingly romantic at every turn if the novelists were able to control its current. Fortunately neither one nor the other has much influence, and the result, in the long run, is that most novels are shockingly tame, while the large body of history is loaded down with picturesque incidents, which if used in fiction, would be thought absurdly romantic and improbable.

Were our simple story of old Vincennes a mere fiction, we should hesitate to bring in the explosion of a magazine at the fort with a view to sudden confusion and, by that means, distracting attention from our heroine while she betakes herself out of a situation which, although delightful enough for a blessed minute, has quickly become an embarrassment quite unendurable. But we simply adhere to the established facts in history. Owing to some carelessness there was, indeed, an explosion of twenty-six six-pound cartridges, which made a mighty roar and struck the newly installed garrison into a heap, so to say, scattering things terribly and wounding six men, among them Captains Bowman and Worthington.

After the thunderous crash came a momentary silence, which embraced both the people within the fort and the wild crowd outside. Then the rush and noise were indescribable. Even Clark gave way to excitement, losing command of himself and, of course, of his men. There was a stampede toward the main gate by one wing of the troops in the hollow square. They literally ran over Beverley and Alice, flinging them apart and jostling them hither and yonder without mercy. Of course the turmoil quickly subsided. Clark and Beverley got hold of themselves and sang out their peremptory orders with excellent effect. It was like oil on raging water; the men obeyed in a straggling way, getting back into ranks as best they could.

"Ventrebleu!" squeaked Oncle Jazon, "ef I didn't think the ole world had busted into a million pieces!"

He was jumping up and down not three feet from Beverley's toes, waving his cap excitedly.

"But wasn't I skeert! Ya, ya, ya! Vive la banniere d'Alice Roussillon! Vive Zhorzh Vasinton!"

Hearing Alice's name caused Beverley to look around. Where was she? In the distance he saw Father Beret hurrying to the spot where some of the men burnt and wounded by the explosion were being stripped and cared for. Hamilton still stood like a statue. He appeared to be the only cool person in the fort.

"Where is Alice?—Miss Roussillon—where did Miss Roussillon go?" Beverley exclaimed, staring around like a lost man. "Where is she?"

"D'know," said Oncle Jazon, resuming his habitual expression of droll dignity, "she shot apast me jes' as thet thing busted loose, an' she went like er hummin' bird, skitch!—jes' thet way—an' I didn't see 'r no more. 'Cause I was skeert mighty nigh inter seven fits; 'spect that 'splosion blowed her clean away! Ventrebleu! never was so plum outen breath an' dead crazy weak o' bein' afeard!"

"Lieutenant Beverley," roared Clark in his most commanding tone, "go to the gate and settle things there. That mob outside is trying to break in!"

The order was instantly obeyed, but Beverley had relapsed. Once more his soul groped in darkness, while the whole of his life seemed unreal, a wavering, misty, hollow dream. And yet his military duty was all real enough. He knew just what to do when he reached the gate.

"Back there at once!" he commanded, not loudly, but with intense force, "back there!" This to the inward surging wedge of excited outsiders. Then to the guard.

"Shoot the first man who crosses the line!"

"Ziff! me voici! moi! Gaspard Roussillon. Laissez-moi passer, messieurs."

A great body hurled itself frantically past Beverley and the guard, going out through the gateway against the wall of the crowd, bearing everything before it and shouting:

"Back, fools! you'll all be killed—the powder is on fire! Ziff! run!"

Wild as a March hare, he bristled with terror and foamed at the mouth. He stampeded the entire mass. There was a wild howl; a rush in the other direction followed, and soon enough the esplanade and all the space back to the barricades and beyond were quite deserted.

Alice was not aware that a serious accident had happened. Naturally she thought the great, rattling, crashing noise of the explosion a mere part of the spectacular show. When the rush followed, separating her and Beverley, it was a great relief to her in some way; for a sudden recognition of the boldness of her action in the little scene just ended, came over her and bewildered her. An impulse sent her running away from the spot where, it seemed to her, she had invited public derision. The terrible noises all around her were, she now fancied, but the jeering and hooting of rude men who had seen her unmaidenly forwardness.

With a burning face she flew to the postern and slipped out, once more taking the course which had become so familiar to her feet. She did not slacken her speed until she reached the Bourcier cabin, where she had made her home since the night when Hamilton's pistol ball struck her. The little domicile was quite empty of its household, but Alice entered and flung herself into a chair, where she sat quivering and breathless when Adrienne, also much excited, came in, preceded by a stream of patois that sparkled continuously.

"The fort is blown up!" she cried, gesticulating in every direction at once, her petite figure comically dilated with the importance of her statement. "A hundred men are killed, and the powder is on fire!"

She pounced into Alice's arms, still talking as fast as her tongue could vibrate, changing from subject to subject without rhyme or reason, her prattle making its way by skips and shies until what was really upper-most in her sweet little heart disclosed itself.

"And, O Alice! Rene has not come yet!"

She plunged her dusky face between Alice's cheek and shoulder; Alice hugged her sympathetically and said:

"But Rene will come, I know he will, dear."

"Oh, but do you know it? is it true? who told you? when will he come? where is he? tell me about him!"

Her head popped up from her friend's neck and she smiled brilliantly through the tears that were still sparkling on her long black lashes.

"I didn't mean that I had heard from him, and I don't know where he is; but—but they always come back."

"You say that because your man—because Lieutenant Beverley has returned. It is always so. You have everything to make you happy, while I—I—"

Again her eyes spilled their shower, and she hid her face in her hands which Alice tried in vain to remove.

"Don't cry, Adrienne. You didn't see me crying—"

"No, of course not; you didn't have a thing to cry about. Lieutenant Beverley told you just where he was going and just what—"

"But think, Adrienne, only think of the awful story they told—that he was killed, that Governor Hamilton had paid Long-Hair for killing him and bringing back his scalp—oh dear, just think! And I thought it was true."

"Well, I'd be willing to think and believe anything in the world, if Rene would come back," said Adrienne, her face, now uncovered, showing pitiful lines of suffering. "O Alice, Alice, and he never, never will come!"

Alice exhausted every device to cheer, encourage and comfort her. Adrienne had been so good to her when she lay recovering from the shock of Hamilton's pistol bullet, which, although it came near killing her, made no serious wound—only a bruise, in fact. It was one of those fortunate accidents, or providentially ordered interferences, which once in a while save a life. The stone disc worn by Alice chanced to lie exactly in the missile's way, and while it was not broken, the ball, already somewhat checked by passing through several folds of Father Beret's garments, flattened itself upon it with a shock which somehow struck Alice senseless.

Here again, history in the form of an ancient family document (a letter written in 1821 by Alice herself), gives us the curious brace of incidents, to wit, the breaking of the miniature on Beverley's breast by a British musket-ball, and the stopping of Hamilton's bullet over Alice's heart by the Indian charm stone.

"Which shows the goodness of God," the letter goes on, "and also seems to sustain the Indian legend concerning the stone, that whoever might wear it could not be killed. Unquestionably (sic) Mr. Hamilton's shot, which was aimed at poor, dear old Father Beret, would have pierced my heart, but for that charm-stone. As for my locket, it did not, as some have reported, save Fitzhugh's life when the musket-ball was stopped. The ball was so spent that the blow was only hard enough to spoil temporary (sic) the face of the miniature, which was afterwards restored fairly well by an artist in Paris. When it did actually save Fitzhugh's life was out on the Illinois plain. The savage, Long-Hair, peace to his memory, worked the miracle of restoring to me—" Here a fold in the paper has destroyed a line of the writing.

The letter is a sacred family paper, and there is not justification for going farther into its faded and, in some parts, almost obliterated writing. But so much may pass into these pages as a pleasant authentication of what otherwise might be altogether too sweet a double nut for the critic's teeth to crack.

While Adrienne and Alice were still discussing the probability of Rene de Ronville's return, M. Roussillon came to the door. He was in search of Madame, his wife, whom he had not yet seen.

He gathered the two girls in his mighty arms, tousling them with rough tenderness. Alice returned his affectionate embrace and told him where to find Madame Roussillon, who was with Dame Godere, probably at her house.

"Nobody killed," he said, in answer to Alice's inquiry about the catastrophe at the fort. "Some of 'em hurt and burnt a little. Great big scare about nearly nothing. Ziff! my children, you should have seen me quiet things. I put out my hands, this way—omme ca—pouf! It was all over. The people went home."

His gestures indicated that he had borne back an army with open hands. Then he chucked Adrienne under the chin with his finger and added in his softest voice:

"I saw somebody's lover the other day, over yonder in the Indian village. He spoke to me about somebody—eh, ma petite, que voulez-vous dire?"

"Oh, Papa Roussillon! we were just talking about Rene!" cried Alice. "Have you seen him?"

"I saw you, you little minx, jumping into a man's arms right under the eyes of a whole garrison! Bah! I could not believe it was my little Alice!"

He let go a grand guffaw, which seemed to shake the cabin's walls. Alice blushed cherry red. Adrienne, too bashful to inquire about Rene, was trembling with anxiety. The truth was not in Gaspard Roussillon, just then; or if it was it stayed in him, for he had not seen Rene de Ronville. It was his generous desire to please and to appear opulent of knowledge and sympathy that made him speak. He knew what would please Adrienne, so why not give her at least a delicious foretaste? Surely, when a thing was so cheap, one need not be so parsimonious as to withhold a mere anticipation. He was off before the girls could press him into details, for indeed he had none.

"There now, what did I tell you?" cried Alice, when the big man was gone. "I told you Rene would come. They always come back!"

Father Beret came in a little later. As soon as he saw Alice he frowned and began to shake his head; but she only laughed, and imitating his hypocritical scowl, yet fringing it with a twinkle of merry lines and dimples, pointed a taper finger at him and exclaimed:

"You bad, bad, man! why did you pretend to me that Lieutenant Beverley was dead? What sinister ecclesiastical motive prompted you to describe how Long-Hair scalped him? Ah, Father—"

The priest laid a broad hand over her saucy mouth. "Something or other seems to have excited you mightily, ma fille, you are a trifle impulsively inclined to-day."

"Yes, Father Beret; yes I know, and I am ashamed. My heart shrinks when I think of what I did; but I was so glad, such a grand joy came all over me when I saw him, so strong and brave and beautiful, coming toward me, smiling that warm, glad smile and holding out his arms—ah, when I saw all that—when I knew for sure that he was not dead—I, why, Father—I just had to, I couldn't help it!"

Father Beret laughed in spite of himself, but quickly managed to resume his severe countenance.

"Ta! ta!" he exclaimed, "it was a bold thing for a little girl to do."

"So it was, so it was. But it was also a bold thing for him to do—to come back after he was dead and scalped and look so handsome and grand! I'm ashamed and sorry, Father; but—but, I'm afraid I might do it again if—well, I don't care if I did—so there, now!"

"But what in the world are you talking about?" interposed Adrienne. Evidently they were discussing a most interesting matter of which she knew nothing, and that did not suit her feminine curiosity. "Tell me." She pulled Father Beret's sleeve. "Tell me, I say!"

It is probable that Father Beret would have pretended to betray Alice's source of mingled delight and embarrassment, had not the rest of the Bourcier household returned in time to break up the conversation. A little later Alice gave Adrienne a vividly dramatic account of the whole scene.

"Ah, mon Dieu!" exclaimed the petite brunette, after she had heard the exciting story. "That was just like you, Alice. You always do superb things. You were born to do them. You shoot Captain Farnsworth, you wound Lieutenant Barlow, you climb onto the fort and set up your flag—you take it down again and run away with it—you get shot and you do not die—you kiss your lover right before a whole garrison! Bon Dieu! if I could but do all those things!"

She clasped her tiny hands before her and added rather dejectedly: "But I couldn't, I couldn't. I couldn't kiss a man in that way!"

Late in the evening news came to Roussillon place, where Gaspard Roussillon was once more happy in the midst of his little family, that the Indian Long-Hair had just been brought to the fort, and would be shot on the following day. A scouting party captured him as he approached the town, bearing at his belt the fresh scalp of a white man. He would have been killed forthwith, but Clark, who wished to avoid a repetition of the savage vengeance meted out to the Indians on the previous day, had given strict orders that all prisoners should be brought into the fort, where they were to have a fair trial by court martial.

Both Helm and Beverley were at Roussillon place, the former sipping wine and chatting with Gaspard, the latter, of course, hovering around Alice, after the manner of a hungry bee around a particularly sweet and deliciously refractory flower. It was raining slowly, the fine drops coming straight down through the cold, still February air; but the two young people found it pleasant enough for them on the veranda, where they walked back and forth, making fair exchange of the exciting experiences which had befallen them during their long separation. Between the lines of these mutual recitals sweet, fresh echoes of the old, old story went from heart to heart, an amoebaean love-bout like that of spring birds calling tenderly back and forth in the blooming Maytime woods.

Both Captain Helm and M. Roussillon were delighted to hear of Long-Hair's capture and certain fate, but neither of them regarded the news as of sufficient importance to need much comment. They did not think of telling Beverley and Alice. Jean, however, lying awake in his little bed, overheard the conversation, which he repeated to Alice next morning with great circumstantiality.

Having the quick insight bred of frontier experience, Alice instantly caught the terrible significance of the dilemma in which she and Beverley would be placed by Long-Hair's situation. Moreover, something in her heart arose with irresistible power demanding the final, the absolute human sympathy and gratitude. No matter what deeds Long-Hair had committed that were evil beyond forgiveness, he had done for her the all-atoning thing. He had saved Beverley and sent him back to her.

With a start and a chill of dread, she thought: "What if it is already too late!"

But her nature could not hesitate. To feel the demand of an exigency was to act. She snatched a wrap from its peg on the wall and ran as fast as she could to the fort. People who met her flying along wondered, staring after her, what could be urging her so that she saw nobody, checked herself for nothing, ran splashing through the puddles in the street, gazing ahead of her, as if pursuing some flying object from which she dared not turn her eyes.

And there was, indeed, a call for her utmost power of flight, if she would be of any assistance to Long-Hair, who even then stood bound to a stake in the fort's area, while a platoon of riflemen, those unerring shots from Kentucky and Virginia, were ready to make a target of him at a range of but twenty yards.

Beverley, greatly handicapped by the fact that the fresh scalp of a white man hung at Long-Hair's belt, had exhausted every possible argument to avert or mitigate the sentence promptly spoken by the court martial of which Colonel Clark was the ruling spirit. He had succeeded barely to the extent of turning the mode of execution from tomahawking to shooting. All the officers in the fort approved killing the prisoner, and it was difficult for Colonel Clark to prevent the men from making outrageous assaults upon him, so exasperated were they at sight of the scalp.

Oncle Jazon proved to be one of the most refractory among those who demanded tomahawking and scalping as the only treatment due Long-Hair. The repulsive savage stood up before them stolid, resolute, defiant, proudly flaunting the badge which testified to his horrible efficiency as an emissary of Hamilton's. It had been left in his belt by Clark's order, as the best justification of his doom.

"L' me hack 'is damned head," Oncle Jazon pleaded. "I jes' hankers to chop a hole inter it. An' besides I want 'is scelp to hang up wi' mine an' that'n o' the Injun what scelped me. He kicked me in the ribs, the stinkin' varmint."

Beverley pleaded eloquently and well, but even the genial Major Helm laughed at his sentiment of gratitude to a savage who at best but relented at the last moment, for Alice's sake, and concluded not to sell him to Hamilton. It is due to the British commander to record here that he most positively and with what appeared to be high sincerity, denied the charge of having offered rewards for the taking of human scalps. He declared that his purposes and practices were humane, and that while he did use the Indians as military allies, his orders to them were that they must forego cruel modes of warfare and refrain from savage outrage upon prisoners. Certainly the weight of contemporary testimony seems overwhelmingly against him, but we enter his denial. Long-Hair himself, however, taunted him with accusations of unfaithfulness in carrying out some very inhuman contracts, and to add a terrible sting, volunteered the statement that poor Barlow's scalp had served his turn in the place of Beverley's.

With conditions so hideous to contend against, Beverley, of course, had no possible means of succoring the condemned savage.

"Him a kickin' yer ribs clean inter ye, an' a makin' ye run the ga'ntlet, an' here ye air a tryin' to save 'is life!" whined Oncle Jazon, "W'y man, I thought ye hed some senterments! Dast 'is Injin liver, I kin feel them kicks what he guv me till yit. Ventrebleu! que diable voulez-vous?"

Clark simply pushed Beverley's pleadings aside as not worth a moment's consideration. He easily felt the fine bit of gratitude at the bottom of it all; but there was too much in the other side of the balance; justice, the discipline and confidence of his little army, and the claim of the women and children on the frontier demanded firmness in dealing with a case like Long-Hair's.

"No, no," he said to Beverley, "I would do anything in the world for you, Fitz, except to swerve an inch from duty to my country and the defenceless people down yonder in Kentucky, I can't do it. There's no use to press the matter further. The die is cast. That brute's got to be killed, and killed dead. Look at him—look at that scalp! I'd have him killed if I dropped dead for it the next instant."

Beverley shuddered. The argument was horribly convincing, and yet, somehow, the desire to save Long-Hair overbore everything else in his mind. He could not cease his efforts; it seemed to him as if he were pleading for Alice herself. Captain Farnsworth, strange to say, was the only man in the fort who leaned to Beverley's side; but he was reticent, doubtless feeling that his position as a British prisoner gave him no right to speak, especially when every lip around him was muttering something about "infamous scalp-buyers and Indian partisans," with whom he was prominently counted by the speakers.

As Clark had said, the die was cast. Long-Hair, bound to a stake, the scalp still dangling at his side, grimly faced his executioners, who were eager to fire. He appeared to be proud of the fact that he was going to be killed.

"One thing I can say of him," Helm remarked to Beverley; "he's the grandest specimen of the animal—I might say the brute—man that I ever saw, red, white or black. Just look at his body and limbs! Those muscles are perfectly marvelous."

"He saved my life, and I must stand here and see him murdered," the young man replied with intense bitterness. It was all that he could think, all that he could say. He felt inefficient and dejected, almost desperate.

Clark himself, not willing to cast responsibility upon a subordinate, made ready to give the fatal order. Turning to Long-Hair first, he demanded of him as well as he could in the Indian dialect of which he had a smattering, what he had to say at his last moment.

The Indian straightened his already upright form, and, by a strong bulging of his muscles, snapped the thongs that bound him. Evidently he had not tried thus to free himself; it was rather a spasmodic expression of savage dignity and pride. One arm and both his legs still were partially confined by the bonds, but his right hand he lifted, with a gesture of immense self-satisfaction, and pointed at Hamilton.

"Indian brave; white man coward," he said, scowling scornfully. "Long-Hair tell truth; white man lie, damn!"

Hamilton's countenance did not change its calm, cold expression. Long-Hair gazed at him fixedly for a long moment, his eyes flashing most concentrated hate and contempt. Then he tore the scalp from his belt and flung it with great force straight toward the captive Governor's face. It fell short, but the look that went with it did not, and Hamilton recoiled.

At that moment Alice arrived. Her coming was just in time to interrupt Clark, who had turned to the waiting platoon with the order of death on his lips. She made no noise, save the fluttering of her skirts, and her loud and rapid panting on account of her long, hard run. She sprang before Long-Hair and faced the platoon.

"You cannot, you shall not kill this man!" she cried in a voice loaded with excitement. "Put away those guns!"

Woman never looked more thrillingly beautiful to man than she did just then to all those rough, stern backwoodsmen. During her flight her hair had fallen down, and it glimmered like soft sunlight around her face. Something compelling flashed out of her eyes, an expression between a triumphant smile and a ray of irresistible beseechment. It took Colonel Clark's breath when he turned and saw her standing there, and heard her words.

"This man saved Lieutenant Beverley's life," she presently added, getting better control of her voice, and sending into it a thrilling timbre; "you shall not harm him—you must not do it!"

Beverley was astounded when he saw her, the thing was so unexpected, so daring, and done with such high, imperious force; still it was but a realization of what he had imagined she would be upon occasion. He stood gazing at her, as did all the rest, while she faced Clark and the platoon of riflemen. To hear his own name pass her quivering lips, in that tone and in that connection, seemed to him a consecration.

"Would you be more savage than your Indian prisoner?" she went on, "less grateful than he for a life saved? I did him a small, a very small, service once, and in memory of that he saved Lieutenant Beverley's life, because—because—" she faltered for a single breath, then added clearly and with magnetic sweetness—"because Lieutenant Beverley loved me, and because I loved him. This Indian Long-Hair showed a gratitude that could overcome his strongest passion. You white men should be ashamed to fall below his standard."

Her words went home. It was as if the beauty of her face, the magnetism of her lissome and symmetrical form, the sweet fire of her eyes and the passionate appeal of her voice gave what she said a new and irresistible force of truth. When she spoke of Beverley's love for her, and declared her love for him, there was not a manly heart in all the garrison that did not suddenly beat quicker and feel a strange, sweet waft of tenderness. A mother, somewhere, a wife, a daughter, a sister, a sweetheart, called through that voice of absolute womanhood.

"Beverley, what can I do?" muttered Clark, his bronze face as pale as it could possibly become.

"Do!" thundered Beverley, "do! you cannot murder that man. Hamilton is the man you should shoot! He offered large rewards, he inflamed the passions and fed the love of rum and the cupidity of poor wild men like the one standing yonder. Yet you take him prisoner and treat him with distinguished consideration. Hamilton offered a large sum for me taken alive, a smaller one for my scalp. Long-Hair saved me. You let Hamilton stand yonder in perfect safety while you shoot the Indian. Shame on you, Colonel Clark! shame on you, if you do it."

Alice stood looking at the stalwart commander while Beverley was pouring forth his torrent of scathing reference to Hamilton, and she quickly saw that Clark was moved. The moment was ripe for the finishing stroke. They say it is genius that avails itself of opportunity. Beverley knew the fight was won when he saw what followed. Alice suddenly left Long-Hair and ran to Colonel Clark, who felt her warm, strong arms loop round him for a single point of time never to be effaced from his memory; then he saw her kneeling at his feet, her hands upstretched, her face a glorious prayer, while she pleaded the Indian's cause and won it.

Doubtless, while we all rather feel that Clark was weak to be thus swayed by a girl, we cannot quite blame him. Alice's flag was over him; he had heard her history from Beverley's cunning lips; he actually believed that Hamilton was the real culprit, and besides he felt not a little nauseated with executing Indians. A good excuse to have an end of it all did not go begging.

But Long-Hair was barely gone over the horizon from the fort, as free and as villainous a savage as ever trod the earth, when a discovery made by Oncle Jazon caused Clark to hate himself for what he had done.

The old scout picked up the scalp, which Long-Hair had flung at Hamilton, and examined it with odious curiosity. He had lingered on the spot with no other purpose than to get possession of that ghastly relic. Since losing his own scalp the subject of crownlocks had grown upon his mind until its fascination was irresistible. He studied the hair of every person he saw, as a physiognomist studies faces. He held the gruesome thing up before him, scrutinizing it with the expression of a connoisseur who has discovered, on a grimy canvas, the signature of an old master.

"Sac' bleu!" he presently broke forth. "Well I'll be—Look'ee yer, George Clark! Come yer an' look. Ye've been sold ag'in. Take a squint, ef ye please!"

Colonel Clark, with his hands crossed behind him, his face thoughtfully contracted, was walking slowly to and fro a little way off. He turned about when Oncle Jazon spoke.

"What now, Jazon?"

"A mighty heap right now, that's what; come yer an' let me show ye. Yer a fine sort o' eejit, now ain't ye!"

The two men walked toward each other and met. Oncle Jazon held up the scalp with one hand, pointing at it with the index finger of the other.

"This here scalp come off'n Rene de Ronville's head."

"And who is he?"

"Who's he? Ye may well ax thet. He wuz a Frenchman. He wuz a fine young feller o' this town. He killed a Corp'ral o' Hamilton's an' tuck ter the woods a month or two ago. Hamilton offered a lot o' money for 'im or 'is scalp, an' Long-Hair went in fer gittin' it. Now ye knows the whole racket. An' ye lets that Injun go. An' thet same Injun he mighty nigh kicked my ribs inter my stomach!"

Oncle Jazon's feelings were visible and audible; but Clark could not resent the contempt of the old man's looks and words. He felt that he deserved far more than he was receiving. Nor was Oncle Jazon wrong. Rene de Ronville never came back to little Adrienne Bourcier, although, being kept entirely ignorant of her lover's fate, she waited and dreamed and hoped throughout more than two years, after which there is no further record of her life.

Clark, Beverley and Oncle Jazon consulted together and agreed among themselves that they would hold profoundly secret the story of the scalp. To have made it public would have exasperated the creoles and set them violently against Clark, a thing heavy with disaster for all his future plans. As it was, the release of Long-Hair caused a great deal of dissatisfaction and mutinous talk. Even Beverley now felt that the execution ordered by the commander ought to have been sternly carried out.

A day or two later, however, the whole dark affair was closed forever by a bit of confidence on the part of Oncle Jazon when Beverley dropped into his hut one evening to have a smoke with him.

The rain was over, the sky shone like one vast luminary, with a nearly full moon and a thousand stars reinforcing it. Up from the south poured one of those balmy, accidental wind floods, sometimes due in February on the Wabash, full of tropical dream-hints, yet edged with a winter chill that smacks of treachery. Oncle Jazon was unusually talkative; he may have had a deep draught of liquor; at all events Beverley had little room for a word.

"Well, bein' as it's twixt us, as is bosom frien's," the old fellow presently said, "I'll jes' show ye somepin poorty."

He pricked the wick of a lamp and took down his bunch of scalps.

"I hev been a addin' one more to keep company o' mine an' the tothers."

He separated the latest acquisition from the rest of the wisp and added, with a heinous chuckle:

"This'n's Long-Hair's!"

And so it was. Beverley knocked the ashes from his pipe and rose to go.

"Wen they kicks yer Oncle Jazon's ribs," the old man added, "they'd jes' as well lay down an' give up, for he's goin' to salervate 'em."

Then, after Beverley had passed out of the cabin, Oncle Jazon chirruped after him:

"Mebbe ye'd better not tell leetle Alice. The pore leetle gal hev hed worry 'nough."

CHAPTER XXII
CLARK ADVISES ALICE

A few days after the surrender of Hamilton, a large boat, the Willing, arrived from Kaskaskia. It was well manned and heavily armed. Clark fitted it out before beginning his march and expected it to be of great assistance to him in the reduction of the fort, but the high waters and the floating driftwood delayed its progress, so that its disappointed crew saw Alice's flag floating bright and high when their eyes first looked upon the dull little town from far down the swollen river. There was much rejoicing, however, when they came ashore and were enthusiastically greeted by the garrison and populace. A courier whom they picked up on the Ohio came with them. He bore dispatches from Governor Henry of Virginia to Clark and a letter for Beverley from his father. With them appeared also Simon Kenton, greatly to the delight of Oncle Jazon, who had worried much about his friend since their latest fredaine—as he called it— with the Indians. Meantime an expedition under Captain Helm had been sent up the river with the purpose of capturing a British flotilla from Detroit.

Gaspard Roussillon, immediately after Clark's victory, thought he saw a good opening favorable to festivity at the river house, for which he soon began to make some of his most ostentatious preparations. Fate, however, as usual in his case, interfered. Fate seemed to like pulling the big Frenchman's ear now and again, as if to remind him of the fact—which he was apt to forget—that he lacked somewhat of omnipotence.

"Ziff! Je vais donner un banquet a tout le moonde, moi!" he cried, hustling and bustling hither and thither.

A scout from up the river announced the approach of Philip Dejean with his flotilla richly laden, and what little interest may have been gathering in the direction of M. Roussillon's festal proposition vanished like the flame of a lamp in a puff of wind when this news reached Colonel Clark and became known in the town.

Beverley and Alice sat together in the main room of the Roussillon cabin—you could scarcely find them separated during those happy days—and Alice was singing to the soft tinkle of a guitar, a Creole ditty with a merry smack in its scarcely intelligible nonsense. She knew nothing about music beyond what M. Roussillon, a jack of all trades, had been able to teach her,—a few simple chords to accompany her songs, picked up at hap-hazard. But her voice, like her face and form, irradiated witchery. It was sweet, firm, deep, with something haunting in it—the tone of a hermit thrush, marvelously pure and clear, carried through a gay strain like the mocking-bird's. Of course Beverley thought it divine; and when a message came from Colonel Clark bidding him report for duty at once, he felt an impulse toward mutiny of the rankest sort. He did not dream that a military expedition could be on hand; but upon reaching headquarters, the first thing he heard was:

"Report to Captain Helm. You are to go with him up the river and intercept a British force. Move lively, Helm is waiting for you, probably."

There was no time for explanations. Evidently Clark expected neither questions nor delay. Beverley's love of adventure and his patriotic desire to serve his country came to his aid vigorously enough; still, with Alice's love-song ringing in his heart, there was a cord pulling him back from duty to the sweetest of all life's joys.

Helm was already at the landing, where a little fleet of boats was being prepared. A thousand things had to be done in short order. All hands were stimulated to highest exertion with the thought of another fight. Swivels were mounted in boats, ammunition and provisions stored abundantly, flags hoisted and oars dipped. Never was an expedition of so great importance more swiftly organized and set in motion, nor did one ever have a more prosperous voyage or completer triumph. Philip Dejean, Justice of Detroit, with his men, boats and rich cargo, was captured easily, with not a shot fired, nor a drop of blood spilled in doing it.

If Alice could have known all this before it happened, she would probably have saved herself from the mortification of a rebuke administered very kindly, but not the less thoroughly, by Colonel Clark.

The rumor came to her—a brilliant creole rumor, duly inflated—that an overwhelming British force was descending the river, and that Beverley with a few men, not sufficient to base the expedition on a respectable forlorn hope, would be sent to meet them. Her nature, as was its wont, flared into high indignation. What right had Colonel Clark to send her lover away to be killed just at the time when he was all the whole world to her? Nothing could be more outrageous. She would not suffer it to be done; not she!

Colonel Clark greeted her pleasantly, when she came somewhat abruptly to him, where he was directing a squad of men at work making some repairs in the picketing of the fort. He did not observe her excitement until she began to speak, and then it was noticeable only, and not very strongly, in her tone. She forgot to speak English, and her French was Greek to him.

"I am glad to see you, Mademoiselle," he said, rather inconsequently, lifting his hat and bowing with rough grace, while he extended his right hand cordially. "You have something to say to me? Come with me to my office."

She barely touched his fingers.

"Yes, I have something to say to you. I can tell it here," she said, speaking English now with softest Creole accent. "I wanted—I came to—" It was not so easy as she had imagined it would be to utter what she had in mind. Clark's steadfast, inscrutable eyes, kindly yet not altogether sympathetic, met her own and beat them down. Her voice failed.

He offered her his arm and gravely said:

"We will go to my office. I see that you have some important communication to make. There are too many ears here."

Of a sudden she felt like running home. Somehow the situation broke upon her with a most embarrassing effect. She did not take Clark's arm, and she began to tremble. He appeared unconscious of this, and probably was, for his mind had a fine tangle of great schemes in it just then; but he turned toward his office, and bidding her follow him, walked away in that direction.

She was helpless. Not the slightest trace of her usual brilliant self-assertion was at her command. Saving the squad of men sawing and hacking, digging and hammering, the fort appeared as deserted as her mind. She stood gazing after Clark. He did not look back, but strode right on. If she would speak with him, she must follow. It was a surprise to her, for heretofore she had always had her own way, even if she found it necessary to use force. And where was Beverley? Where was the garrison? Colonel Clark did not seem to be at all concerned about the approach of the British—and yet those repairs—perhaps he was making ready for a desperate resistance! She did not move until he reached the door of his office where he stopped and stepped aside, as if to let her pass in first; he even lifted his hat, then looked a trifle surprised when he saw that she was not near him, frowned slightly, changed the frown to a smile and said, lifting his voice so that she felt a certain imperative meaning in it:

"Did I walk too fast for you? I beg your pardon, Mademoiselle."

He stood waiting for her, as a father waits for a lagging, wilful child.

"Come, please," he added, "if you have something to say to me; my time just now is precious—I have a great deal to do."

She was not of a nature to retreat under fire, and yet the panic in her breast came very near mastering her will. Clark saw a look in her face which made him speak again:

"I assure you, Mademoiselle, that you need not feel embarrassed. You can rely upon me to—"

She made a gesture that interrupted him; at the same time she almost ran toward him, gathering in breath, as one does who is about to force out a desperately resisting and riotous thought. The strong, grave man looked at her with a full sense of her fascination, and at the same time he felt a vague wish to get away from her, as if she were about to cast unwelcome responsibility upon him.

"Where is Lieutenant Beverley?" she demanded, now close to Clark, face to face, and gazing straight into his eyes. "I want to see him." Her tone suggested intensest excitement. She was trembling visibly.

Clark's face changed its expression. He suddenly recalled to mind Alice's rapturous public greeting of Beverley on the day of the surrender. He was a cavalier, and it did not agree with his sense of high propriety for girls to kiss their lovers out in the open air before a gazing army. True enough, he himself had been hoodwinked by Alice's beauty and boldness in the matter of Long-Hair. He confessed this to himself mentally, which may have strengthened his present disapproval of her personal inquiry about Beverley. At all events he thought she ought not to be coming into the stockade on such an errand.

"Lieutenant Beverley is absent acting under my orders he said, with perfect respectfulness, yet in a tone suggesting military finality. He meant to set an indefinite yet effective rebuke in his words.

"Absent?" she echoed. "Gone? You sent him away to be killed! You had no right—you—"

"Miss Roussillon," said Clark, becoming almost stern, "you had better go home and stay there; young girls oughtn't to run around hunting men in places like this."

His blunt severity of speech was accompanied by a slight frown and a gesture of impatience.

Alice's face blazed red to the roots of her sunny hair; the color ebbed, giving place to a pallor like death. She began to tremble, and her lips quivered pitifully, but she braced herself and tried to force back the choking sensation in her throat.

"You must not misconstrue my words," Clark quickly added; "I simply mean that men will not rightly understand you. They will form impressions very harmful to you. Even Lieutenant Beverley might not see you in the right light."

"What—what do you mean?" she gasped, shrinking from him, a burning spot reappearing under the dimpled skin of each cheek.

"Pray, Miss, do not get excited. There is nothing to make you cry." He saw tears shining in her eyes. "Beverley is not in the slightest danger. All will be well, and he'll come back in a few days. The expedition will be but a pleasure trip. Now you go home. Lieutenant Beverley is amply able to take care of himself. And let me tell you, if you expect a good man to have great confidence in you, stay home and let him hunt you up instead of you hunting him. A man likes that better."

It would be impossible to describe Alice's feelings, as they just then rose like a whirling storm in her heart. She was humiliated, she was indignant, she was abashed; she wanted to break forth with a tempest of denial, self-vindication, resentment; she wanted to cry with her face hidden in her hands. What she did was to stand helplessly gazing at Clark, with two or three bright tears on either cheek, her hands clenched, her eyes flashing. She was going to say some wild thing; but she did not; her voice lodged fast in her throat. She moved her lips, unable to make a sound.

Two of Clark's officers relieved the situation by coming up to get orders about some matter of town government, and Alice scarcely knew how she made her way home. Every vein in her body was humming like a bee when she entered the house and flung herself into a chair.

She heard Madame Roussillon and Father Beret chatting in the kitchen, whence came a fragrance of broiling buffalo steak besprinkled with garlic. It was Father Beret's favorite dish, wherefore his tongue ran freely—almost as freely as that of his hostess, and when he heard Alice come in, he called gayly to her through the kitchen door:

"Come here, ma fille, and lend us old folks your appetite; nous avons une tranche a la Bordelaise!"

"I am not hungry," she managed to say, "you can eat it without me."

The old man's quick ears caught the quaver of trouble in her voice, much as she tried to hide it. A moment later he was standing beside her with his hand on her head.

"What is the matter now, little one?" he tenderly demanded. "Tell your old Father."

She began to cry, laying her face in her crossed arms, the tears gushing, her whole frame aquiver, and heaving great sobs. She seemed to shrink like a trodden flower. It touched Father Beret deeply.

He suspected that Beverley's departure might be the cause of her trouble; but when presently she told him what had taken place in the fort, he shook his head gravely and frowned.

"Colonel Clark was right, my daughter," he said after a short silence, "and it is time for you to ponder well upon the significance of his words. You can't always be a wilful, headstrong little girl, running everywhere and doing just as you please. You have grown to be a woman in stature—you must be one in fact. You know I told you at first to be careful how you acted with—"

"Father, dear old Father!" she cried, springing from her seat and throwing her arms around his neck. "Have I appeared forward and unwomanly? Tell me, Father, tell me! I did not mean to do anything—"

"Quietly, my child, don't give way to excitement." He gently put her from him and crossed himself—a habit of his when suddenly perplexed—then added:

122

"You have done no evil; but there are proprieties which a young woman must not overstep. You are impulsive, too impulsive; and it will not do to let a young man see that you— that you—"

"Father, I understand," she interrupted, and her face grew very pale.

Madame Roussillon came to the door, flushed with stooping over the fire, and announced that the steak was ready.

"Bring the wine, Alice," she added, "a bottle of Bordeaux."

She stood for a breath of two, her red hands on her hips, looking first at Father Beret, then at Alice.

"Quarreling again about the romances?" she inquired. "She's been at it again?—she's found 'em again?"

"Yes," said Father Beret, with a queer, dry smile, "more romance. Yes, she's been at it again! Now fetch the Bordeaux, little one."

The following days were cycles of torture to Alice. She groveled in the shadow of a great dread. It seemed to her that Beverley could not love her, could not help looking upon her as a poor, wild, foolish girl, unworthy of consideration. She magnified her faults and crudities, she paraded before her inner vision her recent improprieties, as they had been disclosed to her, until she saw herself a sort of monstrosity at which all mankind was gazing with disgust. Life seemed dry and shriveled, a mere jaundiced shadow, while her love for Beverley took on a new growth, luxuriant, all-embracing, uncontrollable. The ferment of spirit going on in her breast was the inevitable process of self-recognition which follows the terrible unfolding of the passion-flower, in a nature almost absolutely simple and unsophisticated.

Vincennes held its breath while waiting for news from Helm's expedition. Every day had its nimble, yet wholly imaginary account of what had happened, skipping from mouth to mouth, and from cabin to cabin. The French folk ran hither and thither in the persistent rain, industriously improving the dramatic interest of each groundless report. Alice's disturbed imagination reveled in the kaleidoscopic terrors conjured up by these swift changes of the form and color of the stories "from the front," all of them more or less tragic. To-day the party is reported as having been surprised and massacred to a man—to-morrow there has been a great fight, many killed, the result in doubt—next day the British are defeated, and so on. The volatile spirit of the Creoles fairly surpassed itself in ringing the changes on stirring rumors.

Alice scarcely left the house during the whole period of excitement and suspense. Like a wounded bird, she withdrew herself from the light and noisy chatter of her friends, seeking only solitude and crepuscular nooks in which to suffer silently. Jean brought her every picturesque bit of the ghastly gossip, thus heaping coals on the fire of her torture. But she did not grow pale and thin. Not a dimple fled from cheek or chin, not a ray of saucy sweetness vanished from her eyes. Her riant health was unalterable. Indeed, the only change in her was a sudden ripening and mellowing of her beauty, by which its colors, its lines, its subtle undercurrents of expression were spiritualized, as if by some powerful clarifying process.

Tremendous is the effect of a soul surprised by passion and brought hard up against an opposing force which dashes it back upon itself with a flare and explosion of self-revealment. Nor shall we ever be able to foretell just how small a circumstance, just how slight an exigency, will suffice to bring on the great change. The shifting of a smile to the gloom of a frown, the snap of a string on the lute of our imagination, just at the point when a rich melody is culminating; the waving of a hand, a vanishing face—any eclipse of tender, joyous expectation— dashes a nameless sense of despair into the soul. And a young girl's soul—who shall uncover its sacred depths of sensitiveness, or analyze its capacity for suffering under such a stroke?

On the fifth day of March, back came the victorious Helm, having surrounded and captured seven boats, richly loaded with provisions and goods, and Dejean's whole force. Then again the little Creole town went wild with rejoicing. Alice heard the news and the noise; but somehow there was no response in her heart. She dreaded to meet Beverley; indeed, she did not expect him to come to her. Why should he?

M. Roussillon, who had volunteered to accompany Helm, arrived in a mood of unlimited proportions, so far as expressing self-admiration and abounding delight was concerned. You would have been sure that he had done the whole deed single-handed, and brought the flotilla and captives to town on his back. But Oncle Jazon for once held his tongue, being too disgusted for words at not having been permitted to fire a single shot. What was the use of going to fight and simply meeting and escorting down the river a lot of non-combatants?

There is something inscrutably delightful about a girl's way of thinking one thing and doing another. Perversity, thy name is maidenhood; and maidenhood, thy name is delicious inconsequence! When Alice heard that Beverley had come back, safe, victorious, to be greeted as one of the heroes of an important adventure, she immediately ran to her room frightened and full of vague, shadowy dread, to hide from him, yet feeling sure that he would not come! Moreover, she busied herself with the preposterous task of putting on her most attractive gown—the buff brocade which she wore that evening at the river house—how long ago it seemed!—when Beverley thought her the queenliest beauty in the world. And she was putting it on so as to look her prettiest while hiding from him!

It is a toss-up where happiness will make its nest. The palace, the hut, the great lady's garden, the wild lass's bower,—skip here, alight there,—the secret of it may never be told. And love and beauty find lodgment, by the same inexplicable route, in the same extremes of circumstances. The wind bloweth where it listeth, finding many a matchless flower and many a ravishing fragrance in the wildest nooks of the world.

No sooner did Beverley land at the little wharf than, rushing to his quarters, he made a hasty exchange of water-soaked apparel for something more comfortable, and then bolted in the direction of Roussillon place.

Now Alice knew by the beating of her heart that he was coming. In spite of all she could do, trying to hold on hard and fast to her doubt and gloom, a tide of rich sweetness began to course through her heart and break in splendid expectation from her eyes, as they looked through the little unglazed window toward the fort. Nor had she long to wait. He came up the narrow wet street, striding like a tall actor in the height of a melodrama, his powerful figure erect as an Indian's, and his face glowing with the joy of a genuine, impatient lover, who is proud of himself because of the image he bears in his heart.

When Alice flung wide the door (which was before Beverley could cross the veranda), she had quite forgotten how she had gowned and bedecked herself; and so, without a trace of self-consciousness, she flashed upon him a full-blown flower—to his eyes the loveliest that ever opened under heaven.

Gaspard Roussillon, still overflowing with the importance of his part in the capture of Dejean, came puffing homeward just in time to see a man at the door holding Alice a-tiptoe in his arms.

"Ziff!" he cried, as he pushed open the little front gate of the yard, "en voila assez, vogue la galere!"

The two forms disappeared within the house, as if moved by his roaring voice.

The letter to Beverley from his father was somewhat disturbing. It bore the tidings of his mother's failing health. This made it easier for the young Lieutenant to accept from Clark the assignment to duty with a party detailed for the purpose of escorting Hamilton, Farnsworth and several other British officers to Williamsburg, Virginia. It also gave him a most powerful assistance in persuading Alice to marry him at once, so as to go with him on what proved to be a delightful wedding journey through the great wilderness to the Old Dominion. Spring's verdure burst abroad on the sunny hills as they slowly went their way; the mating birds sang in every blooming brake and grove by which they passed, and in their joyous hearts they heard the bubbling of love's eternal fountain.

CHAPTER XXIII
AND SO IT ENDED

Our story must end here, because at this point its current flows away forever from old Vincennes; and it was only of the post on the Wabash that we set out to make a record. What befell Alice and Beverley after they went to Virginia we could go on to tell; but that would be another story. Suffice it to say, they lived happily ever after, or at least somewhat beyond three score and ten, and left behind them a good name and numerous descendants.

How Alice found out her family in Virginia, we are not informed; but after a lapse of some years from the date of her marriage, there appears in one of her letters a reference to an estate inherited from her Tarleton ancestors, and her name appears in old records signed in full, Alice Tarleton Beverley. A descendant of hers still treasures the locket, with its broken miniature and battered crest, which won Beverley's life from Long-Hair, the savage. Beside it, as carefully guarded, is the Indian charm-stone that stopped Hamilton's bullet over Alice's heart The rapiers have somehow disappeared, and there is a tradition in the Tarleton family that they were given by Alice to Gaspard Roussillon, who, after Madame Roussillon's death in 1790, went to New Orleans, where he stayed a year or two before embarking for France, whither he took with him the beautiful pair of colechemardes and Jean the hunchback.

Oncle Jazon lived in Vincennes many years after the war was over; but he died at Natchez, Mississippi, when ninety-three years old. He said, with almost his last breath, that he couldn't shoot very well, even in his best days; but that he had, upon various occasions, "jes' kind o' happened to hit a Injun in the lef' eye." They used to tell a story, as late as General Harrison's stay in Vincennes, about how Oncle Jazon buried his collection of scalps, with great funeral solemnity, as his part of the celebration of peace and independence about the year 1784.

Good old Father Beret died suddenly soon after Alice's marriage and departure for Virginia. He was found lying face downward on the floor of his cabin. Near him, on a smooth part of a puncheon, were the mildewed fragments of a letter, which he had been arranging, as if to read its contents. Doubtless it was the same letter brought to him by Rene de Ronville, as recorded in an early chapter of our story. The fragments were gathered up and buried with him. His dust lies under the present Church of St. Xavier,—the dust of as noble a man and as true a priest as ever sacrificed himself for the good of humanity.

In after years Simon Kenton visited Beverley and Alice in their Virginia home. To his dying day he was fond of describing their happy and hospitable welcome and the luxuries to which they introduced him. They lived in a stately white mansion on a hill overlooking a vast tobacco plantation, where hundreds of negro slaves worked and sang by day and frolicked by night. Their oldest child was named Fitzhugh Gaspard. Kenton died in 1836.

There remains but one little fact worth recording before we close the book. In the year 1800, on the fourth of July, a certain leading French family of Vincennes held a patriotic reunion, during which a little old flag was produced and its story told. Some one happily proposed that it be sent to Mrs. Alice Tarleton Beverley with a letter of explanation, and in profound recognition of the glorious circumstances which made it the true flag of the great Northwest.

And so it happened that Alice's little banner went to Virginia and is still preserved in an old mansion not very far from Monticello; but it seems likely that the Wabash Valley will soon again possess the precious relic. The marriage engagement of Miss Alice Beverley to a young Indiana officer, distinguished for his patriotism and military ardor, has been announced at the old Beverley homestead on the hill, and the high contracting parties have planned that the wedding ceremony shall take place under the famous little flag, on the anniversary of dark's capture of Post Vincennes. When the bride shall be brought to her new home on the banks of the Wabash, the flag will come with her; but Oncle Jazon will not be on hand with his falsetto shout: "VIVE LA BANNIERE D'ALICE ROUSSILLON! VIVE ZHORZZH VASINTON!"

CPSIA information can be obtained
at www.ICGtesting.com
Printed in the USA
LVOW01s1212310116

473060LV00020B/1075/P